A BRIGHTER DAWN

In spite of her father's words of warning, Sharon Pritchard decided to give up everything to follow her heart. However, her new life with Hadyn is anything but easy. Although he is handsome and charming, he is also feckless and unreliable. And they soon find themselves sinking ever faster into poverty. The birth of their son should be a joyous occasion, but Sharon fears for him amongst the filth and despair of Tiger Bay. Can her love for Hadyn survive and will she be able to provide a better future for herself and her son...?

A BRIGHTER DAWN

A BRIGHTER DAWN

by

Rosie Harris

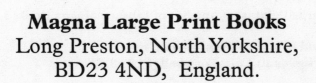
Magna Large Print Books
Long Preston, North Yorkshire,
BD23 4ND, England.

British Library Cataloguing in Publication Data.

Harris, Rosie
    A brighter dawn.

    A catalogue record of this book is
    available from the British Library

    ISBN   978-0-7505-3587-8

First published in Great Britain in 2011 by Arrow Books

Copyright © Rosie Harris 2011

Cover illustration © Samantha Green

Rosie Harris has asserted her right under the Copyright, Designs and
Patents Act, 1988 to be identified as the author of this work

Published in Large Print 2012 by arrangement with
Arrow, one of the publishers in the Random House Group Ltd.

Magna Large Print is an imprint of Library Magna Books Ltd.

Printed and bound in Great Britain by
T.J. (International) Ltd., Cornwall, PL28 8RW

For my Family, Friends and Fans

Acknowledgements

With many thanks to Georgina Hawtrey-Woore for her tremendous help and to the rest of the team at Random House for their continued support, and also to my agent Caroline Sheldon.

Chapter One

Saturday 7 June 1924, the day her brother Parry married Gwen Cogan, would be a day she would never forget, thought eighteen-year-old Sharon Pritchard dreamily. She slipped the peach chiffon dress that she would be wearing over her head and stared at her reflection in the mirror. She was to be their bridesmaid and its frothy loveliness seemed to transform her into a princess.

Parry and Gwen's marriage was looked upon by all of them as a tremendous family occasion and one both the Pritchards and Cogans regarded as a milestone for the future because it was cementing the two families even more firmly.

Elwyn Pritchard and Gwen's father, Lloyd Cogan, had been friends all their lives and their adjacent shops in Cardiff's Queen Street, Pritchard's Paints and Wallpapers and Cogan's Carpets and Curtains, had been established for almost twenty-five years.

They had always worked in close cooperation; indeed, there was a door between the two establishments so that customers could walk from one shop into the next to complete their purchases when they were decorating their homes and wanted curtains or carpets to match the paint or wallpaper they'd selected.

They were family firms in every sense of the word. Parry, who was tall and slim with dark brown hair and eyes, was highly skilled at wall-papering and was in charge of the team of painters and decorators they employed. His bride-to-be, Gwen Cogan, was petite with fair hair and greyish-blue eyes like her mother, Flossie Cogan. Gwen helped her mother to make up curtains and cushions from the fabrics they sold. Gwen's brother, Madoc, who was to be Best Man at the wedding, was of medium height and stocky like the rest of his family. He knew all there was to know about carpets and was a trained carpet fitter.

Sharon's mother, Elaine Pritchard, was the bookkeeper for both shops and Elwyn Pritchard and Lloyd Cogan were not only expert salesmen but also highly knowledgeable in their own field. They had built up their businesses by dint of hard work and were still in control and kept an eagle eye on day-to-day transactions.

Ever since she had left school Sharon had helped customers to co-ordinate their selections. She had a good eye for colour and design and customers sought out her help when trying to decide what would be right for their particular needs. She had even helped Gwen and Parry in their choice of decorations for their new home.

What made this particular day so special for Sharon was that Hadyn Jenkins would be there as one of the wedding guests. She wondered what he would think when he saw her looking so very different from her usual neat but practical white blouse and dark skirt that she wore when she was working in the shop.

Hadyn Jenkins was seven years older than her. He was tall and handsome with wavy auburn hair

14

and deep green eyes. He was the South Wales Sales Representative for Brynmor and Williams, a firm that sold wallpapers and fabrics, so he was well known to them all.

Sharon knew that her father disapproved of her flirtatious friendship with Hadyn because he wanted her to marry Madoc Cogan. In all their eyes that would be the perfect set-up. She liked Madoc but she thought of him in much the same way as she did her brother Parry.

'He's someone I'm very fond of and feel perfectly at ease with but only as a friend. I'm not in love with him and I *certainly* wouldn't want to spend the rest of my life with him,' she told her mother.

'Why ever not? He's hard-working and he thinks the world of you.'

'He's so unexciting; it's like being with Parry,' Sharon explained.

'He's steady and reliable, even if he hasn't been to charm school like that Hadyn chap who keeps chatting you up. I know Hadyn Jenkins has had to learn to be a smooth talker as part of his job as a salesman if he's going to get orders, but don't get carried away by everything he says, cariad.'

Sharon knew better than to argue with her mother but, nevertheless, she didn't believe her. Hadyn was worldly, knowledgeable and extremely handsome and she felt flattered that he paid her so much attention.

She took one final look in the mirror and once again felt delighted that she had insisted on her dress being knee-length with a fashionable dropped waist, even though Gwen would be in a

15

floor-length traditional white wedding dress. She also liked the shimmer effect of the pale peach chiffon over the white satin under dress and once she removed some of the frilly trimmings it would be ideal to wear again afterwards when she went to dances.

She descended the stairs with her head held high, imagining that she was walking down a really grand staircase, and waited to hear the gasp of delight when her mother caught sight of her.

Instead, all she could hear were raised voices and as she entered the living room her father was declaring, 'I will not have that man at my son's wedding. He is not a friend of the family nor will he ever be.'

'Well, he'll be there whether you like it or not,' Parry told him. 'Gwen's family have invited him and since they are the ones paying for the wedding reception they have the right to invite whomsoever they like.'

'He certainly won't be asked back here afterwards,' Elwyn Pritchard said heatedly as he tugged at the points of his dark waistcoat and then ran a forefinger around his starched white collar as if he was finding it was much too tight.

'None of them will be coming back here, will they?' Elaine Pritchard questioned worriedly. 'I thought that after the wedding reception, once we've waved Parry and Gwen off on their honeymoon, everybody would go home. I wasn't planning on entertaining folks.'

'Of course they won't be coming back here, Mam, so stop worrying about it,' Parry told her. 'You get yourself ready–' Parry stopped speaking

16

and gave a low whistle as Sharon walked into the room. 'Duw anwyl, cariad, you look like a princess,' he exclaimed, staring at Sharon in admiration.

'You don't look so bad yourself,' she said, smiling. 'Wait until Gwen sees you all spruced up like that.'

'There's proud I am of the pair of you,' Elaine exclaimed, her voice warm with pleasure. 'They look grand, don't they, Elwyn?'

'I think it is time we all got a move on and headed for chapel or they'll be starting the wedding ceremony without us,' Elwyn told his family. 'You have to be there, Parry, well before the bride arrives. By rights you should be at her house, Sharon, helping her to get ready.'

'I know that, Dada, but she said it wasn't necessary as her mother wanted to do it all. She said I was to be at the door when she arrived at chapel.'

'Come along, then, or the bride will get there before Parry does and that will make tongues wag. One last word of warning, my girl,' he added, addressing himself to Sharon, 'keep well away from that Hadyn Jenkins. I don't want to see you talking to him, not one word. Do you understand?'

'What if he speaks to me? I'll have to answer. It would be downright rude not to do so,' Sharon protested.

'She's quite right, Elwyn, and we don't want any bad feelings, not on our Parry's wedding day,' Elaine protested. 'Surely it's better for her to return his greeting and leave it at that.'

'Yes, as long as she does leave it at that. What I don't want to see is Sharon in deep conversation with him and, from what I've seen with my own eyes, that's what will be happening if he's given half a chance. The man's a menace. He flatters her by singling her out for attention simply to impress her and in the hope that she will persuade me to place a big order with him.'

'That's his job, surely,' Elaine countered. 'He has to get good orders to keep his own boss happy and to make a living for himself. You can't really blame the chap for doing that, now can you?'

'I know all about that but he is ingratiating himself with Sharon far more than is necessary and turning the silly girl's head with his spiel. I wouldn't mind betting that he does it wherever he goes and that he has some girl starry-eyed about him in every damn town he visits. Well, that's his affair, but I don't want him latching on to my daughter.'

Sharon looked across at Parry and pulled a face and was relieved when he gave her a reassuring wink. At least he was on her side, she thought.

She couldn't forget her father's harsh words about Hadyn but she pushed them to one side as she accompanied her parents and Parry to chapel.

Madoc was already there, waiting rather impatiently for Parry to arrive and Sharon had to admit that he did look very smart in his new charcoal-grey suit and white tie and buttonhole.

He wasn't as tall as Parry and was much more stockily built. They'd always been the best of friends; so close that they could have been brothers.

Hadyn, of course, was quite different. He wasn't only tall and good-looking but he also looked so

18

much more grown-up than they did. He also had a wide smile and a lilting voice, which she found very fascinating. He said he came from a village near Caerphilly, but that was all she knew about him. Being a commercial traveller he moved around a great deal but he had several customers in the Cardiff area so he called at least once a month and he always made sure that he had a few words alone with her. On one occasion he had even suggested they should go out together, but her father had overheard what he was saying and had told Hadyn quite firmly that she was far too young for that sort of thing.

She smiled to herself as she recalled his polite acceptance of her father's ruling and how taken aback her father had been when Hadyn had said that he quite understood and that he could wait until she was eighteen, or even older, if that was necessary.

Sharon's wandering thoughts were brought back to the present by the arrival of the bride. Gwen looked lovely in her flowing white dress and as she went to greet her and to take up her position as bridesmaid, Sharon felt almost envious that Gwen was the one getting married that day.

As she walked behind Gwen, so delicate and pretty beside her father, Lloyd, who looked more plump and pompous than usual, Sharon couldn't help feeling how wonderful it would have been if she had been the bride, not the bridesmaid, and if it was Hadyn who was waiting there to make her his wife.

The service began and Sharon kept her thoughts on what she was expected to do. It had all been carefully rehearsed before, so they made no mistakes, and as they emerged from the chapel into the glorious June sunshine, they paused in the doorway to have official photographs taken.

Pritchard's Paints and Wallpapers and Cogan's Carpets and Curtains were both well known and popular in Cardiff and a large crowd of well-wishers had gathered outside to see them and to shower them with confetti.

Once the photographs had been taken the wedding party and their guests set off in a fleet of sleek black cars to the exclusive restaurant in Queen Street where a large room had been reserved for the wedding reception. Sharon was looking forward to this because she was sure that once things got under way Hadyn would find an opportunity to talk to her. She knew her father wouldn't approve but he could hardly say or do anything when they were in the midst of family and friends.

At the reception, however, Sharon found herself seated at the long table that dominated the room between Lloyd Cogan and Madoc. There were lots of speeches and one of the first was from Madoc, who gave a longish one all about the things he and Parry had done when they'd been growing up. Parts of it were received with laughter from those present but Sharon already knew of their escapades, indeed she had taken part in many of them, so most of it was of little interest to her.

It did give her the opportunity, however, to study Hadyn. He was seated halfway down the table which was at right angles to hers and it was so easy to pick him out because of his rich auburn hair.

From time to time their eyes met and she let

herself daydream about what message he was trying to send to her. It made her more and more impatient for the formalities to end and everyone to mingle so that she would have the chance of talking to him.

The speeches and toasts seemed to go on for such a long time that she thought they would never end. Then the newly married couple posed to have yet another photograph taken as they stood with both of them holding a knife poised over the beautifully decorated three-tier wedding cake.

As the reception came to an end, Sharon drew in her breath sharply as she saw Hadyn push back his chair, stand up and move towards the top table. Her heart beat faster but she felt fearful of what her father might say if he saw her chatting to Hadyn for too long. Then she remembered what her mother had said about being polite and she squared her shoulders defiantly. She smiled to herself; she would talk to Hadyn because he was a guest and must be treated courteously.

To her dismay, however, he made no attempt to come and talk to her when the meal ended and people began to move around. Instead he made his way towards Gwen's mother, Flossie, who was wearing the most enormous pale green hat that made her look even dumpier than usual, and engaged her in conversation.

Sharon hovered close by, listening half-heartedly to what Madoc was saying to her because she wanted to be ready to greet Hadyn as soon as she had a chance to do so. The delay was frustrating because she knew that at any minute now she would be expected to go and help Gwen to change out of her wedding dress and into her smart going-away outfit ready to set off with Parry on their honeymoon.

The call from Gwen came all too soon and Sharon still hadn't had a chance to talk to Hadyn. As she helped Gwen out of her wedding dress and into her going-away outfit she found herself forced to listen to her excited comments about what a wonderful day it had been.

'I felt so nervous when I first arrived that I thought I was going to be sick,' Gwen said with a giggly laugh. 'It wasn't until the actual service was over that I started to relax. Since then, though, I've enjoyed every minute of it.'

As Gwen chattered on, Sharon's frustration increased. It was all very well for Gwen, she thought resentfully, everything had gone well for her. She had married the man she loved and had her family's approval and when she returned from her honeymoon there was a nice little house all furnished and waiting for them in Gower Street in Cathays. Gwen would be able to live her own life without her mam or dada interfering with everything she did and telling her what she could and could not do.

'Wouldn't it be wonderful, Sharon, if the next wedding in our family was yours and Madoc's?'

Gwen's words startled her. She knew that was what her own parents were hoping for but the realisation that the Cogan family also thought that she and Madoc were right for each other worried her. As she had explained to her mother when she'd brought the subject up, she liked Madoc well enough but she thought of him as a friend or even as a brother; she didn't want to marry him.

By the time Gwen had changed out of her wedding finery and the two of them returned to the main room where Parry was waiting, Hadyn was no longer talking to Flossie Cogan.

Sharon looked round the big room, her spirits rising hopefully because it meant that at last they would be able to be together, but he was nowhere to be seen. She was about to ask Flossie if he had left but her own parents had joined the group surrounding the newly-weds so there was no opportunity to do so.

The final goodbyes and hugging and kissing seemed to take for ever. Flossie Cogan was in tears as Gwen and Parry were ushered outside to the waiting car that was to take them to the railway station. Once more there were interminable good-byes all round. When the car finally pulled away Sharon breathed a sigh of relief because she was now free at last and could look for Hadyn.

Once again her hopes were dashed. Madoc seemed to be determined to stay by her side as they chatted with the remaining guests and waited for them to leave. Then he took her arm and led her across to join his parents and hers who had decided to have one final glass of champagne to toast the departed newly-weds.

Talk inevitably covered the highlights of the day and there were so many hints and smiles about how long they would have to wait for the next family wedding that Sharon felt trapped.

No matter what any of them said, she resolved determinedly, she would never marry Madoc

Cogan; her mind was made up on that point and nothing anyone said would persuade her otherwise.

Chapter Two

As soon as they were back home again Sharon sought out the sanctity of her bedroom so that she could be alone with her thoughts.

Her room was at the rear of the house overlooking the garden. It was a large, pleasant room and furnished with a good-size single bed, a wardrobe and a dressing table, all in light oak, and a desk and chair as well as a comfortable armchair.

Parry's room was very similar although perhaps not quite so spacious, and her parents' bedroom, which was in the front of the house, was almost twice the size with a walk-in wardrobe and a screened-off section where there was a washbasin and toilet. There were also two other bedrooms, a large one at the side of the house and a slightly smaller one at the very back, which were only used when they had guests. There was also a family bathroom and a separate toilet on the same floor and a large attic up above.

Downstairs there was a square entrance hall with a toilet and cloakroom off them. Oak panelled doors led to three reception rooms as well as a spacious kitchen with a scullery off it. There was also a utility room near the back door where they kept their muddy boots in winter.

The room Sharon liked best was the sitting room which was directly under her bedroom and had a French door leading out into the garden.

They had moved into Pen-y-lan Place when she was about six years old and she had only a vague recollection of living in rooms above their shop before that. She could remember that she'd had to share a bedroom with Parry and that there had only been one living room and everything had been rather cramped. As a small child she had not been able to go out to play because the shop was in such a busy part of Cardiff and she always had to wait until her mother could find time to take her to the park.

Here it was so different. Living in Pen-y-lan Place meant that they were within a stone's throw of Roath Park and she could remember the wonderful feeling of freedom she'd had when she found that she could go to the park on her own whenever she liked. She still loved going there for a walk, especially when there was something troubling her and she wanted to think about it away from family and friends.

The Cogans had also been living over their shop in Queen Street and they had moved only a few months later to Ty Gwyn Avenue. It was a very similar house and only a short distance away so that she and Parry had remained friends with Gwen and Madoc and had even gone to the same schools.

Perhaps it was because of this, Sharon reflected, that she would never want to settle down and marry Madoc. She knew him too well already and he was so identical to her brother Parry in his likes

25

and dislikes that she knew even before he spoke what he wanted to do or what he thought about something.

She thought it improbable that she would ever make either of her parents understand this but she still couldn't understand why her father became so incensed at the idea of her being friends with Hadyn Jenkins. Her mother quite liked him and thought he was very courteous and Flossie Cogan obviously approved of him enough to invite him to Gwen's wedding.

Her father's words when she'd once asked him if she could go to the pictures with Hadyn were etched in her mind, never to be forgotten: 'You might have good taste when it comes to matching up wallpapers and curtain fabrics but you've certainly no taste at all when it comes to picking men.'

At the time she hadn't known whether to laugh or cry. Her father rarely commented on her work; he considered what she did to help customers to select carpets, curtains and paints that went together was her job and he would have been quick to tell her if she wasn't doing it properly. He rarely thought it was necessary to praise anyone working for him, the members of his family least of all. He was extremely hardworking himself and always put the maximum effort into everything he did and because of this he expected everybody else to do the same.

This was another reason why she was baffled by his attitude about Hadyn. Hadyn was a conscientious salesman. He was courteous, brisk and smart in every sense of the word. He was highly knowledgeable about the products he was carrying and quick to point out the advantages of any particular item if called upon to do so. He was always punctual and would go to great lengths to obtain an order. He invariably followed up a big deal with a courtesy call to make sure that the customer was completely satisfied when the product he'd sold them was delivered.

She'd often heard Lloyd Cogan singing his praises but noticed that although her father never said anything, his mouth would tighten in annoyance.

She moved over to the window and stood there staring out unseeingly as she battled with her dilemma. Had Hadyn deliberately avoided her today because he knew it only antagonised her father if he saw them chatting, or had he lost interest in her? How was she ever going to find out? she wondered.

From now on she wouldn't even have Parry to talk to about such things because he would no longer be living there and now that he and Gwen were married he wouldn't have as much time for her anyway.

He'd never expressed any opinion about Hadyn but then, for the last few months, all he could talk about was his forthcoming marriage. She was pretty certain, though, that if she asked him what he thought she ought to do he would tell her to keep away from Hadyn so as not to upset their father. He'd also probably remind her that Madoc was head over heels in love with her anyway, so what more did she want?

How could she possibly tell Parry that it was

because Madoc was so much like him that she considered he was far too dull for her liking? That would only upset him.

No, she determined, this was one problem she was obviously going to have to solve for herself and while common sense told her that it would be easier to conform to her father's wishes, her heart ached for Hadyn.

It was the middle of the following week before Hadyn called at the shop and she was able to set her mind at rest as to whether or not he was still interested in her.

He arrived mid-morning, and her heart beat faster as she saw him entering their shop heavily loaded with new samples. He looked extremely smart in a dark grey suit, white shirt and a dark red tie that almost matched his wavy auburn hair.

She was sitting at the large table at the back of the wallpaper showroom working on a watercolour interpretation of what a room would look like when it was decorated with the paints, wallpapers, carpets and curtains that a particular customer had selected.

It was a service that set them apart from the usual retailers and one which was eagerly sought by customers who were undecided or unable to visualise what the finished result would look like.

She looked up and smiled at Hadyn as he walked towards her and felt her cheeks reddening as he stared critically at her work. She suddenly wanted to hide it from him, afraid that he wouldn't think it very good.

When he commented, 'I must say, you really do

have a talent for that sort of thing', she felt so elated by his praise that tears came into her eyes.

Before she could answer, however, her father had come out of his office into the showroom and immediately Hadyn walked towards him, his hand held out in greeting.

'Good morning, Jenkins, I wasn't expecting you for another week,' Elwyn Pritchard said coldly.

'Really?' Hadyn sounded surprised. Putting down his bundle of samples he pulled out a diary from an inside pocket and leafed through it. 'According to this I am due to see you today,' he affirmed.

'Well, since you are here you may as well come into my office and show me what you have brought along,' Elwyn said briskly as he turned on his heel leaving Hadyn to follow him.

'With pleasure.' Hadyn managed to flash a quick smile in Sharon's direction as he picked up his bundles and hurried after her father.

Sharon tried to concentrate on the work she was doing but her thoughts kept turning towards what was taking place in her father's office. As he was a businessman, she knew that his first task would be to inspect the samples Hadyn had brought and either place an order or tell him that he was not interested in what he was offering.

All that would only take about ten minutes and she waited anxiously for Hadyn to come out of the office. As the minutes dragged by she wondered what else her father was saying to him. He might even be telling Hadyn that he didn't approve of him seeing her and telling him to keep his calls limited to purely business matters.

When she heard the office door open she pretended to be concentrating on her work but she kept glancing sideways and her heart sank as she saw Hadyn walk swiftly from the office and head in the direction of the communicating door between their shop and Cogan's Carpets and Curtains.

Putting down her paintbrush she pushed back her chair and picked up a sheet of paper from her desk which contained instructions about the room she was illustrating, with the intention of going into the curtain department on the pretence of checking some of the details.

Before she was halfway across the room her father came to his office door and called her over.

Biting her lip in frustration she went into his office mentally preparing herself for a warning that he didn't want to see her talking to Hadyn. To her surprise, however, he merely indicated a batch of wallpaper samples that Hadyn had brought in and asked her opinion about them.

They were very striking and completely different from anything they stocked at present and he wanted to know if she thought they would sell.

'I'm not sure; they're very colourful. Have you ordered any of them?' she asked, her voice slightly dubious.

'No, I've placed an order for some of his other ranges but I hardly think these are the sorts of designs we would want to carry as stock. I have said that we will include the samples in our pattern book, however,' he added. 'I wanted to draw your attention to them so that you can point them out to customers in the future so that they are aware that we are abreast of the times.'

'Yes, of course. I'll remember to do that.'

'Good. That's all.' He looked at the piece of paper in her hand. 'Is there a problem? Something you need to know?'

Sharon felt the hot blood rush to her cheeks. 'I ... I was going to check with Flossie about the curtains for the room I'm working on.'

'Why? What's wrong with them?'

'I'm not quite sure if the curtains have to be sill-length or floor-length.'

Elwyn took the sheet of paper from her hand and glanced at it. 'Surely it's obvious from the measurements that they are floor-length,' he commented as he handed it back to her.

Sharon scanned the paper again. 'Yes, of course,' she admitted with an apologetic smile. 'I'll get back to work, then.'

'Good! And there will be no need to bother Flossie with your query after all,' he added with a slightly cynical smile.

'No, Dada,' Sharon agreed as she returned to her desk. She felt angry with herself; she knew her father was well aware that her intention had been to go into the Cogans' shop because Hadyn was in there and he had cleverly outwitted her.

She sighed as she picked up her paintbrush. There was nothing she could do now. He was already suspicious of her intentions and if she moved from her desk again without good reason he'd be sure to ask what she was doing.

She glanced at the clock on the wall above her head. Another hour and she would be free to go for lunch. She usually brought sandwiches and

Gwen did the same and, if the weather was good, they often walked to Cathays Park near the City Hall and sat and enjoyed them there. If it was wet or cold, they ate them in the communal tea room that adjoined the kitchen where either she or Gwen or one of the other girls took turns to make a pot of tea around the middle of the morning and again in the afternoon for the rest of the staff.

Unable to settle to her work she picked up the cup that was on the corner of her desk; it was empty, so she pushed it away again. It was an unwritten rule that they shouldn't make unnecessary cups of tea but for once Sharon decided to ignore it. She needed a distraction and a cup of tea seemed to be the perfect solution.

It was peaceful in the tea room and as she waited for the kettle to boil she day-dreamed about Hadyn. She wondered what he'd thought when he'd seen her all dressed up at the wedding and looking so different.

When someone touched her lightly on the shoulder, she almost jumped out of her skin.

'Hadyn!' She swung round in surprise.

'When I saw you were no longer at your desk I hoped I might find you in here,' he greeted her.

'You shouldn't be in here,' she warned him. 'What do we do if someone comes in?'

'Tell them I asked for a drink of water or that you are making me a cup of tea.'

'Let's hope it's not my father, because he most certainly wouldn't approve of me doing that,' Sharon said, smiling.

'No.' Hadyn raised his eyebrows. 'He doesn't like me talking to you, does he?'

'He gave you an order this morning, didn't he?' Sharon prevaricated.

'Yes, he did, but he was wearing his business hat then and he's well aware that the companies I represent are the best there are and that it's in his interest to stock their lines. When it comes to condoning my friendship with his daughter, now, that is a different matter altogether.'

'He certainly won't approve if he finds you in here with me,' Sharon admitted. 'I'll be free in about an hour, though, for lunch, so can we meet outside somewhere?'

'No, I'm afraid not. I have to be in Newport for a two o'clock appointment,' Hadyn told her. 'What about tonight when you finish work?'

'I'm not sure; I'll have to think up an excuse about why I'm going out,' Sharon explained.

'Surely you can go out in the evenings when-ever you want to,' Hadyn laughed.

The colour rushed to Sharon's cheeks. 'Mam always expects me to tell her where I'm going and whom I'll be with. Usually I go out with Gwen but since she's away...' Her voice trailed off uncertainly as she saw the look of impatience on Hadyn's face. 'I know,' she said quickly, 'I'll tell her that I'm going up to Gwen and Parry's house to tidy up. We left wrapping paper all over the place after they unpacked the wedding presents and I did say I'd sort it out and tidy the place up for them before they came back from their honeymoon.'

'Will she believe that?' Hadyn frowned. 'Can you get in?'

'Yes, Gwen and Parry left a key with us,' Sharon assured him.

'Right,' he gave her a conspiratorial smile, 'we'll meet there. Shall we say seven o'clock?'

'That's perfect,' Sharon agreed happily.

'You haven't told me where their house is.'

'It's twenty Gower Street and that's off Crwys Road; do you think you will be able to find it?'

'I spend my life finding new places; it's all part of my job,' he reminded her. 'I'll be there, so make sure that you are already waiting for me.'

He was gone before she could answer. She pushed her cup away, she didn't really want a drink of tea now – she had far too much to think about.

She wasn't at all sure that she had done the right thing in agreeing to meet Hadyn at Gower Street. Her parents would be extremely angry if they ever found out. She wasn't even too sure what Gwen and Parry would think if they knew she had taken him there even before they'd had a chance to move in.

Chapter Three

By the time she'd reached home Sharon had decided on her plan of action and rehearsed in her mind exactly what she was going to tell her mother about going to Gower Street that evening to tidy up Parry and Gwen's house. There was only one problem, what would she do if her mother offered to come with her?

The moment she walked in through the front

door her plans were scuppered.

'Come on, dear,' her mother called. 'I need a hand; your dada has invited the Cogans round for a meal. Madoc is coming as well; we thought it would cheer you up because I know you must be missing Gwen and our Parry.'

'I was planning to go round to their house this evening and tidy up. I promised Gwen that I would because we left the wrapping paper from some of their wedding presents all over the place.'

'That's very thoughtful of you, cariad, but there's plenty of time before they come back and I'll come with you and help. Not tonight, though. I've prepared a nice meal for us all and I'm sure we'll have plenty to talk about because we haven't really met up since the wedding. There's never time for any chatter when we are at work.'

'Yes, Mam.' Sharon managed a smile, but inwardly she was very upset.

'You go and lay the table, then, cariad, and don't forget that there will be six of us. Make sure you sit Madoc next to you so that the two of you can talk between yourselves if you want to do so.'

'Are you sure that Madoc wants to be sitting indoors on a lovely evening like this?' Sharon asked tentatively.

'If he's in your company, then I am sure he will be happy enough,' her mother said with a smile. 'Anyway, the two of you can go for a walk afterwards if that's what you both want to do.'

Sharon didn't answer but the thought of going for a walk with Madoc and perhaps bumping into Hadyn was certainly something to be avoided at all costs, she thought in alarm.

She'd been looking forward to spending the evening with Hadyn and the thought of him arriving at Gower Street and then hanging around waiting for her only to find that she didn't turn up was very worrying.

For the next half an hour, although she did her mother's bidding, she was trying to think if there was any way of getting a message to him to let him know she couldn't be there but as far as she could see there was no way of doing so.

With the arrival of Madoc and his parents she knew it was too late and the only thing to do was to make them welcome and put all thoughts of Hadyn out of her mind.

The talk was all about the wedding and there were several veiled innuendoes from both her parents and the Cogans about when the next family wedding would take place.

'We'll have to start looking for another nice little property that the company can buy like the one in Gower Street so that there is a home ready and waiting for them,' Lloyd Cogan observed pompously.

'Yes, a proper little love-nest for our Gwen and your Parry to come back to,' his wife stated.

'I couldn't agree more,' Elaine enthused. 'I was only saying to Elwyn this morning how lucky they are. It's so much better than what we had; we started out living in the rooms above the shops, now, didn't we?'

Sharon only half listened to their reminiscing. What was far more important in her mind was whether Hadyn was already pacing up and down outside the house in Gower Street wondering why she was so late and whether she was even going to turn up.

The meal progressed so slowly that she thought it would never end and, what was worse, there was no way of letting Hadyn know that she wouldn't be there, so whatever would he think?

Long after she was in bed that night the problem of how she was going to tell Hadyn that it had been impossible for her to meet him at Gower Street filled Sharon's thoughts.

She fell asleep thinking of him. When she woke the next morning she lay there daydreaming and imagining what their evening could have been like if she had fulfilled her plan to go to Gower Street. She was brought back to reality abruptly when her mother, who had become so exasperated because she didn't answer her call to get up, came and banged on the bedroom door to warn her that she was going to be late for work if she didn't get a move on.

Halfway through the morning she went into the tea room to wash out her paintbrushes and was startled to find Hadyn in there.

'Hadyn!' she gasped, almost dropping the brushes she was carrying. 'I'm beginning to think you live in here.'

'I was going to wait another five minutes and then give up,' he said rather tersely. 'Where were you last night?'

'I'm sorry!' Briefly she told him about what had happened and how impossible it had been to get away.

'Can't you join a tennis club or a dramatic society or something so that you have an excuse to be out one evening a week so that we can meet?'

Sharon shook her head, her eyes filling with tears. 'It's not that easy. My parents expect me to tell them everything I am doing and if I said I had joined a club, they'd want to know all the details and I can't lie to them.'

'You mean they have you lined up for Madoc,' Hadyn retorted sourly.

'What on earth do you mean by that?' Sharon protested as her face flushed uncomfortably.

'You know quite well what I mean. Your brother Parry is now safely married to Gwen Cogan so if you marry Madoc, it will fit in well with your father's plans because it means that the two shops will stay united.'

Sharon stared at him blankly. She'd never thought about it like that before. She knew her father was a hard-headed businessman but she didn't like the idea that she and Parry were expected to marry to fit in with her father's plans.

'We haven't time to stand around talking about this at the moment,' Hadyn said abruptly. 'I want to be out of here as quickly as possible because if your father catches me here and finds out I've been trying to make a date with you, then he might lose his temper and do something drastic.'

'I'm quite sure he would order you to leave,' Sharon admitted with a wry smile.

'So can I see you at lunchtime?' Hadyn asked, looking at his watch. 'It's only in an hour and a half's time but I do have a call to make so it should work out well.'

'Very well, where shall we meet?'

'There's a quiet little restaurant in the David Morgan Arcade. I'll wait for you there.'

The rest of the morning passed in a daze for Sharon. She hoped there would be no customers demanding her attention between now and her lunchtime in case they made her late.

When her father came in to see if she had completed the visual for a job they were doing the next day she found it as quickly as she could and hoped that he wouldn't want her to make any changes.

To her relief he seemed to be quite satisfied with what she had done and went straight back to his office.

At five minutes to one o'clock she tidied her desk and made ready to leave. Normally she would have been spending the lunch break with Gwen so she wanted to slip away before anyone suggested joining her or asking her where she was going.

She wished she could have gone to the park with Hadyn but she realised that as it was such a bright sunny June day that was what most people would be doing so a quiet restaurant was more discreet. They were far less likely to meet anyone who knew them and who might tittle-tattle about seeing them together.

Their meal was a hurried affair because she had to get back to work and Hadyn had an appointment in Penarth for three o'clock.

'I could come back here again this evening. Will you be able to get away?' he asked.

'I think so,' Sharon said, her eyes shining hopefully. 'Where shall we meet?'

Hadyn remained silent as a waitress bringing the plates of ham and eggs that he had ordered put them down on the table in front of them.

'Gower Street, like we planned before,' he said in a low voice. 'Your brother hasn't come back from his honeymoon yet, has he?'

'No, they won't be home until the weekend.'

'Good, then shall we say seven o'clock?'

'Can we make it half past seven? I'm expected to wash the dishes after our meal and if I asked to be excused from doing that then my mother will want to know why.'

'So what are you going to tell her you will be doing?'

'Going for a walk, of course.'

'And she'll believe you?'

'Yes, I'm sure she will. I often used to go for a walk in the evenings with Gwen.' She sighed. 'I don't suppose she will want to do that in future, she will be too busy looking after Parry.'

'Probably, but you won't be lonely because you'll be going out with me,' Hadyn told her. 'Hurry up and eat your meal or you're going to be late back and then you will have your father asking you where you've been.'

'Seven-thirty at Gower Street,' he reminded her as they left the café. He gave her a quick peck on the cheek that made her blush and her heart beat faster with sheer happiness.

Before she could recover her composure he was striding away and was lost in the throng of people passing through the arcade.

Seven-thirty was only just over six hours away, Sharon thought elatedly, and they would be together again. She didn't know how she was going to get through the rest of the day without telling someone; she wanted to tell everyone she knew.

For the rest of the afternoon she was in a world of her own. She did her work almost mechanically as her thoughts, more often than not, were elsewhere.

At home her mother thought she was unusually quiet and as they cleared away after their meal she asked her if she was missing Gwen and Parry.

'Of course I am, but I suppose I'll have to get used to doing things on my own.' Sharon smiled with a light shrug of her shoulders. 'Anyway, I'm not going to sit home and mope about it.'

'Madoc will always take you out, you know,' Elaine Pritchard reminded her. 'He's such a lovely young man, you couldn't ask for anyone nicer.'

'Yes, Madoc is all right, but I don't want to be with him all the time, though. In fact, I'm off out for a walk on my own tonight,' she added quickly.

'Oh, and where are you thinking of going?' her mother queried, looking concerned.

'Probably to Roath Park, it's where Gwen and I always go.'

'All on your own!'

'Yes, nothing wrong with that, is there? I do like my own company, Mam.'

'Yes, of course. I'm not trying to interfere, my lovely. Now you run along and enjoy your walk,' she added, squeezing Sharon's arm as if to signal her approval.

'Yes, Mam. I'll do that.'

'Don't be late home, though, or I shall start worrying about you when it begins to get dark.'

41

'Mam, it's the middle of June and it doesn't get dark until ten or eleven o'clock,' Sharon told her, a trifle irritably.

'Even so it worries me, cariad, when you are out on your own and it starts getting late.'

'Yes, Mam, I'll remember,' Sharon promised as she kissed her on the cheek and then made a quick getaway before her mother could interrogate her any further.

Her heart was light as she made her way from Pen-y-lan Place to Gower Street. It wasn't very far but the houses were very much smaller. It was the sort of area where obviously her family and the Cogans had been thinking of buying another property in readiness for the next wedding in the family. She wondered if they would still feel the same way about it if she told them that she was marrying Hadyn and not Madoc as they all expected her to do.

That was looking ahead a little too much, she told herself. She hadn't really been on a proper date with Hadyn yet. She might be head over heels in love with him but she still had to discover how he really felt about her.

As she turned into Gower Street she could see Hadyn was there ahead of her and her pulse as well as her step quickened. He was so very tall and handsome and such a man of the world that she couldn't understand why he wasn't already married.

Perhaps he has been waiting for the right girl and that's going to be me, she told herself.

She was within a short distance of reaching him when she heard the pounding of footsteps behind her and someone calling her name. As she half turned to see who it was, she was furious to find that it was Madoc running after her.

With a feeling of panic she waved a hand in Hadyn's direction to try and indicate to him to go away and he turned on his heel and walked quickly down a nearby passageway between two houses. Sharon breathed a sigh of relief and hoped that Madoc hadn't recognised him or seen her warning him.

'I missed you; I got to your house seconds after you'd left and your mam said that you were probably coming here to Gower Street,' Madoc puffed as he reached her.

'I'm not going to the house. I'm on my way to Roath Park. I'm meeting a friend there in ten minutes,' she told him, hoping her voice was loud enough for Hadyn to hear what she was saying.

'Oh, that's a shame, because I was going to put up those shelves your Parry didn't get time to finish doing before they went away. I thought it would be a nice surprise for him to find them done when he arrived back. I'll be at the house for a couple of hours so why don't you drop in after your walk and then we can tidy the place up together and I'll walk you home?'

'I can't really promise that I'll come back because it all depends on what my friend wants to do so it might be best if you didn't wait for me,' Sharon told him hurriedly.

'We haven't had a chance to be together since the wedding,' Madoc grumbled.

'You saw me only last night when you came to our place for the evening,' she reminded him.

'We didn't get a chance to be on our own though, did we?'

'Look, I can't stop talking because I'm late already and my friend doesn't like to be kept waiting,' Sharon told him. 'If I don't call back, then I'll see you in work tomorrow morning,' she added evasively.

Chapter Four

Sharon found Hadyn waiting for her as she approached Roath Park. He was leaning against a wall smoking a cigarette and looking anything but pleased. He didn't even kiss her when she reached him.

'So what are we going to do now?' he asked rather impatiently as he dropped the stub of his cigarette on to the pavement and ground it out with the heel of his shoe.

'Go for a walk, I suppose.' She tried to sound positive but she could see that he was cross because their arrangements had gone so wrong. 'It's a lovely evening,' she added rather tritely.

'Yes, it's such a lovely one that everyone else has the same idea!' he muttered. 'I want to be on my own with you, somewhere.' He lowered his voice to a seductive whisper. 'Where no one can see us or even hear what we are saying,' he added as he took her hand and tucked it through the crook of his arm, pulling her close against his side.

Sharon felt reassured and smiled up at him.

'We'll find a secluded spot somewhere,' she promised.

'Not nearly as private as the house in Gower Street,' he reminded her. 'Can't we go back there later?'

'I don't think it's safe to do that because I've no idea how long Madoc will be there.'

'We could give it a try; we could go back and see in, say, a couple of hours,' he persisted.

Sharon shook her head. 'We can't risk doing that because if he saw us together, he would be sure to say something at work and then my father would get to hear about it.'

'I didn't mean you should take me there while he was there.' Hadyn scowled. 'No, we'll go back and you can go into the house on your own and I'll wait a short distance down the road. If he has gone, then you can come to the door and I'll come over.'

'What if Madoc is still there and I'm unable to let you know or to get away?' Sharon asked worriedly.

'If you haven't come to the door within five minutes, then I'll know he is still there and that he will be taking you home. I did hear what the two of you were saying, you know.'

Sharon felt the blood rush to her cheeks. She wasn't sure what Hadyn had overheard and the last thing she wanted was for him to get the wrong idea about her and Madoc but she said nothing. Trying to explain would only make the situation worse, she decided.

They walked for a while in silence. The park was crowded and although she racked her brains she was unable to think of any spot where they could go where they could be sure of being on their own.

'Well?' Hadyn demanded as he stopped to light another cigarette. 'Have you decided what you want to do? I'm fed up with walking around here, so are we going to go back to Gower Street?'

'Like I said, it's a bit tricky doing that,' Sharon demurred.

'Not if you do as I suggested and you go in there first to make sure that the coast is clear.'

Although she felt uneasy about such an arrangement Sharon decided she had no option but to comply. To her immense relief when she went into the house it seemed that Madoc had already gone home. Even so, she checked upstairs as well as the two rooms downstairs to make sure that there was no one there before she signalled to Hadyn who was waiting across the road that it was safe for him come on in.

As soon as the front door closed behind him the tension between the two of them vanished. While they were still in the tiny hallway Hadyn pulled her into his arms, expressing his desire for her, murmuring tender words of love and kissing her ardently.

Sharon felt overwhelmed. It was as if all her dreams and fantasies were coming true at once. She responded eagerly; all her doubts about his feelings for her vanished in a matter of minutes.

Still holding her close he guided her into the living room and began unbuttoning the front of her dress.

Nervously she caught at his hand to stop him,

whispering, 'We can be seen by people passing by outside.'

He frowned and was about to pull the curtains but she shook her head. 'Don't do that, it makes it too obvious.'

Hadyn's frown deepened then, grabbing her by the arm, he hurried her towards the stairs. 'No one will see us up here,' he whispered.

Upstairs in the pristine new bedroom that Parry and Gwen had not even occupied Sharon gave herself up to Hadyn's passionate lovemaking. She knew what she was doing was wrong and she couldn't imagine what her father would say if he ever found out, but at that moment she didn't care. All she wanted to do was to please Hadyn and she was willing to submit to anything he asked in order to do so.

At first she found responding to his sensuous touch as his fingers and lips explored her body was so utterly sublime that she floated on wave after wave of the most exquisite pleasure she had ever known. Then his caresses changed and became more intimate, invasive even, and immediately she felt fearful about what was happening.

There was no time to protest; suddenly there was a sharp pain that left her gasping and the next minute Hadyn flopped exhausted at her side. She didn't know what to say or do. She felt utterly different and from the weak groans he was making so did he.

He reached up and tenderly stroked her face, then pulled her head down so that he could kiss her. His lips were so soothing that she felt an overwhelming rush of love for him. At that moment she would have done anything in her power to keep them there, but at the back of her mind was the nagging worry that Madoc or even her father might walk round to Gower Street to make sure everything was locked up properly and she became anxious for them to leave.

Hadyn had no such worries and was prepared to take his time in getting dressed. He thought she was being exceptionally fussy about making sure that everything was restored to order.

'No one's lived in this house yet so it's important nothing is out of place,' she explained.

'The young lovers will be too tired after their journey and too eager to get into bed to notice if the pillows are creased or the bedding not exactly as it was when they went away.'

'You don't know Gwen,' Sharon told him. 'She's got a very keen eye for details of that sort.'

Hadyn gave a huge yawn. 'I think you are worrying too much,' he told her as he finished dressing. 'Will we be able to come here again?'

'No, it's out of the question,' Sharon told him quickly. Although they wouldn't be back until the weekend, she didn't want to take any more risks. They'd been lucky that no one had found them there but they might not be as fortunate the next time.

'We'll have to try and find somewhere else, then,' Hadyn mused. 'Perhaps I could come round one night when your parents are out and you're at home on your own. Now that Parry is married he will be well out of the way so that could be a perfect meeting place.'

Sharon shook her head. 'No, that would be

quite impossible,' she gasped in a horrified voice.

'Why?' Hadyn's eyebrows shot up. 'Surely they must go out sometimes and leave you at home on your own?'

Sharon was so taken aback at the audacity of his suggestion that she couldn't find the right words to answer him. More than anything else she wanted to see Hadyn again and for them to be on their own, but the thought of them behaving as they had just done in her own home took her breath away.

'I thought you knew my father well enough to know that there is no possibility of us ever being able to do that,' she prevaricated.

'Then in that case you'd better see if they will let you come away one weekend and I'll book into a hotel somewhere and you can join me there.'

'Share a room in a hotel with you!' she gasped in astonishment.

He walked across the room and took her in his arms. 'I really do want to have you all to myself again very, very soon, cariad,' he breathed softly, holding her close.

She sighed as she leaned into his embrace.

'Can you suggest anything else?' he asked as he knotted his tie and looked at her questioningly.

Sharon shook her head; she felt dazed by his proposition which was not only terribly romantic but really did mean that she mattered so much to him that he was determined to find a way for them to be together.

'Think about it and let me know what's best,' he said as he ran a comb through his thick, wavy hair. Picking up his jacket from where he had

49

dropped it he shrugged himself into it and gave her a fleeting kiss. 'I'll be off now; it will be much safer if we leave here separately and it's still light enough for you to walk home on your own.'

Sharon was about to protest but then she saw the sense of his decision and smiled and nodded. 'When will I see you again?'

'I'll be calling in for an order in about ten days' time. I'll see you then and you can tell me when I have to book that overnight stay in a hotel.' He winked and was gone.

Sharon was so distracted and dreamy over the next couple of days that even her parents commented on it.

'Anyone would think she was in love or sickening for something,' Elaine Pritchard sighed.

'In love? Well, I hope it's with young Madoc and not that upstart Hadyn Jenkins; he's far too old for her and far too glib,' Elwyn stated.

'Hadyn is a lovely chap, well spoken and such nice ways with him,' Elaine protested. 'I can't for the life of me see why you don't like him.'

'I know his sort too well,' her husband told her sharply. 'Take my word for it, that charm of his has no depth at all. I don't want him anywhere near our Sharon. He's a wily character and I wouldn't trust him an inch; mark my words, he probably has girls mooning after him in every town he visits. I don't want Sharon to be another scalp to add to his list. It worries me the way lately he always manages to talk to her whenever he comes in to see me.'

'I'm sure there's no harm in it. She's missing Parry and Gwen but they'll be back tomorrow and then she'll be too busy catching up with all their news to be interested in anyone else.'

Elaine was wrong; Sharon could think of nothing but the evening when she had been with Hadyn and she wondered how she could manage to persuade her parents to let her go away for a whole weekend so that she could spend it with him as he'd suggested.

There was an impromptu family gathering at Gower Street to welcome home the newly-weds and Gwen proudly showed off her new home. She thanked Sharon for clearing up in the living room where the wrappings from all the wedding gifts had been left strewn all over the place and then dropped a bombshell by asking, 'Whatever happened up in our bedroom? The bed looked as if someone had slept in it.'

Sharon felt the hot blood rush to her cheeks as all eyes turned on her. 'I've no idea, Gwen,' she said quickly.

'You were the only one who had a key to get in. Did Madoc come with you to help clear up?' she asked archly.

'No, I did it on my own.'

'Oh well, I suppose I imagined it, or it must have been the fairies, then,' Gwen laughed snidely.

Sharon said nothing but she felt overwhelmed by embarrassment and guilt. She was so sure that she had smoothed out the pillows and the rest of the bed so that no one would ever know that it had been used. She'd even checked again when she'd gone back the next day on her own to do the tidying up.

She was still thinking about it when she went to

51

bed and wondered if perhaps someone had seen her and Hadyn either going in or coming out of the house and mentioned it to Gwen.

She waited in trepidation for either her mother or her father to question her about it but, when no one did, she decided there was nothing to worry about and put it out of her mind.

Both her parents, like most of the other people in Cardiff, were worried about all the talk there was about the possibility of a miners' strike and what a bad effect that would have if it happened. As well as the miners being out of work there would be repercussions everywhere and their own businesses would suffer.

Once men were out of work there would be no money to spend on luxuries like improving their homes. The main concern for most families would be finding money for basics like food and heating, especially if the strike extended on into the winter months.

Gwen, however, was more persistent and several times asked Sharon if she had changed anything around in their bedroom while she had been tidying up during their absence. Even though Sharon assured her that she hadn't, Gwen was far from satisfied and several times in a roundabout way questioned whether she had been there with Madoc. It made Sharon very uneasy in case she mentioned it to him and, as a result, the truth came out.

She waited anxiously for Hadyn's next visit so that she could share her worries about this with him. At the same time she wondered how he would react when she told him that, so far, she hadn't found a way to ask her parents if she could go away for a weekend.

He didn't seem to understand the restrictions of living in a close-knit family like hers and having a father who was so protective that he wanted to know everything she did. Hadyn had suggested that she should say that she was going away with a friend but this wasn't as easy as it sounded because her family knew all her friends and were bound to mention the proposed trip to someone in the girl's family and find out that she was lying.

She didn't know an awful lot about Hadyn's family, except what she had heard from her father.

'He's the sort of chap who has grown up living on his wits to get by,' he'd once said in a derogatory tone when her mother had asked about Hadyn. 'As I understand it, he comes from up the Valleys; his father was killed in the Senghenydd Pit disaster when he was about fourteen. He more or less had to fend for himself after that, by all accounts.'

'Poor boyo!' her mother said sadly. 'You have to admire what he's managed to make of himself. Look at him now, so smart-looking and confident and holding down such a good job.'

She'd heard her father mutter, 'Too smart, too damn confident,' and she'd clapped her hands over her ears because she knew his next words would be 'and with girls hanging on to his coat tails in every town he visits.'

The fact that her mother liked Hadyn was comforting but it didn't solve the problem of her father disliking him, because Sharon knew that it was her father's approval that was so important.

She waited on tenterhooks for Hadyn's next visit but as the days went by she began to think she must have missed him. She couldn't think how that could have happened because she had made sure she was around when he was due to call. In the end she plucked up the courage to casually comment that he was overdue for his appointment.

'He came last week during our lunch hour,' her father informed her. 'Very bad timing, so I sent him away without an order.'

Sharon felt shocked but she did her best to remain expressionless because she knew her father was waiting for her reaction.

'I've no time for commercial travellers who don't turn up during business hours,' he said relentlessly.

'Did you give him a chance to explain?' she asked defensively.

'No point. He'd have some glib cock and bull story all ready on the tip of his tongue but that doesn't wash with me.'

Sharon knew it was pointless saying any more but, as soon as her father went out of his office, she looked through his appointment diary to see when Hadyn's next visit was listed and it worried her when she couldn't find any entry at all.

July seemed to drag by as she waited to hear from Hadyn but it was almost as if he had never existed. Then, during the second week in August, the company he represented sent a new man and, for one awful moment, Sharon thought that Hadyn must be ill.

When she enquired later she was shocked when

her father told her that Hadyn wouldn't ever be calling on them again because he was no longer working for Brynmor and Williams.

'Have you any idea why he's lost his job?' she queried, hoping he couldn't hear the way her heart was pounding because she was so upset by the news.

'Due anwyl, why should I know that?' her father said evasively.

'If you know he isn't working for Brynmor and Williams, then I thought they would have said why that was so.'

'Something to do with the way he was carrying on with the daughter of one of his customers.'

Sharon stared at him in alarm, the colour draining from her face until it was almost as white as the blouse she was wearing. 'It was you who reported him, wasn't it!' she said accusingly.

Although Elwyn Pritchard's face was under control as he looked at her, his dark eyes gleamed with anger. 'Now why do you say that? Is there any reason that I should do so?'

Sharon shook her head, unable to speak. Her father had sent away the only man she would ever love but she knew that anything she said would only make matters worse.

That night she cried herself to sleep, afraid that it meant she would never see Hadyn again. Next morning she woke bleary-eyed but determined that she would contact him somehow. The only way she could think of doing so was by sending a letter to the company where he had worked and asking for it to be forwarded on to him.

She puzzled for hours about what to say in her

note to Hadyn. It had to be something that no one would know what it meant or where it came from, in case it fell into the wrong hands.

Finally she wrote a cryptic message to say that he had left something behind so could he please call and collect it as soon as possible. She didn't put her address; she only signed it with her first name.

As the days passed and there was no response her disappointment increased. Her only hope was that he had not received her letter yet.

The alternative was that he was no longer interested in her and she couldn't bear to think that because she would have nothing to live for if Hadyn went out of her life for ever.

Chapter Five

Sharon felt restless; she carried out her duties at work automatically but without her usual verve. She listened to their customers' requirements and made suggestions but her responses lacked her usual spontaneity.

Her father was quick to comment on her lack of enthusiasm as she responded to customers.

'Aren't you feeling well?' he asked.

Sharon gave a little shrug. She wanted to tell him that she was concerned about what had happened to Hadyn; that she was miserable at the thought that she might never see him again and that she would never forgive her father for getting Hadyn sacked. She knew better than to do so; instead she mumbled, 'I feel rather tired, I haven't been sleeping well.'

His mouth tightened but he didn't pursue the matter and she was pretty sure that he knew what the underlying cause was.

In an attempt to cheer her up, her mother kept asking Gwen and Parry around but seeing them so happy together only added to Sharon's feeling of depression.

To make matters worse, Gwen was constantly saying how much she loved having her own home that it was time that Madoc and Sharon got married.

'After all, you've been going around together since you were at school,' she pointed out. 'Surely you must have made up your mind by now, Sharon. It's high time you stopped playing hard to get or our Madoc will get tired of being fobbed off and start looking elsewhere.'

Each time Gwen said this Sharon was tempted to tell her that she wished he *would* forget about her and find someone else. There was only one man she wanted to marry and that was Hadyn Jenkins and, if she couldn't have him, then she'd stay an old maid until the end of her life.

Instead, because she knew it would only cause trouble with her father and perhaps even with her mother, she merely smiled and tried to pass it off by changing the subject or asking Gwen something about how she was managing in her new home.

Gwen's first attempt at entertaining was regarded as a big occasion and although Sharon tried her best to find an excuse not to go, it was impossible not to. She cringed inwardly as they all assembled at Gower Street. As Gwen proudly served the meal, helped by Parry, Sharon found herself remembering her visit there with Hadyn and she felt sick with worry although she was quite sure that none of them knew anything at all about it.

Madoc was seated across the table from her and he kept raising his eyebrows as Parry brought in the dishes from the kitchen and set them down on the table.

'It looks as though I will have to take a course in being a waiter before I get married,' he joked. 'I never do anything at home. Mam waits on me hand and foot.'

'Parry enjoys helping me,' Gwen defended. 'I bet you'll be the same when it comes to helping Sharon,' she added with an arch look at them both.

'Take no notice, Sharon. Our Madoc does help around the place so you'll have no worries there,' Flossie assured her.

'And we've already seen a nice little property not too far from here,' Lloyd added.

'Come on then, you two, name the day, can't you, so that we can start planning and then get back to normal.'

Sharon merely smiled and said nothing but Madoc seized the opportunity to insist that he was only waiting for Sharon to make up her mind as he was more than ready to settle down and have a place of his own.

As she listened to their banter Sharon found it hard to keep back her tears. Why couldn't they leave her alone; how could she marry Madoc when she was so desperately in love with Hadyn? Yet, if she tried to tell them that, it would cause such an uproar that she knew she dared not say anything. All she could do was wait for Hadyn to contact her and in her heart she was sure he would do so as soon as he could.

Every morning when Sharon came downstairs the first thing she did was look to see if there was a letter from Hadyn. Hiding her disappointment when there wasn't one was difficult and often she felt so upset that she felt sick and found it hard to act as though everything was normal and sit down and eat breakfast with her parents.

Days became weeks; summer cooled into autumn and with their summer holidays behind them people once more began making changes to their homes. Both shops were so busy that during the day Sharon didn't have very much time to think about Hadyn. At night, though, it was different. She went over and over in her mind the things he had said and finally, before sleep claimed her, she would remember in detail their last meeting when they had made passionate love at Gower Street.

Her mother constantly nagged her that she wasn't eating enough to keep a bird going but she had no interest in food, especially first thing in the morning when the smell of bacon frying made her want to heave.

'I'm eating plenty,' she kept telling her mother. 'I must be, because I'm putting on weight; all my skirts are tight at the waist.'

59

'Well, I don't think you are. You don't seem to have any energy and you certainly have no interest in anything or anyone outside of work. I wonder that Madoc puts up with you. Whenever he suggests going to a dance or to the pictures you say you are too tired and that you want an early night.'

'We're very busy at work, as you very well know. You say yourself sometimes that you are worn out with it all.'

'At my age, and with a home to take care of, it's only natural that I should feel worn out at times. You're too young to be tired. Even your dad says you don't seem to have the interest in things that you used to have.'

'I do my duty and none of the customers has complained now, have they? And that is all that matters.'

'You've always got an answer for everything, my girl,' her mother told her slightly crossly.

Sharon didn't reply. There were so many questions buzzing around in her head to which she would dearly love an answer. Topping the list was why hadn't Hadyn been in touch?

She was convinced that there must be a problem of some sort because she couldn't bring herself to believe that he had forgotten her; not after the wonderful lovemaking they'd experienced at Gower Street. Surely that momentous occasion would stay alive in his mind as it had done in hers because it had been so breathtakingly wonderful.

The other thing that troubled her deeply, and which she wished she could talk over with her mother, was why she felt so tired and lethargic.

60

Some days even wielding a small paintbrush to do the watercolour interpretations for customers of what their rooms would look like seemed to take so much effort that she could hardly be bothered to do them.

In fact, it took all her energy to concentrate on what they were asking her and then to remember what colour scheme she had suggested or they had requested.

Countless times she saw her father watching her with a frown on his face and, once or twice, he had even gone as far as to say rather sharply, 'You're not paying attention, are you?' or else, 'Do you have to stand around daydreaming? Haven't you any work to be getting on with?'

She wasn't daydreaming, though; leastwise not in the accepted sense. She was either trying to puzzle out what was wrong with her these days or else asking herself why Hadyn hadn't been in touch and what other means she could use to contact him.

Most of all she was worried about herself in case she had some sort of strange illness. At one point she wondered if she had TB. A school friend, Morag Williams, had contracted tuberculosis shortly after they had left school and she had died less than six months later. During that time she had grown painfully thin and weak and looked like a walking skeleton.

Whatever it was it certainly wasn't a wasting disease of that kind, Sharon reflected as she studied herself in the mirror each night when she undressed for bed. Every day her skirts seemed to get tighter because she was putting on weight

61

around her waist and there were times when she was sure her hands looked a bit puffy. Yet it wasn't because she was overeating or indulging in sweets or chocolate. The only thing she was doing more of was smoking, and she had to do that on the sly.

She couldn't smoke while she was at work and her mother didn't like her smoking at home. Elaine was old fashioned in regard to smoking; it was all right for the men to do it, but she said it wasn't considered to be ladylike when she was growing up and she didn't like to see her daughter with a cigarette in her hand, even though nowadays it was regarded as being sophisticated by most young flappers.

Finally, in desperation because she felt she must confide in someone or go mad with worry, she mentioned to Gwen one morning when they were both in the tea room about how out of sorts she was feeling.

Gwen clapped her hand over her mouth and her eyes widened like saucers. 'Oh no! Are you sure, cariad?' she breathed enraptured.

Sharon stared at her in bewilderment.

'I knew you and Madoc had been in our bedroom while we were away,' Gwen babbled excitedly.

Sharon felt annoyed by Gwen's silly reaction. 'What on earth are you talking about, Gwen?' she demanded. 'I told you before I was never in your bedroom with Madoc. Anyway, even if I had been, which I hadn't, what does that have to do with the way I'm feeling?'

Gwen removed the tin kettle from the gas ring and poured the boiling water into the big brown teapot that was standing on the draining board before she answered. 'Are you pretending, or do you really not know what I'm talking about?'

'No, I don't, because you're not making any sense at all,' Sharon told her sharply as she placed cups on to a tin tray and began putting milk into each of them. 'You keep harking back to your bedroom and I keep telling you that I was never in there with Madoc, though what that has to do with the way I feel I really don't know.'

Gwen stirred the tea in the big brown pot thoughtfully. 'Well, from the way you say you feel, I'd say it means you are pregnant, Sharon,' she stated, her cheeks going bright red with embarrassment. 'The thing is, what are you going to do about it?'

'What on earth are you talking about! How can you say something like that?' Sharon said indignantly.

'You're putting on weight as well and that's another sign that you're pregnant,' Gwen hurried on. 'I've noticed how tight your skirt is around the middle and even your blouses are stretched so much it's a wonder the buttons don't pop off.'

'You're making it all up, what do you know about such things anyway?' Sharon defended herself. 'Come on, pour out the tea and I'll take it through or they'll think they're never going to get any this morning.'

'You either don't believe me, do you, or you don't want to believe me,' Gwen added firmly as she picked up the tea strainer and began to pour tea into the cups.

'I don't think you know what you are talking

about, that's why,' Sharon retorted.

'That's where you're wrong. I do know what I'm talking about because they're exactly the same symptoms as I am having and the doctor has confirmed that I am pregnant.'

'You and Parry are starting a family already?' Sharon gasped, her own problem forgotten for the moment as she stared at Gwen in amazement.

'Yes, but we don't want to tell the family yet, not until I am a full three months' pregnant, because the doctor said that things can go wrong in the first three months with a first baby so don't go saying anything to your mother. When we are quite sure that everything is all right then we'll make the announcement to both our families at the same time.'

Before Sharon could reply Gwen had pushed her to one side and picked up the tin tray and marched out into the shop with it.

Left on her own Sharon held her head in her hands. She didn't want to believe Gwen but the more she thought about it and remembered all that had happened between her and Hadyn on that wonderful night back in June the more it seemed possible that Gwen could be right.

She felt dizzy as waves of panic and guilt swept over her. Why hadn't she worked this out for herself? she wondered. Her mother had sat her down and told her all about babies and how they were born when she'd been twelve years old. She remembered how she and Gwen had whispered to each other about it for weeks afterwards, mystified by the knowledge and only half believing what they'd been told.

Now every detail came rushing back into her mind; there was no doubt about it, her symptoms did indicate that she was pregnant. She didn't want to believe it, she didn't want it to happen. She went hot and cold as she thought of the reaction there would be from her parents once she was forced to tell them about it.

No one must know yet; she needed time to think and to plan. Perhaps she could get Gwen to promise to say nothing if, in return, she promised to keep the fact that Gwen herself was pregnant a secret.

That, of course, would only be a temporary measure but at least it would give her a chance to decide what to do for the best and a little longer to try and make contact with Hadyn.

She recalled other scraps of information that had come their way as they were growing up; lurid details of how it was possible to get rid of unwanted babies before they were born. She didn't even know how to go about doing something like that and she didn't think that she would have the courage to do it anyway.

She paced up and down waiting for Gwen to come back. She needed to talk to her, perhaps she could advise her what to do. She shuddered; it was going to be bad enough admitting to Gwen that her diagnosis was correct, but what was going to be even more difficult was telling her that Madoc had not had anything at all to do with it.

How long would it be before everyone knew that it was Hadyn Jenkins who was the father of the baby she was carrying?

Chapter Six

The more Sharon thought about what Gwen had said the more she realised that Gwen was right and that all her symptoms pointed to the fact that she was pregnant.

In desperation she wrote another letter to Hadyn telling him her news. She omitted her own address and didn't even sign it in case someone else read it and guessed whom it was from. She sent it to his old firm, marked it 'Urgent' and requested that it should be forwarded on to him.

The waiting seemed to be interminable; each morning she made sure that she collected the letters when the postman called so that she could make a quick check to see if there was one for her. The despair when there wasn't one was almost intolerable.

Fortunately, her nausea each morning had now gone and in many ways she seemed to be in the peak of good health. Even her feeling of tiredness had abated and her only problem now was one of putting on weight.

Madoc was as attentive as ever and although she did everything possible to avoid his company he seemed always to be around and she suspected that he was being aided and abetted both by her family and his own; especially by Gwen, because she thought it was his baby.

Whenever her father heard her decline to go to

the pictures or for a walk when Madoc asked her, he would suggest that they all sat round the table and played one of his favourite board games.

'You and Madoc can be partners,' he would always say as he dealt out the counters or cards and set the board up ready for them all to play.

Sharon hated these sessions at home even more than going out for a walk with Madoc. Since there seemed to be no way of getting out of it, she had no option but to take her place at the table and join in with as good grace as possible.

In the middle of October, Gwen and Parry announced that Gwen was expecting a baby. Immediately all attention was fixed on Gwen. She was showered with congratulations and advice on what she must and must not do, on the sort of foods she must eat, and her general well-being was foremost in everyone's mind.

Sharon was well aware that her own shape was changing as rapidly as Gwen's and although so far no one seemed to have noticed, she knew that any day now someone would. She had no idea what she would tell them when they did.

Madoc seemed to be the only one not joining in all the excitement; it was almost as if he was jealous of his sister's good news. He kept asking Sharon to marry him and suggesting that Christmas would be a good time for them to announce they were engaged.

Each time he proposed she managed to avoid giving him an answer although, as the days went by and there was still no response from Hadyn, there were times when she was tempted to accept. If she married Madoc, she reasoned, then her baby would have a father. Even so, she couldn't bring herself to do something like that to Madoc and, anyway, it was far too late; he was no fool and he'd be quick to discover why she had accepted him.

She toyed with the idea of telling him the truth; admitting that she was pregnant but she knew that if she did that then she would have to disclose who the father was.

That would do one of two things, she told herself. It would either stop Madoc from having anything else to do with her or she would find herself committed to marrying a man she didn't love.

By November they were well into the pre-Christmas rush and Sharon found that because of Gwen's delicate condition she was expected to cover for Gwen when she wasn't feeling well. This also meant that she was the one who was expected to make the tea every morning and afternoon for the rest of the staff. She didn't really mind because it gave her time away from the shop floor and the watchful eye of her father.

Sometimes she managed to slip out for a breath of fresh air under the pretext of going to one of the nearby shops to buy tea or sugar or fresh milk.

It was on one of these occasions that, a few days before Bonfire Night, she was approached by a scruffy young boy of about ten. Instead of asking for the usual 'Penny for the Guy', as she had been expecting him to do, he handed her a grubby piece of paper and then ran off before she could question him.

Her heart leapt, even though it wasn't signed and she didn't recognise the handwriting. Instinctively she knew it must be from Hadyn. She caught her breath, the whole world seemed to be suddenly spinning round and her hand was shaking so much that for a moment she could hardly make sense of the few words scribbled there:

Meet me tonight when you finish work.
I'll be waiting around the corner.

Her relief that he had at last contacted her was so great that she wanted to laugh and cry all at once. He hadn't forgotten her; she'd been right all along and there had been some very real reason why he hadn't been able to get in touch.

For the rest of the day her thoughts were in turmoil. She wanted to tell the world the good news that she had heard from him but she knew that the slightest whisper and her father would forbid her to meet him. One minute the day dragged, then the next, it seemed to be racing forward.

When they closed she hurriedly collected her outdoor clothes and left. Outside it was cold and dark and there was a fine misty rain falling. Sharon turned up her coat collar and tightened her scarf as she hurried around the corner to where she hoped she would find Hadyn waiting.

She wished she had thought to tell her father that she would be late home to save her mother from worrying when she didn't turn up at her usual time. It was too late to go back and do so, she decided. If she did that then she might miss Hadyn. The best thing to do was meet him first and then they could walk in the direction of her home so that she could pop indoors and let her mother know that she was going to be out for the evening.

If it had been anyone else but Hadyn then she could have taken him home, she thought wryly, but she knew that to do that would infuriate her father. Knowing how he felt about Hadyn, she feared he might even tell him to leave.

Hadyn was sheltering in a doorway and as he stepped out on to the pavement in front of her she felt a wave of panic go through her. For a brief moment she was not sure if it was him. He seemed taller and thinner than when she had last seen him. He was wearing a raincoat with the collar turned up and his trilby hat pulled well down over his eyes and from what she could see of his face he looked drawn and haggard.

'Sharon!' The moment he spoke all the fears and worries that had been troubling her for so many months vanished. As he took her in his arms and she returned his hugs and kisses she knew everything would be all right now. As long as they were together then somehow they would find a way to build a future of some sort for the baby's sake, she told herself as she linked her arm through his and they started walking.

'You got my last note, then,' she breathed.

'Note? What note? When did you send it?'

'Last week, but I did write to you once before,' she told him. 'I couldn't understand why you never replied or weren't in touch.'

'I've never received any notes or letters from you,' he stated firmly.

'You should have done; I sent them to your firm and marked them for you.'

'Why send them there? You knew I had been given the sack,' he said tersely.

'It was the only way I could think of for getting in touch with you because you've never told me your home address,' she explained contritely.

'So why were you so eager to see me again? Have you missed me all that much?' he teased, kissing her on the cheek.

'Of course I've missed you and wondered why you've never been in touch. Then, as soon as I knew that I was pregnant, it was more important than ever to get in touch with you.'

'Pregnant! You're pregnant?' His voice registered shock and he stopped walking and took her by the shoulders and spun her round to face him. 'Are you telling me you're expecting a baby ... and that it is my baby?'

'That's right, and I've been worried sick about what to do. I daren't tell my family. Gwen knows; she was the one who told me. At first I had no idea, I thought I was just feeling ill and sick with worry because I was missing you, but then she had the same symptoms and she knew that hers were because she was having a baby,' Sharon told him breathlessly.

Hadyn shook his head as if mystified by what she was telling him. 'Are you sure you aren't imagining you're pregnant simply because of what Gwen has been telling you?' he protested.

'No, I'm pregnant all right. I've put on so much weight that I can hardly fasten my skirts at the waist and there are so many other things too,' she affirmed. 'I'm pregnant, there's no doubt about that. What's more, I'm almost five months gone

71

and I won't be able to hide the fact from every-one for very much longer.'

'And Gwen knows but she hasn't said anything to anyone; not even to your brother?'

'She promised not to breathe a word and, so far, she seems to have kept her word.'

Hadyn's arm went round Sharon, drawing her close. 'So there's still time for us to do something before your family find out,' he said with relief as they started walking once more.

'Do something? What can we do? I'm almost five months' pregnant,' she reminded him.

He frowned. 'Yes, you have left it rather late, but I think I know someone who can help.'

'Help?' Sharon turned her head to stare at him in bewilderment. 'I don't understand, what do you mean?'

'Help you to get rid of it, of course. You don't want to have this baby, do you?'

'Do you mean that I should have an abortion?' Sharon gasped, placing a hand over her extended stomach protectively. 'I couldn't do that. It's alive! I've felt it moving!'

'So you are going to have it, then, are you?' His voice registered surprise.

Sharon shrugged indecisively. 'I don't know what else I can do,' she admitted.

'You are going to have to tell your family about the baby,' he reminded her.

'I know, and they will be so terribly upset when I do. That's why I have said nothing.'

'They certainly won't be very pleased when you tell them who the father is,' Hadyn said dryly.

'They'll have to know sometime soon,' Sharon

agreed with a shudder. 'Will you come with me?' she pleaded, clutching hold of his arm.

'You mean now? Tonight?'

'I can't hide the truth for much longer, now, can I?'

'I think we need more time to decide what we are going to say to them. Thanks to your father I haven't even got a job at the moment,' he added bitterly.

'If we explain all that to them, then Dad might give you a job,' Sharon said optimistically.

'You don't believe that any more than I do,' Hadyn commented cynically.

'I thought you would want us to get married and be together now that you know about the baby,' said Sharon wistfully.

'Well, I do, but let's think about it for a while and see if we can find any other way of dealing with the situation,' he added as he pulled a packet of cigarettes out of his pocket and lit two of them and passed one to her.

'There isn't,' Sharon told him. 'I've racked my brains for weeks and weeks but there is no way out other than facing up to the truth and seeing what happens.'

'Was that what you were prepared to do if I didn't turn up?' he asked, blowing out a long plume of smoke.

'It was the only option,' Sharon admitted. 'It seems it still is,' she added dolefully.

'Unless we run away.'

Hadyn's suggestion hung on the air for a minute before Sharon responded.

'How can we do that when you haven't got a

job and I have only a few pounds saved up?'

'We can't do it right this moment,' Hadyn agreed, 'but if you can keep your secret for another week or so to give me time to find work and somewhere for us to live, then you can leave home and we can move in together. With luck we'll be nicely settled before the baby is born.'

'That means you will go away again and I won't be able to get in touch with you,' Sharon mused.

They smoked in silence for a couple of minutes, each deep in their own thoughts.

'Listen,' Hadyn took a final draw on his cigarette then dropped the butt on to the pavement and ground it out with the heel of his boot, 'you go on home before they miss you and start asking awkward questions. Give me a few days to see what I can come up with. I'll meet you again, same time, same place, and let you know what I've decided.'

'How can I be sure you will come back again?' Sharon asked. 'I haven't heard a word from you for the past five months.'

'I couldn't help that. It won't happen again,' Hadyn promised. 'Now go on home and try not to worry.'

'How can I be sure that you'll come back unless you tell me why you've stayed away all this time?' she persisted.

He took her half-smoked cigarette from her and tossed it into the gutter. 'It's a long story, I'll tell you all about it when we have more time.' He held her face gently between both his hands. 'I will be back. I promise.'

'You must tell me when. Name a day.'

'I'll be back on Friday night and I'll be waiting

round the corner when you leave the shop. Tell your mother you are going straight out to the pictures or something and then we will have plenty of time to talk. Understand?'

Before Sharon could argue, Hadyn had kissed her fleetingly and was gone. She remained standing in the middle of the pavement, shivering in the damp night air.

Then with a sigh she headed for home, counting the days, the hours and the minutes until she would see him again.

Chapter Seven

Hadyn came back on the Friday night as he had promised to do, but his news was not good. He still hadn't found work or anywhere for them to live.

'Give me time; there's not a lot I can do in a few days,' he pointed out rather grumpily. 'Give me the rest of the month. By the beginning of December I'll have found work and somewhere for us to live. Once that is fixed up then you can leave home whenever you like.'

He took her in his arms, tilting her head back so that he could look into her eyes as he whispered, 'I promise everything will be all right, cariad. Don't worry. I love you and I can't wait for us to be together all the time. We'll have our own home before the New Year and that's a promise. Give me a month, that's all I'm asking.'

'Does it have to take that long? I'll be six months' pregnant by then; someone is sure to notice because I am putting on so much weight,' Sharon protested tearfully.

'You've managed all right up until now, so what difference will another couple of weeks make? I'll be back at the beginning of December and that's a promise.'

Sharon knew it was no good arguing but it did seem a long time to have to wait. Every time she caught a sideways glimpse of herself in a mirror she felt sure that other people must notice how her shape was changing.

Added to that, because she was working full time in the shop and doing much of Gwen's work as well as her own, she felt so tired that at the end of the day she found it hard to go home and act as normal.

Gwen was making the most of her pregnancy. Everybody was fetching and carrying for her and insisting that she must put her feet up and rest, making sure that she didn't lift anything heavy or do anything strenuous.

To save Gwen having to go home at the end of the day and cook a meal for Parry either his mother or her mother took it in turns to provide an evening meal. Sharon hated it when they came to their house. She knew Gwen was watching her closely and she suspected she was secretly laughing because she was attracting all the attention even though both of them were pregnant.

There were even times when Sharon was tempted to confide in her mother, then common sense prevailed. Her mother might accept the situation but she knew that her father wouldn't – especially once he knew that Hadyn was the father.

Instead, she focused on the future and counted the days until Hadyn came back. The first day of December was on a Monday and the closer it came the more confident Sharon felt that very soon everything would be all right.

She fantasised about whether they should tell her parents that she and Hadyn were getting married and that she was moving out to go and live with him or whether it would be better to simply slip away quietly and leave a note telling them why she had gone.

On the last weekend in November, Elaine invited all the Cogans to their house for a meal. Gwen arrived in a new loose-fitting dress in a pretty shade of deep blue which her mother had made for her.

'Oh, you do look nice,' Elaine enthused. 'You've made a lovely job of it, Flossie; that style and colour suits her so well,' she added admiringly.

'I enjoy doing a bit of dressmaking now and again,' Flossie admitted. 'It makes a pleasant change from curtains,' she added with a laugh.

'Perhaps you should ask my mum to make one like this for you, Sharon. You have enough material left over, haven't you?' she asked, looking at her mother enquiringly.

'Well, yes, and I'd be happy to do so, but I don't think Sharon would want one quite the same style as yours because yours is a maternity dress and designed so that the seams can be let out as necessary over the next couple of months.'

'I meant something along the same lines,' Gwen

said with a dismissive shrug. 'It's so very slimming that I thought it might suit Sharon.'

'Well, I must admit my Sharon could do with looking a bit slimmer,' Elaine agreed. 'I think I've been feeding her too well or something because I was only noticing the other day that she seems to have put on a bit of weight lately,' she said, softening her criticism with a smile. 'You look healthy enough, mind, my lovely,' she added turning to Sharon with a warm smile.

'You're right,' Flossie observed. 'Sharon was always the slim one but now she's as plump as my Gwen.'

Gwen smothered a giggle and the quick look with raised eyebrows that she gave Sharon alerted Elaine that Gwen knew more than she did and she looked at Sharon suspiciously.

'What's going on, then, cariad?' she questioned frowning, as she looked first at one and then the other. 'Some sort of secret between the two of you?'

'It's Sharon's secret, not mine,' Gwen said quickly in a smug voice.

Elaine stared at her daughter with a look of dismay on her face. 'Duw anwyl, don't tell me you're in the family way as well as Gwen,' she gasped.

When Sharon turned red but said nothing Elaine said angrily, 'Speak out, girl; let's know the truth. Tell me now before your father comes in.'

'Tell you what, before I come in?'

They had all been so engrossed that none of them had heard the front door opening or realised that Elwyn Pritchard was home. Now he stood there, frowning and looking from one to the other of the four women, waiting for someone to tell him what was going on.

Realising that there was no way she could hide the truth any longer, Sharon took a deep breath as she faced her father. 'I suppose you've got to know sometime that I'm expecting a baby and it's due next spring, round about March.'

'That's the same time as our Gwen's baby is due,' Flossie exclaimed.

'I knew that you and Madoc had been in our bedroom while we were away on our honeymoon, even though you said you hadn't,' Gwen declared triumphantly.

'I've never been in your bedroom with Madoc,' Sharon defended heatedly.

'If you are pregnant, cariad, and it's not Madoc's, then whose baby is it?' Elaine questioned.

Sharon took another deep breath as hot colour rushed to her cheeks then looked at her mother. 'The father is Hadyn Jenkins.'

There was a moment's stunned silence then her father, who was normally so calm, let out a roar of anger that left them all trembling.

'You've been seeing that blackguard! I thought he was out of our lives for good when he lost his job at Brynmor and Williams.'

'When you got him the sack from there, you mean,' Sharon challenged.

Elwyn's face darkened with anger. 'Watch your tongue, my girl,' he cautioned.

'I can't believe you're pregnant, cariad. My own

79

daughter in trouble. Why have you said nothing about it all these months?' Elaine wailed. 'Not a word to any of us; not even to me, your mother.'

'Too damned ashamed of herself, that's why she's said nothing,' Elwyn stated forcibly. 'She knows what I think of that man.'

'So where is he now? Does he know you are pregnant? Is he going to marry you, cariad? Is he going to make a home for you and the baby?'

The questions tumbled from Elaine's lips like a waterfall. Her face was drawn and her dark eyes anxious as she clutched at Sharon's arm.

'He'd better, because she's not staying here and bringing disgrace on our family. I want her out of this house before anyone else knows about this,' Elwyn stated harshly.

'Elwyn, what are you saying! We can't turn her out into the street, not in her condition in the middle of winter,' Elaine exclaimed aghast.

'If we wait until spring when she has had the baby, then the whole world will know,' he retorted grimly.

'It is our grandchild she's expecting,' Elaine murmured timidly.

'Grandchild! It's no grandchild of mine when it's been sired by that rogue! I don't want to hear another word, understand? As for you,' he added, his eyes full of anger as he stared at Sharon. 'I disown you. I want you out of this house and out of our lives before the end of the week. In the meantime, keep out of my sight. Eat your meals up in your bedroom not at the table with us. Stay away from the shop and speak to no one outside these four walls.'

Before Sharon could plead for some understanding her father had turned on his heel and walked out of the room, slamming the door behind him.

Gwen was the first to break the ominous silence that followed.

'Whew, was your dad angry!' she exclaimed breathlessly. 'What are you going to do now? Are you really still in touch with Hadyn Jenkins?'

'Yes, cariad, are you still seeing him? Does he know about the baby? You still haven't told us,' her mother questioned, frowning anxiously.

Sharon bit down on her lower lip. 'What does it matter, he's not welcome here, is he?'

'Well no, your father wouldn't let him over the doorstep, but that's not the point, is it? I would like to know, though, whether he is going to marry you and make a home for you and the baby,' Elaine told her. 'Has he even managed to get another job?' she went on when Sharon remained silent.

'He knows about the baby and he's getting a home together for us right now.'

'Well, that's something, I suppose,' Elaine said in relief. 'Will it be in Cardiff?'

'I don't know, I've left it all for him to arrange,' Sharon told her, shrugging her shoulders dismissively. 'Can we talk about something else?'

'So when are you getting married and moving in with him?' Gwen persisted, her eyes gleaming with curiosity. 'It will have to be a register office wedding because you can hardly doll yourself up in white and have a proper wedding like I had, now can you?' she giggled.

81

'Gwen, that is quite enough,' Elaine told her sharply.

Gwen pulled a face. 'People are bound to ask questions and if we want to avoid a lot of malicious gossip, then we ought to know the answers.'

'There is no need for you to say anything to anybody; this is a private family matter.'

'Customers are bound to start asking where Sharon is when she suddenly disappears,' Gwen went on, ignoring her mother-in-law's warning.

'Then you can tell them she is away on holiday.'

'In the middle of winter! Who is going to believe a tale like that?' Gwen laughed.

Elaine didn't answer. She turned and walked away and Sharon followed her into the kitchen.

'Mam, do you think Dad really meant it when he said I was to leave by the end of the week, or did he only say that because he was so upset by my news?' she asked tearfully.

'He was extremely angry; you know how much he dislikes Hadyn. Whatever were you thinking about, cariad, to let that man have his way with you when it's Madoc who is in love with you?'

'I don't love Madoc, Mam. I've told you over and over again that I like him as a friend but that is all. I don't want to marry him.'

'There's twp you are, girl. He's been a friend of Parry's and almost part of our family since childhood.'

'No, Mam, I'm not stupid, so don't say that. I like Madoc very much as a friend but I know him far too well to ever marry him. I don't love him.'

Elaine shook her head in despair. 'In my eyes you are more than silly; you are plain daft,' she sighed as she took down a saucepan from one of the shelves and began filling it with cold water from the tap and putting it on the gas ring to boil.

Sharon reached into the vegetable basket for the cabbage and began to trim off the outer leaves to prepare it to go in the water as soon as it boiled but Elaine took the knife out of her hand.

'You'd better get up to your room before your dad sees you; you know what he said.'

'He didn't mean it, though, did he?' Sharon argued.

'I think he did. Anyway, get upstairs and stay there until I've had a chance to speak to him and see if I can reason with him.'

'The Cogans are all here for a meal; won't they think it strange if I'm missing?'

Elaine shrugged her shoulders. 'I'm sure Gwen and Flossie will enlighten the others,' she commented as she finished chopping the cabbage, plunged it into the boiling water and put a lid on the saucepan.

'I'm sorry about all this, Mam,' Sharon murmured contritely, putting an arm around her mother's shoulders and hugging her. 'I wanted to tell you but I knew how upset you would be.'

'Well, it's too late now, the Cogans know and so does your father and you know how angry it has made him.'

'He would have to know sooner or later,' Sharon sighed.

'True, but if you had told me about it before this, then I could have picked the right moment to tell him and that might have softened the blow perhaps. Anyway, it's too late for that now.'

'So what should I do, then?' Sharon sniffed as tears of remorse trickled down her cheeks.

'Try and keep the peace by doing as your father told you. Go on up to your room and stay there. I'll bring your meal up to you when it's ready,' her mother told her firmly.

Chapter Eight

Alone in her bedroom Sharon felt isolated. Several times she opened the door and crept out on to the landing to listen to the babble of talk from below but she couldn't quite make out what they were saying.

She wondered if it was about her although, since her father was present, they probably wouldn't dare talk about her, she reasoned. She had never seen him so angry as he'd been when he realised that she was still seeing Hadyn.

It was such a long time before her mother brought her up some food that she was feeling sick with hunger. When she removed the saucepan lid that her mother had placed over the plate she was dismayed to find that the slice of roast lamb and vegetables on the plate were almost cold. Never-theless, she ate it and waited hopefully for her mother to bring up some pudding and also a drink, but as time passed she realised that her mother wasn't going to bring her anything else.

She didn't mind so much about the pudding but she was gasping for a drink and wondered if she dared creep down to the kitchen to get herself a glass of water.

Once more she went out on to the landing to try and work out what was happening downstairs. From the voices and occasional laugh she assumed they were still all sitting around talking.

Very cautiously she began to creep down the stairs towards the kitchen. She was almost at the bottom when the dining-room door opened and her mother came out. The moment she saw Sharon she placed a finger on her lips and waved her other hand wildly to indicate to her that she should go back up to her room.

Sharon's first instinct was to defy her because she was so thirsty but the anxious look on her mother's face stopped her. Nodding that she understood she turned and made her way back but not before the dining-room door opened again and Madoc came out.

Ignoring Elaine, he ran up the stairs towards Sharon, calling out to her to wait because he wanted to speak to her.

'Can you bring me up a glass of water, then?' she said in a low voice.

She had barely reached her room when he was on the stairs carrying the water.

She took it from him and gulped down a mouthful. 'I needed that,' she told him. 'I was dying of thirst.'

'Gwen told me about what happened earlier and the scene with your father,' he said tersely. 'Are you going to tell me what this is all about and what is going on?'

'Gwen's already told you, so what else do you

want to know?'

He stared at her, running a hand through his hair. 'I can't believe it's true. Why didn't you say something before? I thought you were in love with me, that we were going to be married.'

'You may have thought that, but I never have. I don't love you, Madoc. I like you as a friend–'

'You certainly like leading me up the garden path,' he interrupted bitterly. 'I'm not the only one who thought we were going to get married and settle down,' he added, squaring his broad shoulders almost aggressively. 'Both your dad and mine have already started negotiating for a property for us to live in near Gower Street. They hinted about it not so long ago and yet you never said a word to them either. Now look at the mess you're in; your dad's talking about throwing you out, so where will you go if that happens?'

Sharon stiffened, her dark eyes flashing angrily. 'That is none of your business. I think you had better go.'

Madoc stuffed his hands into his trouser pockets and placed his foot over the threshold so that she couldn't shut the door. His face was red and he looked very upset.

'I'm not moving from here until you've heard what I have to say,' he told her.

Sharon shrugged. 'Please yourself. There's nothing you can say that I haven't heard already either from your Gwen or from my own mother.'

'I want you to know that I still intend to marry you.' His face went an even deeper shade of red. 'I know you are expecting another man's baby, but that doesn't make any difference. I love you,

Sharon. I always have and I always will.'

'So much so that you are prepared to bring up another man's child? What do you think your mam and dad would have to say about that? Would they be prepared to accept it as their grandchild?' Sharon questioned.

Madoc hesitated. 'I thought perhaps when it is born you could have it adopted,' he said awkwardly.

Sharon stared at him in disbelief. It was the sort of thing she could imagine her brother saying.

Hadyn was so different from them in so many ways. What really made him stand out from the crowd was the way he dressed. He always wore tailored suits, white shirts with crisply starched collars and eye-catching ties. Her dad called him a dandy but she thought he looked very smart and handsome.

'If you didn't want to do that, then I would bring it up as though it was my own child, no matter what they said,' he added quickly when he saw the look of disbelief on Sharon's face.

'You're saying that you'd marry me even though I've told you I don't love you and that I love someone else?'

'Yes, I would, because I am sure you've simply been led astray by that man's charm and that he seduced you. Deep down I am the one you really love,' he told her rather pompously.

As he moved forward into the room and tried to embrace her, Sharon pulled back and pushed him away. 'No, Madoc. I don't love you and I won't marry you. Now go!'

He hesitated for a moment then, with a resigned

shrug, walked away. Sharon shut the door behind him and placed a chair against it so that no one could come in, then she flung herself down on the bed and sobbed her heart out, knowing that she had completely burned her boats. If Hadyn didn't return, then she had no one.

If her father carried out his threat to turn her out, she'd be homeless and practically penniless and she had no idea what she would do or where she would go.

Hadyn would return for her, she told herself. He'd said he'd be back at the beginning of December and that was less than a week away. She hadn't very long to wait and then they'd be together and everything would be all right.

She pulled herself up off the bed and wiped away her tears with the back of her hand. What was she crying for? She'd never wanted to marry Madoc, so she'd done the right thing in sending him away. Instead of moping, she'd start getting her things together so that she was packed and ready when Hadyn came back for her.

By the time her mother came upstairs with a cup of cocoa and a couple of biscuits for her just before bedtime, all her possessions were laid out on the bed.

'What on earth are you doing, cariad?' her mother asked, frowning.

'I thought I'd sort out what I would be taking with me when I move out,' Sharon told her. 'All I need now is a suitcase.'

'Well, you'll have to wait until tomorrow for that. I can't fetch you one now because it's on the top of the wardrobe in our bedroom and your dad has already come up to bed.'

As she reached the door Elaine paused. 'Sharon, do you think you are doing the right thing in going off with that man?' she asked quietly.

'What else do you expect me to do? Dad says he is going to throw me out...'

'Hush, hush, cariad. Leave things as they are for the moment and he'll come round. He was very upset by your news, that's why he said that.'

'Come round? What does that mean? Am I going to have to stay locked up here in my room for evermore?' Sharon scoffed.

'Give it time and he'll relent. It's terrible what's happened but it's not the end of the world. Once the baby's born you can have it adopted and then–'

'You've been listening to Madoc, haven't you?' Sharon said scornfully.

'Madoc?' Her mother frowned and looked bewildered. 'I don't know what you're talking about.'

'Madoc asked me to marry him. He said we could get the baby adopted. When I told him I wouldn't do that, he said he would agree to bringing it up.'

'He did!' Elaine's face brightened. 'Then isn't that the answer to all your problems?' she asked hopefully.

'No it isn't. I've told you countless times that I won't marry Madoc. I love Hadyn and if I can't marry him, then I won't marry anyone.'

'You are being very foolish, cariad. If you marry Madoc, then that will put things right between you and your dad and provide a father for your child. You have a good man there; one that will make sure you have a home and everything you need for a comfortable life. Your child will grow up alongside our Parry's baby and, in time, the past will all be forgotten.'

Before Sharon could reply her mother had gone, closing the door quietly behind her.

In the days that followed, while she waited for Hadyn's return, Sharon kept thinking about what her mother had said. She knew it was good advice but there was no way she could accept it, not even for the sake of her unborn baby.

The first day of December was dull and grey and for Sharon the wait until evening seemed to be endless. All her belongings were packed into a large brown fibre suitcase and at half past five she debated whether to take her case with her or make sure that Hadyn was there and then come back and collect it.

She was dressed and ready in her thick brown tweed coat, with a red scarf round her neck, a red felt cloche hat pulled down over her ears, and matching woollen gloves.

Sharon heard her mother come into the house shortly after five o'clock and go into the kitchen and from the sounds that followed she knew she was preparing their evening meal. It meant that it was time for her to leave if she was to get to Queen Street by six o'clock. She would have to be careful not to bump into her father who would be on his way home very soon.

Again she debated whether it would be best if she took her case with her rather than come back to the house for it, but when she picked it up, she realised that it was far too heavy for her to carry all the way from Pen-y-lan Place to Queen Street.

As quietly as possible she crept down the stairs, hoping that her mother wouldn't hear her. As the hall clock started striking the half-hour, she had a feeling of panic in case she was late and Hadyn thought she wasn't coming.

It had turned six by the time she reached Queen Street and as she saw Lloyd and her father locking the shop doors ready to leave for home, she quickly turned down the side road.

It was ten minutes before Hadyn arrived but to Sharon it seemed like ten years. She flung herself into his arms and her cheeks were damp with tears as he kissed her.

'What's wrong, what's all this about?' He frowned.

'I was afraid you mightn't come,' she gulped. 'Have you got a job and somewhere for us to live?'

When he hesitated she clutched at his arm in panic. 'I can't stay at home any longer. My father is furious about what has happened. Since I last saw you I've been confined to my room and not even allowed to come downstairs for my meals.'

'I was hoping that you would wait a bit longer; I want everything to be perfect for you,' he prevaricated as he stroked her face and kissed her tenderly.

Sharon pulled away impatiently. 'No, I must come now. My case is packed. If we go to Pen-y-lan Place now then I can slip into the house while they're having their evening meal, collect my case and we can be gone before anyone is any the wiser.'

'Surely they are going to wonder where you are if you aren't there for your meal?'

'You've not been listening; I told you I have been confined to my room ever since my father found out about us.'

'You mean you've not even been working in the shop?'

'No, my father can't bear the sight of me. I'm not even sure if he knows I am still living at home. My mam brings me up some food when they've finished eating. I can't go on living like that any longer,' she added tearfully.

Instead of taking her in his arms and comforting her as she'd expected him to do, Hadyn consulted his watch, frowning as he did so.

'If we go back now for your suitcase, we might bump into your father,' he said worriedly. 'Look, why don't you go home and I'll come back tomorrow and collect you while he's at work?'

'I'd sooner go with you now.'

'Be reasonable, Sharon. If we run into your old man there will be hell to pay,' Hadyn said irritably.

'I don't care; I want to come with you now.'

'It's impossible. I haven't fixed up anywhere for us to live. Give me another day...'

'If you haven't done it in all the time you've had since I last saw you, then how are you going to manage to do it overnight?' Sharon wailed.

'I don't know, but I will. I promise you. I'll come for you tomorrow the moment I have managed to find somewhere for us to live. Come on, I'll walk you home and don't worry, I'll be back tomorrow,' he said, taking her arm. 'I'll come straight to Pen-y-lan Place so be ready.'

'What time? Will it be in the morning?'

Hadyn hesitated. 'Let's settle for the afternoon, I'll make sure that it's before your dad gets home.'

'My mam is home at five, so it had better be early,' Sharon warned.

'All right, all right!' Hadyn said impatiently. 'I understand. I'll be there by four o'clock, now does that keep you happy?'

'Not really, I was hoping that it would be to-night. You've no idea how miserable I am. I want to be with you,' she added piteously.

'I do understand and I promise that I will be back for you and you'll never be miserable again,' he told her as they stopped at the corner of her road.

'I'll leave you here; we don't want to take any risks,' he murmured as he gave her a parting hug.

Sharon blinked back her tears. 'Until tomorrow, then,' she whispered.

Chapter Nine

Sharon put her hand through the letterbox to find the key and cautiously opened the front door. She stood there for a moment, listening to make sure it was safe to go in. She was on the third step of the stairs when the dining-room door opened and her father came out. There was nowhere to hide so she froze, hoping he would turn left into the sitting room and not notice her.

'What are you doing out of your room?'

His voice was cold and accusing and left her startled and silent. She wondered what his reaction would be if she said she'd been out to meet Hadyn and make plans to leave home.

'Answer me! Why have you disobeyed my orders?'

'I needed some fresh air. I can't stay caged in like an animal,' she declared defiantly.

'Don't answer me back,' he said curtly. 'Think yourself lucky that I haven't thrown you out. Your behaviour is a disgrace and if it ever gets out that you are pregnant, it will bring shame on our family name and on our business.'

'So what do you intend to do, keep me locked up for ever?' she challenged. 'What will you tell people when they ask where I am?'

'I shall have to say that you have been sent to look after a sick relative.'

'That's a lie! I thought you always said that it was wrong to tell lies.'

Elwyn's thin face darkened. 'Don't be insolent. I am doing it to save you bringing disgrace on our family. You are to stay in your room until after the child you are carrying has been born and we can arrange for it to be adopted.'

'That's months away!'

'Which means you will have plenty of time to think about what you have done and to pray for forgiveness.'

'It's not possible,' she said in a low voice, shaking her head determinedly. 'I can't stay locked up and, what's more, I don't intend to give up my baby when it is born.'

'Now listen to me, my girl,' Elwyn Pritchard

said sternly. 'In the first place, I can't believe that you disobeyed me and went on seeing that man. He's a bad lot and I warned you about him, but you took no notice and now look at the mess you're in. You either do as I say or I throw you out; that's something I should have done the moment we found out.'

'You daren't do that because you know perfectly well that it's your grandchild and that tongues will wag if you do,' Sharon retorted defiantly.

'That's enough!' Elwyn's hands clenched into fists. 'This is my last warning. Are you going to do as I say or not?'

'I'm not going to stay locked up in my bedroom and I am certainly not going to have my baby adopted,' Sharon told him, tossing her head in disdain.

'Then go. You've got your coat on and there's the door. Five minutes to pack your bag. Move, girl, I mean it,' he roared as Sharon stood stock still on the stairs.

There were tears in her eyes when she came back down a few minutes later. Her father was still standing in the hallway. Hearing the noise as Sharon bumped her heavy case down the stairs Elaine came out of the dining room to see what was going on.

'What on earth are you doing, Sharon? Where are you going with the case?'

'You'd better ask him,' Sharon sniffed.

'Surely you are not throwing her out, Elwyn, not at this time of night?'

'The choice is hers,' he muttered. 'She knows what the alternative is.'

'Why don't I go and make a pot of tea and then the three of us can sit down and talk it over,' Elaine suggested, laying a hand on her husband's arm.

'I've done all the talking I intend to do; the decision is up to Sharon now. It breaks my heart to do it because I've loved her deeply from the moment she was born. I've wanted only the best for her and I still do. I can't stand by and see her ruin her life.'

'Please, cariad,' Elaine pleaded, pushing past her husband and putting her arms around Sharon and holding her close. 'Listen to what your dad is saying and do as he asks. Believe me, he has only your interests at heart.'

'My interests! You mean his, don't you? He's worried in case people tittle-tattle about me and it reflects on his good name and on the business.'

'That will do!' Elwyn's roar silenced them both. Opening the front door he picked up Sharon's suitcase and put it outside on the path then turned round and shoved her roughly over the threshold and slammed the door shut behind her.

Sharon stood there on the doorstep listening to their raised voices. She could hear her mother pleading with him to let her back in and her groan of despair as he refused to do as she asked.

She tottered slightly as she picked up the heavy suitcase. It was almost nine o'clock. She lugged the case as far as the nearest tram stop but she had no idea where to go at that time of night. The only place she could think of was the railway station where she could sit in the waiting room until morning.

Huddled in the corner of one of the bench-type seats Sharon felt it was the longest night she'd ever known. Around midnight a porter opened the door and called out, asking whether there was anyone there. Sharon kept perfectly still, holding her breath and hoping that he was in such a hurry that he wouldn't see her.

As soon as he had turned the lights off, she stretched out on the long seat and tried to sleep. She dozed fitfully but at the first light she was wide awake and shivering with cold, worrying about how she could get out of the station without being spotted.

As soon as it became busy with early morning travellers she asked one of the porters if there was anywhere where she could leave her case so that she could come back later and collect it. He wanted to know where she would be going so she made up a garbled story about arriving too early and that she was supposed to be meeting someone and she wasn't sure about their destination.

It was clear he didn't believe her story and for a moment she thought he was going to refuse to help, then, with a shrug and a big grin, he directed her towards the left luggage office.

It was still very early in the morning and the shops weren't open. She walked across Wood Street and along St Mary Street and was about to walk towards Queen Street when she realised that was a foolish thing to do in case her father saw her.

Instead, she walked back to the David Morgan Arcade and waited until the café halfway along it opened so that she could get something to eat and drink.

She lingered over her meal for as long as possible but it was still early morning and she had no idea how she was going to spend the rest of the day. It was cold outside and there was a raw easterly wind blowing. She walked through both David Morgan's and James Howell's department stores to kill time, then finally went into the public library, which was almost opposite, and whiled away an hour or so scanning the newspapers and magazines.

She longed for it to be time to go and meet Hadyn but because he was to meet her near Pen-y-lan Place and there was nowhere near there where she could shelter, she stayed in the city centre wandering in and out of the arcades and finally went into the café again and lingered over another hot drink until almost the middle of the afternoon.

When she reached Pen-y-lan Place, her feeling of relief when she saw that Hadyn was already knocking on her front door was overwhelming. All day she'd been worrying about what she would do if he didn't come back.

She knew she could never return home and admit defeat but the only alternative seemed to be suicide. She wondered whether it would be quicker to throw herself under a train, or into the canal or the River Taff. She couldn't swim and the thought of sinking down into the icy waters seemed to be worse than being hit by a train.

She imagined the dramatic headlines in the *South Wales Echo* and her father's face when he read the lurid story that would accompany it. That would bring even more disgrace on the family and his precious business, she thought, and her mother didn't deserve to be upset like that.

Finding that Hadyn was waiting for her brought her back to reality. Quickly she explained that her suitcase was at the railway station and they'd have to go and collect it.

'That's all right. It's on our way,' he told her.

'We're going somewhere by train?' she asked excitedly.

'No, not exactly,' he murmured as they set off for the nearby tram stop.

'You have found somewhere for us to live?' she questioned anxiously as they boarded the tram and found seats.

'Yes, but it is only a temporary measure. It was such short notice that I could only manage to get a bedsitter and we have to share the kitchen and so on with someone else.'

'That won't be very convenient.' Sharon gave him a disapproving look.

'I know, cariad, but, as I said, it is only a temporary arrangement until I can find some work, so we'll have to make the best of it. Anyway, first things first, you must be tired and hungry; I don't suppose you've even had a proper meal today?'

Sharon shook her head. Everything seemed to be going wrong. She had been building her hopes on Hadyn telling her he had a wonderful job and then whisking her off to her new home.

'Come on, then, let's go and find a café or a restaurant and celebrate being together at last,' he said.

'What about my suitcase?'

'We'll pick that up afterwards on our way home.'

She felt too tired to argue. Perhaps she would feel better after some food. At the moment she felt so utterly despondent that life really didn't seem to be worth living, even though Hadyn had come back for her as he'd promised.

The good food and the glass of red wine that Hadyn ordered brought the colour back to her cheeks and restored her vitality. As he insisted on buying her a glass of port to finish off their meal she wondered where on earth he had managed to find the money to pay for such an expensive meal if he wasn't working, but she decided it was best not to ask.

Laughing and full of high spirits, they went and collected her suitcase and then walked across the road to the nearest tram stop.

'Where are we going?' she asked as they boarded the tram and Hadyn handed the conductor their fare.

'To our new home, of course,' he whispered, slipping his arm around her waist and holding her close.

'Yes, I know that, but where is it?'

'Clwyd Court.'

'I've never heard of it, nor have I ever been on a tram going in this direction before.'

'This is Bute Street and it's not very far now,' he added, giving her a squeeze and kissing her on the cheek.

'Bute Street!' Sharon sat up straight with a look of shock on her face. Pulling way from him so that she could turn and face him, she asked in alarm, 'Do you mean that Clwyd Court is somewhere in Tiger Bay?'

'Yes, I suppose it is. Does that bother you?' he asked, raising his eyebrows as though amused.

'I don't know. I've never been there before but I've heard some terrible tales about how dangerous a place it is and that no one should go down there on their own, especially after dark,' Sharon said suppressing a shiver.

Hadyn roared with laughter, slapping his thigh and shaking his head. 'You don't believe everything you hear, do you?'

Sharon looked taken aback. 'I'm only telling you what I've been told,' she said stiffly.

Hadyn reached out and pulled the cord to request the tram to stop. 'Come on, this is our stop, so you will be able to judge for yourself in a few minutes.'

With Hadyn carrying the suitcase they crossed the road and walked down several side streets until Sharon felt completely lost. By the time Hadyn turned into a narrow alleyway that opened out into a square with terraced houses on three sides, she was clutching at his arm and looking over her shoulder nervously because all the people they passed seemed to be of different nationalities.

'This is Clwyd Court,' he told her. 'Three doors along is where we will be living.'

Sharon bit her lip to try and hold back her tears. This wasn't at all the sort of place she had imagined but she didn't know what to say. She didn't want Hadyn to think that she was always complaining and she was sure that he only intended it to be for a few nights until things were sorted out, so she resolved she'd try and make the best of the situation.

When he took her inside the house, led her up the grimy staircase and then opened the door to a small, airless room, however, she couldn't restrain her gasp of horror. It was only about half the size of her bedroom at home and it was so grubby and dank that she hesitated in the doorway, not sure that she even wanted to go in.

Hadyn dropped her suitcase and, putting his arm around her waist, propelled her towards the bed.

Before she'd regained her breath he'd pulled the suitcase inside the room and closed the door. Pulling her to her feet he started to remove her outdoor clothes, kissing her hungrily as he unfastened her dress and pulled it away from her shoulders.

Almost roughly he pushed her down on to the bed and threw himself down beside her. She wanted to protest but his mouth was on hers and as he removed his own clothes and the rest of those she was wearing, his frenzy mounted.

She'd looked forward to them making love again like they had the first time at Gwen and Parry's house. That had been a tender, loving session that had ended so sweetly and so satisfyingly that she had dreamed about it ever since.

This coupling was nothing at all like that; it was more like animals rutting, she thought with a shudder as it ended and, with a satisfied grunt of exhaustion, Hadyn rolled off her and almost immediately fell asleep.

She lay there in the darkness for a long time sobbing into the pillow and wondering if the bedding was as grubby as the rest of the room appeared to be.

She was sure she would never sleep but eventually her eyes closed and she sank into darkness. When she wakened it was to the grey light of a December morning. The bed beside her was empty and for one panic-stricken moment she thought that Hadyn had left her and she began to sob hysterically.

'Cariad, what's all the noise about?'

Sharon pushed back her hair from her face and stared up at Hadyn in relief. 'I thought you'd gone and I was left here on my own,' she sobbed.

'I was making you a cup of tea.' He smiled. 'I hope you can drink it without milk because there isn't any. As soon as you are dressed, I'll show you where the shops are before I go off to look for a job.'

'Do you have to do that today? I would sooner you stayed with me,' she pleaded.

'We need money for food and to pay the rent at the end of the week,' he said abruptly. 'That's, of course, unless you have some?' he added hopefully.

Sharon reached out for her handbag and searched around inside it for her purse. 'Here, this is all I have,' she murmured, handing him two white five-pound notes.

He frowned as he took them from her. 'Haven't you any savings tucked away as well? You've been working ever since you left school, haven't you?'

She shook her head. 'I was only given pocket money,' she explained almost apologetically. 'I didn't have to pay anything for my keep, you see, so Dad only gave me a few shillings' spending money each week. It was enough to go to the pictures and buy make-up and so on. Instead he put away money in a savings account for when I got married.'

'Well, this won't go very far but it will buy us some food and pay a week's rent, I suppose. Perhaps you can get yourself a job for a few weeks – just to help out,' he added quickly when he saw the startled look on her face.

Sharon didn't answer. She reached out and picked up the cup of tea he had made. She took a sip and shuddered. It tasted so awful that she could hardly swallow it.

As she looked down at the grubby sheets she wondered how she had ever managed to sleep at all in them and the thought that this was now her home, at least for the present, filled her with dismay.

She gazed around the small, shabby room again. The window was so dirty that it let in hardly any light but, even so, she could see the bedbug trails on the walls and the grime everywhere. The table in the far corner of the room with the kettle and gas ring on it was pitted with grease. The open shelves above it were crammed with a jumble of plates, cups, saucers and a miscellany of bits and pieces, most of which were cracked or stained. Underneath the table were two buckets; one with clean water in it and the other for dirty water. There was also an old wooden box for rubbish. It was the most squalid place she had ever been in.

'Did you say we had to share the kitchen and bathroom?' she questioned awkwardly. 'I need the lavatory, so can you show me where it is?'

'You'd better put your coat on, then, because it

is in the yard and it's damn cold outside this morning.'

For a moment she thought he was teasing her but as he handed her coat to her she realised he was serious.

They went down the stairs and into the hallway then down a passageway towards the back of the house and out through a door into a small yard piled high with rubbish. There was a wooden shed at the far end; the smell coming from it made her heave and she hesitated about going inside.

She pushed open the door then pulled back when she saw the cracked, soiled wooden seat but her need was so great that she knew she had no option but to go inside, even though she felt physically sick as she did so.

'Don't be too long in there if you want me to wait for you,' Hadyn called after her.

'You can find your way back upstairs to our room, can't you?' he asked when she came out. 'I need to use the bog as well while we're down here.'

'No, I'll wait for you; I can't go back up there on my own.'

'Shelter in the doorway, then, out of this sleeting rain and I'll be as quick as I can.'

They couldn't possibly stay in this dreadful place a moment longer than they had to; they must get away before her baby was born, she told herself as she waited in the doorway while Hadyn took her place in the lavatory.

For one, wild moment she thought of giving in and going back home and doing what her father wanted: staying out of sight until the baby was born and then having it adopted.

Chapter Ten

For the first few days Sharon couldn't bring herself to leave their room except to make a scurrying trip downstairs to the lavatory outside in the yard. Each time she did so she hoped she wouldn't meet any of the other people living in the house.

She persuaded Hadyn to do the shopping and by the third day she could tell that his patience was wearing thin and that she had to overcome her fears.

Things came to a dramatic head when he came home without the shopping but reeking of drink. The row that followed between them was so loud that it brought the landlady, Karmu, puffing upstairs and banging on their door.

When Sharon opened it she gave a scream of fright at her first glimpse of Karmu. She was wearing a vivid orange and red dress and she had a matching bandeau tying her immense shock of black hair back from her broad African features. She stood there with her bare brawny hands on her hips and her mountainous bosom rising and falling.

As she delivered a strong warning, threatening to 'chuck them out into the street if they didn't quieten down', Sharon was more scared of Karmu than of what she was saying.

When Hadyn stumbled across the room to see

who it was, Karmu's voice changed from aggression to laughter as she stepped into the room, her arms held wide, and gathered Hadyn to her immense bosom in a warm embrace.

'You're a bad boy,' she scolded. 'You promised to behave if I let you have a room in my house and here you are squabbling like alley cats. Why aren't you out working at this time of day?'

Hadyn hiccupped loudly. 'I've found myself a job and I was celebrating,' he told her with a fatuous grin. 'This is Sharon, by the way, and she doesn't like the idea of having to do the shopping. Do you know, Karmu,' he paused and belched noisily, 'she hasn't been outside these four walls since we arrived here.'

'Don't you give it another thought,' Karmu told him with a wide smile. 'I'll make it my business to take her shopping tomorrow morning and introduce her to all the best shops in Tiger Bay; ones where I am so well known that they won't dare to cheat her when she goes back again on her own.'

'That's good.' Hadyn settled himself down in the battered armchair and put his feet up on the table. 'Now both of you leave me in peace,' he added as he closed his eyes.

'What about this job you say you have found. When do you start work?' Karmu asked.

'This evening, that's why I need some kip now, so keep your chattering down.'

'Evening? Doing what? Doorkeeper, chucker out?'

'Running the roulette table.'

'Watch your back, my boy. Make sure that what you do is legal or you'll have the Bobbies after you. There're some bad types when it comes to gambling.'

'Don't worry, I can take care of myself,' Hadyn grunted.

Sharon listened to them with growing dismay. If Hadyn was going to work at night then he wouldn't be coming home until the early hours of the morning. The thought of being left there all on her own all night petrified her.

Karmu laughed uproariously. 'Come on, honey, get your hat and coat on and we'll go out to the shops and leave his lordship to kip,' she told Sharon.

Although she would much rather have stayed and found out exactly what Hadyn's job was, Sharon did as she was told. By the time she was ready and found the housekeeping money which they'd put to one side and which was now greatly depleted after Hadyn's drinking spree, Karmu was calling out to her to hurry or all the best pickings would be gone.

When she went out into the hallway and saw Karmu standing there still wearing her bright red and orange dress but with a thick green and purple shawl around her shoulders, a rainbow-coloured turban on her head and a huge wicker basket on her arm, she was so embarrassed at the thought of being seen with her that she would have given anything not to have to go out.

Karmu seemed to be quite unaware of how she looked. She breezed down the road like a ship in full sail and in her plain brown tweed coat and red cloche hat Sharon felt like a sombre little tug boat as she walked alongside her.

They went to James Street where everyone seemed to know Karmu and even the shop-keepers from the shops they didn't go into called out a cheery greeting to her.

When it came to actually buying, Sharon learned a great deal in that one visit. Karmu was prepared to haggle, ready to quibble and had no qualms at all over turning down produce which she didn't think was of the very best quality.

Sharon had never seen her mother or anyone else she knew do anything at all like this and, to her amazement, the shopkeepers seemed to res-pect Karmu's judgement. Some laughed and then produced a better quality item; others hag-gled with her but invariably reduced their price. It was all done with laughter and such good humour that it left Sharon astounded and by the time they returned home she felt a great deal of respect for Karmu.

'Now don't go disturbing that man of yours because he needs his sleep. He will want all his wits about him when he goes to work tonight; you need to be sharp as a razor for the gambling game. You cheat them and they cheat you,' she added with a raucous laugh.

'Gambling is illegal, isn't it?' Sharon asked frowning.

'Most things you enjoy are,' Karmu said with a broad smile. 'Now you come and sit yourself down in my kitchen and have a rest and enjoy a cup of tea.'

As Sharon anticipated, once the tea was made and Karmu was also sitting down, she began to question her about how she came to be living in one small room at Clwyd Court and about the baby she was so obviously expecting.

To her surprise, Sharon found that she quite enjoyed telling Karmu all about her past. It felt such a relief to share all her doubts and worries with someone else that she kept nothing at all back. She even admitted with a deep sigh that she and Hadyn weren't married.

'Get a ring on your finger before the baby is born,' Karmu advised. 'That way you make him responsible for the child and even if he leaves you, then you can make him pay towards its upkeep. Well,' she added, her body shaking with laughter, 'that is, if you can find the bugger.'

'I have been married three times,' she went on. 'My first husband was a white man, my second was a Chinaman and the third a Nigerian. You would have thought that a man of my own nationality and colour would have been a good choice but, in fact, he was worse than any of them.'

'You mean he left you?'

'Yes, and now I live on my own and, believe me, I love it. I need please no one. I earn money from letting out my rooms and, from time to time, in other ways.'

Sharon waited for her to explain further but Karmu drained her cup and stood up so Sharon hastily did the same.

'I'd better go and cook a meal,' she murmured, picking up the shopping bag from beside her chair.

'Yes, give him something to sharpen his wits and sustain him until the early hours of the morning; something stodgy to soak up all the booze he's bound to get down him. If you are worried or lonely later on this evening, then you know where to find me. I don't go to bed until well after midnight so come back down if you want to, honey, and we can have another chat.'

Knowing she had Karmu's support, Sharon felt reassured. Perhaps life wasn't going to be as bad here as she'd thought. The fact that Karmu's skin was black was suddenly of no importance. She was warm and friendly and Sharon felt she could turn to her if she needed advice or help.

Hadyn was still asleep so Sharon left him snoring while she cooked a meal for them both. She wished there was an oven; all she had was a gas ring, a couple of saucepans and a frying pan.

She cut the meat into smallish chunks, put a lump of lard into the frying pan and browned the meat. Then she sliced up an onion and cooked that and then transferred the whole lot into the biggest saucepan, added some diced potatoes and carrots, and moistened them all with a little water. She left the stew to simmer over a very low gas, stirring it occasionally to make sure it didn't stick to the pan until it was time to wake Hadyn.

Remembering Karmu's advice about something stodgy she wondered if she could make dumplings but, in the end, decided it might be safer to serve the stew along with some chunks of bread. It was so difficult to do anything more than simply heat things up on the stove and she didn't want to ask Karmu to make them for her.

She had no idea what time Hadyn was supposed to start work but by six o'clock she felt so hungry herself that she decided to wake him.

At first he kept pushing her away and going

back to sleep but when she persisted he sat up with a groan, running his hands through his dishevelled hair and belching noisily.

'What time is it?'

When she told him it was after six he sprang out of the chair, cursing because he was late and dashed into the kitchen to splash his face with water straight from the bucket.

Sharon wanted to protest that it was water she needed to fill the kettle but she bit back her angry words, afraid of what his reaction might be.

Drying his face on the towel hanging there he picked up his jacket and headed for the door.

'I've cooked you a lovely meal,' she said petulantly. 'Aren't you going to sit down and eat it?'

'No time,' he told her brusquely. 'Don't wait up for me because I'll be late, very late,' he called out as he raced down the stairs.

Sharon felt her eyes fill with tears as she took the lid off the pot of stew that she had spent so much time preparing. She ladled out a small plateful for herself and forced herself to eat it and wondered if the rest would keep until the next day.

She kept herself busy doing odd jobs until it was time for bed. As she undressed and crawled between the covers she was sure she wouldn't sleep but the moment her head touched the pillow she was lost to the world.

She had no idea how long she was asleep but she was wakened by the sound of crashing furniture and then Hadyn falling across the bed and lying there completely inert and remaining immobile even when she spoke to him.

His breath reeked of alcohol and she was unsure

what to do. She shook him violently to try and rouse him but it had no effect at all. Hadyn simply lay there, out cold and, in a moment of panic, Sharon thought he was dead and ran down the stairs calling to Karmu to come and help her.

Karmu came sailing into the room garbed in an enveloping white cotton nightgown that reached from her neck to her ankles.

'Oh dear, were you in bed?' Sharon murmured apologetically. 'I don't know what to do, Hadyn seems to be unconscious.'

'He's still breathing, honey,' Karmu puffed as she laid a hand on his chest. 'He reeks of alcohol. He's not dead, honey, only dead drunk. Leave him where he is until morning and let him wake up of his own accord. Expect him to have a terrible hangover, though,' she added with a raucous laugh. 'He'll have a mouth like the bottom of a bird cage and a head full of thumping hammers,' she chortled.

'Now you get some sleep yourself. You'd better make yourself comfortable in the armchair, though,' she warned as she pulled the blanket off the bed and handed it to Sharon. 'If you get into bed alongside him and he turns rough in the night, then you and your baby might both get hurt.'

Sharon slept fitfully. It wasn't comfortable in the armchair and the small fire in the iron grate had gone out and she was shivering with the cold. Shortly before dawn she crept into bed beside Hadyn, spreading the blanket over them both and enjoying the warmth from his body.

She had no idea how long she slept but a hefty shove in the middle of her back sent her sprawling

113

out of bed and on to the floor. As she struggled to her feet she remembered Karmu's warning.

Shaking with fright she padded over to the corner of the room and lit the gas ring and put the kettle on to boil so that she could make herself a cup of tea.

Knowing that she wouldn't get back to sleep again even though it wasn't yet seven o'clock, she decided to get dressed. Hadyn was once more deep in sleep and snoring loudly.

She felt depressed at the thought of what their life was going to be like from now on. He was so very different from the suave, debonair, handsome man who had called at her father's shop for orders; the man who had bewitched her into thinking he loved her as much as she loved him. Now he looked like a stranger, he was so unkempt and dissolute.

As she looked around the small, shabby room she felt sick with worry and regret about what she had done; together they had sunk about as low as it was possible to do.

The chances of them having a proper home before the baby was born seemed remote yet the thought of bringing up a child in such surroundings was even more bleak.

Karmu had told her all about what making a living from gambling entailed. There were days when they had money but even more when they were completely penniless. Karmu had told her to try and squirrel away some of his winnings so that she had enough to keep herself in food. At the moment, she thought desolately, she had no money of her own at all. What little she'd had when she'd left home she'd handed over to Hadyn and the jam jar where they'd kept it was now completely empty.

Yet Hadyn must have had money to buy the drink the previous night, she reminded herself. She wondered if he still had any left and whether she dared search his pockets.

If she took it while he was still asleep, then that would be stealing, she told herself. He'd taken her money and said it was needed for house-keeping so if he wakened and caught her, then she'd tell him the same, she resolved as she approached the bed.

The moment she touched him his eyes opened and he struggled to sit up, staring at her in bleary confusion.

'What's going on?' he grunted. He cleared his throat noisily and held his head between his two hands.

'I need some strong black coffee,' he muttered. 'Go on, then, don't just stand there, make some.'

'We haven't any coffee,' Sharon told him. 'I could go out and buy some if you gave me some money,' she added quickly.

To her surprise he put his hand in his trouser pocket and pulled out some notes. 'Here,' he muttered, thrusting several of them into her hand. 'Go to the chemists and get something to stop this pain in my head.'

'I'll try.' She grabbed the notes from him. 'The chemist mightn't be open yet, it's too early.'

'Well, get the coffee; perhaps that will do it,' he groaned, flopping back on the bed and closing his eyes.

As she was putting on her hat and coat he opened his eyes again and gazed at her in a befuddled way. 'You got any money?'

She was about to remind him that he had just given her some but when he began fumbling in his pocket and pulled out another note, she took it from him without a word.

As soon as she was outside the house she counted what he had given her. In all there were four pound notes. It was a small fortune. She could leave him right now and move not just to a better room but also right away from Tiger Bay.

Her elation was short-lived. Four pounds might seem a fortune but how long would it last, and where would she get any more once she'd spent that? she thought despairingly. She'd never be able to find any work in her condition.

Common sense told her that she should wait until after the baby was born before she tried to do anything like that. In the meantime, she would hide three of the notes and use the other one to buy coffee and other groceries that they needed and put the change in the jam jar and hope he wouldn't remember about the rest.

As she walked home with her shopping, Sharon schemed about how she would try and get money out of Hadyn whenever possible. It wouldn't be easy to hide it away in their confined space and she wondered if she ought to confide in Karmu and ask her to look after it for her.

Chapter Eleven

Christmas 1924 was the bleakest Sharon had ever known. Hadyn didn't return home until the early hours of Christmas morning and he was so drunk that he slept until almost midday.

Knowing that there was no way that Sharon could cook a Christmas dinner in her room, Karmu had invited them to join her. She roasted a plump chicken in the oven of the range in her kitchen and Sharon helped her prepare all the vegetables; some they roasted alongside the chicken and some they cooked on top of the range.

Hadyn was in a dark mood when Sharon roused him but after a lot of grumbling he promised to spruce himself up before he came downstairs to join them.

When they sat down to their meal he was charming, entertaining and full of praise for Karmu's cooking. Sharon smiled to herself at the transformation; it was as if the old Hadyn, the one she'd fallen for and had left home to be with, was back again.

Sharon declined to have a drink at the end of the meal because she was afraid it wouldn't be good for the baby. When she offered to wash up, Hadyn insisted on helping to clear the table and then left her to get on with it while he and Karmu settled down with a bottle of port and a couple of glasses.

As she worked away at the sink Sharon wondered what they were doing at Pen-y-lan Place. Christmas had always been special in the Pritchard house when she'd been at home and something she and Parry had looked forward to for weeks and she couldn't help wishing she was back there now.

Her mother always started preparations early in November, making the Christmas pudding and ensuring that they all had a stir and a wish. That was followed a week or so later by baking the Christmas cake. The rich fruit cake was put away until a few days before Christmas and then covered with marzipan and icing and decorated with sprigs of holly.

They'd all bought presents for each other and taken great care to wrap them up in such a way that no one could guess what was in their package until they unwrapped it on Christmas Day.

When they were little she and Parry had always hung up their sock before they went to bed on Christmas Eve. The joy of waking on Christmas morning and finding it bulging with mysterious gifts had been something she would never forget.

Soon she would be doing the same for her own child, she mused, but would it have anywhere near as happy a childhood as she'd had? she wondered.

Sharon felt so tired by the time she'd finished washing, drying and putting away all the dishes that she left Karmu and Hadyn to their drinking and went upstairs to lie on her bed and have a rest. How long she slept she wasn't sure but Hadyn flopping down beside her awakened her.

118

When he began to caress her she found herself stiffening and pulling away from him.

Hadyn sensed her reluctance and his mood changed from mildly maudlin to outright aggressive. As he forced himself on her she felt tears spilling down her cheeks. This wasn't the romantic love life she had envisaged. There was no tenderness, no real affection, merely lust on his part and fear on hers.

She remained passive until it was over then as he fell asleep she went over to the corner of the room and ladled out some fresh water and washed herself from top to toe. Christmas was over and so were her dreams. In a week's time it would be 1925, the beginning of a new year, and she resolved that she wouldn't go on living like this.

It was time for a fresh start, she told herself as she dressed in clean clothes, and put the kettle on to the gas ring. As soon as it boiled she brewed a pot of tea and roused Hadyn. She intended to have it out with him right now.

She waited until he had almost finished his cup of tea before saying anything.

'I don't like the way we're living,' she told him. 'I hate you earning a living by gambling, I want you to get a proper job.'

He stared at her as if she was mad, spluttering as he almost choked on his tea.

'Are you a bloody witch or have you second sight or something?' he asked with a bitter laugh.

'I don't understand.' She stood up and took his cup from him.

'You don't have to worry about my nightclub job; I've been given the push,' he told her.

She stared at him, a mixture of relief and dismay on her face. 'So that means no more gambling?'

'I didn't say that. How else can I earn enough to keep a roof over our heads? Perhaps you should try looking for a job.'

'Me!' She stared at him scornfully. 'Aren't you forgetting that I'm six months' pregnant? Where do you think I am going to be able to find work? Anyway, I should be resting, not working. It's up to you to do that,' she added spiritedly.

Hadyn gave her a hard speculative stare but he didn't argue and she wondered what he was thinking.

There was an uncomfortable atmosphere between them for the rest of the week. Hadyn would lie in bed until almost midday then he would smarten himself up and say he was going out to look for work but she discovered this meant taking himself off to the nearest pub. When he came back late in the afternoon he was reeking of drink and would sleep for a couple of hours.

In the evenings he went off out again; where he went she'd no idea and as the money in the housekeeping pot remained intact she wondered how he was managing to pay for beer and for the cigarettes that he chain-smoked when he was at home.

On the Wednesday night, which was New Year's Eve, Karmu invited them to come down and share a bottle with her to let in the New Year. Even though she knew she couldn't drink, Sharon accepted, hoping that it would be a good way to clear the terrible atmosphere between her and Hadyn.

She'd had so many dreams about 1925 being a new start for them both; a chance to make something of their life together. More than anything else she wanted them to get married before their baby was born so that it would not be illegitimate.

Several times she had wondered whether that really was the right direction or whether she would be better to swallow her pride and creep back home and hope that her father would forgive her. It was always the dread that he would expect her to have the baby adopted that stopped her from doing that.

When it was time for them to go downstairs Hadyn said he was out of cigarettes and that he was going to pop out for some, so would she tell Karmu that he'd be back in about ten minutes.

'Men!' Karmu laughed when Sharon explained why he wasn't with her. 'He says ten minutes but you can count on that being an hour. If he has gone to the pub to buy them, he is bound to meet up with one or two of his cronies and one drink always leads to another. What a pity you can't enjoy a drink with me because I don't like drinking on my own,' she sighed.

'I could join you in a cup of tea or coffee,' Sharon said smiling.

'Coffee! That's the answer. Then I can add a shot of whisky to mine and really feel that I am celebrating.'

They sat there enjoying their drinks and reminiscing about past Christmases they had known. Some of Karmu's stories were so extraordinary that Sharon found herself wondering if they could possibly be true.

As midnight approached and they heard the sound of ships, klaxons and horns and the shouts of revellers outside in the street, Sharon wondered where Hadyn was.

It was almost one o'clock in the morning when they heard a noise outside like some heavy object falling against the front door and Karmu went to see what had happened.

As she opened the door she called out sharply to Sharon who hurried out into the hall to see what was wrong. Hadyn was lying on the doorstep at Karmu's feet. He was not only drunk but he had obviously been beaten up. His eyes were like puffballs, his face cut and bleeding and his clothes dishevelled as though he'd been in a fight of some sort.

Between them they dragged him into Karmu's kitchen and bathed his face and Karmu made some extra strong black coffee and forced it down him in an attempt to sober him up.

The laceration on his face was deep and jagged and they had difficulty in stemming the bleeding. Each time they touched it he winced and, because it was so close to his left eye, Karmu thought it ought to be stitched.

In addition, he seemed to be in great pain and was holding his hand and arm protectively over his right side.

'I think he has broken ribs,' Karmu pronounced. Deftly she slipped her hand inside his shirt and very gently felt his chest.

'What do you think we ought to do?' Sharon asked worriedly.

'He needs to go to hospital and have his injuries attended to properly,' Karmu pronounced.

'No!' Hadyn grabbed at Karmu's arm. 'I'm not

going to any hospital. Stick a dressing on my face and my ribs will soon heal of their own accord.'

'If we do that, it's more likely than not that you'll get blood poisoning in that cut on your face,' Karmu warned.

'If you take me to hospital, it's more than likely that they'll inform the scuffers and I'll end up with a jail sentence,' Hadyn muttered.

'Why? What have you done? How did you get hurt?' Sharon asked worriedly as she cradled his head in her arms, smoothing back his hair and kissing his brow.

'Never mind about that now, take my word for it,' Hadyn told her. 'If they start looking into what happened and track down the other fellows involved there'll be hell to pay and I'll probably be the one taking the can back.'

When Sharon looked at Karmu to see what she thought about all this the older woman shook her head and clenched her thick lips tightly, so Sharon said nothing. She was far from satisfied but she realised it would be better to ask Hadyn about it all later on when they were alone.

With Karmu's help she managed to get him up to their room and into bed and tried to make him comfortable, hoping that a good sleep would help his injuries to heal.

The next morning, while Hadyn was still asleep, Karmu came upstairs with the morning newspaper in her hand. Sharon's heart was thumping wildly as she took it from her. The picture on the front page was of a brawl that had taken place the night before in Bute Street and showed three men fighting.

According to the caption, two of them had been taken to hospital suffering from knife wounds; the third man had managed to run away but it was understood that he had also been injured and the police warned people to keep away from him because he'd been the one wielding a knife.

'The full story is inside on page four,' Karmu told her. 'Believe me, it's enough to make your toes curl up,' she added with a shudder.

'I don't want to read it,' Sharon told her as she handed the newspaper back. 'What I've seen on the front page is quite enough for me.'

'Well, the police are looking for the third man involved in the fight but, from the sounds of it, they don't know who he is any more than we do,' Karmu said with a knowing look.

It was almost a week before Sharon was able to hear the whole story from Hadyn; a week when she slept as near the edge of the bed as she possibly could so as not to disturb him, but alert whenever he moved or cried out in his sleep.

Then she would wipe the sweat from his brow and moisten his lips with cold water and comfort him the best she could.

She dressed the wound on his face each day, feeling reassured as she removed the old dressing and saw how well it was all healing. His ribs were another matter. The slightest exertion caused him agony; when he coughed he almost blacked out with pain.

She sat at his bedside for hours, wondering how she could earn a living for the next couple of months or until Hadyn was back on his feet again. She toyed with the idea of renting a stall in the market but was unable to make up her mind about what to sell. She was sure that Karmu could advise her but she didn't want to take her into her confidence over this.

She was afraid that if Karmu knew they were practically penniless, she might turn them out. As it was, they owed two weeks' rent and Karmu had agreed to wait until Hadyn was better because he was the one who'd rented the room.

Grateful though she was to Karmu, Sharon hated to be under an obligation and, as Hadyn was making such slow progress, she decided to pay the rent out of the money she had secretly saved from the housekeeping Hadyn had given her.

She waited until Hadyn was asleep before she pulled up a corner of the linoleum and moved the loose floorboard that was underneath it so that she could reach down and retrieve her little hoard.

She ran her hand round in a circle but she found nothing there. Puzzled, she got down on to her knees and pushed her hand in further until her arm was under the floorboards almost up to her elbow. She still couldn't find anything.

Breathless from the exertion she clambered to her feet and sat on the edge of the bed to get her breath back and to give herself time to think. Her forearm was scratched and hurting and as she sat there gently rubbing it she tried to puzzle out why she was unable to find the money she'd hidden there.

Determined to give it one last effort, she started to get down on to her knees again when Hadyn reached out and grabbed hold of her arm and stopped her.

'You might as well give up looking, because you're wasting your time. It's not there. I found it weeks ago.'

'You mean you've taken it ... and spent it?' The colour drained from her face as a feeling of hopelessness swept over her.

'I'm sorry, cariad, but where else do you think I got the money to pay for our food and rent and all the extras for Christmas?'

'We didn't have any extras for Christmas. As for the rent, it hasn't been paid for two weeks now. The reason why I was looking for the money I'd pinched and scraped to save up was so that I could pay Karmu before she chucks us out.'

Hadyn smiled weakly. 'Don't give me that clap trap; and before you say anything about me taking the money, it was mine anyway. We spent the miserly few quid you had weeks ago so any money you managed to hide away was money you'd taken from my pockets when you thought I was out for the count.'

Sharon looked at him in dismay. 'You mean you knew!'

'Of course I knew. I might have been drunk but I wasn't senseless. If I had money when I came home at the end of the evening and it wasn't there the next day, then there was only one explanation, wasn't there?'

As Sharon started to cry, Hadyn said contritely, 'Darw! Don't turn the waterworks on, cariad. I know you thought you were doing it for the best. I hadn't earned the money; it was what I'd won gambling so I didn't really care about it.'

Her sobs deepened as she realised how far apart

126

they appeared to have drifted. It seemed that she might as well discard all her plans for the New Year. The only thing that she could be certain about was that it would bring the birth of her baby and she had no idea how they were going to manage then.

She still loved Hadyn, even though he was turning out to be as feckless as her father had said he was, but she'd cut herself adrift from her home and unless she was prepared to give up her baby there was no going back.

As if reading her thoughts, Hadyn pulled her down on the bed beside him. 'I know I've made a mess of things but you know you can't go home because your father won't have you there. The baby is due soon, so let's try and make the best of things and pull together from now on.'

She looked up into his green eyes, studying him closely. Could she trust him to do that? she wondered.

'Does that mean you will give up gambling and get a proper job?' she asked in a small, anxious voice.

'Yes, I promise I will, as soon as I am fit enough to do so,' he told her solemnly.

They stared into each other's eyes and she felt the last few weeks roll back and he was no longer the dissolute drunkard and gambler but the handsome young businessman she had fallen for and who had swept her off her feet all those months earlier.

She placed a hand over her distended stomach as she felt her baby moving and, for the first time since she'd moved into Clwyd Court, she felt confident about the future. She was determined that they would have a happy life together; they must, for the baby's sake.

As she made a cup of cocoa for Elwyn and herself before going to bed, Elaine Pritchard wondered what sort of a Christmas Sharon had enjoyed.

Ever since Sharon had left home at the beginning of December she had been hoping that by some lucky chance she would bump into her or that she would pay them a visit on some pretext or other.

Although Elwyn never mentioned her name or her absence, she was pretty sure that he was missing Sharon as much as she was. She prayed that one day soon the two of them would be reunited. Sharon needed their support now more than she ever did because soon her baby would be born.

Every time Elaine saw Gwen and realised how soon she would be having her baby, her thoughts turned to Sharon. Gwen would have every possible love and attention when her time came, but what about Sharon? She would have no one but Hadyn Jenkins; that was, if they were still together.

In the hope that she might one day meet up with Sharon she had put together some baby clothes and other things that she thought Sharon would find useful.

She kept them hidden away where Elwyn wouldn't see them. She didn't want to make it even more unbearable for him or for him to think she was reproaching him in any way. He had done what many fathers would do to try and protect their family name from shame.

If only Sharon had accepted his terms, but she had been adamant that she wouldn't give up her baby for adoption any more than she would stop seeing Hadyn Jenkins.

In some ways Elaine felt proud of Sharon's determination to keep the baby. Whether or not she was doing the right thing by going off with Hadyn was quite another matter.

He was good-looking and very charming, and she could understand why Sharon had fallen for him, but he was not only older than she was but, according to Elwyn, he was also something of a reprobate. He certainly didn't like him and had strongly disapproved of Sharon seeing him.

Both of them had always thought that Sharon cared for Madoc and they knew that he worshipped the ground she walked on. He would have made her a wonderful husband and Elaine felt so sorry for him because he was so obviously missing her.

She would always remember that when he had heard that Sharon was expecting a baby he had still wanted to marry her and had even said that he would bring the child up as if it was his own.

Chapter Twelve

For the next few weeks Hadyn seemed to be doing his best to find work. He didn't manage to get a full-time job but he usually managed to find some casual work, either at one of the shops or cafés or down on the quayside, which brought in enough money for them to pay the rent and buy their food, and for him to buy cigarettes and the occasional beer.

Sharon told herself that this was all that mattered and that she should make the best of it. A full-time job would come along sooner or later and he did seem to have stopped gambling, which was something she had hated.

The following week, however, he returned without any money but with a bag full of drawing and painting materials. He looked at her questioningly as he unpacked them and waited for her comments.

They were all the special materials she had used to create the impressions of room settings which had always so delighted their customers when she had been working at her father's shop.

Sharon bit her lip, unsure of what to say because they brought back so many memories, but didn't, however, make a meal, and that was what she was more interested in now.

'Surprised?' Hadyn asked, his eyes dancing with enthusiasm.

'Well, yes. They're all good-quality materials but what about money for our food and the rent?' she asked hesitantly.

Hadyn's smile deepened. 'That's the whole point. Now that you have these, you can help to earn some money,' he said jubilantly.

'Me?' She looked at him bewildered.

'Paint some of the big shops or houses and then I'll take the pictures and sell them to the owners,' he explained.

They argued for a while about whether or not it was ethical to do this without first getting the consent of the owner but, as Hadyn pointed out, people took pictures of houses and shops, so what was the difference in painting them?

'I'm not sure about people's homes but I'll do one of a shop and see what happens,' she agreed.

The next day, sitting at the table with all the pencils and paints laid out in front of her, Sharon felt the old excitement she'd known when she was working. As a first attempt she simply made a watercolor picture of Howell's in St Mary's Street. It was the largest department store in Cardiff and she was sure that other people had either photographed it or painted an impression of it many times before, so she wasn't breaking any law by doing so.

Hadyn was surprised by her choice but he seemed to understand her reasoning. The next day he carefully wrapped the finished painting in a protective piece of newspaper and took it with him when he went out.

'It would look a lot better if it was in a nice frame,' Sharon told him.

'We haven't the money to do that. Perhaps next time, if I manage to sell this one.'

'Sell it? Who do you think is going to buy it?'

'That's something we'll have to wait and see,' he told her. 'I have one or two ideas,' he added cheerfully.

When he came home that night it was without the painting and he looked elated. 'I've not only sold it but two people have asked if you will do paintings of their homes,' he told her as he hugged and kissed her.

'I don't think that's possible without seeing their houses; do you know where they live?'

Hadyn fished in his jacket pocket and brought out some photographs. 'See what you can do with these,' he said, grinning.

Sharon studied them in growing dismay. 'They're all black and white, I have no idea what colours to use.'

'That's the whole point; use your imagination and show them what they ought to do to brighten up the outside of their places,' he explained.

'You mean I have a completely free hand?' Sharon frowned. 'It sounds crazy to me, especially when I have never seen any of these houses and I have no idea what sort of people live there.'

'You do as I ask, and they'll pay for your work and that's all that matters,' Hadyn insisted rather impatiently.

For the next few weeks Sharon found that she was fully occupied painting watercolour interpretations of photographs Hadyn brought home. All their customers seemed to be completely satisfied with her work and paid up as soon as he delivered the paintings to them.

There was only one exception; a man who insisted that Sharon must come and see the house for herself as he didn't have any photographs of it.

The house was quite near Roath Park and Sharon was very reluctant to go there.

'It's too near to Pen-y-lan Place,' she protested. 'Supposing I bump into Gwen or any of the neighbours I knew when I lived there?'

'They probably wouldn't recognise you,' Hadyn told her. 'You're twice the size you were then so you don't look like the same person.'

'No, you're right about that,' Sharon agreed, 'but they might recognise my clothes. I'm still wearing what I left home in and none of it fits me these days so I look like a scarecrow,' she added bitterly.

'Sell a few more paintings and then you can buy some new clothes with the money,' he promised.

'I need money for baby clothes and that's more important than worrying about what I have to wear,' she pointed out quickly.

'All in good time. As long as I manage to find work each week to pay the rent and buy our food, then you can keep the money you make from your painting to spend on whatever else you want,' he promised.

'I'll need quite a lot more materials if I'm going to carry on painting.'

'You make a list of what you want and I'll get them for you,' Hadyn assured her. He pulled her into his arms and hugged her. 'It's a great way to earn some money and, what's more, you enjoy doing it, don't you?'

Sharon had to admit he was right about that. Since she'd started painting again she'd felt so much happier and more relaxed. Her increasing bulk made it uncomfortable to sit for very long but she was free to get up and walk about or make herself a cup of tea whenever she wanted to do so.

It was a fairly mild March morning when she

and Hadyn set off for the house in Roath. She really didn't want to go because she wasn't feeling at all well and she dreaded the thought of having to sit outside to work. What was more, her intuition warned her that her baby would be born any day now.

'All the more reason to get this job under your belt before it happens, since Mr Morgan has promised to pay double the money I usually charge for your paintings,' Hadyn told her when she mentioned it to him.

'You've nothing to worry about; I'll stay with you all the time you are there working and I'll lay out your paints and so on, so all you have to do is sit there and do the actual painting.'

Sharon still felt she ought to be staying safe and warm at home and as they passed Karmu's door on the way out she, too, called out a warning that Sharon was in no fit state to go gallivanting off out and that if she had any sense she'd stay indoors out of the cold.

'Come on, you don't want to listen to Karmu prophesying doom and gloom. The next thing you know she'll have the bones out and she'll be dancing around in her grass skirt doing some sort of witch doctor dance.'

'Hadyn, what a thing to say!'

Although she tried to sound serious, Sharon couldn't help smiling at Hadyn's comments about Karmu. Straightening the thick scarf she'd put on over her coat to keep warm, because the coat no longer fastened up over her bulk, she waddled beside him to the tram stop.

Once they were on the tram, the jolting and

bumping made her feel even worse. Her back ached and she kept having sharp jabs of pain in her side but she gritted her teeth and said nothing.

Once they reached the house, she wasn't at all sure she could go through with doing the painting. Aware that because Hadyn had agreed to stay there with her it meant that he wasn't able to go and find any work himself, she forced herself to do the painting, knowing that they would have no money if she didn't. By midday she had finished, but she felt so ill that she couldn't wait to get home.

When the owner of the house, a middle-aged, austere-looking man wearing a dark grey three-piece suit, came out to look at what she had done, he was very enthusiastic about the result and insisted that they went inside for something hot to eat and drink before setting off for home.

The bowl of hot chicken soup was comforting but the moment she relaxed in his warm, comfortable kitchen, Sharon found that her entire body seemed to suddenly cramp up and, before she could help it, she let out a small scream and doubled up with pain.

'I think your wife has gone into labour; we'd better call an ambulance,' Mr Morgan told Hadyn.

Sharon found the rest of the day more frightening than anything she had ever experienced.

She had talked to Karmu about having the baby and she had been so reassuring, telling her not to worry because she would be at her side the entire time and would do all that was necessary. She had even prepared various potions in readiness and put them into screw-top glass jars so that they would be to hand when needed. What they were for, exactly, Sharon had no idea but she was confident that Karmu knew what she was doing and she was prepared to leave everything to her.

Now, instead of being confined in her own bed, she was being whisked off to hospital with strangers all around her giving orders and telling her what to do. She felt so frightened that even the severe labour pains she was experiencing were as nothing compared with the terrible fear she had of the unknown. It was almost as if her body was no longer her own; as if she had no say at all in what was happening or what was being done to her.

She longed for her mother to be at her side, and, if that wasn't possible, then she wanted Karmu to be there. She kept saying this to the nurses in their stiffly starched uniforms but they paid no attention to what she said.

Pains came and went in rapid succession and when she felt she could endure no more she heard a strange sound like the mewing of a kitten. A bundle was put into her arms and as she looked down at the puckered little face tightly swathed in white sheeting she wondered for a moment what it was.

Then Hadyn was there and she felt relief flooding through her. He'd know what it was and what they had to do with it.

'They tell me it's a boy, so what are we going to call him?' he asked as he gazed proudly at the sleeping baby and ran a finger under its chin.

Sharon shook her head. It was something she hadn't thought about. She'd always expected the baby would be a girl and she'd thought of several pretty names to call her.

'You don't want to name him after your dad, do you?' Hadyn said, frowning.

'No!' She shook her head emphatically. 'No, of course not.'

'We'll have to think of something, so why not call him Morgan?'

'Morgan,' Sharon repeated in a puzzled voice. 'Why should we call him that?'

'Because it was Mr Morgan's house you were painting and he was the one who sent for the ambulance. I have to go back there to collect our money so I'll tell him we are calling the baby after him. He'll probably be so pleased and flattered that he'll give me a bit extra for the kid and we need every penny we can get because you won't be able to work for a while.'

Sharon didn't like the idea of doing that but she also knew that what Hadyn was saying was true. She pulled back the sheet so that the baby's face was more exposed and murmured, 'You're to be called Morgan then', as she kissed the tiny scrap of humanity on the brow.

Sharon was kept in hospital for ten days and once she got used to the rather strict regime she began to enjoy the luxury of lying in a comfortable bed that had crisp white sheets and being served regular meals.

All she seemed to have to do in return was feed little Morgan every few hours after which he was taken away to the nursery ward where she couldn't even hear if he cried.

She slept a great deal for the first few days and then gradually her feelings for her new son became so strong that she resented the fact that he was taken out of her sight and so prolonged the feeding as long as she could.

The moment she was allowed out of bed she went in search of the nursery ward only to be reprimanded and sent back to her own ward. As she lay there in bed with nothing to do she was sure she could hear her baby crying and she was sure that he was unhappy at being parted from her.

When she mentioned this to Hadyn when he came to see her, he laughed. 'You make the most of being able to rest, cariad. Once you're back on your feet and out of here you'll be wishing that someone would take him off your hands when he cries.'

'No, never,' she told him. 'Having Morgan is the most wonderful thing that has ever happened to me.'

'To both of us.' Hadyn grinned. 'When I told Mr Morgan what we'd called him, he offered me some part-time work at his house.'

Sharon's eyes lit up. 'You mean he's giving you a proper job? Doing what?'

'I'll be doing all sorts of odd-jobs like repairs, a bit of gardening, polishing his motor car and goodness knows what else. Who knows, he may even let me drive his wonderful green Wolsey one of these days. Anyway, the important thing is that he'll pay me every Saturday, so our money worries are over for the moment.'

'That's wonderful news.' Sharon beamed. 'Does it mean that we can move to somewhere better? It's going to be awfully crowded living in that one room now that we have the baby.'

'We can't move at the moment; you'll have to be patient for a few more weeks. We'll have to save up enough money to be able to pay two weeks' rent in advance, if we go somewhere else.'

'That will be impossible because there are so many things we are going to need for the baby,' Sharon sighed. 'We haven't anywhere for him to sleep except the bottom drawer of the chest of drawers and he'll soon be too big to fit in there.'

'Don't worry your head about that, cariad,' Hadyn told her with a forced laugh. 'I'm sure you don't really want to move at the moment and lose touch with Karmu.'

'No, you're probably right about that,' Sharon admitted. 'I know so little about babies that for the first few weeks when I come home I am going to need all the help I can get from Karmu.'

Chapter Thirteen

Although Morgan was quite a good baby, Sharon found that feeding and looking after him took up far more of her time than she had expected it to do.

One of the reasons was that living in one room meant that she was in a continual state of muddle. Every day there was a pile of washing to be done and wet nappies and baby clothes were draped over every available space in an attempt to get them dry.

139

Hadyn constantly grumbled that there was no-where to sit down and about the constant trips downstairs that had to be made to bring up pails of fresh water and to dispose of all the dirty water and other rubbish.

It also meant that Sharon had less time to do any painting and this led to angry tiffs between them.

'If you want me to go out and view the house I have to paint, then why don't you take a turn in looking after Morgan?' she challenged when he grumbled because she hadn't started a painting as he had asked her to do.

'If I'm sitting here, then I'm not earning any money,' Hadyn retorted. 'What's more, I can't risk losing my job by taking a day off, now can I? If you don't want to take the baby with you when you have to go and look at a house, then why don't you ask Karmu to keep an eye on him?'

'No,' Sharon shook her head, 'I don't want to take advantage of her kindness. Time enough for that if there is some kind of an emergency.'

'Earning money is an emergency and, anyway, she's the one who benefits from us having some money, otherwise she won't get paid her rent.'

'You finish work at Mr Morgan's house at five o'clock so on those days, if you come straight home, you could look after Morgan while I go and take a look at the outside of the house that has to be painted,' Sharon argued.

'I thought you didn't like having to go out after dark because of the sort of people who live around here?'

'I don't, but it's not all that dark in the evenings now that spring is here and from now on it will get even lighter; in fact, in a few weeks' time it will be light almost up until bedtime.'

Reluctantly, Hadyn agreed to come straight home after he'd finished work so that Sharon could go out and, for a few weeks, it seemed to be working quite well. By the time Hadyn arrived home Sharon had fed Morgan and settled him down to sleep. She had also prepared something for Hadyn to eat so all he had to do was sit down and eat his meal and pick Morgan up and comfort him if he was restless.

When Morgan was a year old, Sharon insisted that the next money she earned must be spent on a second-hand cot because he was far too big to go on sleeping in the drawer.

The other thing she was anxious to buy was a pram to take him out in. So far she had been carrying him, Welsh-fashion, wrapped in a big shawl that enveloped both her and the baby but soon he would be far too heavy for her to go on doing that.

Her hopes that there would be no more problems about money now that Hadyn had regular work at Mr Morgan's house had been dashed when Hadyn told her that he still owed money to the gambling club where he had once worked.

Early in the New Year he had started going there again on Saturday nights, insisting that he was working there to pay off his past debt, but Sharon didn't believe him. She was pretty sure that he was spending some of his wages there and she could tell by his mood whether he had won or lost.

'Once they've gambling in their blood, you'll

never stop them betting. They'll beg, borrow, cheat, lie or even steal in order to get their hands on some money to do it,' Karmu told her, shaking her head regretfully, whenever Sharon went to her in tears and asked if she would wait a few more days for their rent.

In desperation, and intent on finding some way of breaking the pattern and stopping him from gambling all their money away, Sharon told Hadyn that she had to go out that evening to view a house and asked him if he would come straight home.

'On a Saturday?' he argued.

'It will have to be, if I'm to have the painting ready by Monday.'

When she pointed out that they needed the money to pay the rent which was already overdue, he capitulated but made her promise to be home before six o'clock.

'If I don't turn up to do my stint at the club and pay back what I still owe, then they'll be sending somebody round to know why and if it's one of their heavy boyos, then more than likely he'll beat me up,' he warned.

'Don't talk daft,' Sharon argued as she packed a sketch pad and some pencils into a canvas bag. 'You've worked there every Saturday night for months, so you can't owe them very much now. You've paid them back far more regularly than you pay Karmu her rent.'

'Never mind about that, you make sure you are home well before six o'clock,' Hadyn insisted, his handsome face darkening into a scowl.

'I'll be as quick as I can, but it depends on how

142

the trams are running because this place I'm going to is out by Victoria Park and that means I have to change trams twice.'

It was a lovely early May afternoon and as she approached the park she was unable to overcome the temptation to take a quick walk in the fresh air.

She had only meant it to be ten minutes but she was enjoying the fresh air and the spring flowers so much that it wasn't until she came within sight of the clock tower that she realised she had spent over half an hour there.

As she hurried down the nearby roads to the house she had to draw, she resolved that the very next thing she would buy would be a pushchair for Morgan so that she could bring him here to enjoy the sun and fresh air.

It was almost six o'clock by the time she reached home and as she went in, Karmu called out to her to come into her place and have a cup of tea.

'I'd love to, but Hadyn is waiting to go out and I'm late as it is,' she called back as she made for the stairs.

'No need to worry about him,' Karmu told her, coming out into the hallway. 'He went out well over an hour ago.'

'Oh, I'm sorry! I suppose that means he's left little Morgan with you?'

'No.' Karmu shook her head. 'No, he never mentioned anything about the baby. That means little Morgan must be sound asleep, because I haven't heard a sound. Come on,' she urged, 'ten minutes isn't going to make all that much difference and we'll hear the baby if he starts to cry.'

'Well, I could certainly do with a cuppa,' Sharon agreed as she followed Karmu into her kitchen. 'The miners were having a protest march and there was a lot of trouble in the city centre, so the tram was held up for ages because it couldn't turn down St Mary Street until the police moved them on.'

'Sit down then, cariad, and take the weight off your feet,' Karmu told her. 'Why don't you slip your shoes off and put your feet up for a few minutes?' she added as she busied herself with the teapot and milk jug.

'Here you are, then,' she murmured as she passed the cup of tea to Sharon and pushed the sugar bowl towards her so that she could help herself.

For the next half an hour they sat relaxed and comfortable, gossiping about things in general, what might happen to the country as well as in Cardiff if the miners did decide to go on strike, and how it might affect their own lives.

'I really ought to go upstairs and make sure that Morgan is all right and then get started on some washing and try to tidy the place up a bit before Hadyn comes home,' Sharon said guiltily when Karmu offered to refill her cup.

'Stay where you are, what's the hurry? He won't be home for hours yet.'

'No, you're probably right,' Sharon agreed. 'Even so, I ought to go and check that Morgan is all right.'

'Go on, then. You do that while I wait for the kettle to boil so that I can make us a fresh pot of tea.'

Sharon's scream a few minutes later brought not only Karmu but also several of the other people living in the house out on to the stairs to find out what had happened.

'What's wrong, cariad? What's all the yelling about?' Karmu puffed as she lumbered up to Sharon's room.

'Help me, please help me; tell me what to do,' Sharon sobbed. 'It's Morgan. He's breathing in a funny sort of way, almost as if he had a rattle stuck in his throat.'

'What on earth are you talking about?' Karmu frowned as she waddled over to the corner of the room and bent over the cot to take a closer look at the baby.

'Duw anwyl, you're right about that, cariad,' she gasped as she straightened up. 'It sounds bad; perhaps you should get him to a doctor.'

'Move over and let me have a look.'

Alwyn Jones, a bold-looking middle-aged woman with black shining hair pulled back in a coil at the nape of her neck, who'd come to see what Sharon was making such a fuss about, impatiently pushed Karmu to one side. 'Poor little mite, it looks as though he's spewed up and he's choking on his own sick,' she stated.

Sharon stared at her nervously. She had never spoken to Alwyn Jones all the time she'd been living at Clwyd Court and whenever they'd passed each other in the passageway, Alwyn had always ignored her. Now, finding the older woman's sharp, dark eyes fixed on her accusingly, Sharon felt frightened. 'So what do I do?' she asked nervously.

'When my little one chokes like that I always find that the best thing to do is to sit down and lay him across your lap and then thump his little back,' advised Caitlin Thomas, a young fair-haired wisp of a girl who had also come to see what was going on.

Sharon smiled at her gratefully. She liked Caitlin; they had chatted once or twice and she knew that Caitlin came from the Valleys. Her husband had been a miner but had hated working underground and so they had come to Cardiff about six months ago and he was now working down at the docks.

'I'll deal with it,' Alwyn said. 'I've had six kids of my own so I know what to do.'

Before Sharon could say anything, Alwyn had picked Morgan up, sat down on the side of the bed, put him over her knee and slapped him hard across the back.

Morgan made a strange gurgling noise, gulped loudly and then was violently sick all over Alwyn's red cotton skirt. He followed that up with a long wailing cry of protest.

'That sounds better,' Caitlin muttered. 'My youngest always yells his head off when he's feeling sick; it's a wonder you didn't hear this little one crying?'

'She probably didn't hear him because he was all on his own when it happened and, at his age, that's neglect in my book,' Alwyn opined tartly. She took the towel Sharon held out to her and began dabbing her skirt.

'Here, you can take him now and make sure you look after him better in future,' she added as she wiped around Morgan's mouth with a corner of the towel and then held the screaming child out to Sharon.

Sharon murmured her thanks as she took Morgan from Alwyn and cradled him in her arms. If only she had checked that Morgan was all right the minute she got home instead of sitting drinking tea and gossiping with Karmu. And had Morgan been all right when Hadyn had gone out, or had he not even bothered to check and make sure before he left?

She sighed aloud, wondering if Hadyn really did love little Morgan as much as he said he did or had he been in such a hurry to get to the club because he wanted a glass of beer and the thrill of putting on a bet that he'd forgotten all about him?

She was equally to blame, she reminded herself. She should have come straight upstairs when she got home instead of staying with Karmu drinking tea and gossiping. She looked round the dingy, squalid room with distaste. She hated being there so much that even Karmu's cluttered kitchen seemed to be a haven.

Her longing to go back home to Pen-y-lan Place was overwhelming. She missed her mother so much as well as the pleasant surroundings and her own big bedroom with all her own favourite things around her.

For the rest of the evening she sat cuddling Morgan as if afraid something else might happen to him.

Finally, because she was so tired herself, she decided that it was pointless waiting up for Hadyn since she had no idea what time he would come home. She fed Morgan once again and then undressed and took him into her own bed.

As she settled down with the sleeping baby cradled in her arms she wondered what sort of life she was going to be able to make for her little son. Already there seemed to be so many pitfalls in caring for him and, unless she had Hadyn's support, she didn't think she was going to be able to deal with them all.

If only she could turn to her mother for advice, she thought sadly. She envied Gwen; she could turn not only to her mother but also to Sharon's mother as well. They would both be eager to help if ever there was any emergency. They would always be right there showering love and attention on Gwen's child.

Because Sharon had left home she had denied her child this privilege. Morgan would grow up never knowing his grandparents; Hadyn's parents were dead and hers might just as well be.

For the first time she worried about what would happen to Morgan if she was taken seriously ill, or even if she died. Somehow she didn't think that Hadyn would be able to manage single-handed, so what would he do with Morgan?

She wondered if he would get someone like Karmu, or perhaps Alwyn Jones, to look after him while he was out at work. Or would he put him in an orphanage?

She had fought so hard to prevent the baby she had been expecting from being adopted. Now that he had been born and was a personality in his own right, the thought of that happening to him terrified her even more now.

Once again she wondered whether, for her child's sake, she ought to try and make peace with her family. She felt sure that if her parents met Morgan and saw how adorable he was they would accept him. They would take him to their hearts and she would be able to rely on them to care for him if ever there was any need for them to do so.

Although Hadyn seemed to be more or less happy with the way they lived, she wasn't. She was fed up with trying to exist in one squalid room where they had to eat and sleep and where there was no sink or running water. She longed to have a proper home with space for Morgan to toddle around and perhaps even a strip of garden so that he could be outside when the weather was fine.

She still didn't understand why they were so desperately poor. The housekeeping money that Hadyn handed over wasn't enough to keep them in basic foodstuffs so she had to use the money she earned from her paintings to eke out their frugal budget so that she could buy things that little Morgan needed.

She had never been so shabby. Her clothes were threadbare and she had cut pieces of cardboard to go inside her shoes to keep the cold and damp out because there were holes in the soles.

Hadyn was also working most evenings at the club in Bute Street so that he could afford to buy clothes for himself. He still worked three days a week for Mr Morgan so it was important that he looked fairly smart.

He insisted that half the money he earned at the club was to clear off the money he still owed them but she was sure he'd done that a long time ago and that he was using the money they paid him to gamble again. She could always tell from his mood when he arrived home whether or not he'd had a winning streak.

Chapter Fourteen

Sharon was wakened from a deep sleep by Morgan crying and she was still drowsy as she went to attend to him. He was soaking wet so she changed him and put him down again in his cot. It was only when she went back to her own bed that she realised that Hadyn was still not home.

When she looked at the clock she was surprised to find that it was almost seven o'clock. She drew back the curtain and as the early morning May sunshine came into the room she wondered where on earth Hadyn could be.

She was worried in case he'd had an accident or was in some kind of trouble. She kept remembering what he was always saying would happen if he didn't turn up at the club. But, as far as she knew, that was where he'd gone the night before.

Memories of what had happened the previous evening came rushing back and she went over to check that Morgan was all right even though it had only been moments earlier that she'd put him down.

He looked so perfect and peaceful as he lay on his back, arms and legs spreadeagled, that she wanted to pick him up and cuddle him.

150

Knowing that it would be foolish to disturb him, she turned away. As she stripped off her nightdress and then had a wash and got dressed, she began to feel increasingly concerned about why Hadyn hadn't come home.

As soon as Morgan was awake she went down to ask Karmu what she thought about it.

'You mean you haven't heard?' Karmu said, her voice tinged with disbelief.

'No, what should I have heard?' Sharon asked, shifting Morgan into a more comfortable position.

'I think you'd better sit down and take a look at this, cariad,' Karmu told her as she pushed the previous night's late edition of the South Wales Echo into Sharon's hand. 'You can read all about what happened in St Mary Street yesterday.'

'I told you there was some sort of trouble when I was coming home,' Sharon said as she took the newspaper and sat down in an armchair and settled Morgan on her lap. 'The police had to deal with some sort of disturbance and move them on before the tram I was on could pass along St Mary Street,' she reminded Karmu.

'I don't know if that was when this was happening or later on,' Karmu told her, jabbing her finger at a picture which was captioned: ARREST AT MINERS' MARCH.

Sharon stared in disbelief at the picture; three policemen were grappling with a man who was carrying a bucket in one hand and, in the other, a large placard that read:

Funds For Miners.
Give Generously.

151

'That looks like Hadyn!' Sharon exclaimed as she stared at the picture in disbelief. 'It can't be him, though, can it, because at that time he was here at home looking after Morgan.' Her voice trailed away as she read what was written there and learned the time the incident had taken place.

'Are you sure about that? He wasn't here when you arrived home now, was he!' Karmu reminded her.

Sharon studied the picture and read the write-up again. 'I don't know what to do about it,' she said resignedly, looking at Karmu as if expecting her to advise her.

'Nothing much you can do about it, is there? They've arrested him.'

'For doing what?'

'Well, you've just read about it,' Karmu said impatiently. 'He's been arrested for pretending to be a miner and collecting money on their behalf.'

'He was probably trying to help them,' Sharon said lamely as she looked at the paper yet again. 'Don't forget, he comes from up the Valleys; his father and brothers were all killed in the Senghenydd pit disaster.'

'More likely he was trying to line his own pocket, and you know it,' Karmu told her flatly.

Sharon stared at her in dismay, her eyes filling with tears. 'So what will happen to him?'

'They'll consider him to be a thief and he'll get sent to jail, of course.'

'Are you quite sure about that, or are you just surmising?' Sharon asked worriedly.

'You can bet your boots that is what will hap-

152

pen. What's more, I'll bet any money you like that he'll get a stiff sentence,' Karmu prophesised.

'I think I'd better go to the police station and see if I can say something to help him. If I tell them that he was at home looking after our baby they might let him off,' Sharon said. She transferred Morgan from her lap into her arms as she stood up.

'He wasn't, though, and if the police find out that you are lying, then they might arrest you as well as an accessory or whatever it is they call it.'

'Don't talk daft, I wasn't there; I was here with you,' Sharon said spiritedly.

'They might accept that as your alibi but I doubt it. If Hadyn says he stole the money in order to help support you and his child then they still might consider you to be equally guilty,' Karmu reasoned.

Sharon took refuge in her room for the rest of the day, shaking like a leaf every time she heard footsteps on the stairs outside in case it was a policeman coming to arrest her.

Morgan seemed to sense the tension in the air and was unusually fractious. Every time he started crying Sharon picked him up and either played with him or walked up and down the room rocking him in her arms to soothe him.

That night she was haunted by tortuous night-mares. She dreamed that Morgan had been taken away from her by some stranger in a forbidding uniform and that she was shut up in a tiny cell with people outside jeering and calling out abuse at her.

The next morning, as she fed Morgan, she

153

decided she could stand the uncertainty no longer. She would ignore Karmu's advice and go to the police station and find out what was happening.

If she could persuade them to let her speak to Hadyn, then she could at least find out if Mr Morgan owed him any wages so that she could go and ask him for them because she had no money at all.

At first, because she wasn't legally Hadyn's wife, the desk sergeant refused to tell her anything other than that Hadyn was under arrest and that he would be brought before the magistrate for sentencing in due course.

When, with tears trickling down her cheeks, she explained that her reason for wanting to speak to Hadyn was that she had no money and she couldn't go out to work because she had their young child to look after, he relented.

'Wait here, then,' he said, indicating a wooden bench, 'and I'll make some enquiries.'

She sat waiting for such a long time that she began to think that he had forgotten all about her. Then, finally, she was taken along a cold corridor to a small bare room at the far end and told to sit down at a scrubbed table.

A few minutes later a sharp-faced policeman brought Hadyn into the room and then took up a position by the door within earshot while they talked.

Hadyn looked haggard, as if he'd had no sleep, and his face had a deep cut down one side and one of his eyes was badly bruised. His jacket was torn and dirty and she supposed that it had happened when he'd been intercepted in St Mary Street.

As she began to say something about his appearance he shook his head very slightly and pressed a finger to his mouth warning her not to do so.

'I've got no money to give you, if that's what you've come here for, so you'll have to make do somehow with what you have,' he said bluntly.

'I haven't anything left; I spent my last penny on the tram fare yesterday,' she retorted. 'You must be owed some wages so I'd better go and collect them, hadn't I?

'Ssh!' He frowned and shook his head, casting a swift glance over at the policeman who was still standing by the door and obviously listening to what they said.

'Keep your voice down,' Hadyn muttered softly. 'I don't want anybody in here to know I work for Mr Morgan. It might be better if you didn't go there, anyway.'

'I must, I haven't any money to live on or to buy things I need for the baby.'

Lowering his voice, Hadyn muttered, 'Ask Mr Morgan to let you have an advance on my next lot of wages; the police have taken the money he paid me on Saturday.'

'What do I say about you not being at work?' she asked in a hesitant whisper.

'Duw anwyl, you won't need to say anything; don't go making up any excuses for me,' Hadyn said bitterly. 'He will have read all about it in the newspaper, the same as you did. That's how you found out, isn't it? It must be, since I never told them where I was living or your name because I didn't want you to be involved.'

Sharon nodded, too choked to answer him. He

seemed to be so offhand that for a moment she couldn't help wondering if that was the truth or whether the real reason was that he was planning to abandon her and little Morgan.

'If Mr Morgan has read the papers, he might not want you working for him ever again anyway,' she said eventually, 'so it won't be any good my asking for an advance on your wages.'

'Time's up.' The policeman who'd been standing by the door walked towards them and motioned with his baton to Hadyn to stand up.

As Sharon moved closer, intending to kiss Hadyn goodbye, the baton was raised to form a barrier between them and she pulled back with an exclamation of shock.

'No touching or making any sort of contact with the prisoner,' the officer told her curtly as he grasped hold of Hadyn's arm to make sure they stayed apart.

'When ... when will I see you again?' she asked forlornly, her eyes filling with tears.

'I won't know anything at all until after the trial. Watch the newspapers, they're bound to report it,' Hadyn told her as he was led away.

It was raining when Sharon left the police station, fine, drizzly rain, and although she wrapped the big flannel blanket as tightly as she could around herself and Morgan, it had soaked right through them both long before she reached Clwyd Court.

Cold and shivery, she towelled herself and little Morgan as dry as she could. He was whimpering so much that she sat down and fed him in an attempt to comfort him. It also gave her time to think about whether or not she could go and ask Mr Morgan if she might have an advance on Hadyn's wages.

She wished she'd thought to ask Hadyn the name of the people to whom he had intended to sell the picture he'd asked her to paint. She still hadn't had time to finish it but if she knew how much money was involved then that would be an incentive to get on and do it.

As soon as Morgan settled to sleep she laid out her brushes and paints. The moment she settled down to work Morgan woke up crying for attention but she did her best to ignore him.

Morgan was making so much noise that Karmu called out to know what was the matter. 'Bring him down here for a while and have a cuppa,' she invited.

Sharon hesitated; she knew she ought to be working but she was finding it impossible to concentrate on her painting, so perhaps the break would do her good, she told herself. Anyway, she was longing for a cuppa and she had used up every scrap of tea there had been in the caddy.

As she made her way downstairs with Morgan in her arms, she wondered optimistically if Karmu might even have some advice about where she ought to apply for help if Hadyn was sent to jail.

Karmu busied herself making the tea and waited until Sharon was sitting down nursing Morgan before she started questioning her about her visit to see Hadyn.

'He looked terrible; he had a gash on his face and one of his eyes was badly bruised,' Sharon confided as she sipped her tea.

157

Karmu's eyebrows shot up. 'Did he say how he'd got those and whether it was in the scrimmage with the miners or since he's been in the police cell?'

Sharon put her cup back on to its saucer with a clatter. 'Surely the police wouldn't do something like that to him while he's in custody,' she gasped.

'You never know. I don't trust them an inch,' Karmu told her. 'Did he say when his trial would be?'

'No, he didn't know. He didn't really say very much because there was a policeman standing close by all the time, listening to everything we said.'

'So really it was a waste of time you going there.'

'Not altogether. He said I could go and collect the wages that are due to him so that I would have some money for food. He said that I was to pay you, of course,' she added quickly.

'Surely you don't mean you're going to risk paying a visit to that gambling den he goes to in Bute Street!' Karmu gasped, her eyes widening in alarm. 'You'll be taking your life in your hands if you do that, cariad!'

Sharon was about to say that it wasn't there that she was going but held back. She'd never thought about going to the gambling club. If Hadyn was telling the truth and he really was working there, then perhaps there was some money due to him, she mused. If she went along there and told them how desperately she needed some money to live on there was always the possibility that they might let her have it.

Going there was a considerable risk but if she went fairly early in the evening before it was dark, then surely she'd not come to any harm, she told herself.

If she had that money as well as any that Mr Morgan was prepared to let her have, then she might be able to get by until Hadyn came home again, she thought hopefully.

Chapter Fifteen

The next morning, remembering Karmu's warning about the dangers she might encounter if she went to the gambling club, Sharon decided that it might be better if she went to see Mr Morgan first.

She had no idea how much Hadyn was owed, but she hoped she would be able to make it stretch until he came home again. If she could do that, then she wouldn't have to take the risk of going to the club.

She washed and dressed Morgan, then put his dirty clothes and nappies in a bucket of water to soak while she fed him. After she'd put him down to sleep she did the washing and then took the wet items downstairs and put them through the big wooden mangle that stood in the yard outside.

Singing softly to herself she brought them back upstairs and draped them around the room, hoping they would be almost dry when she got back. Then she took off the apron she'd been wearing to protect her best skirt and blouse and combed her hair ready to leave.

Although it was quite a warm day she wrapped Morgan and herself in the big flannel blanket so that she could carry him Welsh-fashion.

As she set off on the long walk to Roath she told herself that at least she could count on having enough money to pay her tram fare on the way back.

By the time she reached Cathays Park she felt so exhausted that she sat down for a few minutes on one of the seats to rest her feet and get her breath back.

One of the first things she intended to buy as soon as she had some money was a second-hand pram or pushchair. The weather was already much too warm for them both to be wrapped up in a heavy flannel blanket but it was the only way she could carry Morgan any distance.

With a feeling of relief Sharon unwound the heavy blanket the minute she walked through the front gate of Mr Morgan's house. Little Morgan was asleep, so she folded the blanket into a thick pad and placed it down on the wide doorstep, then laid him down on it, making sure that he couldn't roll off.

Standing up, she stretched and took a deep breath as she flexed her arms to relieve the stiffness in them. The day was warm and sunny and she couldn't resist the temptation to take a few paces around the immaculate garden. It would help her to regain her composure as well as go over in her head what she was going to say before she knocked on the door, she told herself.

As she came in sight of the front of the house again her pace quickened. The doorstep where she had left Morgan was bare; even the blanket had gone.

With a feeling of panic in case someone had come into the garden and taken him, she ran towards the gate and looked up and down the road. Her heart thudded with fear. There was no sign of anyone and the street outside was deserted.

Thoroughly alarmed she banged on Mr Morgan's front door, calling out at the same time. The long pause before she heard footsteps approaching seemed like an eternity.

Finally, a formidable-looking middle-aged woman with grey hair swept up in a topknot opened the door. She was dressed in a severe black dress and starched white apron.

'Yes? What do you want?' she asked, eyeing Sharon up and down suspiciously.

The woman's voice was as sharp as her appearance and Sharon drew back, feeling intimidated. As she did so she heard a child's cry from somewhere inside the house and knew instinctively that it was Morgan.

'That's my baby crying,' she gasped, her voice trembling with relief. 'I only put him down on the doorstep for a rest, so can I have him, please?'

'You mean you abandoned your child, don't you, and now you've had second thoughts and you want him back. Well, I suppose it means you have a conscience.'

'I didn't abandon him,' Sharon told her heatedly. 'I simply put him down there for a moment while

161

I got my breath back. I've carried him all the way from Clwyd Court, near Bute Street, and he got heavier by the minute, let me tell you.'

'Exactly who are you and why have you come here?' the woman questioned.

'I've come on behalf of Hadyn Jenkins and to collect his wages. He works for Mr Morgan as a handyman. He hasn't come to work because he wasn't feeling very well and–' Sharon stopped as another loud wail came from inside the house. 'Have you left little Morgan all on his own?' she asked accusingly.

'Your child is quite safe; far safer than he was when you left him abandoned on the doorstep,' the woman told her. 'Do you realise that he might have been there for several days before anybody found him? You are lucky I heard him crying because Mr Morgan is away on business and won't be home again for two weeks and I'm off on holiday myself for a few days as well.'

The news that Mr Morgan was away hit Sharon like a body blow because it meant that her long journey had been in vain and she still wouldn't have any money.

'I didn't abandon little Morgan,' she muttered. 'Like I told you before, I put him down on the step to give myself a breather, that's all, so if you give him to me now I'll be on my way,' Sharon repeated dully.

'I thought you said that you'd come to collect Hadyn Jenkins's wages,' the woman said suspiciously.

'I had, but if Mr Morgan is not at home, then I've had a wasted journey,' Sharon sighed.

The woman studied her for a long moment then, holding the door wide, said, 'I'm Nanwen Williams and I'm Mr Morgan's housekeeper. You'd better come in. Since you know his name and I know all about why your baby's called Morgan, I'm prepared to accept that you are the person you claim to be.'

She led the way across a polished parquet floor strewn with colourful Persian rugs into the largest kitchen Sharon had ever seen. The first thing she noticed was a huge cane wash-basket on top of the big scrubbed table and that Morgan was sitting in the middle of it, his eyes screwed up in anger as he yelled for attention.

Half laughing, half crying with the relief at finding him safe and sound, Sharon gathered him up in her arms, crooning to him and covering him with kisses.

'You'd better sit down and nurse him and I'll find him a biscuit and make us both a cup of tea and you can answer a few more questions about why Hadyn Jenkins hasn't come to work,' Nanwen Williams stated. 'This time I want the truth,' she added ominously as she indicated to Sharon that she should sit in the high-backed wooden armchair that was at the head of the table.

When Nanwen Williams brought their tea over to the table Sharon attempted to get up from the armchair but Nanwen gently pushed her back down.

'You stay where you are,' she murmured. 'There's no need for you to move. I can sit on one of these other chairs. Now,' she said as she stirred sugar into her tea, 'shall we start all over again?

You were about to tell me why Hadyn Jenkins hasn't come to work.'

Sharon's face burned and she remained silent for a couple of minutes. She realised from Nanwen Williams's voice that she knew the truth and she was also aware that the older woman suspected that she'd been about to lie.

'You read all about what happened to him in the newspaper, didn't you?' Sharon said at last.

The older woman nodded. 'I'm afraid I did. Was he telling the truth when he said he intended giving the money he was collecting to the miners, or was he going to keep it for himself?'

Sharon looked her straight in the eyes. 'I'm sure he was going to give it to them because he came from a mining family,' she stated defensively.

'Yes, I read all about his family being killed in the Senghenydd pit disaster. You won't remember it, of course, but it's etched in my mind because I knew people who died there on that day. It was a terrible accident, one of the worst ever known. I come from the Rhondda, you see, so I know all about what the miners have to put up with and I can't say I blame them for striking. The pit owners make all the money and live off the fat of the land while most of the miners and their families are on the bread line.'

They drank their tea in silence for a while, each of them occupied by their own thoughts. Morgan finished his biscuit and Sharon wiped his mouth and then held the glass of milk to his lips.

'Here, let me hold him while you eat that piece of cake I cut for you,' Nanwen offered, holding out her arms to take Morgan. 'Refill your cup and you can pour me another one while you're at it,' she added as she sat Morgan on her lap.

'So you've come to collect Hadyn's wages,' she commented thoughtfully, looking down at the child as she gently jogged him up and down. 'Did he ask you to do that?'

Sharon hesitated for a moment then shook her head. 'I know he hasn't much due but I have no money at all and nothing to buy food,' she said in a low voice.

'So you walked all the way here from Tiger Bay on the off-chance that because you knew he worked here there was some money due to him?'

'No,' Sharon shook her head, 'Hadyn hoped that perhaps Mr Morgan would let me have an advance. Since he's not here then it's been rather a waste of time,' she added ruefully.

'Not really, because before he went away Mr Morgan left Hadyn's wages with me both for this week and for next week, so I can give that to you.' She sniffed. 'I don't approve of what Hadyn was doing and I told Mr Morgan we ought to sack him in case he was sent to prison, but Mr Morgan's so soft-hearted that he insisted on giving him another chance.'

'Mr Morgan would do that? Give him two weeks' wages?' Sharon asked in surprise. 'Hadyn mightn't even be able to come next week either,' she said quickly. 'It all depends on whether they let him off when his case is heard or send him to prison.'

'Either way, you are going to need money to live on,' Nanwen Williams pointed out. 'If they let him go without giving him a sentence of any kind, then I shall expect him to be here for work next week as usual.'

'Yes, but what if they do put him in prison?' Sharon asked worriedly.

'If that happens, then he will have to make the time up when he is free and can come back to work. Either way, you will have enough money for food and to keep a roof over your head. What's more, you won't need to try abandoning this precious little soul on someone's doorstep again,' she murmured as she looked down at the child on her lap.

'I wasn't abandoning him, Mrs Williams, really I wasn't,' Sharon told her earnestly.

'I know that,' Nanwen Williams told her, smiling for the very first time. 'I was only jesting, cariad. I can see you're a devoted little mother and would never do a thing like that.'

'I've given up a great deal to have Morgan,' Sharon told her seriously. 'I'm not married to Hadyn, you see,' she confessed, the blood rushing to her face. 'My dad has never liked him and he said I must forget about him, but I was so much in love with Hadyn that I couldn't do that.'

'I suppose that means you've gone against your parents' wishes and they turned you out,' Nanwen mused.

'That's right. They think I've brought disgrace on the family and they wanted me to have the baby adopted.'

The next minute she found herself telling Nanwen Williams all about how she had left home and was now living in one room in Tiger Bay.

'Duw anwyl, you mean the three of you are

166

living in one room! That's no way to be bringing up a baby,' Nanwen said in a shocked voice. 'You can't give your little one a proper home life under those sorts of conditions.'

'I know that, and I want something better for him as soon as possible,' Sharon agreed.

'How do you manage to do his washing, and how do you manage to cook when you have only a gas ring? Does your mother know how you are living?'

'No, I haven't dared go back home since I left,' Sharon said sadly. 'I miss them all so much,' she added, brushing away her tears with the back of her hand. My brother Parry's wife Gwen was expecting and her baby will be the same age as Morgan, and I don't even know if she has had a little boy or a little girl.'

'Why don't you go and visit them all? Little Morgan is their grandchild, remember, and it's not right that they have never even met him.'

'I know that, and I have thought of going to see them, but the fear that they still won't want anything to do with me has stopped me from doing so.'

'I'm sure that once your mam and dad have had a chance to see little Morgan they'll be so enchanted with him that they'll not only forgive and forget about what happened in the past but will want to help you,' Nanwen Williams said encouragingly.

'I don't know. I think I may have left it too late to do so, because of what has happened with Hadyn. They're bound to have read all about it in the newspaper.'

167

Nanwen Williams pursed her lips but said nothing for a few minutes. 'Promise me you'll think about paying them a visit quite soon. Put your pride behind you and do it, for the little one's sake,' she said quietly.

Sharon nodded. 'I will think about it. I must be on my way,' she said as she stood up.

'Very well. Now you wait here for just a minute and I'll go and get that money for you,' Nanwen told her as she passed Morgan back to her.

There was a spring in Sharon's step as she left Mr Morgan's house half an hour later and made for the nearest tram stop. She had enough money in her pocket to hand over two weeks' rent to Karmu. What was more, Nanwen Williams had given her a basket of food. Exactly what was in it she had no idea but it would help her to eke out Hadyn's money for several weeks. Nanwen Williams might disapprove of Hadyn's behaviour but she seemed a kindly soul at heart.

Elaine Pritchard hastily shoved the newspaper she'd been reading under a cushion as her husband came into the room.

'There's no need to do that,' he told her in a resigned voice, 'I've already read all about it.'

'Poor Sharon, I really think we ought to try and get in touch with her,' Elaine murmured, shaking her head sadly.

'No!' Elwyn's mouth tightened into a thin line. 'She's made her bed and wouldn't listen to reason, so that's the end of it.'

'She's had her baby now; in fact, he will be over

a year old, the same as our Parry's child. How will she manage with no man to provide for her?'

'Man!' Elwyn's lip curled. 'Hadyn Jenkins was no man; he was nothing but a rogue,' he sneered. 'What's happened has proved that. I want nothing at all to do with him; it's a pity that our paths ever crossed.'

'It's Sharon I'm worried about,' Elaine persisted, 'and of course the baby. It's our grandchild, you know, Elwyn.'

He turned away frowning and she knew better than to pursue the matter any further. He was a good husband and a hard-working businessman, but he expected others to obey his wishes. Sharon had defied him and that was something Elaine knew he would find hard to forgive.

Nevertheless, she was worried about Sharon and would have given anything to find out where she was living and to go and see her. She was bound to need help if Hadyn was sent to prison because there would be no money coming in at all and she wouldn't be able to work herself because she had a young child to look after.

Chapter Sixteen

It was a Friday morning early in June when Hadyn was released on probation after the trial was over. He looked thin and haggard when he returned home and was very disgruntled about the way he'd been treated.

When Sharon told him that while he'd been inside she had been to Mr Morgan's and been given an advance on his wages, he looked surprised. 'I suppose that means that I still have a job to go back to. They'll expect me to put in some extra time to make up for that, though, I suppose,' he added with a grimace.

'Mrs Williams did point that out to me but I thought you wouldn't mind. After all, I had to have something to live on and she was trying to help.'

'Who the hell is Mrs Williams and what has she got to do with it?' Hadyn demanded.

'She's Mr Morgan's housekeeper. I would have thought you knew that.'

'Oh, you mean the frosty old biddy who gives me a cup of tea sometimes when I'm working there.'

'She's not frosty at all; in fact, I thought she was very kind. She gave me a lovely basket of food to bring home with me as well and that made all the difference in the world, I can tell you.'

'So you spun her a hard-luck story, did you? Perhaps instead of going to work myself I should send you out begging since you seem to be so good at it.'

Sharon felt very hurt by Hadyn's remark but she tried not to show it. He'd had a rough time of it, she told herself, and so she must be patient. In a couple of days when he was back at work once more and had put all that had happened behind him, everything would be all right again.

In an attempt to placate him she handed him the watercolour of the house that he had asked

170

her to paint before he went to prison. Instead of being pleased, he seemed to be annoyed that she hadn't delivered it and collected the money.

'I did think of going back and knocking on the door,' she told him spiritedly, 'but because you never told me the name of the person who'd asked for it, I wasn't sure if it was the right thing to do. Anyway, you can deliver it now and that will mean we'll have some money for food over the weekend,' she added with a bright smile.

'Probably too late now,' he muttered as he took it from her and scrutinised it.

'Well, it's worth a try because I have only a few coppers left in my purse and that won't go very far and, in addition, we also owe two weeks' rent to Karmu.'

'Wrap it up, then, and I'll see what I can do. Judging by the size of the place they can afford to buy it, so let's hope they're still interested in doing so.'

Hadyn was gone so long that Sharon started to think he was never going to come back. Now she was worried in case they didn't want to buy the painting because they knew he'd been arrested during the miners' strike.

She was starving hungry and there was only half a loaf and a scrape of margarine left in the cupboard. She had given him the coppers to pay his tram fare and to bring back some fish and chips for their meal out of the money he would be collecting.

Morgan was tired and hungry so she gave him a crust of the stale bread smeared with margarine and put him down to sleep. She was about to hack off a wedge of the dry bread for herself when Hadyn appeared. The smell of the newspaper-wrapped package he was carrying made her mouth water.

'They paid you, then; were they pleased with it?' she asked as she rushed to put two plates on the table so that they could enjoy their feast.

'They seemed happy enough with it but they couldn't pay me all the money, so I'll have to go back there again this evening to collect what they still owe,' he mumbled as he tucked into the chips and fried fish.

Sharon wasn't too sure if he was telling the truth or not. She suspected that it might be an excuse to go to the gambling club that night but she deemed it best not to say anything. At least he was home and, for the moment, they had money to pay their way and tomorrow or the next day he would be going back to work at Mr Morgan's house.

Everything began going so well over the next few months that Sharon felt content. Hadyn seemed to be eager to please her in every way, as though anxious to atone for what had happened. He was once again the man she had fallen for and she felt quite hopeful about their future together.

Morgan was thriving and she had at last managed to buy a second-hand pushchair, which made it so much easier when she took him out. Furthermore, she was sure that he would soon be walking well on his own.

Even life in Clwyd Court had improved because they now had two rooms and, although the second one was not very large, it did mean that

172

they had a separate room in which to sleep.

Sharon still secretly longed to move right away from Tiger Bay but she was grateful to Karmu, who had been almost like a mother to her with all her help and advice.

Hadyn had been asked for several more paintings. They were usually of big houses in the more exclusive area around Roath Park and usually he was willing to look after Morgan while she went to look at them and do a rough sketch.

He had agreed that each time he was paid for them they should save some of the money and, although when Christmas came they dipped into it for extras, they now had quite a little nest egg towards eventually moving to somewhere better.

It was the middle of June 1927 when Hadyn said he wanted Sharon to do a special view of a large house in Whitchurch. He was so anxious to have it done immediately that he offered to look after Morgan while she went to view it.

'I'll get Morgan dressed and put him in his pushchair so that he is all ready and then you can take him out for a walk while I go there,' Sharon agreed.

'Duw anwyl, there's no need to do that, cariad,' Hadyn said quickly. 'He's big enough to walk and I hate pushing that damn thing. I would sooner carry him on my shoulder.'

'Well, be careful; he's only just turned two, even if people think he's a four-year-old.'

'Don't you worry; I'll take good care of him. You get off and do that view then you can come straight back and sit down and paint it and that will be a bit more to go in our savings pot,' he told her with a grin.

Sharon quite enjoyed her outing. It was a lovely sunny day, a taste of early summer. Much as she loved little Morgan, it was nice to have the freedom of being out on her own.

As she boarded the tram to go home she felt pleased that her work was completed. When they reached the city centre she decided that as she was on her own she would break her journey and take a quick look at the shops.

She had no money to spend but for the next half an hour she enjoyed looking in all the shop windows and fantasising about what she would like to buy.

With the few coppers left in her purse she went into a cake shop near the tram stop and bought a gingerbread man to take home for little Morgan.

All the way home on the tram Sharon thought about how his face would light up when he saw it. He loved little surprises and treats and he didn't have anywhere near as many of them as she would have liked.

She felt vexed when the tram came to such a sudden stop as they were travelling down Bute Street that she was thrown forward in her seat so violently that the gingerbread man shattered into several pieces.

With an inward smile she consoled herself that Morgan would still enjoy eating it. Then, like all the other passengers on the tram, she became concerned about why the tram had stopped so abruptly and why they were not continuing on their journey to the Pier Head.

The conductor and driver were already out in the road and one of the passengers decided to go and find out what was happening. When he returned he looked grave.

'There's been an accident and the police have been called to deal with it,' he told them.

Sharon was debating whether or not to walk the rest of the way home when a policeman boarded the tram and told them they would not be able to continue their journey for quite some time. A man and a small child had been knocked down and the child was seriously injured and they were waiting for the ambulance to arrive to take them both to hospital.

Several of the passengers decided that the best thing to do was walk the rest of the way and Sharon decided to do the same. As she alighted from the tram the ambulance arrived and, as they lifted the injured man and child on to a stretcher, she gasped in horror. The child was little Morgan. She was sure of it because of the vivid red jumper he was wearing.

She pushed her way forward and then saw the man and, even though his face was so covered by blood that it was almost unrecognisable, she knew from his auburn hair that without doubt it was Hadyn.

'That's my man and my little boy,' she gasped as she ran towards the stretcher.

'Are you quite sure?' One of the policemen grabbed hold of her by the arm and tried to restrain her.

'Yes, I'm positive. What happened to them?'

'As I understand it the toddler ran out into the

roadway and the man dashed after him to try and stop him. They were both hit by the tram.'

'It is them; please let me go to them,' she begged. 'Hadyn was looking after little Morgan while I was out. He must have brought him this way to meet me. Why don't you ask him, if you don't believe me.'

The policeman hesitated for a moment then went over and spoke to the man who was now lying on the stretcher. The next minute he was nodding at her and she found herself being bundled into the ambulance along with them.

'Can I hold my little boy, please,' she pleaded as they pulled away but the attendant who was carrying little Morgan in his arms shook his head.

'Don't worry, cariad, he's being taken care of,' Hadyn murmured. He reached out to take her hand then gave a sharp grunt of pain. 'I think it's broken,' he muttered as he clasped hold of his arm with his other hand.

When they reached the Royal Infirmary, Hadyn was wheeled away in one direction and little Morgan in another and Sharon was told to wait.

A nurse in a blue dress and starched white apron and cap came and spoke to her and took down details about both Hadyn and Morgan. She was then once again told to wait. About ten minutes later a policeman came and began asking her more or less all the same questions.

'I've told you everything, so now can I see my little boy?' she pleaded when he had finished writing.

'What about your family? You haven't mentioned them,' he said as he scrutinised his notes.

'Yes, I have, Hadyn and Morgan are my family,' Sharon told him emphatically.

'I meant your own parents. If you tell me where they live, then someone can go and let them know what has happened, if you would like us to do so. They will probably want to be here with you at a time like this.'

'What do you mean by that?' Sharon asked, her suspicions suddenly aroused. 'Hadyn and little Morgan are both going to be all right, aren't they?'

'Wait here and I'll ask the sister to come and talk to you,' the policeman told her gruffly.

Once again the waiting seemed to be interminable. By the time the sister came over to speak to her, Sharon's mind was in such confusion that at first she didn't comprehend what the sister was telling her.

'Now do you understand what I'm telling you? I'm afraid your child is dead, my dear,' the sister repeated, laying her hand gently on Sharon's arm.

Sharon stared at her in disbelief. It was all so unreal that she couldn't believe it was happening. It was as though she was having some sort of nightmare. Any minute now, she told herself, she would wake up and find Hadyn in bed beside her and little Morgan sleeping contentedly in his cot.

As she clapped her hand over her mouth to prevent herself from being sick, the sister signalled to one of the nurses to bring a glass of water.

She waited until Sharon had taken a couple of sips of it and then suggested that she might like to go somewhere quiet for a few minutes to get over the shock.

'No, no!' Sharon shook her head vehemently. 'I

177

want to see my little one. You must have made a mistake. Little Morgan isn't dead. He can't be.'

'Wait here a moment,' the sister murmured.

Sharon watched as she summoned another nurse over and tried to hear what they were saying to each other but their voices were so low that it was impossible.

'We will take you to see your little boy if that is what you want us to do,' the sister told her.

'Good. Then I'll take him home and look after him. Karmu will know what to do to make him better,' Sharon told them as she stood up.

As the nurse accompanying them began to speak the sister shushed her to silence.

When they reached the door to the mortuary the sister paused and once more tried to prepare Sharon to accept that Morgan was dead.

'Why do you keep on trying to stop me from seeing him?' Sharon said agitatedly, her voice quivering.

'I am trying to make you understand that your child is dead, my dear,' the sister said quietly as she opened the door and indicated to the nurse to precede them.

'It's too cold in here for him,' Sharon protested but her words were cut short. Bile rose into her throat as the nurse pulled back the green sheet to reveal a tiny form lying in a cot looking for all the world like a china doll with red hair.

Chapter Seventeen

Sharon was inconsolable. The sister gave orders for her to be sedated and then to be taken into a small side ward and kept under observation.

When she woke up several hours later, Hadyn was at her side. One of his arms was in plaster and supported in a sling and the cuts on his face had been stitched or covered with plasters. For a minute or so she stared at him unseeingly, almost as if she didn't recognise him then, as she recalled all that had taken place, she held out a hand to take his.

'When you feel up to it, I'll take you home,' he told her as he kissed her awkwardly on the brow.

'What about Morgan?' she asked in a trembling voice as tears trickled down her cheeks.

Hadyn shook his head. 'No, his body will have to stay here until we arrange the funeral,' he said quietly.

Sharon was in floods of tears when they reached Clwyd Court. She flung herself down on the bed, repeating Morgan's name over and over again, and refused to be comforted by either Hadyn or Karmu.

She left it to Hadyn to make all the arrangements for the funeral; she didn't even ask where they were going to find the money to pay for it.

Sharon and Hadyn were the only ones who attended the short service followed by interment at Cardiff cemetery. As the tiny white coffin topped by a simple wreath of white flowers was lowered into the grave, Sharon felt that a part of her life was being buried at the same time.

For a long time afterwards Sharon seemed to live in a daze. She carried on each day as though Morgan was still alive. She regularly prepared meals for him and then threw them away at the end of the day. She kept his cot made up ready as if she was intending to put him to bed at any moment.

Hadyn tried to divert her attention by taking her to the cemetery to put fresh flowers on Morgan's little grave. He also took her shopping and bought her some new clothes. When she protested that they couldn't afford them, nor all the flowers he was buying, he laughed away her fears, telling her that he'd had a stroke of luck recently.

'You mean you've been gambling again,' she said reproachfully. 'How could you, when Morgan is barely cold in his grave?'

'Yes,' he admitted, 'I took a gamble, a very big one, in fact, but it paid off so well that I will never have to do it again.'

His answer puzzled her but she said nothing. It didn't really seem to matter any more. As long as they had enough money to pay their rent and buy food, she didn't really care where it came from.

Hadyn had recovered from his injuries; the lacerations on his face had all healed and his arm had mended and he was back working for Mr Morgan.

During the daytime while he was out, Sharon spent hours looking at the rough drawings she'd

180

made of the houses that he'd asked her to paint. She even took some of them down to show Karmu.

Karmu picked one of them up and scrutinised it more closely. 'That looks exactly like the house that was mentioned in the South Wales Echo last week because there'd been a robbery there and the thief or thieves got away with a hoard of silver items as well as a great deal of cash,' she exclaimed.

'Are you sure?' Sharon asked, the colour draining from her face as she stared at her, wide-eyed.

'Of course I am,' Karmu asserted. She turned to rummage amongst a pile of old newspapers by the side of her chair. 'Here you are,' she said triumphantly as she handed the newspaper to Sharon. 'That's the same house now, isn't it, and you can read the whole story for yourself.'

Sharon stared at the newspaper in disbelief then, without a word, she gathered up all her pictures and fled back up to her room, sobbing her heart out.

She was still lying on the bed crying when Hadyn came home. When he put his arms around her and tried to comfort her she pushed him away.

'It was you, wasn't it?' she sobbed, jabbing her finger at the tear-soaked page of the newspaper. 'You were the thief. That's where the money for my new clothes came from; that was the big gamble you were boasting about.'

Hadyn pulled back, his face taut. 'Duw anwyl! Who's been putting such damn ridiculous ideas into your head and who gave you that?' he demanded hoarsely, snatching the newspaper out of

181

her hand.

'It's the house in Whitchurch that I painted. Karmu recognised it when I was showing her some of my paintings. How could you do such a thing?'

'You're talking absolute rubbish,' Hadyn blustered, struggling to regain his composure. 'I might have known that black witch had put the idea into your head. Now, who are you going to believe, her or me?'

Before Sharon could answer there was a loud knocking on their door. The colour drained from Hadyn's face as he looked round the room as if wondering where he could hide. Speedily he dived into bed. 'Tell them I'm out,' he muttered as he pulled the covers up over his head.

When she opened the door and saw the two policemen standing there Sharon's throat went dry and she was too frightened to say anything as they came into the room and started turning things over. She gave a scream of protest and tried to stop them going into the bedroom to search. Within minutes one of them had pulled back the bed covers and dragged Hadyn to his feet.

Sharon heard the policemen caution him and then start firing questions at him after he admitted that he was Hadyn Jenkins.

She tried to make sense of what they were all saying but in the end she sat down in a chair and put her head in her hands to try and shut out what was going on.

She felt that she was in some sort of nightmare as they searched through the chest of drawers and the two cupboards. She gave an anguished cry of outrage when one of the policemen upturned Morgan's cot and rifled through the bedding.

In numb disbelief she watched them slip handcuffs on Hadyn and then march him away with his hands securely fastened behind his back.

It was three weeks before Hadyn's case came to trial and Sharon still had not come to terms with what had happened. She walked around in a daze, neglecting her home as well as her appearance and not even bothering to eat unless Karmu made her do so.

Karmu went to court with her and Sharon listened in horror as a policeman said that the hoard of silver items that had been stolen from the house in Whitchurch had been found buried in Morgan's grave in Cardiff cemetery.

Memories of their frequent visits and the fresh flowers that Hadyn had insisted on taking each time to lay on the grave flooded into Sharon's mind and made the evidence all the more poignant.

She listened dumbfounded when a sentence of fifteen months in prison was served on Hadyn.

There were still tears streaming down Sharon's cheeks as they left the court. Once they were outside they were hounded by reporters who were eager to find out how much they knew about what had happened and who bombarded them with questions. Karmu, a striking figure in her vivid yellow dress and yellow and orange turban, fended them off. She was almost twice the size of most of them and looked such a formidable character that they soon dispersed.

'Come on,' Karmu took hold of Sharon firmly

by the arm, 'let's get home and have a nice cuppa.'

Sharon nodded. She was still in such a state of shock that nothing made sense. She kept going over in her mind all that she'd heard in court that day and wondering why she had not realised what was happening. Hadyn's exultation over what he had called his wonderful stroke of good luck kept going round and round in her head. She had thought he meant he'd put on a bet and had a good win but now it seemed he'd been referring to the robbery.

When they reached home it dominated her thoughts and as she sat in Karmu's kitchen she could think of nothing else. When she mentioned it to Karmu and said that she must go and explain to Mr Morgan about what had happened, the older woman shook her head vigorously.

'Leave well alone; let sleeping dogs lie,' she cautioned. 'He will have read about it and, if you go to his house, he may claim you are pestering him and send for the police and then you might find yourself locked up as well. Stop brooding about what has happened and start making some plans for the future,' Karmu told her as she poured her a cup of tea. 'How are you going to earn a living for the next fifteen months?'

'I don't know,' Sharon told her listlessly. 'Your rent is due again at the end of the week,' Karmu reminded her.

Sharon pushed her cup to one side and stood up. 'I thought you were my friend.'

'Of course I am. I won't turn you out, but you already owe me for two weeks and this time Hadyn will be in prison for over a year. I can't

184

wait for it for ever.'

Sharon didn't answer. She felt betrayed. She wanted sympathy and understanding and all Karmu was interested in was the money that was due to her.

Back in her room she felt loneliness wrap itself tightly around her. She was alone in the world and surviving was up to her. She toyed with the idea of going back home. Would they welcome her now that there was no longer a child to bring disgrace on the family name?

The fear of rejection was so strong that in the end she resolved to face the world on her own rather than sacrifice her self-respect. She tried to decide what sort of work she could do. She'd served in her father's shop and she could sketch and paint. It was not a lot to go on, but surely there was a need for her skills somewhere out there.

Before she went to bed that night she sponged and pressed her dark skirt and ironed her best white blouse. At least she would look businesslike when she went job-hunting the next day, she told herself.

She started looking methodically, visiting all the shops in St Mary Street and Queen Street. At each one she was told the same thing; they were putting people off, not hiring them.

They all blamed it on the miners' strike that had started in May the previous year and not ended until November. It had held up shipping and transport and it had also spread dissension amongst other manual workers not only in Cardiff but also countrywide.

As a result of the hard times people were still experiencing, many shops were closing down and even offices were laying off their staff. No one seemed to know when the situation would improve.

Four days later, on a dreary wet September day, hungry and despondent and with still no prospect of work and not even a penny for her tram fare home, Sharon resorted to visiting the soup kitchen that had been set up on The Hayes.

As she took her place in the long queue of people who were also destitute, she wondered what the future held in store. How was she going to manage to survive until Hadyn came out of jail? Perhaps it wasn't even worth trying.

The bowl of hot broth that was ladled out and handed to her with a crust of bread rekindled her energy. She left The Hayes determined to find work of some kind so that she could retain her independence.

As she trudged along the Taff embankment planning to try the shops in and around James Street for work, she told herself that 1927 might be termed the Mean Year but, come what may, she intended to survive.

When she arrived back in Clwyd Court, Karmu came bustling out of her kitchen to say that a man had been there looking for her while she'd been out.

'Do you mean a policeman?'

'Well, he wasn't in any kind of uniform and he didn't look tall enough to be a bobby. He was middle-aged and smartly dressed, though, so perhaps he had come from the court about something, but I don't think so.'

Sharon shook her head. 'I can't think who it could be or what he would want,' she confessed.

'Well, he left this,' Karmu muttered as she pulled a scrap of paper out of her pocket. 'I'm not sure what it means, but perhaps you can make sense of it.'

With a puzzled frown Sharon took it from her. There were letters and figures written on the paper and they didn't make any sense to her either until she realised that it must be a telephone number.

She studied it closely but she had no idea whose it was and even though she thought that it might be Mr Morgan's, she didn't even have the few pennies she would need to ring the number from a telephone box and find out.

For the rest of the day she puzzled over who it might be but she couldn't think of anyone except her father who had a telephone and it certainly wasn't his number.

The next morning, consumed by curiosity, she tried to work out the number from the telephone directory. When she discovered that the number must belong to somebody living in the Roath area, she wondered again if it had been Mr Morgan who had called to see her the previous day.

Saying nothing to Karmu about what she was planning to do she set out to walk to Roath. It was a miserable wet day and she was soaked through as well as exhausted by the time she reached his house.

Conscious of how bedraggled she must look, she hesitated before approaching the front door.

Then, summoning up her courage, she ran a hand over her hair to smooth it down, straightened the collar of her blouse, and then walked up to the front door and rang the bell, telling herself that sooner or later she had to face Mr Morgan and find out what it was he wanted to know.

When the door opened Sharon felt all her courage draining away as she looked into the severe face of Nanwen Williams.

For a minute they stared at each other like strangers then the older woman held out her arms and enveloped Sharon in a hug.

Chapter Eighteen

'Duw anwyl! Just look at the state you are in! You're soaked to the skin. Now get that wet coat off, and those shoes, and I'll fetch a towel to dry you off,' Nanwen Williams stated as she released Sharon from a bear-like hug and took her through to the kitchen.

Shivering with cold Sharon took off her wet outer clothing and dried her face and hair with the towel while the older woman bustled around making a pot of tea. She waited until she had put out a cup for each of them and pushed one across the table to Sharon before she started speaking.

'You've had a rough time of it, cariad. I've read all about it in the *South Wales Echo*. Tragic about little Morgan, and for that to be followed on so closely by Hadyn's misdeed must have been

188

unbearable for you.'

'It has been,' Sharon gulped, blinking back the threatening tears. She felt grateful to Nanwen Williams for her kindly concern but she didn't want to think about little Morgan, let alone talk about him.

'You should have come to see me long before this,' Nanwen scolded. 'You must know that a trouble shared...' her voice drifted off as she replaced her cup and saucer on the table. 'Hadyn's misdemeanour probably added to your grief after little Morgan died,' she sighed, almost as if speaking to herself.

'I don't know,' Sharon admitted sadly. 'So many blows and all at once, I sometimes wish I had been the one who died. Then I got this and it gave me hope,' she added, fishing in the pocket of her skirt and bringing out the scrap of paper on which Karmu had written down the telephone number. 'I thought that perhaps Mr Morgan might intend to give me some work. I did a painting for him once and I hoped he might know of someone else who wanted some done.'

'He's away on business at the moment.' Nanwen frowned as she held out her hand to take the piece of paper. 'What's all this about, then?'

'I thought it was his telephone number,' Sharon explained. 'I hadn't got the money to make a telephone call, which is why I walked here today.'

'I'm afraid this isn't his number,' Nanwen told her, shaking her head.

Sharon's shoulders drooped. 'It must be, I know it's a Roath number, because I checked through the directory in one of the telephone boxes to find out.'

'It's a Roath number, all right, but not for this house. Shall I ring through and find out who it is?'

'Oh, could you?'

Nanwen Williams went out into the hall to the telephone, lifted the receiver and asked the operator if she could be put through to the number on the scrap of paper while Sharon waited hopefully. After a couple of minutes, however, Nanwen replaced the receiver.

'I'm sorry, cariad, but there's no reply,' she explained as she came into the kitchen and handed the piece of paper back to Sharon. 'Whoever it is must be out or away. You'll have to try again another time.'

Sharon shook her head. 'Perhaps it was a mistake. Karmu said the man came to the door asking for me, though.'

'Perhaps he was a reporter from one of the newspapers,' Nanwen mused. 'Anyway, don't worry about it. Now, have you eaten today or would you like a bowl of cawl?'

'That's kind of you, Mrs Williams, but...' Sharon hesitated. She was hungry but she didn't want Nanwen Williams to think that was why she had come there.

'Real good soup it is, though I say so myself, and it won't take me a jiffy to warm it up for you. I made enough for two, forgetting that Mr Morgan wasn't here. I'll have to eat it again tomorrow if you don't have some, and I hate having the same meal two days running.'

'Thank you, Mrs Williams, I'd love some,' Sharon told her.

'Good, and what about having a nice hunk of my newly baked crusty bread to go with it?'

Nanwen Williams watched Sharon tuck into the hot food and the minute her plate was cleared placed a slab of buttered fruit loaf in front of her.

'A slice of my bara brith will round things off nicely and while you're eating it, I'll make a fresh pot of tea,' she pronounced.

Replete from her good meal and feeling better than she had done for many days, Sharon stayed for another hour telling Mrs Williams all her problems and listening to the good advice the other woman gave her.

She even found herself talking about her grief over Morgan's death and blaming herself for leaving him with Hadyn.

'No, my lovely, there's no cause to do that. You were a good mother and of course you felt it was safe to leave him with his father. Don't be too hard on Hadyn either. Accidents do happen, no matter how careful we try to be. What Hadyn did afterwards is another matter; that is unforgivable,' she said grimly, shaking her head from side to side in disapproval. 'And it's not the first time he's behaved badly. Last time he was lucky and got off with a caution.'

Sharon nodded silently as she stood up to leave.

'The rain has stopped so, with any luck, you will get home in the dry,' Mrs Williams told her as she walked to the door with her to say good-bye.

'Here,' she pushed some silver coins into Sharon's hand, 'take this and get the tram home

191

and there'll be enough left over so that you can telephone that number if you want to do so. Anyway, whether you do or not, come back again soon and let me know how you are getting on. Mr Morgan will be home in a couple of weeks and, as you said, he might have some work for you.'

Nanwen's encouraging words were still ringing in Sharon's head when she got off the tram in Bute Street. On the way home she had counted the money Nanwen Williams had given her and the first thing she did when she arrived home at Clwyd Court was to give Karmu two weeks' rent money.

'So where did you get this much money, then, cariad?' Karmu asked suspiciously. 'You've been gone a long time; not been on the game to earn this, have you?'

Sharon felt the hot blood rush to her cheeks. The thought that Karmu could even suggest such a thing filled her with shame. Surely she didn't think she had sunk that low, she thought bitterly.

'I came by it quite honestly,' she said stiffly.

'Well, I was only joking, but how did you come by it?' Karmu pressed.

Sharon hesitated. Then, because she didn't want Karmu to think she had obtained it by some dishonest means, she told her about her visit to Roath because she'd thought it was Mr Morgan's telephone number.

'So if it wasn't him who came here asking for you, then who was it and what did they want?' Karmu mused.

'I don't know,' Sharon admitted. 'I had hoped that it was Mr Morgan offering me some work. I'll try telephoning again but I'm not sure when the person will be at home.'

'You may be wasting your time anyway,' Karmu said dismissively. 'I should leave well alone. It might be a reporter or, even worse, it might be someone from the police and we don't want them round here asking any more questions.'

Sharon nodded as though in agreement. In her heart, though, she was sure that Karmu was wrong. Something told her it was someone who was going to offer her a job.

Even so, first thing the next morning, she decided to see if she could find some work. She had been foolhardy in handing over two weeks' rent to Karmu because it left her with less than a shilling in her purse.

She spent all morning going from one shop to another to see if they needed any assistants but always the answer was the same. They were sacking staff, not taking them on.

Hungry as well as footsore and weary, she came home and went straight to bed, hoping that if she managed to get to sleep then the hunger pangs would go away.

The next morning she was still hungry and found herself debating whether to spend the few coppers in her purse on food or on the telephone call that she'd promised herself she'd make.

If there was no answer when she tried the telephone number, then as long as she was careful to press the right button afterwards, she'd still have her money, she reasoned, so really it made sense to try that first.

It was the sort of gamble that Hadyn would take, she thought wryly as she waited to be connected.

When a man's voice said 'Hello', she was so taken aback that for a moment she couldn't answer. When she finally managed to do so she found herself stuttering as she tried to explain who she was and why she was ringing.

To her surprise he seemed to be expecting her call. 'Can you come and see me at my office in Bute Street at eleven o'clock this morning?' he asked in a crisp voice.

'I could, but I want to know why you want to see me,' Sharon told him.

'I knew Hadyn and I know he's inside and I thought you might want some work. Come and see me and we'll talk about it. I'm over the pawnbroker shop halfway down Bute Street, I'm sure you can find it. Ask for Geraint Humphreys.'

Before Sharon could reply he had replaced the receiver at his end and, for a moment afterwards, she stood in the telephone box wondering what to do next.

Her head was buzzing with questions and doubts. Who was he? What sort of job could he possibly be offering her and, most important of all, if he had known Hadyn, then would it be something that was legal?

The thought of having some regular work was a tremendous temptation. It was only a short walk away so the sensible thing to do was to go and meet this Geraint Humphreys, she told herself. If she didn't like him or the work he was offering her, then she would simply walk away.

As she approached the pawnbroker's halfway along Bute Street, Sharon studied her reflection in one of the shop windows. What she saw didn't please her. She looked drab and because she couldn't afford to have her hair cut, it was pulled back into the nape of her neck so tightly that it made her look thin and sharp-faced.

She found herself thinking back to the days when she had lived in Pen-y-lan Place and had a wardrobe full of clothes. There had been smart ones for work and pretty ones to wear when she went out with Gwen or Madoc and the rest of their friends.

She wondered what had happened to them all; had her mother kept them or given them all away? Not that it mattered, because they probably wouldn't fit her; they'd hang on her because she'd lost so much weight.

When she asked in the pawnbroker's for Geraint Humphreys she was told to go through the black door at the side of the shop and then up the stairs, where she would find his office.

At the top of the stairs she hesitated, wondering what she was letting herself in for, then, pulling herself together, she knocked on the door. A man's voice called out, telling her to come in.

The room was in sharp contrast to the surroundings. It was large with a window looking out on to the street. There was a deep-pile red carpet on the floor and in the centre of the room an imposing highly polished mahogany desk. Matching glass-fronted bookcases flanked two of the walls and the only other furniture were two high-backed black leather chairs on each side of the desk.

Geraint Humphreys was sitting in one and, as Sharon entered the room, he rose and held out his hand to welcome her and then indicated that she was to sit in the chair on the other side of the desk.

They scrutinised each other in silence for a moment. She judged him to be in his late thirties or early forties. He was extremely good-looking and his suave appearance made her feel even more conscious of how down-at-heel she must appear to be.

'You said something about offering me some work,' she said hesitantly.

He leaned back in his high-backed chair, tapping on his even white teeth with his fountain pen. 'Yes, I did, didn't I?' he mused as he continued to study her.

For a moment she wondered if he was laughing at her and she edged forward on her chair, ready to stand up and leave.

'I know you can paint,' he murmured, 'but have you ever worked as a receptionist?'

'No, never. I have worked in a shop, though, and I understand how to deal with people, so I suppose that is something similar,' she added quickly.

'Mmm!' He tapped his teeth thoughtfully. 'I need a receptionist to work at one of my clubs, so perhaps I should give you a trial and see how you get on?'

Sharon clenched and unclenched her hands. She needed the work badly but, because this man claimed that he knew Hadyn, she was worried about what sort of club it was.

'Is it a gambling club?' she asked hesitantly.

Geraint Humphrey's eyebrows lifted and once again she felt that he was laughing at her.

'No,' he said solemnly, 'I don't really think you could describe it as that. It's more a place of relaxation, somewhere people go to meet friends, have a drink and so on.'

'Very well.' Sharon nodded eagerly.

'You will have to wear a uniform, but I will supply that,' he told her. 'Now, when can you start?'

'As soon as you like; the sooner the better, in fact.'

He nodded as though he understood what she meant. 'Very well, what about starting tomorrow? Your hours will be from two in the afternoon until midnight.'

'Midnight!'

'I did tell you it was a club where people met after work for relaxation; if the hours are not suitable, then...' He left the sentence unfinished but, once again, he raised his eyebrows and regarded her speculatively.

'No, no, that will be quite all right and I can start tomorrow,' Sharon said quickly.

'Good! This is where the club is.' He held out a business card with an address written on it and at the same time stood up, indicating that their meeting was over.

Sharon took the card but felt so nervous that she didn't even look at it as she took her leave. It wasn't until she was back home in Clwyd Court that she realised the club was only a few doors away from where she had been and that if she had looked at the address sooner she could have seen what sort of place it was.

Karmu heard her coming in and called out to her to join her for a cup of tea. Sharon knew it was because she was curious about where she'd been and hesitated for a moment about whether or not to tell her.

She was bound to find out eventually, Sharon reflected, so she might as well tell her. Also it meant that she could reassure her that there would be no problems about paying her rent from now on because she'd have a regular weekly wage.

Karmu had never heard of Geraint Humphreys and when Sharon showed her the business card she frowned and shook her head.

'It doesn't really give you much idea of what sort of club it is or what goes on there, does it? There's silly that you didn't go and take a look at the place,' she scolded.

'I wouldn't be able to tell very much from the outside, now would I?' Sharon defended. 'Anyway, it's a job and that's what's most important. I'll find out soon enough what sort of club it is and whether or not I like working there.'

'Well, it is certainly better than nothing and with Hadyn in prison for the next fifteen months you'll have to find some way of earning your living,' Karmu agreed. 'Even so, I think you want to be careful; not all the clubs in Tiger Bay are on the right side of the law, you know, and you don't want to end up in some sort of disreputable place, now do you?'

Chapter Nineteen

Later that day Sharon received delivery of a large flat cardboard box. When she opened it she found a note inside that stated 'Your uniform' and beneath a layer of white tissue paper was a sleeveless dress in heavy black silk and a matching short jacket. There were also some black silk stockings and a pair of high-heeled black shoes with grosgrain bows at the toes.

She stood for a moment fingering the beautiful material before she ran down the stairs to show it all to Karmu.

'I've never seen anything as pretty in my life,' Karmu enthused. 'Come on, then, my lovely, you'd better try it all on to make sure that it fits you, cariad,' she ordered as Sharon stood there stroking the expensive material.

'I could try the dress on and let you see what it looks like, but I'd better not put the stockings on until tomorrow in case I ladder them,' Sharon murmured.

'Well, put the dress and jacket on so that I can see what they're like,' Karmu insisted.

As she slipped the silky sleeveless dress over her head and smoothed the box-pleated skirt down over her hips, Sharon gave an exclamation of dismay. 'It's too short. Look, it barely reaches my knees and the neck is so low that–'

She left the sentence unfinished as she and

Karmu looked at each other and started laughing.

'I think it's supposed to be like that,' Karmu told her. 'Turn round and let me have a good look at you.'

As Sharon twirled round the skirt flared out, revealing even more of her legs.

'When you put those black silk stockings on you'll be able to dance the Charleston in that, it's a right flapper outfit,' Karmu chortled. 'Mind you,' she added more seriously, 'it really does suit you, and it looks gorgeous on you.'

'Yes, and I know what people will think if they see me walking down the street in it, especially if I tell them I am on my way to work,' Sharon said disparagingly.

'Well, yes, you will have to wear your big coat to cover it up, I suppose. Still, at this time of the year, that won't be any problem, now will it?'

'This dress and my shabby coat and clumpy old shoes will go well together!'

'Perhaps it might be best if you went to and from work in your own everyday clothes and changed into this stuff when you get there,' Karmu mused.

'You're probably right.' Sharon sighed. 'Geraint Humphreys did say I had to wear a uniform but I never dreamed that it would be anything like this.'

'I must say, it is rather an unusual sort of dress for a receptionist to have to wear. It must be a very posh sort of club. What did you say it was called?'

'He said that it was called The Secret Retreat.'

'That's a fancy sort of name. I'm surprised you

200

didn't go and take a look at it.'

'I suppose I should have done, but I was so excited at the thought of getting a job that it never entered my head to do so,' Sharon admitted as she carefully folded up the dress and jacket and put them in the box again.

As soon as she was back upstairs in her own room Sharon tried the dress on again. She'd never worn anything with such a short skirt and she felt uncomfortable in it. She wished Hadyn was there to convince her that it would be all right to wear something that was so revealing.

For the rest of the day the words of a popular song 'Poor Little Rich Girl' kept going through her head and she found herself singing the words out loud:

'In lives of leisure
The craze for pleasure
Steadily grows.
Cocktails and laughter
But what comes after?
Nobody knows...'

It all sounded so apt. She realised that Geraint Humphrey's club must be very posh but she had no idea what he was expecting her to do in her role as receptionist and, by bedtime, it was beginning to worry her so much that she was sure she wouldn't be able to sleep.

The following day, before she set out for the club, she checked to make sure that her coat hid her dress. She carried the shoes and the black silk stockings in a bag ready to put on when she arrived at The Secret Retreat.

It took longer than she expected to find the club because although he had said it was only a few doors away from his office in Bute Street, Mr Humphreys hadn't explained that the opening to it was in Hodges Row.

The plain black door was slightly ajar and, as she stepped into the lobby, she found a tall broad-shouldered coloured man sitting there reading a newspaper.

'Can I help you?'

'I'm coming to work here for Mr Geraint Humphreys,' Sharon stuttered.

'Wait a minute.' He picked up a receiver and pressed a button and in the far distance Sharon could hear a buzzing. Then a voice answered. The coloured man looked across at Sharon, 'What's your name?' he asked.

She waited while he repeated it and then he nodded and replaced the receiver and pointed to another door. 'He'll meet you at the top of the stairs,' he told her.

Sharon nodded but her heart was thumping as she made her way up the red-carpeted stairs. She paused on the landing outside the door that had the name of the club marked on it in bold gold lettering on a black background, wondering if she was supposed to knock or to walk straight in.

Summoning up her courage she pushed the door open and immediately found herself in a good-sized room that had large double doors facing her and ornately framed floor-to-ceiling mirrors on the other two walls. There was a deep-pile gold carpet on the floor but the only furniture in the room was a highly polished mahogany desk and a matching four-drawer filing cabinet.

She was still wondering what to do when one of the double doors opened and Geraint Humphreys appeared.

'Aah!' He consulted his gold watch. 'You're in good time. This is where you will be working,' he said, indicating the desk. 'You're not wearing your uniform, though,' he added, frowning.

'Some of it; I have some of it on,' she said, her face reddening with embarrassment as she removed her coat. 'I couldn't walk in the shoes but I'll put them and stockings on now if there is somewhere I can go to do it.'

'I see.' He chewed his lower lip and surveyed her thoughtfully for a moment. 'I'm going to introduce you to Glenda Roberts, my personal assistant. She will look after you and tell you what is needed. She'll be here in a moment and will show you where the staff cloakroom is and help you with your appearance.'

'My appearance?'

'Yes, your hair and all that sort of thing,' he explained dismissively. 'Do whatever Glenda suggests and you will be all right,' he added reassuringly.

Glenda was tall and slim with an oval-shaped face, short blonde hair and bright green eyes. Her tight-fitting red dress emphasised her curvaceous figure and also revealed the longest pair of legs Sharon had ever seen.

Sharon listened in dismay and disbelief as Glenda and Geraint Humphreys began discussing and criticising her appearance. It made her feel that they regarded her as an object instead of a person, especially when she heard him issuing instructions to Glenda to do something to smarten her up.

She felt nervous and rather resentful as Glenda took her along a passage to the staff cloakroom. It was a large room that had pegs and individual lockers as well as washbasins and toilets and a couple of wooden chairs.

'Sit here,' Glenda indicated one of chairs, 'and let me do something about your hair.'

Before Sharon knew what was happening, Glenda had put a towel around her shoulders to protect her uniform, unpinned the neat roll and was wielding a pair of scissors.

Half an hour later, feeling rather self-conscious with her new cropped hairstyle and wearing her black silk stockings and the rest of her uniform, Sharon found herself being critically scrutinised by Geraint Humphreys.

'Yes, that's a great improvement,' he commented. 'We can make further changes as we go along, that's if you are satisfactory. Now let me outline your duties.'

It took a very short time for him to do this. All that was required of her was that she should greet people as they arrived at the club and then book them in.

'You must never ask them their name, only their code number,' Geraint Humphreys emphasised several times. 'Now, do you understand that?'

'What do I do if they haven't got a code number or can't remember what it is?'

'Then you press this little bell here underneath your desk and one of our security men will come out here and deal with the matter,' he told her crisply.

It all so sounded so extremely simple that her earlier fears about whether or not she would be able to do the job vanished.

Geraint Humphreys remained at her side for the first half-hour to make sure she was able to deal with the early arrivals correctly. He seemed to be quite satisfied that she could and, before he left, he even praised her.

'Someone will come and relieve you for fifteen minutes every four hours,' he told her. 'You know where the cloakroom is and next door to that is the staff rest room where you can have a drink and something to eat.'

Left on her own Sharon waited apprehensively for the next arrivals. At first they came in dribs and drabs but later in the evening more and more members arrived.

Everything went smoothly; they all seemed to know their code numbers and all she had to do was record them and the time they arrived in a ledger.

From somewhere inside the club she could hear music as well as laughter. She was curious to know exactly what went on there, so each time she had a break she went along to the staff room in the hope of talking to someone and finding out but, apart from saying hello, none of them seemed prepared to talk to her.

Shortly before midnight Geraint Humphreys came into the office to show her where the registers were to be locked away each night before she left.

'It's a quarter to twelve, so you can leave now and that will give you time to get home before the lamplighters go round putting out all the street lights,' he told her.

Karmu came hurrying out of her room the minute Sharon arrived home. 'The kettle's boiling, I waited up because I thought you'd like a hot drink before you turn in,' she greeted her. Then she gaped in surprise. 'What have you done to yourself? Your hair, where's it all gone?'

'I'll tell you all about it and as much as I know about The Secret Retreat while I have that drink,' Sharon said, smiling.

By the end of the week she was able to relate many more interesting details to Karmu as they sat and enjoyed a cup of afternoon tea in Karmu's kitchen on the Sunday.

'There seem to be a great many rooms and all the ones which I've seen are so elaborately furnished with silk drapes, deep-pile carpets and elaborate crystal chandeliers that it's like being in a palace,' she divulged.

'Have you found out what all these different rooms are used for?' Karmu asked as she poured out their tea and placed a cup in front of Sharon.

'Well, one of them is just for eating and drinking and watching entertainers perform on a small stage. The largest room of all has a highly polished parquet floor for dancing and there are a couple of other rooms with enormous couches that are upholstered in red velvet or gold damask. It seems people use these to simply sit and relax or talk to each other and have drinks.'

'It all sounds very grand. You'd never expect to find anything like that in Bute Street. I thought all the clubs along there were seedy gambling clubs but this place sounds really posh.'

'Well, it is, and there are also some smaller rooms on the top floor but I don't know what they are for because the doors appear to be permanently locked.'

'Perhaps they are offices or store rooms,' Karmu suggested as she stirred sugar into her tea.

'I suppose so.' Sharon frowned. 'They all have numbers on the doors but so far I haven't seen anyone go into them or leave. Give me time and I'm sure I will be able to find out,' she added with a light laugh.

'Well, make sure you remember to tell me when you do,' Karmu told her.

Karmu was also interested to know if she ever recognised any of the people who used the club.

'Not really, although some of the faces do seem to be familiar and I think I may have seen them before. I'm never sure, though, whether it has been a picture in the newspaper or if I've seen them out in the street. Everyone has a code number, you see, so now I automatically think of the regulars by that.'

'I wonder why they don't want their names known or recorded on your register?' Karmu mused. 'There must be more to that club than simply having meals there or dancing.'

'Well, they do have professional entertainers. Stand up comics, singers and professional dancers giving special displays, all that sort of thing.'

'Yes, that's all very well and all legal and above board and no one would mind other people knowing that they were enjoying that sort of entertainment. It's what goes on behind those locked doors at the top of the building that I think is the reason for all the secrecy,' Karmu said thoughtfully.

'You mean you think that perhaps there is some sort of gambling going on up there?'

'That or perhaps it is something else. It's quite obvious that whatever it is they don't want other people knowing about it,' she added ominously.

'You may be right but, for the life of me, I can't think what it could be other than gambling,' Sharon told her as she pushed her cup to one side and stood up ready to go up to her room.

'Never mind, I'm sure you'll find out in time, so don't forget to tell me when you do,' Karmu pronounced as she took their empty cups over to the sink to wash them up.

Sharon found that for a long time after she'd undressed and got into bed she was unable to sleep. She kept trying to think why Karmu was so curious about what went on in the top rooms.

She also found herself wondering what Hadyn would think about her working at The Secret Retreat. This wasn't the club he had worked at, so had that been another one that Geraint Humphreys owned, or was it somewhere completely different?

Apart from saying that he knew Hadyn when he had first met her, Geraint Humphreys hadn't mentioned his name since and she didn't like to ask too many questions. The few that she had asked Glenda had been met with either a blank silence or an expressive shrug of the shoulders that told her nothing.

She wished she could ask Hadyn what he knew about Geraint Humphreys and also about The Secret Retreat but so far she was still waiting to hear if he was being kept in Cardiff jail and, if so, when she could go and visit him.

Chapter Twenty

A month later, when Sharon was allowed to visit Hadyn for the first time, he stared at her as if she was a stranger.

'Duw anwyl! I wasn't sure it was you,' he greeted her. 'What the hell have you done to your hair?'

'I've had it cut.' She raised one of her hands and patted the sleek bob. Twisting her head round as she did so to make sure he could see the full effect.

'I can see that, but why have you done that?'

'I've started a new job and it's the way my boss Geraint Humphreys asked me to wear it.'

'Geraint Humphreys!' There was a mixture of surprise and alarm in Hadyn's voice. 'Don't tell me you've got yourself in his clutches.'

'What's that supposed to mean? You know who he is, then? He said he knew you.'

'I've met him,' Hadyn said tersely. 'What sort of work are you doing for him?'

He listened in moody silence as Sharon explained about her job as a receptionist at The Secret Retreat.

'That's long hours he's expecting you to work,' he muttered. 'How do you get home afterwards?'

'Walk, of course.'

'On your own at that time of night?'

'Yes. There're not many people about and he says that it's all right for me to finish a bit earlier before the lamplighter goes round putting out the lights.'

'You want to ask him to tell one of his guards to walk home with you.'

'I'd sooner walk home on my own in the dark than have one of them walking alongside me,' she told him firmly.

Hadyn said no more about it but she could tell he was annoyed, although whether it was because she didn't want to take his advice or not she wasn't sure.

They sat in awkward silence for a minute or two then she said brightly, 'Well, do you like my new hairstyle?'

'Geraint Humphreys told you that he wanted you to have your hair cut like that, did he?'

'No, Glenda Roberts, his personal assistant, did. In fact, she cut it for me. She said that she used to be a hairdresser before she started working for Mr Humphreys.'

'You want to watch your back with both of them,' he said sourly. 'I wouldn't trust either of them. Do you have to work there? Surely you could have found some other job?'

'I didn't come here to talk about them,' Sharon said firmly, 'I want to know how you are and what it's like being in here.'

'Not exactly a picnic, I can tell you,' Hadyn said bitterly. 'I'm counting the days until I'm out.'

'So am I.' She sighed. 'You've already done a month and it seems as if we've been apart for a lifetime.'

'So what do you think it feels like for me?' Hadyn said with a harsh laugh. 'You're free to do what you like; I'm shut in here and the only time I see daylight is when we are taken out into the yard and marched round like a herd of cattle for an hour each day.'

'Are you in a cell on your own?'

'Duw anwyl! What do you think this place is, a bloody hotel with room service? Of course I'm damn well not. I'm shacked up with two other fellas. One of them is in for manslaughter and the other is a con man.'

Sharon didn't know what to say; it seemed that every topic she mentioned irritated Hadyn. She was almost relieved when the warden supervising the prisoners and the visitors announced that time was up.

Even so, as the prisoners stood up and began to file out of the room, Sharon had to blink back her tears as Hadyn joined them. Even in prison garb he stood out from the others with his auburn hair and handsome features.

She felt sick with love for him and devastated because they weren't allowed to kiss goodbye. She wanted him to hold her in his arms, stroke her face and whisper sweet words of love as he'd done in those far off days when she had first known him.

As Hadyn was marched out along with all the others her heart sank, knowing that it would be another month before she was allowed to visit him again and over a year before he would be able to hold her in his arms.

When she reached home she went straight up to her room, flung herself down on the bed and cried her heart out. She felt so lonely. If only little Morgan was still there she could hold him in her arms and cuddle him and it would have made Hadyn's absence more bearable. His tragic death haunted her like a bad nightmare. Every time she found one of his little toys or an item of clothing it brought it all rushing back and her heart ached. If only she could turn the clock back.

She sat up and scrubbed her eyes dry with the back of her hands and pushed her hair away from her face. It was no good thinking like this. She had a new job, so it ought to be a fresh start. She'd collect up all little Morgans belongings and put them away out of sight. She didn't need pictures of him on display in the room because he would always be in her heart and in her mind, for ever.

Work became her refuge for the next few days. She was pleased they were so busy that she had no time to think about Hadyn while she was working but it did nothing to ease the loneliness of the night when she went home.

The first month had passed by on leaden weights, the next was bearable and, after that, as Christmas approached, they seemed to speed up slightly. Hadyn, however, seemed more morose each time she saw him. He no longer smiled, no longer wanted to hear what was happening in the

212

world outside.

As she stared across the table at his slightly haggard face and dull eyes she couldn't help feeling apprehensive about their future. Would he regain his charm and zest for living when he was once more free? she wondered.

As a special concession there was extra visiting allowed on Christmas Day and, since it fell on a Sunday, Sharon didn't even have to ask for time off. She took along a parcel of foodstuffs from Karmu and cigarettes and chocolate bars from herself. She was bitterly disappointed when she found that even though it was Christmas the strict rules hadn't been relaxed and she wasn't allowed to give them to Hadyn.

'What will happen to it all?' she asked as the warder strode over and took it from her.

'He'll take his pick and then what the bugger doesn't want he'll give back to me,' Hadyn muttered sourly. 'I've told you before not to openly hand anything to me.'

'What else can I do?'

'Slip me some fags under the table like all the other women do for their men.'

'It's not easy to do that, not with the warder watching us all the time,' Sharon protested.

'What does it matter if he does see you? They're not going to slam you in a cell if you're caught, now are they?' he sneered. 'They'll give you a bit of a ticking off and they'll keep the bloody ciggies for themselves, that's all that will happen.'

'They might punish you, though, that's what I'm afraid of,' she told him.

'Don't worry your head about me; I know how

to take care of myself. I've had to learn to do that since I've been in here,' he added bitterly.

Although Karmu had delayed her Christmas dinner until evening so that Sharon could enjoy it with her, Sharon was feeling so miserable at first that she had a job to eat any of it.

'Here, cariad,' Karmu pronounced, handing her a big round glass half filled with what looked like dark red wine, 'I was keeping this for afterwards to drink with our mince pies, but by the look of things it will do you far more good to have it now.'

Sharon managed a weak smile as she took the glass from Karmu and took a good drink. The next minute she was coughing and spluttering.

'Whatever is it?' she gasped. 'It's set my throat on fire.'

'It's rum from Jamaica and it will put new life into you,' Karmu chortled as she poured herself some. 'Go on, drink it up, but take it in sips, don't gulp it down like it was a glass of water.'

Sharon did enjoy the rest of her evening but she had to admit that she felt quite tipsy by the time she went up to her own room to bed.

'You'll sleep like a top tonight, my lovely,' Karmu assured her, 'so have a lie-in in the morning. You don't have to go off to work in the morning.'

As the ships' klaxons and sirens sounded to herald midnight, Elaine Pritchard stood in the midst of her family with her glass raised, ready to toast the New Year.

The Pritchards and the Cogans were all gathered together, as they were every year. Even Parry and Gwen's little boy, who could hardly keep his eyes open because it was so late, was there to welcome in 1928.

Once the celebrations were over they all prepared to depart and, as the house emptied, Elaine once more felt the emptiness she'd known ever since Sharon had left home.

This year it was more poignant than ever because she knew that in the past year Sharon had experienced so much grief losing her little boy.

She had desperately wanted to try and find her after she'd read the account in the newspaper about her child being killed in a road accident. She had begged Elwyn to let her go to the hospital or to the funeral but he had forbidden her to do either.

'A dreadful accident, I grant you, but it is none of our concern, so you are not to go to it,' he'd said sternly.

She'd brooded about his decision for a long time, wondering if there was some other way of getting in touch with Sharon. If only she could speak to her then she might be able to persuade her to come home.

She wondered if the police would tell her where Sharon was living if she explained that she was Sharon's mother, but she was hesitant about asking them in case they followed it up with a visit and Elwyn became involved.

She dare not ask at the newspaper office because they would expect her to tell them the whole story about why Sharon had left home in the first place and then it would be splashed across the newspaper.

When she'd mentioned to Parry how much she longed to see Sharon, and reminded him of how close Sharon and Gwen had been, he was as tight-lipped as his father on the subject.

'Water under the bridge, Mam,' he said. 'Sharon is no longer part of our lives, so we want to forget about her.'

The only other person Elaine could think of to ask was Madoc but ever since Sharon had turned him down he had changed so much that she hesitated to do so in case he rebuffed her. She was sure he was still missing Sharon because all the laughter and banter had gone from him. He was now always so serious and brusque. He had even stopped calling her Aunty and now addressed her as Mrs Pritchard.

Early in the New Year Geraint Humphreys asked Sharon if she would be prepared to help out upstairs for a short while.

'We're rushed off our feet because several people are off sick,' he explained. 'One of the security guards can take on your job and check people in and out for the moment.'

'I don't mind as long as you think I will be able to do it,' Sharon told him.

'There's not a lot involved,' he told her quickly. 'In fact, the work is pretty much the same as what you are doing down here. You will be sitting at a desk and recording code numbers against room numbers, that's all.'

Sharon was intrigued and readily agreed. She'd been working at The Secret Retreat for several months now and she still hadn't found out what went on in the rooms on the upper floor; this would be her chance to do so.

It would also mean that she would get to know some of the other girls who worked there. Up until now, apart from a brief 'hello', they'd all ignored her except Glenda, and she never felt sufficiently at ease with her to ever ask any questions.

'So at last you'll be able to find out what happens up in those top rooms,' Karmu murmured with a satisfied smile when Sharon told her about her new job.

Even though it was well after midnight, Karmu was still waiting up for her when Sharon arrived home after her first stint of working upstairs.

'Come on, through here,' she called out from her kitchen as Sharon let herself into the house. 'Sit down. The tea is all ready,' she added as Sharon came into her kitchen. 'Now then, what news have you for me?' she asked as she poured out a cup of tea and passed it across to Sharon.

'Not very much,' Sharon admitted as she eased off her shoes and rubbed her aching feet.

She took a sip of her tea and then put the cup back on the table because it was too hot. 'It's like Mr Humphreys said, the job is pretty much the same as what I was doing when I was downstairs. I'm just booking people in, using their code number instead of their name against the room they are using.'

'Yes, yes, I understand that,' Karmu told her impatiently, 'but what are they using the rooms for? Does some form of gambling go on in them, like we thought?'

'I honestly don't know.' Sharon picked up her

cup of tea again and this time took a mouthful. 'It's always men who book in. At one end of the landing there's a door with some sort of emblem on it. I can't really make out what it is supposed to be. It's like a star, yet it isn't. Quite a lot of men seem to go into that room and stay in there for hours.'

'And what about the other rooms, what goes on in those, do you know?'

'Not really,' Sharon admitted. 'The only thing I can tell you is that men come up and book into them but they only seem to stay for a limited time and then they leave. Five or ten minutes later another man will arrive and go in there. This goes on all evening with all four of the rooms.'

'Yet the men who've gone into the big room stay there for the entire evening,' Karmu mused.

'Well, most of them seem to do so. Occasionally one or two will leave early.'

'I'm pretty certain that there's gambling going on in that big room. In fact, I'd bet my life on it,' Karmu stated. 'You want to watch yourself, my girl. One of these nights there'll be a police raid on the place, you mark my words.'

'I hope not, I don't want to get mixed up in anything like that.' Sharon sighed. 'Anyway, what do you think goes on in the other rooms, then?'

Karmu's thick lips tightened. 'I think I've already said enough,' she retorted primly. 'You see what else you can find out,' she added ominously.

Karmu's warning about the possibility that there was gambling going on at The Secret Retreat worried Sharon. She wondered if that was why Hadyn seemed to know so much about Geraint

Humphreys when she'd mentioned his name. Thinking back, she realised how naive she'd been. The reason Geraint Humphreys had contacted her in the first place and offered her a job was probably because Hadyn had been one of his clients.

She decided to ask Hadyn about it next time she went in to see him and to find out if he knew if gambling went on there and what he thought she ought to do for the best.

Hadyn was not at all helpful. 'How the hell should I know what goes on there? You certainly ought to. I don't suppose you would take my advice anyway. You didn't take any notice when I warned you in the first place to be careful of Geraint Humphreys and that Glenda Roberts.'

'I don't want to give up my job but at the same time I don't want to risk being arrested by the police,' Sharon pointed out worriedly. 'I only wish I knew what went on upstairs. Even though I'm on the desk up there I'm no wiser about what goes on behind those closed doors than I was before.'

'Never make a detective, would you?' Hadyn smirked. 'Why don't you ask Glenda?'

'I don't really like to do so. Anyway, I'm not sure she'd tell me even if I did.'

'You're probably right about that, she's a snooty cow, as I remember.'

'Well, perhaps if I told Glenda that it was you that wanted to know—'

Hadyn cut her short before she could finish what she was saying. 'Don't you ever mention my name to her or to Geraint Humphreys, is that clear?' he said angrily, thumping his fist on the table so hard that the warder came over to see what was the matter.

'There was no need to get so worked up about it,' Sharon told him when the warder moved away again.

Hadyn scowled at her but didn't answer. For the rest of the visiting hour he was in such a bad mood that Sharon wondered why she had bothered to come at all.

She tried to make allowances, reminding herself that it must be terrible to be locked up in a cell all day, especially since when she'd first known him he'd been used to travelling all over the place. Nevertheless, it did worry her because she wondered what he was going to be like when he came home in a few months' time.

He wasn't the only one who'd changed, she reminded herself. Now that she had a steady job she felt so much more independent that she was no longer prepared to take orders from him or be satisfied with the sort of life she'd known before.

Several times over the Christmas period she had been tempted to call in at her father's shop in Queen Street and see if she could manage to persuade him to let her see her mother and brother again. She still missed them all a great deal and now that there was no baby to bring disgrace on the family name perhaps they could forgive and forget all that had happened in the past.

When she'd mentioned her idea to Karmu, hoping for approval, she'd been shocked when Karmu had tried to dissuade her and told her not to build up her hopes.

'If he wanted you back, then he would have let

you know when little Morgan died,' she'd said cryptically.

'Perhaps he didn't know about it,' Sharon told her but that had cut no ice with Karmu. 'He was bound to have read about it in the *South Wales Echo*,' she'd said scathingly. 'It was headline news and there were placards about it on the news-stands. Of course he would know all about it and, for that matter, so would your mother and the rest of your family.'

Sharon hadn't argued with her because she'd felt far too upset and near to tears to do so. Karmu's harsh words, however, had remained in her mind ever since. Several times she'd walked into the city centre with the idea of calling at the shop so that she could prove Karmu wrong but at the last minute lost her nerve to do so. If her father did turn her away, she would feel even more heartbroken and wish she'd left well alone.

She still harboured the dream that one day she would be lucky enough to meet Gwen out shopping and that they would stop and chat and, in that way, she could get back with her family again but so far this had not happened.

Chapter Twenty-One

Much to Sharon's disappointment she found that even though she was working on the reception desk on the top floor of The Secret Retreat she was still ignored by the other girls working there.

For the first few days she had made a point of smiling and saying hello to them as they arrived. Sometimes all five of them came in together, laughing and talking between themselves, but they always went into separate rooms.

On her first day working upstairs she had inadvertently gone to open one of the doors only to find that it was firmly locked. This puzzled her because whenever a man arrived after checking in with her, he seemed to be able to walk straight in.

At the end of her first week on the top-floor reception desk, when Geraint Humphreys asked her if she would carry on working there for another week, she tried to pluck up the courage to ask him what the rooms were used for but at the last minute her nerve failed.

'If he wanted you to know, then he would have told you,' Karmu opined when she told her about it while they were having a cup of tea together on the Sunday morning.

'Yes, I suppose you are right. I do feel that there is something strange going on, though, and I do hate mysteries or being kept in the dark.'

'There's something odd about the whole set-up at that place, if you ask me,' Karmu stated. 'Remember what Hadyn said when you told him you were working there?'

'He didn't say very much, as far as I can remember.' Sharon frowned.

'Oh yes, he did. You said he told you to watch your back with Geraint Humphreys and with that Glenda Roberts. If that wasn't a warning that the place and the people running it are dodgy, then I don't know what is.'

Sharon didn't argue with Karmu but she re-solved to talk to Hadyn again about The Secret Retreat next time she went to visit him and find out what he knew.

At the beginning of the following week, before she had a chance to do so, Geraint Humphreys asked her if she would consider changing her job yet again.

'The girl you've been deputising for is coming back to work tomorrow but one of the other girls is off sick and I wondered if you would like to do her job. You've been here long enough now to know the ropes and with your pretty face I think you'd probably do well. I'm sure the clients would take to you and, as well as an increase in your wages, you would be in line for some generous tips.'

'I like the sound of that.' Sharon smiled. In-wardly she felt exultant. More money to add to her savings would be very useful. Hadyn wouldn't be out of prison for a long while yet and she wasn't sure if he would still have a job with Mr Morgan when he was released. They would need every penny she could save.

'Good, then I'll ask Glenda to come and explain what will be expected of you. You will need a smart outfit but I'll leave all that to Glenda. She will take you shopping and buy whatever she thinks appropriate.'

When Sharon told Karmu her news the next morning, instead of looking well pleased for her, as she'd expected, Karmu shook her head and gave a heavy sigh.

'Are you sure you know what you are letting

yourself in for, cariad?' she muttered.

'No, not yet, because Glenda hasn't told me what my duties will be but the important thing is that it is a chance to earn more money.'

'Money's not everything, my lovely,' Karmu said sharply.

'You seem to think it is, when my rent is overdue,' Sharon reminded her.

Karmu's lips tightened but she said nothing.

'I'm sorry,' Sharon said quickly as she saw the hurt look on Karmu's face. 'I didn't mean it like that. Money is important, though, especially to me at the moment, because I'm saving hard so that I have money to tide us over for a few weeks when Hadyn comes out of prison so that he has a chance to get back on his feet again.'

'Perhaps you should talk to him about this new job before you decide to do it,' Karmu advised.

'I can't. I'm starting it today. Glenda Roberts is taking me out shopping for a new outfit, what about that!'

'I think you should wait until you see what she buys you before you look so pleased,' Karmu told her drily.

Sharon said nothing but she remembered Karmu's words later in the day when, instead of taking her on a shopping trip, Glenda handed her a bundle of assorted clothing, all of which had obviously been worn before.

'You're about the same size as Maria, so these will probably fit you,' she said off-handedly. 'Run along to the Ladies' cloakroom and try them on.'

For a minute Sharon hesitated, looking at the conglomeration of items that Glenda had thrust into her arms.

'If they're not suitable, then we'll go out and buy something,' Glenda said impatiently. 'Try these on first. I'll be along in a couple of minutes to see what you look like in them.'

As soon as she was on her own Sharon sorted through the bundle Glenda had given her. She couldn't believe her eyes. There was only one dress and that was so tight and so revealing that she felt naked in it.

The rest of the clothes were all fancy underwear; the sort of thing she'd seen displayed in shops but certainly had never worn or even tried on.

She had just managed to squeeze into a low-cut lace-trimmed black bra and matching French knickers and was standing staring at her reflection when Glenda walked in. Sharon quickly snatched up the red peignoir trimmed with white swans' down and wrapped that round her shoulders.

'There's no need for false modesty,' Glenda said with a brittle laugh. 'You'll have to get used to strutting around in your underwear or, for that matter, stark naked, if you are going to make a success of your new job.'

Sharon stared at her in bewilderment, the colour rushing to her cheeks. 'Whatever do you mean?' she gulped.

Glenda raised her pencilled eyebrows. 'Didn't Mr Humphreys make it clear what you would be doing?'

Sharon shook her head. 'No, he said you would explain everything and tell me what I would have to do.'

There was a long moment of silence as Glenda

thoughtfully chewed on her lower lip. 'Very well, you'd better come with me and, as a start, I'll show you where you will be working.'

As she reached out for her own clothes Glenda stopped her. 'Come as you are; bring the rest of the stuff with you. No point in getting changed because you will be starting work in about half an hour.'

'Dressed like this!' Sharon gasped.

Glenda didn't bother to answer; she was already walking away and, after a moment of hesitation, Sharon slipped on the peignoir and picked up all the rest of the clothes and hurried after her.

Glenda went straight for one of the doors that Sharon had always found locked. As she followed her inside and her feet sank into a deep-pile cream carpet, Sharon couldn't believe her eyes, the room was so opulent. There was cream and gold damask wallpaper on two of the walls but on the other two were floor-to-ceiling mirrors with ornate gilded frames and, in the centre of the ceiling, was a matching mirror. A door at the opposite end of the room was ajar and Sharon could see that it was a bathroom and that the washbasin also had gilded taps.

Dominating the room was a huge divan bed, which was piled high with satin cushions and was half covered by an enormous cream fur spread. The headboard was in cream and gold damask and the only other item of furniture in the room was a huge matching armchair.

Sharon had never in her life seen a room like it and she felt petrified as she realised what it was used for and what was expected of her. She wanted to run but she felt unable to move.

From somewhere in the background she could hear Glenda outlining her duties but the words refused to register properly in her mind. All she could hear was a jumble of instructions that she had no intention of carrying out. 'Be nice to them and remember you are here to do whatever they ask you to do'; 'Any trouble, and there is a secret button you can push for help'; 'Make sure they wash first'; 'It is your responsibility to see that they pay for any extras'; 'Remember they're allowed to stay for two hours and no more. Is all that quite clear now, Sharon?' Glenda asked impatiently when she had finished.

Sharon stared at her, utterly stunned. 'You can't expect me to do something like that,' she protested. 'Hadyn would be horrified.'

'Hadyn? Do you mean Hadyn Jenkins, by any chance?' Glenda asked in a highly amused voice.

'Yes!' Sharon nodded. 'I believe that both you and Mr Humphreys know him, don't you?'

'We know him, all right, and there's certainly no need to worry about what he would think; he's done far worse things in his time, I can assure you. Anyway, he was always a very good customer here,' she added rather cattily.

Before Sharon could reply the door was pushed open and a very tall barrel-chested Nigerian wearing a smart navy blue suit came into the room. He was in his early forties and would have been handsome if it had not been for a cauliflower ear, a broken nose and a deep gash down his left cheek that extended from just under his eye to his chin.

'What's all this?' He grinned, showing a mouthful of gleaming white teeth as he stared first at Sharon and then at Glenda. 'Does this mean that I am getting two for the price of one, then?'

'Sampson, the very man.' Ignoring his quip Glenda greeted him with a smile. 'This is Sharon and you will be her first client. As one of our regulars I am sure you will be able to tell her exactly what is expected.'

'It will be my pleasure and, of course, hers,' he leered as his large black hand reached out and pulled Sharon towards him; so close that she almost retched on the strong odour he gave off.

'No, stop. I'm not doing any of this, it's all a terrible mistake, please let me go!' Sharon pleaded.

As she tried to pull away he gave a deep laugh then caught her around the waist and unceremoniously lifted her off the ground and threw her down on the bed. She lay there shivering with fright, apprehensive about what he would do next.

'Right, Sampson, I'll leave everything to you,' Glenda said with a supercilious smile.

Sharon jumped off the bed and snatched up the fur covering and wrapped herself in it the moment the door clicked shut behind Glenda.

'Feeling cold?' he asked as he removed his jacket and hung it up on a peg behind the door. 'Never mind, I'll soon warm you up,' he added with a deep noisy laugh.

'Don't you dare touch me,' Sharon breathed, her eyes widening in distress as slowly but methodically Sampson slipped his braces off his shoulders and began to undo the buttons down the front of his trousers while walking towards the bed at the same time.

'If you take even one more step, I'll ring the panic button for help,' Sharon warned and felt furious that her voice sound muffled and squeaky.

Sampson merely laughed. 'Do you really think I'd let you do that?' He flexed one of his arms, making the dark brown shiny flesh ripple and then become a hard knot of muscle.

'Now let's get this clear, little lady,' he went on impassively. 'You know why I'm here and what I want. I've paid for your services and I want value for my money. Do you understand?'

Sharon shook her head. 'I don't think you understand. I don't know what you want me to do, because I've never done this sort of thing before. Until a few minutes ago I didn't even know what went on in these rooms.' She gulped. 'All I want to do is put my own clothes back on and go back to sitting at the desk checking people as they come in.'

Sampson stared at her for a moment in disbelief then his booming laugh filled every corner of the room. He laughed so loud and for so long that she thought he would never stop.

'Oh my, oh my,' he gasped. 'You're a first-class tease but that doesn't worry me. I'm all for fun. If you are as innocent as you say you are, then it's been money well spent.'

Once again he reached out and pulled her towards him. Sharon fought him off with every ounce of her strength but she was like a small kitten trying to wriggle free from the clutches of a rabid dog. Sampson had his prey and he had no intention of letting it go.

With a deep growl he threw her back on the

bed and was on top of her before she could put up any resistance. Panic gave her a strength she didn't know she had. Using both hands against his sweating barrel chest she tried to push him away but it had no effect.

Determined to get free she clenched her teeth and tried a different tactic. This time she managed to reach up with one hand and scrape her nails as hard as she could down his cheek.

Sampson let out a howl of pain and, as he pulled back, she managed to bring up one of her knees in a vicious jab to his groin. As he rolled over on to his back cursing her and clutching at himself to try and ease the pain, she managed to wriggle free from under him.

Tears blinding her she grabbed at her own clothes then, still carrying them, dashed out of the room and along the corridor towards the stairs, hoping to find someone who would help her.

As she passed the last door on the upstairs landing it opened and two men came out. Their jeering exclamations at seeing her half naked made her cower back against the wall, half afraid that they might attack her.

The sound of Geraint Humphreys' voice as he came hurrying up the stairs demanding to know what all the commotion was about calmed her a little and, for a brief moment, she felt safe.

Then her heart sank as she heard his exclamation of annoyance when he saw her standing there half naked. Before she had a chance to explain Sampson came lumbering along the landing; there was blood trickling down his face and he was shouting and cursing. When he spotted Geraint

Humphreys, he began telling him in an outraged voice what had happened and how she had attacked him like a wild cat and he'd been unable to control her.

His outcry brought gales of laughter from the other two men who were still listening. 'You a boxer and you can't defeat a chit of a girl like that?' one of them teased. 'Did she cut all your hair off, Sampson, and take your strength away?' the other man guffawed.

'That's enough!' Geraint Humphreys held up a hand for silence. 'Come along with me, Sampson, we'll go along to my office and I'll have a look at that scratch and stop the bleeding and then you can tell me all about it over a whisky,' he consoled the irate black man.

'As for you,' he said, turning towards Sharon, 'get your clothes on and leave. I never want to see or hear from you again. We've never had an unpleasant incident of this sort in my club since the day I opened it. I should have known that if you were in any way connected to Hadyn Jenkins then there was bound to be trouble sooner or later!'

Turning on his heel Geraint Humphreys took Sampson by the arm and led him towards the stairs leaving Sharon still standing on the landing shivering and in tears.

As she went back into the room to find her own clothes and get dressed she wondered what on earth Geraint Humphreys had meant by the reference he had made to Hadyn.

Sharon was still shaking when she arrived home

231

at Clwyd Court. It was only nine o'clock and Karmu came hurrying out into the hallway to see who it was.

'What's happened, why have you come home so early? You're shivering! Why aren't you wearing your hat and coat? Aren't you well? You look terrible; you're as white as a sheet. Come on in, then, and sit down in my place. I'll put the kettle on and you can tell me all about it over a cup of tea.'

Karmu listened intently to Sharon's account of what had happened, shaking her head from time to time or nodding in agreement, but remaining silent until Sharon had finished.

'Well now,' she murmured as she refilled Sharon's cup and then her own, 'you can't go back there again, that's for certain.'

'I must go back and get my coat. It's the only one I've got and I need it,' Sharon muttered.

'Better to lose your coat than your virtue,' Karmu told her. 'You keep right away from that place. I always thought it was a den of iniquity when you first told me about it.'

'I know you did and I should have listened to you, but it seemed to be such a wonderful opportunity to earn good money while Hadyn was in prison. Hadyn seemed to be surprised that I'd gone there to work,' Sharon said reflectively.

'I bet he was. He would know all about the place and what went on there, so it's a pity he didn't tell you so and warn you against working there. I hope you tell him so when you next go to visit him.'

'I'm not sure whether to tell him or not. It also means telling him that I've lost my job, remember.'

'You may have found another one by then,' Karmu pointed out. 'Come on, finish drinking your tea and have an early night then tomorrow you can start looking for something else,' she added with an encouraging smile. 'There must be some other sort of work that you can do that is better than selling your body.'

Chapter Twenty-Two

February ushered in high winds and cold drizzly rain. As Sharon trudged the streets, day after day, trying to find work, she shivered with the cold, without a topcoat of any kind.

On her way home each day she would make a point of looking at the second-hand clothes rack in the market on The Hayes to see if she could spot anything but there were never any coats she could afford to buy.

As the weather seemed to get colder she decided that even though she hadn't found work she would have to use her savings to buy a coat before she caught a chill.

After much searching she found a full-length one in dark brown cloth that fitted her perfectly and, although it took all her savings, she was determined to buy it. It had a brown fur collar which made her feel both warm and pampered. It was as good as new and she couldn't understand how anyone would want to part with it.

'Maybe they needed the money,' Karmu pointed

out. 'That's usually the reason why people get rid of things.'

When she went to visit Hadyn at the beginning of March wearing her new coat he raised his eyebrows in surprise. 'Come into a fortune, have we?' he said cryptically.

'No, quite the reverse. I've lost my job and I've now spent all my savings on a warm coat.'

He stared at her in silence, his dark eyes questioning as if expecting an explanation.

Choosing her words carefully she told him about what had happened at The Secret Retreat. His reaction was much the same as Karmu's had been.

'Don't expect any sympathy from me. Right from the start I warned you against getting mixed up with Geraint Humphreys and Glenda Roberts.'

'I know,' Sharon admitted, 'but you didn't tell me why or anything about what went on there.'

'So what sort of club did you think he was running?' Hadyn asked scornfully. 'You must have known he wasn't holding prayer meetings.'

Sharon bit her lip and said nothing. She felt close to tears. She'd hoped Hadyn would understand and even praise her for not doing as they'd asked.

'So have you found a new job, then?' Hadyn asked rather impatiently.

'No, but I'm looking every day. I'm still hoping that trade will pick up soon for some of the big stores will need extra assistants and I might be lucky and get taken on.'

'Pigs might fly,' Hadyn sneered. 'You've never worked in a shop, so why should they hire you when you've no experience and they'd have to train you?'

'I have. I was working in my father's shop, that's how we came to meet.'

'Yes, but you spent most of your time in the background. It was your father and his partner who dealt with the customers that came into their shops. They were the ones doing the real selling.'

Sharon was glad when visiting time was over. Hadyn had done nothing but pull her to pieces the whole hour she'd been there. As she walked out of the prison into Adam Street and along Bute Terrace she felt very resentful about his attitude. As she turned down Bute Street and made her way home she even debated whether she would go and visit him again.

He had less than a year of his sentence to serve and, not for the first time, she wondered what their future was going to be like.

Prison had certainly changed him and not for the better. He seemed to be so hard, so unfeeling and his comments were always so bitter. It was almost as if he was deliberately trying to undermine any decision she took.

By the time she'd reached Clwyd Court her mind had cleared and once more she was dreaming of the time when they would be together again. He was still the man she'd fallen in love with, she told herself, and it was only because she cared so much about him and wanted to shine in his eyes that his critical remarks hurt so much.

Once he was out of prison and back in the real world, he would regain his charm and good humour and, once again, be as loving and kind as she knew he really was.

In the meantime, she told herself, she had to find some work so that she could replace the savings she'd squandered on her coat. Perhaps now that she looked so much more smartly dressed she would be more successful when she went for interviews, she thought optimistically.

Two weeks later she was still out of work and becoming desperate. It was now well into March and as she trudged from shop to shop they all informed her that any additional assistants they required for the coming season had already been hired.

She was on the point of returning home when a woman's voice called out her name and she turned to find Nanwen Williams standing there smiling at her.

'Duw anwyl! Fancy bumping into you like this,' Nanwen greeted her. 'There's well you look, and what a posh coat with that lovely fur collar,' she enthused. 'Out on a shopping spree like me, are you?' she asked, indicating the two heavy bags that were resting on the ground by her feet.

'Nanwen, it's lovely to see you again,' Sharon greeted her. 'No, I'm not shopping, I'm trying to find a job,' she sighed.

'No luck?'

'None at all. None of the shops seem to be taking on any new staff, even though we are always being told in the newspapers that trade is picking up again.'

'Well, if you are not in a hurry, how about giving me a hand and helping me to carry my shopping to the tram stop. We seem to be in the way standing here in the middle of the pavement,' Nanwen suggested. She gave an apologetic smile as several people made impatient noises as they tried to pass them.

When the tram arrived they were still talking and so Sharon helped Nanwen carry her shopping on board.

'Come on, then, sit down,' Nanwen invited, patting the seat alongside her.

'Well, I was on my way home,' Sharon murmured.

'You've left it too late to get off.' Nanwen smiled as the conductor rang the bell and the tram began to pull away.

'I hope you're going to help me get this shopping home,' Nanwen said anxiously as they reached her stop. 'Be a great help if you did,' she added quickly. 'I get breathless these days when I carry too much. I should have known better than to buy such a lot.'

As soon as Nanwen opened the front door Sharon placed the bags down in the hallway. As she turned to leave, Nanwen Williams said in surprise, 'Surely you are going to stop for a bite to eat and a cup of tea now that you've come all this way?'

'Well...' Sharon hesitated. She was starving hungry and the invitation was tempting.

'Come on, cariad, bring the shopping through to the kitchen and then get your hat and coat off and make yourself comfortable while I put the kettle on.'

Over bowls of hot soup and crusty bread they talked some more and Sharon told Nanwen all about The Secret Retreat and what they had wanted her to do.

'Duw anwyl! A nice girl like you! Walking out was the best way of dealing with that sort of situation and no mistake. In fact, it was the only thing you could do. I call it scandalous that such places are allowed to exist.'

As Sharon was leaving, Nanwen reminded her of the days when she had done the painting of the house.

'Mr Morgan was only saying the other day how much he would like to have another picture done to show all the improvements he's had made in the garden. There's a lovely pond out there now, with fish in it, and he's had a nice aviary built as well. Could you paint something like that?'

'I'd love to if only I had the materials to do so,' Sharon said wistfully.

Nanwen looked thoughtful. 'Wait here a minute,' she said. 'I've got an idea.'

In next to no time Nanwen was back, her face beaming. 'Come along, Sharon. Mr Morgan wants a word with you,' she said triumphantly.

An hour later when she set off for home, Sharon was walking on air. She couldn't believe her good luck. It was almost like a dream coming true. Not only had Mr Morgan asked her to paint the rear view of his house but he had also told her she could use a room at his house to work in. He had given her five pounds to go and buy whatever brushes and paints she thought she was going to need.

He had shown her the room and, much to her delight, it had a large window, which meant there would be excellent light. There was a long work bench with storage cupboards underneath, running the full length of one wall and, to her surprise, there was also an artist's easel in there.

'I had dreams of doing a spot of painting myself once,' he told her with a deprecating laugh.

'It's a wonderful studio, so why ever did you stop?' Sharon asked shyly.

'I'm not sure,' Mr Morgan said with a shrug. 'No one to encourage me, for one thing, and I wasn't confident that I had any real ability. In time other things took over in my life and so I didn't bother any more.'

'Perhaps you'll start again one day,' Sharon mused.

'Maybe,' he agreed. 'In the meantime, I would like you to use the room. To start with, I'd like you to do a painting of the garden and after that I may have other commissions for you.'

'It's quite a long journey for you to make each day,' Karmu commented. 'Is it going to be worth it?'

'I'll be paid for the picture, so it is the same as having a job,' Sharon pointed out. 'What's even better, I'll be doing the sort of work that I enjoy. I'd still have quite a long journey if I was working at one of the shops in the city centre and I will be much happier painting than I would be serving behind a counter.'

The studio at Mr Morgan's house was warm and comfortable and Sharon was delighted to find that she was asked to share her meal break with Nanwen. Mr Morgan was so pleased with the garden view that he asked her if she could do several different versions featuring the new pond so that he could send them to friends at Christmas.

When those were finished he wanted another series of paintings of his house, each done from a different angle, but he told her to take her time over them, as there was no hurry. He simply wanted to build a varied collection that he could draw on as presents for his friends whenever the need arrived.

Most days he came to watch her working and stayed talking to her. She enjoyed his company but by April they were both well aware that she was only filling in time. She had painted so many pictures of his home that he now had more than he could ever use and each day she waited apprehensively for him to tell her so.

'Perhaps the time has come for you to teach me to paint,' he suggested. 'I used to be able to do it, so I should be a very apt pupil,' he added with a smile.

At first Sharon thought of refusing, because she suspected that this was simply a way of keeping her employed. Then the thought of being out of work and having to spend any of the money she had so arduously been saving lately stopped her. When Hadyn was released they were going to need every penny she could earn.

The lessons were not much of a success. Right from the start it was obvious that Mr Morgan had no eye for line or perspective and also that he was a very messy painter. After a while, Sharon was more than ever aware that what they were doing was a charade.

Even so, she felt her heart sink when he said, 'I'm not really very proficient at this sort of thing.

I don't seem to be making any progress. I'm not managing to produce anything other than un-recognisable daubs.'

'Do you mean you wish to stop?' she said, trying to keep her voice steady.

'I'm afraid I do, because it's so obvious that I'll never be any good at it,' he said quickly.

'Perhaps you need to concentrate more,' she suggested. 'You said yourself that you hadn't done any painting for a long time,' she added encouragingly.

He shook his head. 'No, Sharon, I'm sorry about this, but I know my limitations. You've been very patient but I am only making a fool of myself.'

She bit down on her lower lip to try and hide her disappointment. 'So does that mean that my work here is finished?' she asked.

'As my teacher, it does,' he agreed with a deprecating laugh.

'I quite understand and I appreciate all the work you've given me,' she said stiffly. 'I'll pack everything away and make sure your studio is tidy before I leave tonight.'

'No, Sharon, you've got it all wrong. I don't want you to stop coming here,' he exclaimed. 'In fact, I don't want you to go home at all. I'd like you to move in with me and stay here for good,' he stated rather wistfully.

Sharon felt bewildered. Before he'd gone to prison, Hadyn had been working for him as a handyman, so was Mr Morgan suggesting that they moved into his house as joint caretakers to look after his needs? She took a deep breath and tried to think clearly about what this would entail.

She knew Mr Morgan was making a very generous offer and she was grateful, but she needed more time to think everything through and to talk to Hadyn about it before either accepting or turning turn down his offer.

If she and Hadyn became his housekeepers, then what was going to happen to Nanwen Williams? She might be getting old but this was her home as well as her life.

Mr Morgan's next words took her breath away.

Taking her hand he said, 'I want you to leave Hadyn, he's no good and you deserve better. I can offer you a far better life than he will ever be able to do. I can give you everything you've ever dreamed about – clothes, jewellery, holidays, and you'll be mistress of this lovely home as well,' he told her eagerly.

Sharon stared at him in disbelief. She couldn't believe her ears. She studied him almost as if seeing him for the first time. He was in his mid-fifties, red faced and had the sort of paunch that told its own story of many years of good living and drinking. He was shorter than she was, and she could see the start of a bald patch at the crown of his short, dark hair.

Mentally she compared him with Hadyn who was less than half his age. To give up Hadyn to live in luxury with Mr Morgan would be almost as bad as selling her body at The Secret Retreat, she thought with a shiver.

She released her hand from Mr Morgan's grip and backed away. He had been so kind to her that she didn't want to hurt his feelings but she couldn't accept.

For all his faults, and she knew there were

plenty, she still loved Hadyn with all her heart. In some ways his misdeeds and their misfortunes had only made her love him deeper. Whatever he did, she would stand by him.

Her relief as Nanwen Williams came to the door of the studio to enquire if they would like a cup of tea was so overwhelming that for a moment she was unable to answer.

'I'm afraid not, I have to go,' she said hurriedly, realising that it was a chance for her to make her escape.

Before Mr Morgan could intervene she stood up and reached for her coat that was hanging behind the door.

'You don't usually leave this early,' Nanwen remarked in a surprised voice.

'You are coming back tomorrow, I hope?' Mr Morgan asked. 'We've some unfinished business to deal with, remember,' he added pointedly.

Chapter Twenty-Three

As the tram bumped and swayed all the way from Roath to the Pier Head, Mervyn Morgan's invitation to move into his house went round and round in Sharon's mind.

As she went over what he had said she even began to wonder if she had somehow dreamed it because he'd never said anything like it to her before.

She wished he'd wanted them both to move in

and work for him but from the look in his eyes, and the way he had held her hand as he detailed all the things he could offer her, she knew that this was not the case.

He had made it clear that he didn't approve of Hadyn or how he had behaved and that he wanted her to leave Hadyn, and come and live with him on her own and there was no way she was prepared to do that.

In the normal course of events she would have been able to talk to Karmu about the dilemma she found herself in and listen to what she thought, but in this instance it was impossible to do so because it was far too personal.

No, she decided this was something she really did have to decide for herself. Nevertheless, she couldn't help wishing that Mervyn Morgan hadn't made such a proposition because she now felt uncomfortable about having to face him in the future.

Perhaps it would be best if she didn't go there again, though it would mean she wouldn't be able to say goodbye to Nanwen Williams and upsetting her was the last thing she wanted to do because Nanwen had always been so kind to her.

It was at times like this, she reflected, when it would have been wonderful to be able to turn to her mam and dad for advice, or even her brother Parry.

By now he and Gwen would be nicely settled in their new home and might even have had a second baby by now, she reflected a little enviously. Perhaps she should have married Madoc Cogan after all, like her family had wanted her to do. Her life would have been so much more orderly.

She hadn't wanted Madoc then and she didn't want him now, she told herself firmly. She still loved Hadyn and once he was out of prison and they were together again things would be all right. Losing little Morgan had been a terrible blow but by next year they might even have another baby, she thought hopefully.

When she woke up the next morning, the situation was much clearer in her mind. She would go along to the studio and pack everything away neatly so that the room was as it had been when she'd first moved in there. Then she would thank Mr Morgan for his hospitality and go and say farewell to Mrs Williams.

She would probably see Nanwen Williams again from time to time to share a cup of tea and talk about what was happening in their lives and that was how she wanted it to be.

Things went nowhere near as streamlined as she had planned. Mr Morgan appeared before she was halfway through clearing out the room.

'Does this mean that you are leaving for good?' he asked sadly. 'When Hadyn comes out of prison you shouldn't take him back, not after all the heartache he's caused you. Mrs Williams has told me what almost happened to you when you were working at that club in Tiger Bay; you mustn't take that sort of risk again.'

'That wasn't Hadyn's fault,' she defended quickly. 'He warned me to be careful when I first went there to work.'

'He will do something that puts him back in prison and you will have to fend for yourself and then something similar will happen again in the future, as you very well know,' he predicted, ignoring her interruption.

Sharon shook her head. 'No, once Hadyn is free he will look after me. Anyway, I'd never do anything like that; I'm surprised that you think I would.'

Mr Morgan shook his head sadly. 'You are still very young and inexperienced in the ways of the world,' he said, his voice full of concern. 'Come and live here with me where you know you will be safe and let me take care of you,' he persisted.

'No,' Sharon shook her head, 'you have been very kind to me, to both of us, in fact, but Hadyn needs me. I thought, when you first mentioned it yesterday, that you meant both of us to come and live here,' she added with a tremulous smile.

'Oh Sharon, you are so sweet but so naive. Surely you must realise that I love you and that I've done so for a long time. I want to spoil you as well as look after you. Come and live with me and you'll never want for anything. I'll shower you with presents. You can have whatever you like, absolutely anything that takes your fancy.'

He pulled her close and began stroking her hair with one of his hands and murmuring tender words of love. Before she realised what was happening one of his hands had gone behind her head, drawing her face close, and his lips were almost on hers.

'No!' She tried to push him away but even though he was not much taller than her he was strong and his hands clasped her arms in an iron grip.

'Listen to me,' he ordered, his voice curt. 'You are being a fool if you reject me and my offer.'

Sharon stared at him hostilely. 'You know that I love Hadyn,' she protested.

'We both know that Hadyn Jenkins is a rotter and that he will go on committing crime after crime for the rest of his days. Is that the sort of man you want? You are still young and beautiful but he will drag you down and in next to no time you will become as evil as he is.'

Sharon clamped her hands over her ears in an attempt to shut out what he was saying. 'Stop accusing him of such dreadful things,' she gasped.

'You'll sink lower and lower in society until you will be an outcast, just as he is,' Mr Morgan went on relentlessly. 'This is your opportunity to save yourself and begin a new life. Think of all the luxury and comfort I can offer you if you come and live with me,' he repeated in a persuasive voice.

Sharon retreated backwards, until there was a chair between the two of them. 'I could never share a bed with any man I didn't love,' she gasped.

'Sometimes friendship grows into love and I can be a very patient man when it is something I want so desperately,' he said softly.

Disregarding the barrier, he once more pulled her into his arms and began running his hands down her arms and back and then trying to nuzzle her neck.

She remained stiff and unresponsive as, again, he tried to kiss her. Then, making a supreme effort, she broke free from his embrace and made for the door and ran headlong down the stairs pausing in the hallway only long enough to pick up her coat and hat and put them on.

She didn't even call out goodbye to Nanwen Williams because she saw that Mr Morgan had come out on to the landing and was standing at the top of the stairs, hopefully waiting in case she changed her mind.

Once outside his house she breathed deeply of the fresh spring air. She'd done the right thing, she told herself. The only man she had ever wanted to be with or to make love to was Hadyn and soon he would be home again.

She didn't feel that she was ready to go back to Clwyd Court and answer all Karmu's questions about why she had returned home so early and since she was only a short distance from Roath Park and it was a fairly mild day for May, she decided that a walk might help clear her mind.

Lost in thought as she debated whether or not to tell Hadyn about her encounter with Mr Morgan and wondering what he would say if she did, she was completely unaware of everybody else in the park. That was until a blow suddenly hit her between the shoulder blades, making her jump in alarm.

As she turned round ready to reprimand whoever had kicked the ball at her and saw that a plump young woman, who was wearing a smart grey coat and hat and was pushing a pram, had stopped and was scolding the small boy at her side.

'Now go and tell that lady that you are very sorry,' she insisted as she pushed the child forwards.

Sharon stared in disbelief. 'Gwen?' she questioned.

For a moment the other woman looked puzzled. 'Sharon? Heavens above, whatever are you doing here?'

Sharon walked towards her and kissed her on the cheek but Gwen didn't return the salutation.

'Sorry about the ball hitting you,' Gwen murmured. 'I keep telling Ieuan that he should always be careful where he is kicking it, but being a boy and only three he takes no notice at all.'

'That's all right. It didn't really hurt; it just took me by surprise.' Sharon smiled. 'And is this one a little girl?' she asked peering into the pram.

'Oh yes, this is Ceri,' Gwen said, pulling back the pink blanket so that Sharon could just see the small pointed face and straggles of dark hair beneath the knitted white bonnet.

'How old is she?'

'She's only three months old and so far she sleeps most of the time, which is more than I can say for Ieuan. Never had a moment's peace with him. We still don't, if it comes to that,' she added with a proud smile.

Sharon felt a momentary pang as she remembered little Morgan who would also have been three by now. Then she pulled herself together and asked 'And how is Parry?'

'Oh, he's all right, and working every hour God sends. You know what he's like; he puts the business before himself all the time. The business is doing so well, of course, and now Parry has his own car and takes us out in it at the weekends. We even went to Barry Island a couple of times last summer. That was before I had Ceri, of course,' she said as she bent over the pram and tucked the blankets in more firmly.

'Mind you, he dotes on these two; he's a proud father, there's no doubt about that,' she added as she straightened up. 'He's always making plans for their future and what schools he wants them to go to so that they have all the knowledge possible before they come into the business.'

'Everything seems to be going fine for you all, then. Is Madoc well?'

'Yes, and he's courting at last. It took him a long time to get over you going off with that Hadyn Jenkins, mind. Broken hearted, he was, for months, I can tell you. Are you still with Hadyn?'

'Of course I am.'

'I did wonder. We read all about the accident he had and about your toddler being killed and then about Hadyn being involved in a big robbery and going to prison. As you can imagine people were ready to tell us a lot more than was in the newspapers. He's led you quite a dance one way or another, hasn't he?' she said tartly. 'Is he still in prison?'

'Yes, but he's due home soon,' Sharon replied, trying to keep her voice steady.

'I don't know how you can live with it, especially when it was his fault that your little boy was killed.'

'We've had our ups and downs,' Sharon admitted. 'I imagine you've had some of those yourself,' she added.

'Nothing as bad as yours! Your poor mam was very upset by what was written in the newspapers, but your dad never said a word. In fact, if he heard any of us discussing it, he'd tell us in no uncertain terms to shut up. He said he never wanted to hear that man's name mentioned ever again,' she added triumphantly. 'We must get back, because Ceri is due for a feed and I can't do anything about that out here,' she murmured when Sharon said nothing. 'Pick up your ball, Ieuan, and I'll put it in the bottom of the pram until we get home,' she told the little boy as she turned the pram around.

'You'll say hello to them all for me, won't you?' Sharon asked as Gwen started to walk away.

'I'm not sure if that would be a good idea or not,' Gwen told her. 'I'll tell Parry that I've seen you, of course, and then see what he thinks I ought to do.'

'You must do whatever you think is best, Gwen, but I am sure my mam would want to know that I am well and that we have met up,' Sharon insisted.

'Perhaps, or then again it might make her sad and despondent like she was after you ran away and that would be a pity now that she's back on her feet. Anyway, it's not so much your mam as your dad I am concerned about. I don't want to risk making him lose his temper and having him shouting at me, now, do I?'

As she made her way home to Gower Street, Gwen debated with herself whether to mention her meeting with Sharon to Parry when he came home that night or to wait and tell the entire family next time they were invited to dinner by

251

Elaine and Elwyn.

At one time there had been so much speculation about what had happened to Sharon and whether or not she was still with Hadyn Jenkins. Then, after the reports about the accident, followed by the news that Hadyn had been involved in a robbery and sent to prison, Elwyn Pritchard had forbidden them to speak about it any more because he could see how much it was upsetting his wife.

Even so, Gwen mused, actually meeting Sharon was something quite different to speculating about what had happened to her. She was sure that Sharon's mother would like to hear all about it, even if Elwyn Pritchard preferred to turn a deaf ear.

She wondered what Madoc's reaction would be. Would it be enough to make him break up with his new girlfriend and start mooning after Sharon all over again?

When she got home she sat and breastfed Ceri and looked around her comfortably furnished little home with a glow of satisfaction. She no longer had to work in her parents' shop; she had two lovely children and a husband who made her happy. She couldn't bear to think how she would feel if she lost Ieuan the way Sharon had lost her little boy.

She had been lucky. They even had the use of a motor car to go out in, even though it belonged to the business and wasn't exactly their own as she'd led Sharon to believe.

As she put the two children to bed and then started preparing dinner, Gwen tried to decide whether it might be better to keep the meeting with Sharon to herself for the moment. If she told Parry then he would probably tell her that she must say nothing to his mother for fear of upsetting her. On the other hand, because he had been quite fond of his sister, he might ask why she hadn't invited Sharon to come back with her.

It had never entered her head to do so because she had never forgiven Sharon for making use of her bedroom while she and Parry had been away on their honeymoon. It had been annoying enough when she'd thought she'd slept in their bed with Madoc before she and Parry had had a chance to do so, but when she discovered that it had been with Hadyn Jenkins she had found that unpardonable.

By the time Parry came home that night she still hadn't decided what action to take. She wasn't sure that she wanted Sharon back home. Everything was going so smoothly that it seemed to be silly to cause ripples.

At present she was the centre of attention both with her own parents and Parry's because she had produced two lovely grandchildren for them. Elwyn Jenkins and her own father both seemed to be able to forget all their business plans and worries when Ieuan was chattering away to them or when they were out in the Pritchards' big back garden kicking a ball around.

Chapter Twenty-Four

Sharon couldn't put her chance meeting with Gwen out of her mind. She thought she had hardened her heart to the past and was managing to concentrate on her new life but suddenly all her memories were revived.

It seemed a lifetime ago when Hadyn had walked into her life, a brash, handsome young commercial traveller full of charm and confidence, and she had fallen head over, heels in love with him and counted the weeks and days until his next visit. In those days, even hearing his voice had filled her with such excitement that she could hardly breathe.

Even after her father had discovered what was going on and forbidden her to have anything more to do with Hadyn, she had still made sure that she knew when he would next be calling. On those days she always made a point of wearing something smart and, making sure that her hair was at its best.

She had put Hadyn on a pedestal, she realised now. Partly because he was that much older than her and so much more a man of the world than either Parry or Madoc, who was always her partner whenever they went out as a foursome.

Madoc never complimented her in any way; Hadyn always managed to say something that was flattering. Madoc in those days had seemed gauche and clumsy whilst Hadyn had always been suave and very self-confident.

She wondered what Madoc was like these days and what sort of girl he had eventually fallen for. From what Gwen had said about her own brother it seemed he was very grown up and self-assured and aiming to be a success in life like their dad.

If she'd married Madoc like everyone had thought she would, by now she would have had her own well-furnished home and perhaps a car standing outside as well as a couple of small children, just as Gwen and Parry had. Little Morgan would have been the same age as Ieuan, she thought wistfully.

She could imagine how proud her own parents were of their two grandchildren and it saddened her to realise that they had never even seen little Morgan. Probably the first intimation they had that he even existed was when they read an account in the newspaper about him running out into the road and being run over.

For the first time she realised what a dreadful disappointment she must be for them. She wondered what they would think if they knew that today a man who was probably as old as her father had asked her to come and live with him; or, indeed, what their reaction would have been if she had gone ahead and accepted Mr Morgan's suggestion.

Possibly, because he was rich and influential and had a lovely home, they would have thought he was a good choice and that it would be far better than living with a ex-convict in the squalor of Tiger Bay, she thought ruefully.

For the rest of the journey home she tried to decide how much she ought to tell Karmu about what had happened. She didn't owe any rent, at least not at the moment, but unless she could find work she very soon would. What little savings she had would be used up in next to no time. For that reason it might be best to tell her as little as possible.

Months later, footsore and weary from trudging from shop to shop trying to find work, and with Hadyn due home within the next few days, Sharon was so desperate that she lowered her sights and went to work in Curran's enamelware factory that was between Taff Embankment and Curran Embankment.

She found the smells obnoxious, the noise deafening and the women and girls so rough and outspoken that she tried to shut her ears to their bawdy conversations.

The work itself was very strenuous, usually dirty and often in unpleasant, steamy conditions. The heavy lifting was supposed to be done by the boys and young men but, more often than not, they left it to the women because many of them were so much stronger than they were.

Sharon found she had no trouble at all mixing with the men who worked there, apart from their wolf whistles and occasional sly remarks that brought a flush to her cheeks. It was the women she feared. As soon as they realised she hadn't grown up in Tiger Bay they teased her unmercifully, played japes on her and made sure that all the most unpleasant jobs came her way.

The forewoman, Betti Lewis, was an Amazonian figure with a very loud voice that sounded like a foghorn over the general crashing, banging and hum of machinery that went on in the factory. Sharon found that she seemed to be perpetually calling out her name and accusing her of some misdeed or other.

'Easy to see that you've never worked in a factory before,' she scoffed whenever Sharon appeared not to know what to do or when the work piled up on the bench in front of her and caused hold-ups further along the assembly line. 'This is the real world, girl, so you'd better learn to keep up. We're all on piecework, so we can't afford to carry laggards.'

'I'm sorry, but I am doing the very best I can to keep up,' Sharon assured her.

'You might think you are, but it's not good enough and my pay packet as well as those of all the others on this assembly line will suffer if the total number of pans we produce are down at the end of the week.'

After that she moved her from one section of the assembly line to the other so that by the end of the week Sharon was so confused about what she was supposed to be doing that she was feeling quite distraught.

None of the girls were particularly friendly and Sharon found that even the few who did pass the time of day with her didn't hold back with their grumbles about how slow she was when they found that their take-home pay was less than usual at the end of the week because they hadn't produced as many items as they normally did.

She was feeling so depressed when she arrived home that evening that she even went as far as to say to Karmu that she wondered if she ought to look for something else.

'Don't talk such nonsense,' Karmu scolded. 'You know that it's a waste of time doing that. Look at how long you spent trying to get some sort of shop work. Stick it out for a bit longer and if you still don't like working there, find something else first before you give in your notice.'

'I don't want to stay there a minute longer because they are all so unpleasant to me.'

'Of course they are, it's because they're short in their pay packets. Next week you'll know the ropes and be able to keep up there will be no problems at all.'

'I hope you are right,' Sharon said, shaking her head rather dubiously.

'Look, cariad, stick it out until your Hadyn comes home. Another few days to go, that's all. Then as soon as he gets himself a job you can pack yours in and look for something you like better.'

'That sounds all right, providing Hadyn can find himself a job when he gets home.'

'He can always go back to work at that Mr Morgan's place where he was before, can't he?' Karmu reasoned.

Sharon shuddered, remembering what had happened there before she'd left. 'I don't know. Mr Morgan mightn't want to employ him again, not after he's been in prison,' she said evasively.

For one brief moment she was tempted to tell Karmu about what had happened between her and Mr Morgan. Then common sense prevailed and she knew it was best to tell no one in case it ever reached Hadyn's ears.

The following week at Curran's was nowhere near as bad. A new girl, Alex Price, started work on the same assembly line. She was about eighteen, small, dark and very pretty with a wide smile that lit up her elfin face. She came from Tonypandy. Her father had been killed in a mining accident a few years earlier and her mother had gone into a decline and had also recently died so Alex had come to live with an aunt in Grangetown.

Since most of the other women came from Tiger Bay she had to stand a good deal of ribbing about being too posh to work there. Any mistakes she made were attributed to this and although there were often tears in her sloe-dark eyes she always managed to turn their critical comments into some kind of light-hearted joke and have them all laughing.

Because they were both new to Curran's and about the same age Sharon not only liked her but found her to be a good companion. She wished she could have known her earlier so that they could have gone out together because now all her plans were focused on Hadyn's homecoming.

Alex seemed to accept this quite happily and to understand when she explained about Hadyn. She didn't even appear to be shocked when Sharon told her that Hadyn had been in prison.

'You say he comes from up the Valleys?'

'Yes, his dad was killed the Senghenydd Pit disaster when he was quite young,' Sharon told her.

Alex nodded sagely. 'Daft old job, going underground, I can see why he wanted to get away. I remember my mam saying that when she was a young girl her mother used to work down the pit.'

'As a miner, do you mean?' Sharon asked in astonishment.

'Well, sort of; they used to put a harness on the women and girls so that they could fasten the coal truck on to them and then they had to pull them along the tacks to where they could be hauled up to the pit face. Terrible work, it was. She said that her mother had said that her grandmother still had the scars where the harness chafed her skin until it was bleeding.'

'That's terrible,' Sharon exclaimed. 'I thought working here in this hell hole was bad enough with all its noise and smells, but it's nothing compared to that, is it?'

'No, this is a picnic,' Alex laughed. 'It's only the women and their catty comments that we have to worry about and you know what they say, "sticks and stones can break my bones but harsh words can hurt me never". At least Betti Lewis doesn't hit us. My gran once told me that the pit foreman would use a strap on them if they weren't pulling the trucks quickly enough.'

'Well, they might say that but some of the sharp comments Betti Lewis makes cut me to the quick,' Sharon said and shuddered.

'You're too soft-hearted, that's your problem,' Alex laughed. 'Take no notice of what she says or else give her back as good as she gives you, the same as I do.'

Although she couldn't bring herself to do that, Sharon found that Alex's attitude did help her and she felt far less miserable. Even though she still didn't like working in a factory.

In the days that followed, whether she was at work or at home, Sharon could think and talk about nothing else but Hadyn's release from prison.

He was due to be released early on Wednesday, so she didn't go in to work that day but was outside the prison gates in Knox Road waiting for him.

In the weeks before he was due to be discharged from prison Hadyn had spent most of his time thinking back about his past and dreaming and scheming about his future.

His life had never been easy, he reflected. Losing his dad when he'd been only fourteen and having to fend for himself afterwards had meant that he'd grown up and become streetwise far younger than most boys.

He'd been determined not to work down the pit so he'd come to Cardiff looking for a new life. At first it had been very hard; he'd hung around the docks hoping for work of some kind. He was even willing to run messages for the dockers as long as they gave him something in return. In those early days he slept in doorways and lived off scraps or even pilfered food and cigarettes from nearby shops and stalls whenever he was forced to do so.

His luck had changed for the better when one of the lorry drivers had asked him to give him a hand with a heavy consignment of linoleum that he was unloading single-handedly from one of the cargo boats and then stay on the lorry and help to unload it if he had nothing better to do.

When they'd got back to the warehouse and the driver had given him sixpence for his trouble, he'd hung around so long that the foreman had said that if he was looking for work he'd give him a trial going out with the van driver making deliveries.

It had been a good start but he still wasn't satisfied. He wanted more and his determination had paid off eventually.

The following year there was a lot of talk of war and rumours were flying that anyone who was fit and healthy was considered to be a coward if he didn't volunteer. It meant that a great many men over the age of eighteen were packing in their jobs and going into the forces.

He'd taken advantage of the fact and when he heard that the chap who worked as a commercial traveller for Brynmor and Williams had gone into the army, he applied for his job.

At first the sales manager had been reluctant to take him on because of his age but Hadyn had pointed out that was something of an advantage because he was too young to either join up or be called up. What was more, because he had been working for a delivery firm, he knew the area well.

He had made the most of the opportunity; women liked him and he never lacked for a bed for the night, whatever part of South Wales he was visiting.

By the time the war ended he was so firmly established and well liked that he expected to be with Brynmor and Williams for the rest of his working life. He probably would have been, he reflected, if it hadn't been for Elwyn Pritchard making a complaint about him. Still, he thought wryly, he'd scored over Pritchard in the end because he'd persuaded Sharon to leave home.

That's when his luck had changed dramatically. Absolutely everything had seemed to go wrong from the moment they'd moved into Clwyd Court.

Sharon had stuck by him, he'd give her that, even after he'd been responsible for their kid being run over. Perhaps little Morgan dying like that had been for the best, he thought ruefully. What sort of life would it have been for the child if he'd grown up in Tiger Bay?

For that matter, what sort of life was he going to be able to provide for himself and Sharon when he was released? He wondered if Mervyn Morgan would be willing to take him back after what he had read about him in the newspapers and now that he had a prison record.

The railway station was only a couple of streets away from the prison so perhaps when he was let out, instead of going home, he should clear off to Liverpool or London or some other big city. If he changed his name he could start afresh and no one need know about his past record.

It would mean deserting Sharon and he didn't want to do that. He sometimes found it hard to believe that she still loved him after all the traumas he had put her through, but she did; and, what was more, he still loved her. Without her there would really be no point in going on at all, no reason to try and start a new life.

As the huge iron gates slammed shut behind him

Sharon saw him stop and take a deep breath. Then he pulled out a crumpled packet of cigarettes from the inside pocket of his jacket and he seemed to be so tensed up that she gave him a moment to enjoy his cigarette before she went up to him.

For a moment he looked so surprised to see her that he didn't even speak. Then he was hugging her close, knocking her hat to one side as he kissed her hungrily.

'I thought you'd be at work. What have you done, told them that you are sick?' he questioned as he released her and took another long pull on his cigarette.

'No, I never thought to do that,' she admitted. 'I wanted to be here to see you and welcome you home the moment you were free so I just took the day off.'

Hadyn pulled a face. 'A bit on the reckless side doing that, isn't it, cariad? You don't want to chance losing your job, now, do you?'

'I never really thought about it. All I wanted was to see you,' she admitted with an eager smile.

'Come on, then, let's go and find somewhere to eat. I'm starving hungry and I'd like nothing better than a good fry-up and a big cup of strong coffee. You have got some money, haven't you?'

Sharon's heart sank. That wasn't what she planned to do but she didn't like to spoil his homecoming by saying so.

'Yes, of course I have, and we'll do what you like,' she agreed. 'Only Karmu will be disappointed because she is counting on us going home and is looking forward to cooking you one

264

of her really special meals.'

'No, I want to be in the outside world for a while and be amongst people, so don't let's argue about it.' Firmly he took her by the arm and steered her in the direction of Bute Street.

'You can tell me all about what's going on and, whatever other news you have while we eat,' he assured her, 'and then we'll go home and see old Karmu.'

As he tucked into a huge plate of bacon, eggs, lava bread, black pudding and fried bread, Sharon nursed a cup of coffee and studied him.

He had not only lost weight but he also had the pallid look of someone who hasn't been out of doors for months. His normally glossy auburn hair looked dull and stringy and when he occasionally looked at her there was a calculating look in his green eyes that hadn't been there before.

He didn't seem to want to talk about himself and she sensed that he was only half listening to what she had to say. The rest of the time his eyes were darting round the café, watching people come and go, almost as if he was weighing the place up. Remembering the past it gave her an uneasy feeling and she was glad when he had finished his meal and they could leave.

Karmu greeted him like a long-lost son and made no mention of where he'd been during his long absence. He responded well enough but Sharon could see he was eager to get away.

Once they were alone in their own room he became the Hadyn she had fallen for when she'd worked in her father's shop. As he undressed her and began to make love to her he was as tender and passionate as she remembered.

While she was in his arms all her fears vanished. She felt as hopeful for their future happiness together as she had been on the day she had left home. This time, she assured herself, things really were going to turn out all right.

Chapter Twenty-Five

Having Hadyn back at home turned Sharon's world topsy-turvy. He didn't seem to be interested in finding work, not as long as she was working at Curran's, and there was enough money coming in to pay Karmu the rent and to buy basic food.

The money she had skimped and saved towards his homecoming was dwindling by the day. She suspected that Hadyn had started betting again and that at the moment he was having a run of good luck, otherwise her meagre savings would not have lasted as long as they had. Nevertheless, she was worried about what was going to happen once it had all gone.

He'd not mentioned going back to work for Mr Morgan so she hadn't said a word about it, either, and kept her fingers crossed that Karmu wouldn't mention it.

Her own social life had certainly been busy since he'd been at home. He'd taken her to the pictures several times and they'd gone dancing twice, and on the second occasion they'd taken Alex with them and all three of them had enjoyed their evening out.

Alex could talk of nothing else when they met in work the next day. She kept remarking on what a nice bloke Hadyn was and how lucky she thought Sharon was to have someone like him.

'That chap Gustav that we met at the dance was good company too and a great dancer,' she enthused. 'He's asked me to go out again with him. It's a pity that he's a sailor and only in port for a couple of weeks.'

'He'll be back again in next to no time and then we can all have a night out together,' Sharon promised.

'I doubt it. He's off to Argentina and when he returns it will be to his own home port in Sweden. They'd only put into Cardiff for a couple of days,' Alex sighed.

'Never mind, you can always come out with us now and again,' Sharon said, smiling.

'That's kind of you, but I don't like playing gooseberry.' Alex pouted.

'You wouldn't be doing that for very long. You'll probably find a partner almost the moment we get inside the dance hall and we won't see you again for the rest of the evening.'

From then on it became established that Alex would join them whenever they went dancing and, as Sharon had predicted, she always met someone because, with her pretty face and lovely figure, Alex seemed to attract men like bees to a honey-pot.

Hadyn still hadn't managed to find a proper job but he seemed to be earning enough money from casual work to eke out her wages and enable them to live without any real money problems.

Even so, Sharon wished he would find a permanent job so that she could give up working at Curran's. She'd been there almost a year now and she still hated all the noise and all the obnoxious smells.

'I'm sure that is what is making me feel ill every morning,' she confided in Alex. 'The minute I put a foot out of bed I feel sick and I can hardly ever eat any breakfast. Cooking something for Hadyn makes me heave.'

'That certainly doesn't sound right. Perhaps you should go and see a doctor. He might be able to give you some pills or something to stop it,' Alex suggested.

'I'm quite sure it's breathing in all those foul fumes and stuff at work because I don't feel the same when I wake up on a Sunday morning.'

'You probably don't get up as early then,' Alex pointed out. 'I know I don't. I really look forward to a good long lie-in on Sunday mornings.'

A few weeks later when Sharon had seemed to have stopped complaining about feeling unwell in the mornings Alex asked her if she was feeling better.

'I'm fine. I think I've found out what was wrong with me. I was going to bed on an empty stomach. Ever since I started having a snack before bedtime I've felt much better. The only trouble is I seem to be putting on weight.'

Alex studied her critically. 'Yes you are,' she agreed.

'I can't help it, I seem to be hungry all the time,' Sharon admitted.

'Oh dear, you're not eating for two, are you?' Alex asked with a giggle.

Sharon stared at her in silence for a moment, the colour draining from her cheeks and her eyes widening with shock. 'Do you know, I never thought of that! Why on earth didn't I? After all, I've been pregnant before so I should have known.'

When she reached home she turned down Karmu's invitation to have a cuppa. Instead, she went straight up to her room and stripped off every vestige of clothing and studied herself as best she could in the small mirror fixed to the wall.

Hadyn came home while she was doing it. 'What's going on here?' he asked with a laugh.

His lips pursed into a silent whistle when she told him her news and he stared at her in disbelief. 'Are you sure?'

She nodded. 'Are you pleased?'

He ran a hand through his hair. 'I don't know what to say or think,' he admitted. He stepped closer and enfolded her in his arms. 'I'm pleased if you are,' he said softly.

Gently he moved her on to the bed and quickly took off his own clothes. As their bodies entwined Sharon gave a deep sigh of happiness as she surrendered to Hadyn's passionate lovemaking.

'I'll have to stop working at Curran's. I can't go on breathing in those poisonous fumes; it would be bad for the baby. You'll have to find a full-time job,' she murmured as they lay there together afterwards and Hadyn lit up a cigarette.

'You'll have to hang on at the factory for a bit longer,' he protested. 'I've been trying for months now to get work, you know that, but there's nothing out there. Leastwise not for someone who has a prison record.'

'You'll have to try harder. There must be someone who will take you on.'

'Geraint Humphreys would probably give me a job but it would be at that place where you worked, or one of his other gambling clubs, and we agreed to have nothing more to do with him.'

'If there is nothing else, then I suppose that is better than nothing,' she said reluctantly.

'Shall we give it another couple of weeks and see if I can get anything better?' he suggested.

'All right, shall we say the end of this month? That will give you ten days to find some work.'

'Right, and it means you will only have to work at Curran's until the end of the year and then you need never go anywhere near that factory ever again.'

Alex frowned when Sharon told her about their plans for the future. 'Does that mean we aren't going to see each other ever again either?'

'No, of course it doesn't. You know where I live so you can come and see me whenever you feel like doing so. I will probably be there on my own most evenings because I am pretty sure that Hadyn will end up working at that gambling place in Bute Street once again, so it will be good to see you.'

'When are you going to tell Betti Lewis and the girls at work that you are leaving?'

'I'm not saying a word. Well, leastwise not until the very last minute. I'll make sure that you are there when I do so that you can see the look on her face.'

'I think you should tell Betti Lewis right now so that she stops asking you to lift anything heavy,' Alex told her.

A week later and Sharon wished she'd taken Alex's advice to heart. They were working flat out to complete a large order before Christmas and Betti Lewis decided that the stone on one of the grinding machines needed changing. As there wasn't a man available it meant that one of the women would have to do it.

'You can do it, Sharon,' she ordered, 'it's about time you came out of your daydreams and put some effort into your work. I've been watching you dawdle all morning.'

As Sharon hesitated Alex quickly stepped in. 'I'll do it,' she volunteered.

'I said Sharon was to do it,' Betti Lewis stated. 'Come on, get a move on,' she ordered, standing by the side of the machine with her arms akimbo waiting for Sharon to come over and replace the grinding stone.

Sharon had difficulty in removing the heavy stone but finally she managed to do it. Holding it close to her body with both arms she stepped back, intending to place it down on the floor. As she did so she stumbled and fell with the huge stone on top of her.

'You clumsy cow,' Betti Lewis yelled. 'You almost dropped that on my toe.'

Alex and two of the other women rushed to help and struggled to move the heavy stone off from Sharon's stomach.

'You're all right now, cariad. Can you sit up?' Alex murmured encouragingly.

271

When Sharon made no effort to do so, Alex bent over her and then, straightening up, said in alarm, 'Can someone get some help? She's unconscious and she's expecting a baby.'

'Since when? She's never mentioned anything about it to me. How far gone is she?' Betti Lewis blustered, pushing to one side the other women who had crowded around.

'Five, possibly six months,' Alex told her. 'She needs to go to hospital.'

Commotion followed. Betti Lewis sent one of the women in search of the floor manager to let him know what had happened and to ask his permission for them to send for an ambulance.

By the time the ambulance arrived Sharon was fully conscious but in such considerable pain that she was unable to sit up. Alex had laid a couple of sheets of corrugated cardboard, which they used as final packing material when dispatching goods overseas, on to the floor for her to lie on and stayed at her side trying to comfort her.

'Will you let Hadyn know what has happened?' Sharon begged, clutching at Alex's hand as she was lifted on to the stretcher ready to be taken to hospital.

'Of course I will, but you are going to be all right, so don't worry. I'll come to the hospital to see you later on after I've finished work,' Alex promised.

It was three days, however, before they would let Alex in to see her. Until then she had to be satisfied with the reports Hadyn gave her each day after he'd been into the hospital. She was saddened to learn that Sharon had lost the baby she'd been expecting.

It was another week before Sharon was well enough to come home. She looked extremely pale and was very listless and she was also depressed. Even so, she had insisted that she wanted to spend Christmas at home.

Hadyn was there to collect her in a taxi when she was discharged from the hospital but, once they reached Clwyd Court, he explained that he would have to go to work that evening and would she be all right if he left her with Karmu?

'Of course I will be. I must be all right, or they wouldn't have sent me home.'

'That's the spirit, cariad.' Karmu smiled. 'It's all over now and, who knows, with any luck, by this time next year there might be another baby on the way.'

'No.' Sharon shook her head emphatically. 'There will never be another baby.'

'Never! That's a long time, my lovely!' Karmu gave a deep laugh. 'At the moment you might think you don't want to go through all that again but in next to no time you will have forgotten and be longing to have a baby in your arms.'

'Please!' Sharon held up a hand to silence the older woman. 'They told me at the hospital that the internal injuries caused by that big grinding stone falling on me were so serious that I can never have another child. Now, I never want to speak about it again. Do you understand?'

Karmu looked shocked. 'I'm so sorry to hear that, cariad; such a terrible thing to happen. What you need right now is a good strong brew. Sit down and make yourself as comfortable as you can while I put the kettle on.'

'No!' Sharon shook her head. 'What I need right now is to be on my own. I'm going up to my room to lie down and, if possible, have a sleep,' she added wearily.

'Would you like me to bring you up a cup of tea?' Karmu asked solicitously.

'I've already said, I want to be on my own. I don't want to listen to your platitudes or to have to answer any more questions,' Sharon said turning away.

It was the beginning of the end of the close friendship she had known with Karmu. On New Year's Eve she even refused to go down and welcome in the New Year with Karmu, even though Hadyn begged her to do so before he went off out to work.

'It's a very special occasion, cariad, because 1930 is going to be a new start for us in every way. I only wish I could be here with you but, as you know, it is one of the busiest nights of the year for clubs and pubs so I must go to work.'

'A new start?' Sharon gave a sad laugh. 'It was going to be a wonderful year. We were having a baby to replace little Morgan but now there is no baby to look forward to and there never will be. How can you expect me to celebrate knowing that?'

'I know you are heartbroken, cariad, so am I,' Hadyn murmured, taking her in his arms and stroking her hair. 'Be brave, my lovely,' he added kissing her on the brow. 'The New Year is the time for starting afresh and forgetting all that has happened in the past. Next year will be good, I promise you. Now I must go or I shall be starting 1930 out of work again,' he added with a forced laugh as he released her.

For several weeks into the new year Sharon didn't want any company other than her own and Hadyn's. She refused to see Alex so many times that in the end Alex stopped calling.

Hadyn tried to reason with her but, although she never argued with him, she took no notice of what he said. She didn't even ask him if he still had the same job. She simply took it for granted that since they hadn't been asked to move out of Clwyd Court he was paying the rent each week to Karmu.

Most of the time she simply lay on the bed in a semi-darkened room staring unseeingly at the ceiling until she fell into a doze or, sometimes, a deep slumber.

Hadyn took care of himself and made meals for her when he was at home. Half the time she wasn't aware whether he was there or out working nor realise that it was usually after midnight when he came home.

At first Hadyn tried to persuade her to take an interest in what was going on.

'Karmu keeps asking after you. Why don't you get up and get dressed and go downstairs and have a chat with her like you used to do?' he urged.

'I don't want to see her or talk to her or to anyone else except you,' she told him.

He did his best to comfort her but she was so apathetic that after a time he even stopped trying to do that. He'd done all he could and he had his own life to live, he told himself.

Since Sharon seemed to have no interest in what he was doing, he had gone back to working at one of the gambling clubs owned by Geraint Humphreys.

At first there had been a decided awkwardness between them and Hadyn wondered why this was but he thought that it was best not to stir up trouble by asking.

It wasn't long before Glenda Roberts enlightened him and said that Geraint Humphreys was annoyed because of Sharon's refusal to accede to his demands to entertain customers when she'd been working at his other club, The Secret Retreat.

Hadyn waited for Geraint Humphreys to say something but since the matter was never openly broached he thought it was best to say nothing.

Life at home was still difficult because Sharon was so depressed and seemed to be unwilling to get back into the real world but he was now enjoying his life. He found it was stimulating being back in the swing of things in the gambling world once again. He'd had one or two profitable wins on the side so he didn't want to stir up any unpleasantness that might result in him losing his job; not now when he'd made contact with so many of his old cronies.

Chapter Twenty-Six

As spring advanced and the days gradually became brighter and longer Sharon stirred out of her apathy and began to take an interest in what was going on around her.

Although she was once again on friendly terms with Karmu there was a distinct change in their relationship. She no longer spent hours sitting in her kitchen drinking tea and gossiping. She even regretted the many hours she had wasted in the past doing this.

Now that Hadyn was home she didn't feel the need for company, even though he went out around seven in the evening and didn't come home again until midnight or even later.

She realised that he was gambling once again and felt strongly enough about it to tell him that he had to stop.

'If I do that, then we will be out on the street quicker than you can snap your fingers,' he told her. 'That's unless you get a job, of course,' he added, raising his eyebrows speculatively.

Sharon appeared to ignore what he said but a couple of days later she started scanning the small advertisements page in the *South Wales Echo*.

'Looking for something?' Hadyn asked when she grabbed the newspaper he was carrying under his arm the moment he came in with the shopping.

'Yes. You told me to get a job, so that is what I am trying to do. I've never had any luck going into shops and asking if they have any vacancies so I thought I would see if I did any better by answering an advertisement in the newspaper,' she told him.

'Depends on what sort of work you are thinking of doing, I would imagine. The ones advertised in the paper are mostly office jobs or ones asking for skilled workers in the building trade.'

'No, there are quite a lot of domestic jobs on offer as well,' Sharon told him.

'You mean cleaning people's houses and that sort of thing?' Hadyn mused, pulling a packet of Woodbines out of his pocket and taking one out.

'That's right. Since I can't get any shop work and I don't want to work in a factory ever again, then being a skivvy is about all that's left for me, isn't it?'

'They usually expect you to wear a uniform and live in, don't they?' he asked, drawing deeply on his cigarette.

'No, you only wear a uniform in the posh places where you are employed as the housemaid or cook or something of that sort. The type of job I'll be expected to do will be as a washerwoman or doing general things like scrubbing and cleaning.'

'Do you want to do that sort of work?' he asked in a puzzled voice.

'No, of course I don't, but if it is the only way to stop you gambling, then that's what I will have to do, isn't it?'

'Oh come on, that's blackmail.' He put his cigarette down in an ashtray that was on the table and

278

pulled her into his arms. 'You'd go that far to stop me gambling?' he asked softly as he tilted her chin so that he was looking directly into her eyes.

'Yes, I'll even go that far,' she whispered as his face came nearer to her own and his lips claimed hers.

'I know you feel strongly about me gambling,' he said resignedly when he released her, 'but there's no need to punish yourself like that. I'm always careful to keep my gambling under control. I'll never run us into debt ever again and at the moment I am on a lucky streak.'

'Lucky streak indeed! How long do you think that will last?' she asked scornfully.

'I've managed to make enough to keep our heads above water ever since you came home from hospital. I promise you I will stop once my luck runs out.'

'Good. I still think it's time I was working again. It might help to take my mind off thinking about little Morgan.'

'Do you have to keep reminding me about that?' Hadyn said contritely. 'I feel guilty enough about it as it is; it's all in the past, so perhaps we should both try and put it behind us,' he added as he picked up his cigarette and once more drew on it heavily, his face grim.

Sharon didn't answer. She turned her attention back to the newspaper, studying the page intently as she ran her finger down the column of small adverts.

'There are one or two that look quite promising,' she said as she marked them with a pencil. 'I'll give this one in Cathedral Road a try and, if that's no good, there is another one in Whitchurch Road that I think looks promising.'

'You do what you like,' Hadyn muttered. 'I'm going to have a kip; it was a long, hard stint last night and it will be the same again tonight, I expect.'

Sharon nodded. She was too busy writing down the two addresses to look up. The sun was shining, it was an invigorating spring day, and suddenly she had the energy to want to go and find some work.

She put on a plain, dark skirt and a white blouse so that she would look neat and tidy and then hoped that her good coat with its fur collar wouldn't make her look overdressed. It was the only one she had so it would have to do. Perhaps if she found some work she would be able to afford to buy some new clothes. Except for her coat, all the rest had that tired, well-worn look about them.

The house in Cathedral Road was more imposing than she had expected. She wondered if there was a back entrance that she ought to use but, taking her courage in both hands, she walked boldly up to the front door and rang the bell.

It was only then that she noticed that there was a brass plate on the door and that it wasn't a private house at all. It was occupied by a company called Isaacs Insurance and she wondered if she had taken down the address correctly.

Before she could make up her mind whether or not she ought to leave it and try the other address in Whitchurch Road, the door was opened by a dapper middle-aged man wearing a pinstripe navy-blue suit, a dark-blue shirt and a light-blue tie. He had receding dark hair and was wearing gold-framed spectacles balanced on his rather prominent nose.

'I ... I've come about your advert in the newspaper for a cleaner,' Sharon stuttered.

'Good, good, come on in. In here,' he added as he opened a door into a cluttered office. 'I'm Mr Isaacs. Sit down, sit down,' he added as he cleared a pile of papers off a chair and balanced them precariously on top of a filing cabinet.

'Now, what is your name? Have you done office cleaning before?' he asked, sitting down at the desk and pulling a blank sheet of paper in front of him.

'My name's–' She hesitated, uncertain whether to say Pritchard or Jenkins, then said, 'Sharon Jenkins.' After all, she told herself, they had been living together long enough for her to call herself that, even if they hadn't got round to making it legally so. 'And no, I have never cleaned offices before,' she added.

'Well, there's nothing very demanding about it. I like my office ready for use by nine o'clock but the other offices should be done first because some of the juniors start at eight o'clock and, of course, there's the outside step to be scrubbed and whitened, but I don't think that needs to be done every day.'

'So does that mean that you want me to start work at seven each morning, Mr Isaacs?' Sharon asked.

'Whatever you think is best. Seven or half past seven. Depends on how quickly you work, doesn't it?'

'I would probably need to start much earlier than seven if the other offices have to be cleaned and ready by eight,' Sharon pointed out.

He nodded. 'Whatever you think is best. When you've finished the cleaning each morning you'll be expected to make tea or coffee for all of us. That will be eight cups altogether unless we have any clients here, in which case it may be more. Oh, and you will have to go out and shop for whatever is necessary to do all that and also buy any sandwiches and so on that we might require for our midday snack. Can you manage all that?'

'Yes, I am sure I can. Is there anything else?'

He studied her for a moment over the top of his gold-rimmed glasses before pushing them firmly back into place. 'You'll have a key to get in, so if you find seven o'clock in the morning is too early for you, then you can clean the offices in the evening. That would mean you wouldn't need to be here until ten o'clock in the morning, wouldn't it?' he murmured vaguely. 'Any other questions?'

'No, that all sounds fine. Perhaps I can decide which is best when I've had a chance to work here for a little while,' Sharon said rather hesitantly.

'Of course. I don't really mind when you do the work as long as it is done. Now let's decide on hours and pay.'

'Will it be Monday to Saturday?' Sharon asked.

'Of course! Let's say five hours each day and you can decide when you work them as long as we have our morning coffee on time, and you collect sandwiches or whatever else we need each morning,' he said a trifle tetchily. 'That's thirty hours a

282

week. So shall we say fifteen shillings a week?'

Sharon drew in her breath sharply. She could hardly believe her good luck. Not only did she have a job but the pay was also far higher than she had dreamed it would be. What was more, the hours were flexible. She could more or less work to suit herself and, with Hadyn out most evenings, then it might well be better for her to work in the evenings than in the early mornings.

'Thank you. When do I start?'

'Tomorrow?' He looked round the office. 'The place is a shambles as you can see, so the sooner you can start the better.'

'Very well, if you show me where all the cleaning materials are kept and where I will have to make the tea, then I'll be here tomorrow at seven in the morning,' Sharon told him.

'Good.' He handed her a key and then led the way down the passageway to the back of the house and into what had obviously once been the main kitchen.

'This is where you make the tea and coffee,' he said looking around the room with a slight frown of disgust. 'It's a bit of a mess; perhaps one of your first tasks should be to clean it up before we all end up with food poisoning.'

'Very well. I'll do that now, if you like,' she offered.

'Are you sure?' He looked at her with raised eyebrows as she removed her coat and hung it up behind the door.

'It will make things a lot easier for me tomorrow morning,' she told him briskly. 'I'll need all the time I have to get the offices into some sort of order, I expect.'

He nodded as if in full agreement. 'Right, then I'll leave you to get on with it.'

Sharon wrapped a kitchen towel around her waist to protect her skirt and spent the next couple of hours throwing out scraps of stale food and sour milk, scrubbing out the cupboards, washing up the stacks of dirty cups and saucers and generally restoring order to the place.

Mr Isaacs came back just as she was finishing and his look of astonishment as he looked around the kitchen gave her an inner glow of satisfaction.

When she told Hadyn about it later that day he shook his head in disbelief that not only had she found work so quickly but also that she was being paid so much for doing such a menial job.

'It must be your lucky day,' he laughed, then his face straightened as he added in a more serious tone, 'but you don't believe in luck, do you?'

'Well, there's luck and luck,' she quipped. 'I don't believe in chancing your luck by putting your last penny on some sort of gamble in the hope that it will pay off.'

'You took a gamble by going to that place in Cathedral Road first instead of to the house in Whitchurch Road and it has paid off, now hasn't it?'

'We'd better wait and see, hadn't we? Mr Isaacs might sack me at the end of the week.'

'Not him! He knows a good bargain when he sees one, the same as I do,' Hadyn laughed as he pulled her into his arms. 'Would you like me to go and get some fish and chips to celebrate tonight and then when you get your first week's wages we'll have a real night out and I'll take you dancing.'

'I'd love some fish and chips but only if you have some money to pay for them. All I have in my purse is two shillings and I'll need that for tram fares for the rest of the week. I don't fancy walking all the way to Cathedral Road when I have to be there by seven o'clock in the morning.'

It took Sharon a week to establish a routine that suited her. There were five rooms in the house that were used as offices as well as the big kitchen where she made the coffee. The kitchen was also used by some of the other men who worked there as somewhere to sit and eat their midday sand-wiches.

She found out from talking to them that, in the past, they had merely rinsed out their dirty cups so that they could use them again and didn't attempt to clear up after themselves. Now, find-ing the place was being kept neat and clean, they even asked what they should do if they used cups later in the day.

'Stack your dirty cups and plates by the sink and I will wash them up, but I am not going look-ing for them,' she told them. 'If you want me to collect anything from the shops for you, then write out a list and give me the money and I will do it, otherwise you will have to go out and get it yourself.'

She made similar rules regarding how she would clean the offices.

'If your desks are littered with papers then I won't attempt to dust or polish them,' she told the clerks. 'If you keep the desktops all neat and

285

tidy, then I'll give them a shine you'll be able to see your faces in.'

In next to no time she found that they were all cooperating and not only did it make her work easier but it also made the whole place look smarter.

She established her own routine by cleaning the offices at night so that she was at home in the morning to cook breakfast for Hadyn. Afterwards it was something of a rush to do the shopping and make up sandwiches and take them back to the office.

Hadyn was delighted by it all. The only problem was that he kept back more and more of his own wages because he didn't think she needed the money now that she was earning.

'That's not fair,' she told him heatedly when, for the third week in succession, he had only given her enough to pay the rent. 'I need my money for new clothes and that's why I went out to work, so that I could buy some.'

'You don't need to be dressed up to go charring,' he told her sarcastically.

'That's true,' she agreed, 'but I do need some new clothes for when you take me out and from now on, since it is summer, I want us to go out and enjoy ourselves more.'

'All right, then here's the deal,' he told her. 'I'll take care of the rent and I'll take you out at least once a week, and you buy the food and anything else we need.'

'We can give it a try,' Sharon agreed, although inwardly she felt that Hadyn was getting the better deal.

At the end of the month, Mr Isaacs called her into his office to tell her that he was well satisfied and informed her that from now on there would be an extra half a crown a week in her pay packet.

Sharon was delighted and couldn't wait to tell Hadyn. Then, on the tram coming home, she had second thoughts. Perhaps it would be better not to tell him, she decided. More than anything else she wanted to start looking for somewhere else to live because she thought it was high time they moved away from Tiger Bay.

Instead of telling Hadyn about the increase in her wages she would put the extra half a crown aside each week so that she had a little nest egg that he knew nothing about. Then, if she could find somewhere better for them to live, she would be able to pay the rent in advance and give him a wonderful surprise by telling him they were moving from Clwyd Court.

Chapter Twenty-Seven

Sharon found she was enjoying her new job far more than she had expected. Mr Isaacs was easy to work for and the other men who worked there were equally accommodating and appreciative of what she did for them.

Just before Christmas Mr Isaacs gave her an extra ten pounds as a present and the rest of the staff all clubbed together and bought her a matching scarf and gloves set as a way of expressing their thanks for the many changes she had made since she'd been working there.

She was very tempted to tell Hadyn about the generous bonus but in the end decided it would be better to put it away to swell her funds for the future.

As well as saving the half-crown increase Mr Isaacs had given her she had also managed to save an extra shilling or two each week so that, along with her bonus, her nest egg now amounted to a very healthy sum of almost fifteen pounds.

She was glad that she had said nothing to Hadyn or to Karmu. Once the Christmas holidays were over, though, she would tell Hadyn about it and then they could start looking for somewhere else to live, she promised herself.

Christmas week, however, brought unexpected problems. Karmu tackled her about the overdue rent.

'The pair of you are working, so you ought to be able to pay me what is owed and I'd like you to do it before the end of the month so that we can start the new year with a clean slate,' Karmu told her a couple of days before Christmas.

'Surely we don't owe you any rent,' Sharon challenged 'Hadyn has taken care of it each week.'

'He might have told you that, but he hasn't paid me a penny piece for the last six weeks and I simply can't afford to wait for it any longer,' Karmu told her emphatically.

'Six weeks? Are you saying that our rent hasn't been paid for the last six weeks!' Sharon exclaimed in disbelief.

'That's right.' Karmu squared her broad shoulders as if defending every word she said.

'Why on earth didn't you say something about it earlier?' Sharon asked in dismay.

'I've mentioned it often enough to Hadyn. I've not said anything to you because, if you remember when you started work, you said that he would be the one paying me each week,' Karmu stated.

'Yes, I did say that,' Sharon admitted, 'and I thought he was doing so. I am very sorry about this, Karmu. Give me a day or two to talk to Hadyn and find out how this has happened. Don't worry about it. I'll sort things out and will let you have every penny that is owing to you.'

'Not much good talking to him,' Karmu sniffed. 'He says he's had a run of bad luck and is stony broke, but then I suppose you know all about that.'

'As I said, leave it with me for a couple of days and I'll sort it out,' Sharon promised.

Although Sharon managed to keep a smile on her face as she spoke to Karmu, inwardly she was fuming. She hadn't known that Hadyn had any money problems and she didn't like being told about them by Karmu rather than by Hadyn himself.

The moment he came in from work that evening, before he had time to take off his coat and hang it up, Sharon tackled him about the overdue rent and demanded to know why it was that Karmu had not been paid.

'I was afraid you would find out before I had a chance to settle up with her,' he muttered as he sat down on a chair and began unlacing his shoes.

'So you had no intention of telling me?' she railed. 'How do you think I felt about being informed by Karmu that we owed her six weeks' rent and that you couldn't pay her because you'd been betting and were on a losing streak?'

'I told her I'd square up with her as soon as I could,' he defended, pulling out a packet of Woodbines and then taking one out and lighting it up.

'Yes, but you didn't tell her when that was likely to be, now did you? She relies on our rent to buy her food and so on, so it's unfair to keep her waiting.'

Hadyn drew deeply on his cigarette before answering and when finally he looked across at her Sharon was shocked to see the abject misery in his face.

'I couldn't give her a firm date because I don't know when I will be able to give her the money,' he admitted. 'As Karmu has already told you, I've had a run of bad luck lately. She's not the only one I owe money to and the others are getting pretty impatient about it, the same as she is.'

Sharon's heart sank. She'd been feeling so happy, so convinced that the bad times were over and that the future was bright and full of promise and now it seemed everything was back to where it had been before.

'I don't understand. What exactly do you mean by a run of bad luck? Why have you kept me in the dark about it?' she demanded angrily.

'I didn't want to worry you, cariad,' Hadyn said apologetically. 'They're threatening what they'll do to me if I don't pay up but I haven't any money so there's nothing I can do.'

'Does that mean that you have lost money because you have been gambling?'

'Yes,' Hadyn admitted, avoiding her eyes as he stubbed out his cigarette.

'After you promised that you would stop the moment you started to lose?' she accused.

He dropped his head into his hands in a gesture of despair. 'I know, I know. Not only did I promise you but I vowed to myself that I would stop the moment I started losing and, believe me, I meant every word of it.'

'So what happened? Why didn't you?'

'I had a small loss but I thought if I had just one more bet and won then I would be able to clear it. It didn't work, though, and I tried again and lost. Three times lucky, I thought, and had an even bigger bet and when I lost that I just went on and on hoping the next one would be a win even though I knew I was getting deeper and deeper into the mire each time.'

'So the people who are after you are the ones who let you go on betting, even though they knew that you were losing each time?'

Hadyn nodded, running his hand through his hair in a despairing gesture.

'Well, in that case it serves them right and, in my opinion, they deserve to lose every penny of the money you owe them,' Sharon told him heatedly.

Hadyn shook his head. 'Cariad, it doesn't work like that. I owe them and they are insisting on being paid and somehow or other I have to find the money.'

Sharon was silent for a moment. She needed to know how much was involved but Hadyn appeared to be so worried that she was afraid to ask.

'You know what will happen if you don't pay

291

them back whatever it is you owe them. They'll make a few threats but it's probably all bluster,' she said at last.

He shrugged his shoulders. 'It'll be more than that. I'm scared, Sharon. You don't know what they're really like. They've threatened to break my arms and legs, slash me with a razor, even burn my face with their cigarette butts.'

'They wouldn't dare do any of those things, would they?' Sharon said worriedly.

'Don't you believe it. They're a tough gang. I wish to heaven I'd never got mixed up with them.'

'Then why do you keep going back there to work each day? Surely you could try and get a job somewhere else.'

'I will as soon as I have paid them off. If I leave now they will hunt me down. If they can't find me then they'll turn on you; they've already threatened to do that if I don't pay up what I owe them.'

'So it means that if you pay off this money they'll leave us alone and you will be free to leave and find some work elsewhere?'

'Yes,' he nodded, 'but how can I do that when I owe them so much? They've been keeping back the bulk of my wages each week as it is, and that's why I've not had enough to be able to pay the rent here to Karmu.'

Sharon walked across the room, turned on the gas ring and placed the kettle over it to give herself time to think. She still didn't know how much money Hadyn owed but by what he said she was pretty sure it would take every penny she had saved up, if not more, to clear his debts.

If she paid off the money and cleared his debt

would he really stop betting or would they be back in the same pickle in another few months' time?

As she spooned some tea into the pot and poured boiling water over it Sharon tried to make up her mind whether or not she ought to help Hadyn. And what if they really did come for him? Could she really leave him to their mercy?

She still loved him with all her heart, she reflected, but she didn't want to go on struggling to exist for the rest of her life. She had a decent job herself now and she was sure she could find somewhere else to live and manage on her own if she had to. But did she want to do that?

If she was on her own, would her family take her back? she wondered. Meeting Gwen and seeing how nicely dressed and happy she looked and hearing how well set up she and Parry were had made her dissatisfied with what was happening in her own life because of the shambles it had become.

If she left Hadyn and decided to go back home and admitted she had made a mistake in defying her father, then it would mean eating humble pie. Even that, she reasoned, couldn't be worse than living in fear of every knock on the door in case it was one of the men Hadyn talked about, coming to take revenge.

As she poured out their tea and passed a cup to Hadyn, their hands touched and she felt the old thrill run through her. What on earth was she thinking of? she asked herself. She couldn't live without Hadyn. Their life together had been traumatic right from the very start but that had knitted them so close together that now they were inseparable.

'I'll take care of the rent we owe Karmu with the Christmas bonus I was given by Mr Isaacs,' she said quietly.

'You never mentioned you'd had a bonus.' Hadyn's green eyes widened in surprise.

'No, I was going to spend some of it on extras for us for Christmas and then put the rest towards moving away from this place,' she told him.

'A new year and a fresh start – well, we could certainly do with that,' he muttered.

'Yes, but it doesn't look as though that's going to be possible, does it?' she said sadly.

'No, not unless you can pay off the other money I owe. Let's think about it before you hand over any money to Karmu,' he said quickly. 'If you paid off my gambling debts and there was enough left for rent for a new place, then we could scarper and not bother about paying the rent we owe here.'

'You mean you'd cheat a poor old woman out of the money that is due to her but pay those sharks who helped you to run up debts by gambling?'

'I know it sounds pretty ruthless but it's a question of survival,' Hadyn explained. 'Make no mistake; they'll have their revenge if they're not paid. Karmu will grumble about the way we treat her but she won't try to kill us, now will she?'

'Perhaps not but it's still pretty despicable to defraud her like that, especially when she has always been so good to us ever since we moved in here.'

'I know, but it's a question of our survival,'

294

Hadyn reminded her again grimly.

Sharon finished drinking her tea in thoughtful silence. As she collected up their cups she asked, 'Exactly how much do you owe, Hadyn?'

'Fifteen pounds.' The words hung on the air and when she said nothing he added, 'It was a lot more but I have been paying off every penny I could over the last month or so.'

'Are you still betting?'

'Duw anwyl! Are you listening to what I'm telling you?' he said angrily. 'I've been trying to pay off my debts, not add to them. I haven't put on a bet for ages.'

'Would that be because they won't give you any more credit?' Sharon asked dryly.

'No, it's because I know what a fool I've been and that I should have listened to you,' he said humbly.

Sharon tightened her lips. She'd heard his apologies and assurances so many times before that they had ceased to have any real meaning. 'Why should I bother to bail you out when we are not even married? All these years together and I've stood by you through thick and thin and yet you've never put a ring on my finger.'

'Married? I never thought you wanted us to be married,' he said in a bewildered voice. 'Of course I'll marry you; I can't live without you.' He took her hand. 'No more betting for me ever again and I promise you that this time I really mean it. I swear to you that once I have paid off my gambling debts I'm getting right away from Geraint Humphreys and his cronies.'

Geraint Humphreys' name sent a shiver through

Sharon as she pulled her hand away. 'I didn't know he was the one you were involved with,' she said in an uneasy voice.

'Yes, he's a nasty piece of work, but then you know all about that, don't you?'

She nodded emphatically. His name made her decide what she must do.

It was imperative that she help Hadyn to clear his debts as speedily as possible, even though it would take all of her savings to do so and would mean abandoning her dreams of getting away from Tiger Bay.

She didn't want to hand over her nest egg and certainly not to a man like him, but she realised that when Hadyn talked about the threats that had been made it was not idle speculation. She was sure that they were very real and suddenly she felt fearful not only for his life but also for her own.

Keeping her nest egg intact or even having to give up all hope of moving away from Clwyd Court seemed a small price to pay in return for freedom from worrying about such possibilities.

Hadyn waited with bated breath for Sharon's decision. He'd suspected that she had received a Christmas bonus and had been waiting for her to mention it. When she didn't, he felt forced to make her do so.

He had not exactly lied when he said that he hadn't been able to give Karmu their rent because of his debts. He had needed the money that should have paid the rent to gamble in the hopes of winning and paying her and the rest of his debts all in one go before the end of the year.

He had also meant it when he said he wanted to start the coming year debt-free but he wasn't at all certain whether or not he would keep to his other promise of not betting ever again.

Sharon didn't seem to understand his need to gamble. When he was on a winning streak the whole world was his oyster. As he pocketed his winnings he let his imagination about plans for his future and hers widen.

Moving away from Tiger Bay was most certainly top of his list. Equally high on the changes he wanted to make was to own his own club. He knew exactly how it would be run. It would be better than all Geraint Humphreys' enterprises put together.

He wasn't sure that Sharon would approve of this idea but once they were married, if he could persuade her to cooperate, then between them they could create an empire that would take not only Cardiff but also the whole world by storm.

All he needed was the capital to get started and in no time at all he would rule Bute Street and attain far more power than Geraint Humphreys had ever dreamed of having.

After that he would expand countrywide. Newport, Barry and then London, Birmingham, Bristol, Manchester and Liverpool. One day there might even be one of his clubs or casinos in Las Vegas.

For the moment, though, he'd have to be satisfied if Sharon paid off his current gambling debts and he no longer had to look over his shoulder whenever he was walking down the road and heard footsteps behind him.

He hoped there would be enough left to cover the rent that they owed to Karmu. He hated living at Clwyd Court but at least it was a roof over their heads.

Chapter Twenty-Eight

Sharon found that handing over every penny of her precious savings to Hadyn, knowing that he would be using them to pay off Geraint Humphreys, was so agonising that she almost changed her mind at the last minute. It was only the fear of what might happen if she didn't that convinced her that she must do it. She also hoped that if she kept her side of the bargain, then Hadyn would keep his promise and marry her.

She'd had so many dreams about them finally leaving such a notorious area as Tiger Bay and moving to somewhere more respectable like Cathays or Canton or even Grangetown.

Now that all her plans had gone awry she didn't want to think about the future. She wouldn't even be able to start saving again unless Hadyn found himself a new job. Until he managed to do that it would take every penny of what she earned for them to keep their heads above water.

First and foremost, though, she was determined that, by some means or other, she would pay Karmu her rent regularly each week even if it meant that they had to go hungry to do so. She also resolved to try and get her friendship with Karmu back on its old level.

She knew the fault was hers and that she was the one who had caused the rift and she was sorry about that now because she felt very lonely. She rarely spoke to anyone else in Clwyd Court except to pass the time of day and she missed the cosy chats she'd had with Karmu a great deal.

When she handed over the money to Hadyn she begged him to come straight back home as soon as he'd delivered it.

'What's the matter, don't you trust me?' he asked, his voice tinged with bitterness.

'Of course I do,' she assured him, 'it's just that I'll be on edge until I know you've done it and we're safe.'

On his return the look of relief on his face and his words of gratitude as he hugged her went some way to recompensing her for the sacrifice she'd made.

'I hope that's the very last we ever hear or see of Geraint Humphreys,' she told him.

'So do I,' he agreed. 'I've learned my lesson. No more gambling for me, I promise you. Tomorrow I'll be out looking for work and it will be as far away from Bute Street as possible.'

Hadyn discovered that finding a new job seemed to be impossible. The depression that still held the whole country in its grip meant that more and more men were on the dole. Eventually, in late February, he managed to get taken on by a delivery company called Davis's Deliveries as a temporary co-driver.

'That's wonderful, but how on earth did you

manage it? You've never driven a car, have you?' Sharon exclaimed in astonishment when he came home and told her.

'Of course I can drive. Most men can, it comes naturally,' he told her loftily.

'You didn't have a car when you were a representative carrying wallpaper and carpet samples from shop to shop.'

'No one did in those days except the sales manager who went round checking up on you and making sure that you were doing a good job and keeping your customers happy. These days, more and more commercial travellers have cars or vans and they can do a better job because they can carry far more sample books than I ever could.' He sighed.

'So does that mean you can still drive a car or van?' Sharon pressed.

'Duw anwyl! Once you know how to drive that's all there is to it.' Hadyn laughed. 'I'll soon get back into the swing of things, don't you worry. Anyway, as the co-driver, I will probably be expected to do most of the deliveries and the other chap, Bryn Dutton, will simply sit there in the cab while I do it.'

'So if it all works out, then, with both of us working again, perhaps 1931 is going to be a good year for us after all,' Sharon said tentatively.

'You mean we will be able to pay the rent regularly from now on without you having to pawn your best coat and your bits of jewellery like you've had to do recently,' Hadyn agreed. 'It breaks my heart when I've seen you having to do that these last few weeks, cariad,' he added softly.

'There are plenty of other people in the same boat because poverty seems to be everywhere,' Sharon sighed. 'I sometimes wonder what the world is coming to.'

'I know,' Hadyn agreed. 'Standing in one of those long queues outside the dole office each week I hear the others talking about all the hunger marches that are taking place all over the country. Even women are banding together and marching in Hyde Park in London and I understand they're carrying banners with "Fighting for Bread and Beans" written on them.'

Sharon nodded. 'I overheard Mr Isaacs saying the other day that a man called Sir Oswald Mosley has been trying to form some sort of new political party, though what good that will do, I don't know. He's been attracting huge crowds in London so that will probably stir up even more unrest.'

'Yes, the country is in a terrible state,' Hadyn agreed. 'All the hard-luck stories I heard from the men in the dole queue over the last few weeks makes me more than thankful to have landed a job, I can tell you.'

All through the spring they felt grateful that they were so well off. Sharon was relieved that Hadyn no longer seemed to be interested in betting or going to the club in Bute Street that had been the root of so much trouble for them.

Hadyn started work at seven o'clock each morning, so once again Sharon decided to change the hours she worked to fit in with his. Instead of cleaning the offices in the evening, she now did them in the morning. It meant that she was finished work and was back home again by early afternoon.

Gradually the old habit of dropping in for a cuppa and a chat with Karmu started up again. By early summer not only had their life fallen into an established pattern but also Sharon's precious savings were mounting up once more and she was feeling extremely happy and contented.

Hadyn, too, was more settled. His co-driver, Bryn Dutton, occasionally let him take the wheel and this gave Hadyn a great deal of satisfaction, as he found that he loved driving.

The blow when it came was so unexpected that Sharon couldn't believe what had happened. It was a bright summer's day when she turned up at Cathedral Road at her usual time of seven o'clock only to find that there was a notice pinned on to the front door to say that the business was closed down.

At first she thought it must be some kind of mistake but when she tried to open the front door she found that she was unable to do so because her key wouldn't turn and she realised that the locks had been changed.

It took her over a week to find out what had happened and when she did, it was to learn that Isaacs Insurance was no more. Mr Isaacs had gone bankrupt.

'Another victim of this damned recession,' Hadyn commented when she told him what she had found out. 'Bryn Dutton was saying that apparently things aren't going at all well in our firm either,' he added gloomily.

Although she tried to find some other kind of work Sharon found it was impossible. They lived in such cramped conditions and there was so little to do that she began spending more and more of her time sitting in Karmu's kitchen drinking endless cups of tea.

Even so the days dragged and as she was forced to dip into her meagre savings more and more she became increasingly concerned.

Another thing that worried her was that Hadyn was frequently bringing home odd items. They were very varied and there was no pattern to them. It could be anything from a bag of oranges or apples to a small ornament or sometimes kitchen items like a frying pan or a pudding basin.

If they weren't edible, then he'd suggest that if she didn't have any use for them she should take them along to the pawnbroker's and see if he would give her a bob or two for them.

Because they were so hard up she usually did as Hadyn suggested but it always made her feel uneasy. Deep down she didn't believe what he said about them having been left on the van and that they were things no one wanted, and she was worried in case he had come by them dishonestly.

Her own inability to get work worried her and, because she couldn't afford tram fares into the centre of the city or further afield where the big houses were, once again she began looking for work nearer to home. She was so desperate to earn some money that she was willing to take any kind of job she was offered, even if it was only temporary.

Over the next couple of months she did short stints that ranged from being a charwoman and a barmaid, to helping out on an open-air fruit and vegetable stall and even washing up at the hostel for seamen in Bute Street.

When Hadyn found out that she was working there he told her to pack the job in immediately.

'Keep well clear of Bute Street, especially that area near The Secret Retreat,' he warned. 'I don't want you running into any of that lot ever again.'

'I'm only going to be there for a couple of weeks or so while the woman who usually helps them out in the kitchen is away ill with bronchitis,' she told him. 'Anyway,' she pointed out with a smile, 'I'm hardly likely to bump into Geraint Humphreys in the seamen's mission, now am I?'

'No, you mightn't, but you might be seen by one of the girls from The Secret Retreat or someone else who works for him and then they might trace back through you and find me.'

'I thought you'd paid him the money that was owing to him and that you'd finished with him completely,' Sharon said, frowning.

'I paid him and cleared off my debt, but that's not the end of the matter,' he said evasively.

'Why not?'

For a moment Hadyn didn't answer. He pulled out his packet of cigarettes and concentrated on selecting one.

'Men like Geraint Humphreys don't like letting people like me ever get out of their clutches,' he told Sharon after he had lit up and taken a long draw on his cigarette. 'I told him I was taking a boat and leaving the country.'

Sharon looked perplexed. 'Why tell a lie like that?' she asked. 'You're not scared of him, are you?'

'Not of him personally, but it's best not to know some of the others who work for him.'

Sharon tried to get him to explain what he meant but Hadyn remained tight-lipped and it worried her. She had thought that they had both put the past behind them and that their only worry was earning enough money to pay their way. Now she wondered if there was some secret in Hadyn's past which he didn't want her to know about.

The more she thought about it the more agitated she became because memories of some of the things he'd done in the past and which she'd managed to forget about kept going round and round in her mind.

They'd been together now for seven years and yet they had made no progress at all. She looked round their small squalid living room in disgust. Coming to Clwyd Court had been supposed to be a temporary measure so why had they stayed there all this time? She hated the area and, apart from Karmu, she had no one she could confide in and she certainly couldn't talk to her about this.

She walked over to the cupboard and took out the tin in which she kept her savings. She sat down and tipped the contents out on to the table. There were a few silver coins, some coppers and one single pound note. She counted it all up. Altogether there was one pound and fifteen shillings.

It wasn't really enough to start making plans to move but then again, maybe she should do just that. Instead of looking for work perhaps she should find somewhere else for them to live first and then see if she could find a job in that area.

She wondered whether to talk to Hadyn about

her idea but she was pretty sure that he would say they were better off staying where they were so it might be more sensible to find the new place first and then tell him.

If she found a job as well as somewhere better for them to live, then probably it would be fairly easy to persuade him that it was necessary for them to move so that she could be nearer to where she would be working.

Three weeks later, her feet blistered from walking so far each day in the hot July sun, Sharon admitted defeat. There were plenty of rooms available but the landladies all wanted far more rent than they were paying Karmu.

The other thing was that there were no jobs to be found. The depression was biting in deeper and shop takings were down and a great many shop assistants had been laid off. Like her they had lowered their sights and were willing to do absolutely any sort of work they could get. Whenever there was a vacancy, even if it was for a daily cleaner or a char, there was always a long queue of applicants eager to fill it.

Sharon was shocked to see that even in the more respectable areas of Cardiff there were ragged, barefoot children who looked half-starved. She also saw women waiting at the butcher's and baker's at the end of each day hoping to be able to buy any food that might be left, and which wouldn't still be saleable the next day, for a few coppers.

There were a great many unfortunate people as well as them, she reflected, as she made her way home. At least Hadyn had regular work and wasn't standing in a dole queue every week like so many other men were.

Karmu called out to her the moment she went through the door. Smiling and looking forward to the cup of tea that she knew Karmu would have waiting for her Sharon went straight through to Karmu's kitchen.

To her great surprise Karmu was not alone. There was a youngish woman with light brown hair and deep blue eyes sitting in Karmu's armchair. She was nursing a small child wrapped in a black shawl who seemed to be fast asleep.

'You've got a visitor to see you,' Karmu announced, her dark eyes inquisitive.

'I have?' Sharon looked surprised. 'I wasn't expecting anyone, are they coming back?'

Karmu gave one of her deep laughs. 'This is your visitor,' she said, indicating the young woman with a nod of her head. 'Haven't you recognised her?'

Sharon looked again. She had no idea who the girl was and yet there was something faintly familiar about her.

'I'm Wanda West. Don't you remember me from The Secret Retreat?'

A brief image of a slim girl with long shining hair and a bright smile flashed through Sharon's mind but this girl was nothing at all like the Wanda she had known there.

'I saw you there a few times. I stopped working there a long time ago. I had to, because I was pregnant,' Wanda told her. 'I've had a pretty rough time since then,' she added and there was a tinge of bitterness in her voice as she looked down briefly at the child in her arms.

'I'm sorry to hear that,' Sharon said sympathetically. 'Were you hoping that I might be able to help you in some way?'

'Not really.' Wanda sighed. 'It was your Hadyn that I really came to see.'

'Hadyn!' Sharon stared at her in bewilderment. 'How do you know Hadyn?'

'He's the father of my kid, that's how I know him,' Wanda retorted. 'By the sound of things he's never mentioned it to you, so that's probably why I've had such a hard time getting any help from him. Most of the time I've been left to beg on the streets to get enough food for myself and for the little one.'

Sharon clutched at the back of the chair Karmu was sitting in for support. Her head was spinning. She thought Karmu had called her in to have a cup of tea and a gossip. To be faced by this news was like something out of a nightmare.

Taking a deep breath to try and pull herself together she faced Wanda defiantly. 'It's a good story but, do you know, I don't believe one word of it.'

'Then why the hell am I here?' the girl challenged, her blue eyes hardening.

'You've obviously heard Geraint Humphreys mention Hadyn's name because he once worked for him and you thought that he'd be a soft touch and give you a few bob to help you out. I don't blame you for one minute,' she added quickly. 'I know what it's like to be on the bread line and I also know how impossible it is to find work. It must be even worse for you with a small child.'

'Don't talk such rubbish,' Wanda said heatedly. 'This kid is your Hadyn's. Here, take a look.'

Pulling back the black shawl she thrust the child in her arms forward so that Sharon had no option but to look at him.

When she did, her heart thudded so wildly that she felt giddy. The child was lovely, with an appealing round face, firm little nose and a rosebud mouth. What Sharon noticed most of all, though, was the colour of the child's hair; it was dark auburn, exactly the same colour as Hadyn's.

Chapter Twenty-Nine

Sharon couldn't put the image of the child that Wanda had been holding in her arms out of her mind. She felt devastated. She tried to work out when it could have happened; was it since Hadyn came out of prison? she wondered.

They had seemed to be so happy together since then that it must have been before then she reasoned. She tried to decide how old the child was but he had seemed to be so small and so cocooned in the black shawl that she was unable to do so. In fact, she didn't even know if it was a girl or a boy, only that it had a shock of auburn hair that was identical to Hadyn's.

She was on the point of going downstairs to talk to Karmu and see if between them they could throw any light on the matter, when Hadyn came home. She stared at him intently, almost as if he was a stranger, wondering if she knew him at all. When he put his arms round her and attempted to kiss her she stiffened and pulled back abruptly.

'Duw anwyl, what have I done wrong this time?' he asked irritably.

Sharon blinked back the tears that threatened to spill from her eyes and shook her head. There were so many questions bubbling in her mind but she felt too emotional to speak.

'Well, if you don't tell me what's wrong, then I won't know and I can't do anything about it,' Hadyn commented as he unlaced his boots and kicked them off.

'Do you know,' he went on, 'my feet ache more from driving than they do from walking. I think it's because it gets so damn hot in the cab of that van. Now then, tell me what's upset you.' He reached out and took her arm and pulled her towards him. 'Karmu gave me one of her deep black threatening looks as I came in through the hallway so is it a row between the two of you that's upset you?'

'No,' Sharon shook her head, 'it's got nothing to do with Karmu, except that she knows all about it. Wanda West came here while I was out so Karmu asked her in and they were still talking when I came home. You haven't forgotten who Wanda West is, have you?' she asked, her voice trembling.

Hadyn let go her arm and ran his hand through his hair in a worried manner as his brows knit together in a deep frown. 'Wanda? What did she want?'

Sharon tried to tell him but the words wouldn't come. Shaking her head she ran into the bedroom, slamming the door shut, afraid he might follow her.

As she flung herself down on the bed she knew she was being foolish. There was only one way of dealing with the matter and that was to face up to it and that meant asking Hadyn if it was true that the child was his.

As she lay there curled up under the bedspread trying to stop the shivering that convulsed her, she tried to formulate the questions she knew she must ask him. The answer to the one that mattered most rang all too plainly in her ears.

The moment she'd seen the colour of the child's shock of hair she knew that Wanda was telling the truth. What she still didn't know was when it had happened or why.

Pulling herself together she combed her hair and straightened her clothes, determined to face Hadyn and demand the truth no matter how much it might hurt.

When she went back into the living room it was empty and her misery increased. She wondered where he had gone. And in her heart she feared it was to see Wanda.

The hours ticked by and when Hadyn still didn't come home she was beside herself with worry. Had he gone to see Wanda as she had anticipated, or had he simply cleared off for good? She was tempted to go and look for him, but she had no idea where to start.

She lit the gas ring and put the kettle on to boil. She needed a hot drink but when she went to the cupboard where she kept the packet of tea there was none.

There was no money left in her purse so she

311

reached for the tin where she kept their savings. She hated dipping into it except in an emergency but that's what this was, she told herself.

The tin was empty.

Sharon couldn't believe it. She shook the tin vigorously, turned it upside down and banged it, even ran her fingers around inside it, but there was nothing at all in there. Then she sat down and put her head in her hands and sobbed out loud.

It was bad enough that Hadyn had taken their precious savings but the thought of him handing it all over to Wanda was an even bitterer pill because in her mind it proved without any shadow of a doubt that the child was his.

She was still sitting at the table holding the empty tin in her hand when Hadyn returned.

'I had to take the money to help Wanda out,' he said abruptly. 'She's desperate and she needed it to buy food and medicine,' he added.

'Is it Wanda who's sick, or is it the child who needs the medicine?' Sharon asked.

'Wanda is. She's not got long to live. That's why she came here today. She wanted to ask me if we would look after the baby if anything happens to her.'

'Care for her baby!' Sharon's voice rose in a shriek of horror. 'Of course we can't! How could I possibly look after the child you'd had with another woman?'

Hadyn shook his head in a gesture of despair but he said nothing.

'Why did you do it? How old is the child? Is it a boy or a girl? How could you deceive me like this?'

The questions shot out like bullets and she gave him no opportunity to answer them before she asked the next. She felt beside herself with such a mixture of grief and anger that she wanted to vent on him that she felt demented.

'I think we need to sit down quietly and talk this through,' Hadyn told her.

'Talk about it! You've left it a bit late to do that, haven't you? The harm's done. You've got another woman in your life and, what's more, she's given you something that you know I can never give you; she's given you a child. The son we had, yours and mine, died because of your carelessness. Why did you get my child killed and not hers? Answer me that.'

Even though she tried to resist him, beating him off with her clenched fists, Hadyn refused to let her push him away. With his arm tightly round her shoulders he pulled her into his chest, stroking the back of her head to try and calm her.

When eventually she stopped shaking he sat down in the armchair and pulled her on to his lap. 'Let me try and explain,' he said gently.

'No! I can't bear to talk about it.' Sharon shuddered, putting her hands over her ears.

Hadyn moved her hands away. 'It started a long time ago; before I went to prison, in fact. What happened with Wanda was simply a fling. I know what I did was wrong, cariad, but you had so little time for me.' He sighed.

As Sharon was about to protest he raised a hand to silence her. 'Let me finish. I know I had no excuse and I've regretted it ever since. When you went to work at The Secret Retreat I was afraid you would find out about it either from Geraint Humphreys or Glenda Roberts. That was why I warned you to be careful of both of them. It was because I didn't want you to become too friendly with any of them there, especially with Glenda, in case she told you.'

'Why did you have to keep it from me all this time?' Sharon whispered.

'It was my problem, not yours, and I didn't want you to be upset by what had happened.' He sighed. 'I have tried to support Wanda by giving her as much money as I could whenever I've had a decent win to try and help her out.'

'So why has she come here now wanting me to help look after her child?'

'I think she was looking for me, not you, because she is so worried about what will happen to him now that she knows how desperately ill she is,' Hadyn explained. 'I think we must expect her to come back here again asking for our help now that she knows where I live,' he warned.

'No, no! I can't bear that. I don't want to see her or the child ever again.'

'I understand,' Hadyn said quickly, 'but obviously there is some urgent reason why she's so anxious to find me. After all,' he added with a grim smile, 'she's never troubled us before, now has she? Perhaps the best thing I can do is go and see her and find out exactly what she has been told by the doctor.'

Sharon bit her lip then nodded in agreement, although it wasn't really what she wanted. She didn't like the idea of Hadyn meeting up with Wanda but, most of all, she couldn't bear the thought of him being with the child especially now that she knew it was a little boy. It brought back too many painful memories that she had managed to push to the back of her mind.

For the next week or so she found herself looking anxiously at the clock if Hadyn was a few minutes late coming home from work and worrying in case he'd gone to visit Wanda again.

Common sense told her that Hadyn didn't need to wait until after he had finished work to visit Wanda; there were probably plenty of opportunities during the day when he could do so. Whenever he was out driving one of the vans, or even in his lunch beak, he could go and see her.

As the weeks passed she waited for him to say something, to tell her he had been to see Wanda and why she had started pestering them, but he said nothing and so she thought it was best not to raise the subject.

It was like living on a knife edge. Every time she came home from one of her part-time jobs she dreaded that Karmu might say that the woman with the baby had called again.

The visit, when it finally came, was not from Wanda but from Geraint Humphreys.

She was laying the table for their evening meal when she heard a man's step on the stairs and thought it was Hadyn. When the door was pushed open and Geraint Humphreys barged into the room she was so taken aback that she couldn't speak.

To Sharon's relief Hadyn arrived hot on Geraint Humphrey's heels before he even had a chance to speak to her.

'What's going on?' Hadyn frowned as he looked from one to the other of them.

'This is what's going on.' Geraint Humphreys tossed a bundle he was carrying at Hadyn.

'What's this?' Hadyn asked as he caught the bundle and saw that it was a pile of children's clothes.

'It's your kid's clothes,' Geraint Humphreys told him. 'His name is Martyn, by the way, and he'll be three years old next month. As his father, you probably know that already without me telling you,' he added in a sneering tone.

'Hold on,' Hadyn said in alarm. 'He's not with us, so who told you to dump all his stuff here. Was it Wanda?'

'Wanda couldn't care less about him now and there's no one else to look after him. He's your kid, so it's up to you to do so. Either that or put him in a home.'

'What do you mean? Is she too ill to care for him any more?'

'Wanda's dead. She died last night. She's had TB for the last six months. I've left the kid out in the car asleep, so one of you'd better come out and get him – that's if you are going to have him, otherwise I'll have to take him to a home because he can't stay at the club.'

Geraint Humphreys' harsh tone sent a shiver through Sharon. She watched in silence as the two men went out of the room and tried to pull herself together and get to grips with what was happening.

When they returned, Hadyn was carrying the

316

child who was still wrapped in the enveloping black shawl. It was the same one Wanda had been carrying him in when she'd called there only a few weeks earlier.

As he pulled back a corner of the shawl and the child's little round face was revealed with its shock of auburn hair, Sharon caught her breath. It was like looking at a replica of little Morgan and she felt tears of compassion welling up as she thought what a dreadful life the child had known.

Freed of the encumbering shawl the little boy stirred, rubbed the sleep from his eyes and started to wriggle free. Hadyn put him down on the floor where he stood swaying unsteadily almost as if his little legs were too thin to hold him upright.

'Is it true that he will be three years old next month?' Sharon asked in disbelief.

'Yes, that's right,' Geraint Humphreys affirmed. 'Small and weedy for his age, I know.'

Sharon stared at the child, then she went down on her knees and opened her arms to him. The child hesitated for a minute but when she spoke his name very softly he tottered towards her and she hugged him close.

Geraint Humphreys watched for a moment in silence. Then he demanded, 'Does this mean that you'll look after him and give him a home?'

'Yes, of course we will,' Sharon said quickly before Hadyn could reply.

'I can assure you that it will be a much better one than he appears to have had up until now,' she added bitingly, as Geraint Humphreys rubbed his hands together in satisfaction and prepared to leave.

317

There was silence for a moment after he left the room. Then Hadyn said, 'You don't have to do this, you know. I do understand how you must be feeling and I always hoped that you would never find out about Martyn.'

'Do you mean you'd rather put him in a home than have him living here with us?'

'Of course not but I would be prepared to do that if it was necessary rather than lose you or make your life miserable,' Hadyn said quietly.

Sharon looked down at the child she was cuddling and shook her head. 'This child didn't ask to be born and it's your responsibility to try and make up to him for the awful life he has had up until now.'

As the child looked up and gave her a little smile and then snuggled closer into her arms, Sharon said quietly, 'I think little Martyn needs a bowl of bread and milk before we tuck him up in bed, so would you go and make it for him?'

Chapter Thirty

Sharon found that having Martyn to live with them brought tremendous changes to both their lives. She was no longer able to go out to work which meant budgeting ever more tightly. In addition, having a small child meant so much extra washing to do and in their already cramped accommodation she had nowhere to dry the wet things except to hang them around the living room or in front of the fire.

At first it seemed best for Martyn to sleep in a small bed in their room because he was so nervous which meant it was very crowded in there.

'As soon as he is a bit more settled, perhaps we should ask Karmu if we can have that small room again, the one we used for Morgan,' Hadyn suggested.

'Yes, but he's not ready for it yet,' Sharon pointed out. 'Anyway, I don't think that we can afford it.'

'I'll make sure we can. I'll see if I can get some overtime and, if that's not possible, then another job on the side.'

'Either that, or, perhaps, I could get some evening work serving in the bar of one of the pubs around here and you could stay in and look after him,' Sharon suggested.

They tossed the ideas backwards and forwards but both of them agreed that for the time being it would be better if Hadyn worked extra hours and Sharon was at home with Martyn because he had taken to her and seemed to feel safe when she was around.

Martyn was so undernourished and nervous that Sharon's heart went out to him. His legs and arms were so pitifully thin that he didn't seem to have any strength in them. When she stripped off his clothes and stood him in a tin bowl in front of the fire to bath him, it was almost like looking at a skeleton.

Although he was within a few days of being three he seemed to have no energy and walking tired him out in next to no time. It was easy to see from the misery on his face that he found it hard to keep up, even when they walked to the nearby shops, so the first thing she bought for him was a push chair, having sold the one she'd had for Morgan. His delight in riding in it was worth every penny it had cost.

He never complained – in fact, for the first few weeks he hardly spoke at all. Sharon spent a great deal of her day encouraging him to repeat things after her.

At first his appetite was pitiful and he stared at everything she prepared for him as if he wasn't sure what it was. Crusts of bread, chips from the fish and chip shop, buns and doughnuts seemed to be the only foods he recognised.

It took several weeks of careful coaxing to make him accept a wider range of foods but in time he would eat practically everything she put in front of him. As a result he began to put on weight and because she took him out every day he started to get some healthy colour back into his cheeks. In a surprisingly short time he began to take a lively interest in what was going on around him.

Martyn also began to grow taller as well as fill out and the few clothes that were in the bundle that Geraint Humphreys had handed over to them no longer fitted him. Most of them were meant for very young toddlers and he had outgrown them all.

In desperation Sharon opened up the big brown fibre suitcase in which she had stored all Morgan's things after he had died. At first the sight of them brought tears to her eyes. She felt so emotional that she couldn't bring herself to go through them and quickly she shut the lid down.

Marty was standing alongside her and as she raised the lid again he reached out and grabbed hold of the teddy bear that she had packed away with Morgan's clothes.

When she held out her hand to take it back he clutched it to his chest, burying his head in its soft fur with such a cry of happiness that she hadn't the heart to make him give it up.

From that moment it was his constant companion and he carried it wherever he went. At night it had to be tucked up alongside him before he would settle down to sleep.

Sharon remembered that it had been Morgan's favourite toy so in some strange way she found that it made it easier to sort out the rest of the things in the suitcase and even to derive pleasure from seeing Martyn dressed in Morgan's clothes.

For the first week or two Hadyn's attitude towards the child worried Sharon. She had already taken Martyn to her heart and felt that he was a replacement for Morgan but Hadyn seemed hesitant about even talking to him.

It wasn't until one Sunday when Hadyn was at home and Martyn fell over while playing and banged his head against the table leg and then burst into noisy sobs that she realised how much Hadyn cared for the child.

His concern as he picked Martyn up astonished her. Very gently he bathed the bruise on the boy's forehead, talking to him and consoling him until the child's sobs gave way to smiles and he was quite sure that he was all right.

'We really, must make an effort to get out of

this place and find something bigger,' Hadyn said as Sharon handed him a cup of tea. 'Anyway, Tiger Bay is no place to bring up a child. We must try and do it before he goes to school and starts getting mixed up with the wrong sort of friends.'

Sharon nodded in agreement but said nothing. Inwardly she was elated that at long last Hadyn had come round to her way of thinking, even though she didn't know how they could possibly afford to move.

Tentatively, she again suggested that she should find some part-time work. 'If you don't like the idea of me working behind the bar in a pub, then perhaps I can find some office cleaning that I can do in the evening.'

'No, Martyn needs you here. He's coming along so well. He's a different child from the scared little scrap that arrived here a few months ago. We don't want to undo all the good work you've done to achieve that, now do we?'

Sharon did her best to save a couple of shillings each week but she found it difficult. No sooner had she done so than Martyn would need new shoes or Hadyn new trousers for work.

It was almost Christmas and she was determined that they would make it a special occasion for Martyn. Her ambition was to buy him a scooter and she had been paying off sixpence a week towards it for several weeks. She hadn't even told Hadyn because she wanted it to be a real surprise.

Hadyn was also doing all he could by working overtime whenever it was available in order to earn more money. Often in the evenings, after she had put Martyn to bed and she was doing the ironing or tidying around, Sharon thought about the changes that having Martyn had brought.

She loved the little boy so very much that she couldn't imagine ever being without him. She would never forget that his real mother was Wanda but she felt no resentment towards her, only sadness that she had died so young and would never have the joy of seeing her son grow up into a fine young man.

Having Martyn living with them had also changed Hadyn. He was so much quieter and more thoughtful than he had been before. It was as if he had drawn a line under the past and discarded all his unsuitable gambling friends who had led him into so much trouble and become a responsible family man. For that alone Sharon felt very grateful.

One evening, when her chores were all done and she was still waiting for Hadyn to come home, she opened up the package containing some of the paintings she had done in earlier days. She had kept them as a reminder of what her life had once been like and now, as she looked through them, she wondered if perhaps she could earn some money if she started to paint again.

When Hadyn came home she mentioned the idea to him. He went through the paintings that she had kept. There were a few of interiors that she'd done when she'd been working for her father and also several of the exterior of his shop. There were also one or two exteriors of houses that Hadyn had asked her to paint but which he had never managed to sell.

Hadyn studied them critically and then shook his head regretfully. 'I can't see you selling anything like this again,' he said reluctantly.

'No, I know that. Anyway, they caused too much trouble for us one way and another. No, I was wondering about portraits. If I can paint interiors, then why can't I paint people? I thought I'd start by doing one or two of Martyn to get my hand in and see how they turned out.'

'You do that and then, if we think they are any good, I'll take them along to work and see if any of the other drivers would like a picture of their kids.'

It sounded such a good idea that she spent some of her savings the next day to buy some brushes and paints. She set to work eagerly but the results didn't really please her.

'Don't give up yet,' Hadyn encouraged her, 'perhaps if they give you an ordinary sepia photograph they've had taken of their kids you could turn it into a colour picture by working straight on to the photograph?'

'Probably,' she said doubtfully, 'but it wouldn't be quite the same thing, would it?'

'No, but I'm sure it would work,' Hadyn said enthusiastically. 'One of the chaps was only saying the other day that his family had all been along to Jerome's in Queen Street to have their pictures taken and they'd had to buy the sepia ones because they couldn't afford coloured ones.'

'They won't want to pay very much though, will they?' Sharon said doubtfully.

'Not as much as if it was a picture painted by a

professional artist, but it wouldn't take you all that long to do and it would only need the minimum outlay for paints. Why don't you give it a try?'

The idea caught on and in the run-up to Christmas Sharon found herself so busy carrying out orders that she was hard pressed to fit everything in.

When she was working, Martyn was so intrigued by what she was doing that he would pull a chair up by the table and climb on it and remain quiet for long stretches as he watched intently what she was doing. He was utterly fascinated by the way she transformed a dull sepia picture into a glowing one that seemed to bring the people in it to life.

One day Sharon gave him one of her well-worn paintbrushes and the picture of a young girl that she had cut out of the newspaper and told him to try and see if he could paint the same as she did. To her delight he not only thoroughly enjoyed himself but proved to be quite dextrous.

By Christmas, Martyn had also come to accept Karmu and was always happy to be taken down to see her. When he had first arrived at Clwyd Court he had seemed to be scared of the big black woman with her vividly coloured clothes and striking headdress.

Karmu had eventually won him over by handing him a crust she had cut from the loaf and smeared with strawberry jam; his face had broken into a beaming smile as he took it from her and from then on he was always eager to go and see her again.

When she discovered how fond he was of jam doughnuts she often bought one specially for him and in no time they were firm friends.

'Now the bad weather is coming if you ever want to go to the shops on your own, Martyn can always stay here with me, you know,' Karmu told Sharon.

'That's kind of you, Karmu, but I'm not too sure that he is ready to be left with anyone else yet.'

Karmu rolled her eyes and gave one of her hearty laughs. 'Don't you worry about it, cariad,' she chortled. 'I can always bribe him with a jam doughnut if he should get worried or restless,' she said confidently.

There were very few occasions when Sharon found it necessary to take advantage of Karmu's offer but a few days before Christmas she was grateful for the opportunity to do so. She had a pile of orders completed and ready for delivery and Hadyn was working overtime so, rather than ask him to go out again after he came home, she decided to do one of them herself.

Hadyn had told her the address and it was only a few streets away, but it was a damp, dreary day so she decided it was better to leave Martyn with Karmu.

Her mission completed, she was hurrying back home to Clwyd Court again when a man she did not recognise stopped her and asked after Hadyn.

'You don't recognise me, do you?' He grinned. 'Percy Roberts is the name; I did time with Hadyn and I saw you several times when you came to visit him in the clink.'

'He's fine, thank you,' Sharon said stiffly.

'Has he managed to get a job, or are you the one who's out working?'

Sharon didn't answer. She felt intimidated. The man was unshaven and ragged and there was something evil about him that sent shudders through her.

'I think I'll walk home with you because I'd like to see him again. We were very good mates back in the old days,' Percy Roberts commented.

Sharon struggled to keep her nerve. She didn't want to be seen with this man and she certainly didn't want him to find out where they lived.

'I'm not going home,' she stated. 'I'll tell Hadyn we've met,' she added as she began to walk away.

'If you're not going home, then where are you going?' he persisted. 'Going up to Queen Street to beg a few bob from your old man? He still owns Pritchard's Paints and Wallpapers, doesn't he?'

Sharon didn't wait to hear any more. Taking to her heels she started to run, looking back over her shoulder now and again to see if he was following her.

Hadyn was already home when she got there and most concerned when he saw the distressed state she was in. He looked very troubled when she told him the reason for her panic.

'I hoped never to see or hear from him ever again,' he groaned. 'He's a bad lot. He's a thief, a thug and a very dangerous man; he'll stop at nothing to get what he wants.'

'Well, I didn't tell him anything. He wanted to know if you had a job but I didn't answer him and I'm pretty certain he didn't follow me home. I kept looking back to make sure, so he doesn't know where we live.'

'Are you sure he didn't ask you anything else?'

Hadyn persisted.

'No!' Sharon shook her head emphatically. 'The only other thing he said when I wouldn't tell him where I was going was that he supposed I was off to see my father at his shop in Queen Street to ask for a handout.'

The colour drained from Hadyn's face and he stared at her in dismay. 'We'll have to do something; we ought to warn your father,' he said worriedly.

'What are you talking about?' She frowned. 'Why do we need to warn him?'

'Percy Roberts is not only a thief but he's also got a huge chip on his shoulder and he takes offence very quickly if he think he is being snubbed.'

Sharon looked perplexed. 'I don't understand. Are you saying I should have told him where we lived or even invited him to come back here with me?'

'No, no, of course not. You did the right thing. My worry, though, is that he will think you were giving him the brush-off and that he'll take his revenge.'

'How can he when I didn't tell him where we live?' Sharon asked in a puzzled voice.

'He knows where your father lives – or at least where his business is.'

'If he goes there looking for us he will get short shrift. My dad hasn't had anything to do with me since he threw me out after our Parry's wedding when he discovered that I was pregnant, as well you know,' Sharon said bitterly.

'I'm not worried about him going there to try and find us; it's far more serious than that. I keep telling you, he is a thief and not a petty thief either. He's carried out some of the biggest thefts in Newport and Cardiff in his day. Breaking into your dad's shop would be small fry for him.'

Sharon's eyes widened. 'You've been mixed up with him in the past, haven't you?' she said accusingly.

'Yes,' Hadyn admitted. 'I have, and that is how I know how dangerous he can be.'

'So what are we going to do about it? Do you think we should inform the police?'

'I don't think that would do a lot of good because they are hardly likely to take any notice of anything I tell them, knowing that I'm an ex-convict. No, the only thing we can do is to go along and see your father ourselves.'

'That's only possible if my dad will talk to us. Or even take any notice of anything we say.'

'If he won't, then perhaps your mother will listen if we confide in her,' Hadyn said worriedly.

'I don't think so. Perhaps we should think about it for a while because I'm pretty sure that we would be wasting our time telling either of them,' Sharon said resignedly.

Chapter Thirty-One

Although they said no more about it Sharon could see that Hadyn was on edge for the rest of the evening. When they were undressing for bed he brought the matter up again.

329

'Let's leave things as they are,' she told him. 'Why are you so concerned about my dad when he's never worried about us? I don't understand you. Surely you haven't forgotten that it was because of him that you lost your job as a commercial traveller at Brynmor and Williams.'

'That's all in the past and I know only too well what a ruthless thug Percy Roberts can be. I wouldn't like to think that your father got hurt simply because I didn't swallow my pride and go along and warn him.'

'Let's sleep on it and decide tomorrow what's the best thing to do,' Sharon insisted.

The next morning they woke up late and Hadyn was in far too much of a rush to discuss anything. In fact, Sharon didn't give it a thought either until she was clearing away the breakfast dishes.

As she dressed Martyn ready to go out for a walk and to do the shopping, she recalled how worried Hadyn had been the night before. She toyed with the idea of going up to Queen Street and walking past her father's shop in the hope of catching sight of him. If she did, and he spoke to her, then she could warn him to be on the alert for trouble, she told herself.

Even as the thought went through her head she rejected it. He probably wouldn't speak to her, perhaps not even recognise her, and then she'd feel mortified.

Hadyn was probably being overanxious because he knew the sort of reputation Percy Roberts had. They had obviously been in jail at the same time, so he had probably heard rumours about him from other prisoners.

She began to wonder if he had been involved in the robbery Hadyn had been arrested for and which had resulted in him being sent to prison. The thought troubled her so much that she could think of nothing else.

To try and distract her thoughts she popped Martyn into the pushchair and set out to walk to the Pier Head. He loved watching the huge ships coming into port after making their way up the Bristol Channel and she hoped the sharp, clean air would help to clear her mind.

She was still undecided about what to do as she prepared their evening meal but resolved to talk it through again with Hadyn and do whatever he thought best. She wasn't too sure about him being the one to go and tell her father, but if he was willing to do so then she would support him.

It might even be the start of some sort of reconciliation between them all, she thought hopefully. If her father enquired how she was and seemed to be at all interested, then perhaps she could go along and see him and her mother.

That would be wonderful, she reflected. It was so long now since she had seen them and yet rarely a day went by when she didn't think about them and her brother Parry because she missed them all so much.

She brought her thoughts back to the present as Martyn began saying that he was hungry. When she looked at the clock she could understand why. Hadyn was almost an hour late and she wondered if he was doing overtime and had forgotten to mention it to her before he'd left that morning.

'Of course you're hungry,' she told Martyn. 'Come along, sit up at the table and we'll have ours, we won't wait for your daddy any longer.'

Their meal over, she read him a story and then played Snakes and Ladders with him until it was almost seven o'clock.

'Can I stay up until Daddy comes home?' he begged as she started getting him ready for bed.

'Well, only for a little while longer. He might be very late, so if you go to bed I'll tell him to come and kiss you goodnight as soon as he gets home, OK?'

'No.' Martyn shook his head. 'If I'm asleep, I won't know if he's kissed me.'

As the time ticked past Sharon found it difficult to concentrate on the story she was reading to Martyn and when his eyelids began to droop she took advantage of his tiredness to pop him into bed and, within minutes, he was fast asleep.

As she cleared away the remnants of their meal and tidied up in the living room she kept worrying about why Hadyn was so late and wondering where he could have gone.

She hoped he hadn't gone to see Percy Roberts and been inveigled into either a drinking or a gambling session with him. She shuddered as she thought back to those days and all the problems Hadyn's gambling habit had caused them.

She was tempted to go downstairs and have a chat with Karmu to take her mind off her problem but she didn't like to risk leaving Martyn on his own. Although he was fast asleep, he might very well have one of his troublesome nightmares, when he woke up screaming because he still had a fear of being left on his own.

No, she resolved, she wouldn't worry or panic but get on with something to take her mind off it. She had some darning that needed doing so she collected her workbox and settled down in a comfortable chair to get on with it.

She had just finished darning a hole in the heel of Hadyn's sock and was about to put everything away when she heard raised voices in the hallway and went to the door to see what was happening.

To her surprise she saw two policemen standing there talking to Karmu and the next thing she knew, they were coming up the stairs heading for her door.

'Mrs Jenkins? Mrs Hadyn Jenkins?'

Sharon nodded a trifle uncertainly. Although she now always called herself Mrs Jenkins, she and Hadyn were still not officially married. While she didn't think that concerned anyone else, when it came to the law she wondered if she was committing some sort of crime by doing so.

'Can we come in and talk to you in private?' one of them asked as other doors started opening and people looked out to see what was happening.

'Yes, of course.' Her heart thundering like a sledgehammer, she opened the door wider and then backed into the room to let them come in.

'I'm afraid we have some bad news,' the older policeman told her. 'There was an attempted armed robbery in Queen Street this evening and your husband was shot and has been taken to the Royal Infirmary.'

Sharon felt her head spinning and she reached

out and grabbed hold of the back of a chair to steady herself. The words 'robbery' and 'Queen Street' were going round and round in her brain.

'Was it at Pritchard's Paints and Wallpapers?' she asked.

The two policemen exchanged glances. 'Yes, as a matter of fact it was,' they affirmed. 'Do you know anything about it? Does your husband work for them?'

'No.' Sharon shook her head. 'No, he doesn't work there. Was anyone else hurt?'

'Fortunately, not. From our investigations, we think the shot was aimed at the owner of the store, Mr Elwyn Pritchard, but it seems that Hadyn Jenkins intervened and he was shot in the process. Now would you like us to take you along to the Royal Infirmary to see your husband?'

Sharon hesitated. She desperately wanted to see Hadyn, not only to find out how badly hurt he was, but also for him to tell her exactly what had happened, but she didn't know what to do about leaving Martyn.

'Can you wait while I waken my little boy and get him ready?' she asked.

'Is that necessary? Isn't there someone here who would keep an eye on him while you are at the hospital?'

Again Sharon hesitated, wondering if it would be too much for Karmu or whether she should ask either Alwyn Jones or Caitlin Thomas to listen out for him.

In the end her problem was solved by Karmu coming upstairs to see if everything was all right. The moment she heard that Hadyn was in hospital she insisted that Sharon must go and see him and she would look after Martyn.

'I'm sure he will sleep because he has only just gone to bed and he was very tired,' Sharon told her as she struggled into her outdoor coat and pulled on her hat.

'Off you go, cariad, and don't worry about him, he'll be safe enough with me,' Karmu confirmed. 'I'll be around because I know he doesn't like the dark,' she added reassuringly.

'Thank you, Karmu. I'll be as quick as I can,' Sharon promised.

All the way to the Royal Infirmary in Newport Road the older policeman kept questioning her in a roundabout way to try and find out if she knew anything about the robbery.

'We know Hadyn Jenkins finished a long sentence for theft not very long ago,' he said at last, 'so why not come clean and admit he was involved in this break-in.'

'He most certainly wasn't,' Sharon told him heatedly. 'Since he came out of prison he has had a regular job as a van driver for Davis's Deliveries. He has not been involved in anything like that or broken the law in any way.'

Even as she said it she wondered if she ought to mention Percy Roberts and to explain that Hadyn had probably been there because he wanted to warn her father in case Percy Roberts tried to break in, but she felt that it was better not to do so in case she only incriminated Hadyn.

When they arrived at the hospital they were asked to wait while someone checked to make sure that Hadyn was out of theatre and suffi-

335

ciently recovered to be allowed visitors.

The minutes seemed to drag by and she was acutely aware of how conspicuous she was standing there flanked by two uniformed policemen. She was very much afraid that they intended accompanying her to Hadyn's bedside and she wondered how he would react if they did.

When she was finally told that she could go in and see Hadyn for a few minutes, her heart sank as they both walked alongside her to the ward.

The sister who was in charge of the ward met them at the door and she frowned in a disapproving manner. 'Only one of you at the bedside at a time,' she stated, 'and then only for ten minutes, no longer. Mr Jenkins has only just come out of surgery and he will tire easily, so he needs to rest.'

'I'll go in first, I'm his wife.' Sharon quickly stepped forward, determined to make sure that she spoke to Hadyn before the police started questioning him.

The sister led her towards a curtained-off bed and, after checking the time on her watch, left her after reminding her that she was only allowed ten minutes.

Hadyn could barely open his eyes but he smiled weakly as she bent over and kissed him and when she took his hand he managed to give it a squeeze.

'The police are waiting outside, they accompanied me here,' she said in a low voice, hoping that no one except Hadyn could hear what she said.

He frowned and she could see how worried he was by what she'd said. Then he gave a weak smile and nodded. 'They would be. What have you told them?'

'Nothing, really. They reminded me that you were in prison not so long ago after committing a serious theft and I told them you now had a steady job and all that sort of thing was in the past.'

'Did you mention Percy Roberts?'

'No, I was wondering if I should do so when they were questioning me on the way here, but I thought it might be better if I said nothing, in case I said the wrong thing.'

'Good!' He gave a deep sigh of relief then closed his eyes as if the effort of talking to her had exhausted him.

The two policemen were waiting to drive her home and once again they questioned her to see if she could help with any information about the robbery.

'Didn't your husband have any idea who was involved in the robbery?' the policeman sitting in the back of the car alongside her asked as they drove down Newport Road towards Bute Street. 'After all, he must know most of the petty criminals in Cardiff, considering the length of time he was inside.'

'Perhaps it wasn't anyone from Cardiff who did it,' Sharon countered.

'Do you want us to take you straight home, or would you like to go and see your father and make sure that he is all right?' the policeman who was driving asked.

'No, I must get back in case my little boy wakes up,' she said quickly.

The rest of the journey was made in silence and

Sharon felt trapped. All the time she was waiting for them to start questioning her again and she went over in her head how much she would tell them if they did.

'Well, since you don't seem to be able to help us, then we will have to go back to the hospital and question your husband,' the older one commented as he brought the car to a stop in Clwyd Court to let her out.

'He may be well enough to tell you more tomorrow after he's had a good night's sleep,' she agreed.

She stood for a moment on the pavement after they'd driven away, trying to control her shaking and wondering if, after all, she should have mentioned Percy Roberts's name. The only thing was she'd been afraid that if she did, because he had been in prison at the same time as Hadyn, they would think it was a put-up job between him and Hadyn.

She'd go back to the hospital again in the morning, she resolved, and find out exactly what had taken place in Queen Street and how Hadyn had come to be shot.

The next morning, even before she'd finished her breakfast, Karmu was knocking on her door, waving the morning edition of the *South Wales Echo* at her and jabbing her finger at the glaring headlines.

LOCAL HERO THROWS HIMSELF IN
FRONT OF ROBBER AND SAVES THE
LIFE OF SHOP OWNER

Underneath, in smaller print was the lurid story of what had taken place at Pritchard's Paints and Wallpapers in Queen Street the evening before. Hadyn's name was mentioned as the hero and his bravery applauded in lengthy detail.

Sharon read it all through, wondering if it meant that they had apprehended Percy Roberts, because she was sure he was the villain behind it. At the end, though, all it said was that the police were continuing their inquiries and it was expected that an arrest was imminent.

'Well, cariad, what do you make of all that?' Karmu beamed. 'Your husband a hero! Everybody here is singing his praises and saying what a fine fellow he is. Alwyn and Caitlin say we ought to have a party to welcome him home when he comes out of hospital. Have you any idea when that will be?'

'No, not really. He wasn't saying very much at all last night because he had only just come out of the operating theatre.'

'Was he badly hurt when he got shot, then?' Karmu asked, her voice full of concern.

'I'm not even sure about that. They only let me speak to him for a few minutes. I'm hoping to be able to find out more when I go in to see him today.'

'You can leave Martyn with me, if you like, while you do that,' Karmu offered.

'That's very kind of you but I think I'll take him with me because I am sure Hadyn would like to see him. I know Martyn wants to see his daddy because he can't understand why he didn't come home last night.'

In that case, then perhaps I'd better come to the hospital with you, cariad,' Karmu pointed out, 'because I'm not at all sure that they will let Martyn in and you don't want to leave him with a stranger.'

Chapter Thirty-Two

Sharon decided to wait until the afternoon before going in to see Hadyn, confident that if the police had been in to interview him they would have left by then. She also hoped that he would be more himself than he had been the day before because she was anxious to hear exactly what had happened and why he had been there.

Karmu kept calling up to her to come down and join her for a cuppa but because she knew that all Karmu wanted to do was talk about the robbery she pretended not to hear.

In the end Karmu came lumbering up the stairs, loudly huffing and puffing from the exertion, and knocked on Sharon's door. The vivid green and orange bandeau she had on her head had slipped sideways, giving her such a comical look that Martyn started giggling as she came into the room.

'Have you any news?' Karmu gasped as she flopped down on a chair and struggled to get her breath back.

'No, I'm trying to get things in order here before I go to the hospital because I'm hoping they will say that Hadyn can home with me,'

Sharon told her.

'Duw anwyl, there's silly you are being, cariad,' Karmu chided. 'They won't let him out of hospital this quickly. Not only will they be treating him for shock but, remember, he's also had an operation to remove a bullet.'

Although she was pressed for time Sharon made a pot of tea and sat down for a few minutes to talk to Karmu. Once again she told her exactly what had happened when she'd been to the hospital the night before.

'You really ought to leave Martyn with me when you go to visit Hadyn; a hospital is not the sort of place you want to take a young child.'

'Well, I'm not sure,' Sharon said hesitantly. She knew Karmu meant well and she didn't want to offend her, so she chose her words carefully.

'I think I ought to take Martyn with me because if they don't discharge Hadyn today, then both of them will be longing to see each other.'

Karmu pursed her big lips thoughtfully as she looked down at Martyn who was sitting on the floor by her feet playing with a toy train. She reached out and ruffled his mop of auburn hair. 'Yes, cariad, you could be right. It would probably be a tonic for Hadyn to see him,' she agreed.

She handed her empty cup and saucer back to Sharon and pulled herself up out of the chair. 'You'd better get on, then, or you won't be ready in time to go this afternoon. If you change your mind about taking Martyn with you, then remember he can always stay here with me for an hour or so.'

The moment Karmu left Sharon began preparing herself and Martyn to visit Hadyn. She insisted that he had something to eat, even though he said he wasn't hungry.

'A couple of biscuits and a glass of milk,' she coaxed, 'and then I have a very special treat planned for you. Instead of you going in your pushchair, we're going to have a ride on a tram.'

Martyn's green eyes lit up with excitement and, without another word, he scrambled up on to a chair by the table, eager to do as she asked.

As soon as he had finished his snack, Sharon wiped around his mouth with a damp flannel and then put on his outdoor clothes ready to leave.

They arrived at the hospital shortly after half past one. She knew visiting didn't start until two o'clock so, instead of going to the reception desk, she decided to walk down to the ward and wait outside. That way they would be first in and every minute they could spend with Hadyn was precious.

'What do you think you are doing? You're not allowed to hang around here.'

The sharp, officious voice of a nurse in a pink and white uniform who was coming out of the ward made Sharon jump.

'I'm waiting to see my husband,' she explained.

'Visiting time doesn't start until two o'clock. You're far too early; you'd better go back to Reception. What's your husband's name?' she asked when Sharon still hesitated.

'Hadyn Jenkins.'

'Oh, the chap who was shot in the shoulder during the robbery yesterday.' The nurse's voice became more friendly. 'And is this his little boy?'

342

'Yes, and he's longing to see his daddy.' Sharon smiled.

'Young children are not allowed on the ward, but I think we can make an exception since his daddy is such a hero. Wait here a minute and I'll make sure it is all right for you to come in.'

When she came back and led them to a bed at the far corner of the ward, Sharon was quick to notice that the curtains were drawn back, Hadyn was sitting up, and there was no policeman there either.

Hadyn's chest was bandaged and his left arm was in a sling. He winced and his jaw tightened as Martyn bounded on to the bed to hug him. Cuddling him with his other arm, Hadyn smiled up at Sharon over the top of Martyn's head. 'They're going to let me out later today – or tomorrow – providing I have someone at home to look after me,' he told her before she had time to say anything.

'Have you told the police the name of the man who did this to you?' she asked anxiously.

'I didn't need to do so because they already knew and they've made an arrest.'

'Are you sure they have the right man? It was Percy Roberts, wasn't it!'

Hadyn nodded but said nothing.

'What if he gets off, though, and then comes looking for you?' Sharon asked worriedly.

'Don't worry, cariad; Percy Roberts won't trouble us again because he will be behind bars for a long time to come,' Hadyn assured her.

Sharon didn't argue but she didn't feel too confident about that. Percy Roberts was such an

343

evil man that she was quite sure he would want revenge when he came out of prison and she was afraid that he might come looking for Hadyn.

'By the way, your father has been in to thank me for saving his life. He was brought in by one of the newspaper reporters because they wanted to write another piece about what happened and wanted a picture of the two of us together. It will be in today's *South Wales Echo,* so look out for it.'

'My father!' The colour drained from Sharon's face. 'Did he recognise you?' she gulped.

'Of course he did. After I finished work last night I went round to warn him that there was the possibility that there might be a robbery at one of the shops. I was there when Percy Roberts and his mob attempted to break in.'

'So that was the reason why you were late home,' Sharon murmured. 'It's all coming clear now. When I read the report in last night's paper, I couldn't understand how you came to be there at the same time as Percy Roberts...'

She stopped speaking as she saw the expression on Hadyn's face and she reached out and took hold of his hand.

'Duw anwyl! You didn't think that I was part of the robbery set-up, did you?' Hadyn exclaimed uneasily.

'No, never for one minute! I know full well that you've drawn a line under all that sort of non-sense,' she added in a firm, clear voice as she squeezed his uninjured hand and bent over the bed and kissed him.

'So what did my dad have to say when you called on him yesterday?'

'He was very cordial and he thanked me for taking the trouble to come and warn him,' Hadyn said solemnly. 'Mind you, I think he was so startled to see me that he only half believed what I was saying,' he added with a smile.

'Did he ask about me?' Sharon asked hesitantly.

'He didn't get a chance to do so. The next minute we heard the door being opened and Percy Roberts and his mob were in there wielding crowbars and a gun at us. He believed me then, all right,' he added grimly.

'Was my dad in the shop on his own?'

'Yes, the rest of the staff from both the paint shop and the shop next door had all gone home so there were just the two of us there.'

'I'm so glad my mam had already gone home because it would have been enough to give her a heart attack if she'd been there,' Sharon said with a shiver.

'Percy Roberts and his cronies weren't expecting anyone to be there so they panicked and, as Percy fired his gun, I pushed your father to the ground but the bullet got me as I was trying to duck down and take cover.'

'Oh, Hadyn, it must have been a terrible ordeal. You could have been killed!'

'Yes, that's very true,' Hadyn agreed. 'Fortunately, Percy's not a very good shot.' Hadyn grinned. 'Anyway, from then on it was pandemonium and then the police arrived and I don't know what happened after that because I was put in an ambulance and brought here.'

'I still can't get over the fact that you saved my dad's life, especially after the way he treated you in the past. It's a funny old world, isn't it?'

'He probably thought that as well when he'd time to get over the shock,' Hadyn agreed.

'But he didn't mention me or ask after me?' Sharon persisted wistfully.

Hadyn shook his head. 'No. He didn't have time to do so,' he reminded her quickly.

'What about when he came into the hospital today, didn't he ask about me then?'

'Well, there were nursing staff, policemen and a newspaper reporter as well as the photographer all hovering around us so he could hardly do so then, now could he?'

Sharon bit her lip trying to hide her disappointment. 'No, I suppose not.'

Although she knew that Hadyn was probably right and there hadn't been any opportunity, she still felt very unhappy that her father hadn't asked how she was.

Perhaps he wasn't sure if we were still together and so didn't want to embarrass Hadyn when he'd just saved his life by asking him about me, she consoled herself.

Even so, it made her sad; she missed her family so much. She wished she had been the one who had gone and warned them earlier in the day that there might be trouble and not left it for Hadyn to do so. Yet, if she had done that, her father might have been the one who was shot, she reasoned.

The arrival of the ward sister to tell her that they were discharging Hadyn but that he would have to come back in a week's time to have his dressing changed brought her thoughts back to the present.

'In order to give the wound in your chest and shoulder a chance to heal, you must keep your left arm strapped across your chest and not attempt to use it at all until after we have seen you again,' the sister told him.

'I think he's going to find that very difficult to do,' Sharon said worriedly.

'He should consider himself lucky that his injuries are no worse,' the sister told her briskly. 'Now, will you take your little boy out into the corridor and wait out there with him while the doctor comes and makes a final check on your husband and then he can go home with you.'

By the time Hadyn was ready to leave it was late afternoon so they took a taxicab home. Hadyn was still in considerable discomfort and afraid that someone might bump into him or that the jolting of the tram would make the pain worse.

The moment they arrived at Clwyd Court and stepped inside the door Karmu came bustling out to meet them. She insisted that they went into her kitchen so that Hadyn could have a rest and get his breath back before he walked upstairs.

'The kettle's boiling so you may as well have a cup of tea, and I know little Martyn would like a glass of my homemade lemonade and one of my special cookies,' she said, beaming. 'While you are drinking your tea you can take a look at this,' she added, producing a copy of the midday edition of the *Echo* which had a new article about the robbery and a picture of Hadyn and Mr Pritchard blazoned across it.

Sharon felt the tears building up as she took the

347

newspaper from Karmu and studied it; her father looked exactly as she remembered him. Although she said nothing in front of Karmu she felt desolate to think that he hadn't even asked Hadyn how she was.

The journey home and all the excitement of the past couple of days seemed to have tired Hadyn a great deal. As soon as he had finished his cup of tea he stood up and said he wanted to go and have a lie down.

'A nice sleep in your own bed will be as good as any medicine,' Karmu told him. 'Now you take him on upstairs, Sharon, and look after him well. If you want me to have Martyn or to get you anything from the shops or need any help at all, night or day, then you have only to call out.'

'I think you should get Martyn off to bed first, he looks so tired that he can hardly keep his eyes open,' Hadyn said as they reached their own room. 'I wanted to get away so that I could sit down quietly for half an hour and gather my wits together.'

'Right, well, I must give Martyn something to eat, although I don't suppose he's very hungry because he ate three biscuits while we were down with Karmu. I'll undress him ready for bed first and then give him a bowl of bread and milk. That's still his favourite,' she added with a smile.

She had just settled Martyn into bed and come back into the living room when there was a knock on their door.

'If it's Karmu, then tell her you're helping me to get undressed,' Hadyn said in a whisper.

When she opened the door, Sharon's heart

thundered. A man was standing there; a tall, thin man with dark hair that showed signs of grey at the sides. Was it her father? she asked herself, or was it a trick of the light?

For a brief moment she wasn't sure because he didn't seem to be quite tall enough; she had always looked up to her father but she was more or less on eye level with this man and he looked so much older than she remembered.

'Sharon!'

The moment he spoke and she heard his voice, she let out a long sigh of sheer happiness.

'Dad! Is it really you?'

'Yes, it's me, Sharon. I thought it was about time I came to see you and make things right between us at last. I'm not much good at saying sorry, cariad, but I've greatly regretted what happened and the things I said.'

For a long moment they simply stared at each other as if not quite knowing what to do then, the next minute, they were enfolded in each other's arms, hugging and kissing and both of them trying to talk at once.

Sharon felt overwhelmed. She had dreamed so often of this happening that now that it was actually taking place she felt she must be imagining it. She clung on to him, wanting this wonderful moment to last for ever.

When they finally drew apart she couldn't resist reaching up and kissing him again on the cheek.

'Look who's here, Hadyn!' Her eyes were shining like stars as she took her father's hand and led him into the room.

'I've already seen Hadyn once today and I also

saw him last night as well,' Elwyn Pritchard reminded her.

'Of course, none of us will ever forgot about that, will we?' she agreed.

'You are going to sit down and have a cup of tea and something to eat with us?' she invited eagerly as she propelled him towards a chair.

'A cup of tea will do me fine. What I wanted more than anything else was to find out how you are and what's been happening to you. Your mother has been out of her mind with worry because we haven't heard from you all these years.'

They spent the next hour catching up with family news. When Sharon told him that she had seen Gwen some time ago and asked if she had told him, he shook his head.

'She never said anything to me or to your mother, but she might have mentioned it to Parry and perhaps they thought it best not to mention it for some reason or other. I don't know. Anyway, it doesn't matter. I've found you again at long last and that is all that matters.'

'It's wonderful to see you again and know that you and Mam are all right. I've dreamed about it happening for so long that it's hard to believe it's come true at last.' Sharon sighed as her father stood up ready to leave.

'I know, I know,' he murmured, stroking her hair tenderly as he gave her one last hug.

'Please will you bring Mam to see us as soon as you can,' Sharon begged.

Elwyn Pritchard hesitated before replying. As she saw him look around their living room, a wave of shame swept over her as she realised how shabby and squalid the place must appear to him compared to the home she had grown up in.

'Perhaps it would be better if you came to see her,' he said quietly.

Silently she nodded in agreement. She felt too choked to say anything.

'We'd like to do that,' Hadyn said quickly, filling in the awkward silence. 'Give me a day or two for this to settle down,' he said, indicating his shoulder.

'Of course. You must take great care of that wound for the next couple of weeks,' Elwyn Pritchard agreed. 'Perhaps you could come on your own, Sharon,' he added as he saw the look of disappointment on her face.

'I'd like us to come and see you both together, so that it will be a proper reunion,' she demurred.

'As you wish.' Elwyn smiled as he put on his topcoat and fastened it up. 'Another few days won't make all that much difference, not after all this time.'

Chapter Thirty-Three

Elaine Pritchard, her round face anxious, came bustling into the hallway the moment she heard her husband's key in the door.

'Well?' she demanded as Elwyn walked into the house. 'Did you find them? Did you see Sharon? Is she all right? What sort of place is she living in?'

'Hold on, cariad, let me get my coat off and my

351

breath back and then I'll tell you everything.'

'Here, let me hang those up,' Elaine said impatiently as she took his hat and coat from him. 'Come and sit down. Do you want a cup of tea?'

'No, I don't want tea; I need something stronger than that. I think I need a whisky,' he added as he walked over to a cupboard and took out a bottle. 'Do you want a nip as well?'

'Perhaps I should have one; it sounds as though you have some grim news, judging by the look on your face. I only want a very small one, mind. I'll get some water to go in it,' she added as she headed for the kitchen.

'Now,' she said forcefully when they were both sitting down and had taken a sip of their drink, 'what news do you have? You did see Sharon?'

'Yes, I saw her. She looks very thin and older than when she left home.'

'Well, she's bound to because that's seven years ago and she's had a lot to contend with. She lost her child, for one thing. What sort of place is she living in?'

'Two squalid rooms in a lodging house in Clwyd Court, which is not far from Bute Street and in the heart of Tiger Bay. I think that says it all,' Elwyn said grimly.

'We can't leave her living there in those sorts of conditions!' Elaine gasped.

'I know that, but what is the best way of helping her? I have a feeling that neither Sharon nor Hadyn would be prepared to accept help from us, but I wondered if perhaps I could give him a reward for saving my life.'

'You mean give him some money,' Elaine

352

mused as she took another sip of her whisky and water. 'Well, fair-dos, I suppose that would help them out a bit, but what about us seeing them? I want to see my Sharon again.'

'I know, I know.' Elwyn put his empty glass down on the table. 'I have asked Sharon to come and see you and she has promised that she will do the moment that Hadyn is a bit better and feeling well enough to do so.'

'When on earth is that going to be?' Elaine murmured in a disappointed voice. 'Hadyn's still in hospital, isn't he?'

'No, he's home. They discharged him from the hospital this afternoon, so it should only be a day or two before they come to pay you a visit,' he added as he rose from his chair and went over to pour himself another drink.

He was on the point of telling Elaine that Sharon had told him that she had met Gwen not so very long ago but at the last moment he decided that it might be better not to do so since Gwen hadn't mentioned it to them.

Sharon felt bitterly disappointed the next day when Hadyn said he wasn't feeling too well and suggested that they should postpone their visit to see her mother.

'Perhaps it's for the best,' she commented philosophically. 'I didn't think to ask my dad if she was still only working part-time at the shop, so we might go all the way to Pen-y-lan Place and then find no one at home.'

'We could go along to the shop first and find out if she was there or not. We will have to change trams in the city centre, anyway,' Hadyn reminded her. 'Or you could go and see her on your own one evening after you've put Martyn to bed.'

'No, I want us to go there as a family, so it might be best if we leave it and go on Sunday,' Sharon said firmly. 'That gives you time to feel a bit stronger and we know she will be at home then.'

'If your dad has told her that he's asked you to call on them and you don't turn up, won't she think that rather strange?' Hadyn persisted.

Sharon was not to be dissuaded. She wanted her reunion with her mother to be special, not in such a public place as the shop. Furthermore, she was longing to go and see her old home again and find out if it really was as comfortable as she seemed to remember it used to be.

Visiting her old home in Roath after years spent in Tiger Bay would be such a contrast that it would be like visiting another world, she told herself. There were moments when she wanted to drop everything and go there, she felt so emotional about the thought of seeing her mother again.

Sunday dawned bright and sunny and, after breakfast, as she dressed Martyn and strapped him into his pushchair and then helped Hadyn into his coat, she felt as if they were setting out on some exciting mission.

'I think you should have asked your father to warn your mother that we were coming,' Hadyn said worriedly.

'If I'd done that, then it wouldn't be a surprise for her,' Sharon protested.

Hadyn's words were still echoing in her ears as

she lifted the big brass knocker, but then it was too late and it was actually happening. She could hear her mother's quick footsteps coming along the parquet floor and then the door was opening and her mother was there, staring at her as if she was seeing a ghost.

Leaving Hadyn to hold the pushchair, she moved into her mother's arms as their murmurs of happiness and tears of reconciliation mingled.

'Come along inside this minute, we're making a scene out here on the doorstep,' Elaine Pritchard scolded, stepping backwards into the hallway.

The moment the door closed she hugged Sharon again. 'I feel I want to pinch you to make sure you're real,' she sighed as she mopped at her eyes.

'Come along into the kitchen for a minute; your dad's gone for his usual Sunday morning walk. I was preparing a roast for lunch when you knocked. Let me pop the joint in the oven and then we'll all sit down and have a cup of tea. Are you feeling better, Hadyn? Is your shoulder healing well?' She stopped and drew in a sharp breath as she looked at Martyn. 'Who is this lovely little boyo, then?' she asked with a wide smile.

'Our little boy Martyn, and he's nearly four,' Sharon said quickly before Hadyn could answer.

An hour later when Elwyn returned from his walk in nearby Roath Park they were all still sitting in the kitchen trying to catch up with all that had happened in the intervening years since Sharon had left home.

'Elwyn, you never told me that Hadyn and our Sharon had another little boy,' Elaine said reproachfully as she poured him out a cup of tea.

355

'That's because I didn't know,' he told her as he helped himself to sugar. 'Fine little chap, isn't he?' he added as he picked Martyn up and began to give him a ride on his knee. 'He has the same colour hair as his daddy.'

Sharon felt her pulse race. She felt she ought to explain about Martyn but she couldn't bring herself to do so because she wasn't sure how her parents would react or even if they would understand.

It was late on Sunday afternoon before they set off for home and they only left then because Sharon could see that Martyn was very tired and needed to go to bed.

'You've no idea what a joy this has been for me,' her mother told her as she helped Sharon to tuck Martyn into his pushchair. 'I'll just get a paper and pencil and write down your address and I'll come and see you next Wednesday on our half-day.'

The idea of her mother coming to Clwyd Court and seeing for herself their small, squalid rooms was unthinkable and Sharon tried to think of a way out of it.

'Why don't I come here and then we can take Martyn for a walk in Roath Park, if it's a nice day?' she suggested.

'Yes, all right, if you'd prefer to do that,' her mother agreed as she hugged and kissed her goodbye.

'Hadyn, you'll be coming as well on Wednesday?' Elwyn Pritchard asked quickly.

'I don't know, I thought it might be better to let Sharon bring Martyn on her own.'

'I'd like you to come; there's something I want to discuss with you and we can stay here and do that while they are at the park,' Elwyn Pritchard insisted.

'Very well,' Hadyn agreed.

Sharon could see that he was not too pleased by the idea and on the way home she tried to find out why.

'Your dad has already given me what he called a reward for saving his life,' Hadyn reminded her rather irritably, 'I don't want any more handouts from him and I'm pretty sure that's what this is all about.'

'Well, like he said, if it had been a stranger, he would have rewarded them and, since you are not able to work until your shoulder is better, we need something to live on.'

'I still don't like taking his money. I hope when I go back to the hospital this week they will say that I am fit to work again.'

'If your job is still there waiting for you,' Sharon pointed out. 'There hasn't been a word from them all the time you've been at home. I would have thought they would have sent someone round to see if you were all right.'

'They probably think I'm the one who should have sent them a message to let them know what had happened and a doctor's note to say I wasn't fit for work.'

'Rubbish! They will have read all about what happened in the newspaper. It was in for two days running and with your picture each time.'

They didn't mention the subject again but Sharon knew that Hadyn was brooding about it.

When he visited the hospital the following Tuesday to have his dressing changed, he asked when he would be able to go back to work.

'Not for at least another month,' the sister told him.

The news depressed Hadyn so much that Sharon wondered whether it would make things better or worse if she suggested that she found herself a job again.

Karmu would give him a hand to look after Martyn and, anyway, she might be able to find an evening job and be able to have Martyn ready for bed before she went out. If she could arrange something like that, then all Hadyn would have to do was read Martyn a story and then listen out for him if he should waken.

Hadyn seemed to be so upset and so resentful at the moment that she decided it would be best to leave it for a day or so before mentioning it. His mood was bad now and she didn't want to make things any worse before they went to visit her parents the next day.

Wednesday was cool but bright and Sharon was looking forward to their visit as she dressed Martyn. It was ages since she'd been to Roath Park and when she was younger it had been one of her favourite spots.

'Do we have to take Martyn in that? Surely he's big enough now to walk,' Hadyn said grumpily as Sharon strapped Martyn into his pushchair.

'If my mam wants us to take him for a walk in Roath Park then I think it's best that we take the pushchair,' Sharon explained.

'Not really,' Hadyn argued. 'If he gets tired of

walking I'll carry him.'

'With your bad shoulder?' Sharon teased. 'Anyway,' she went on quickly as she saw Hadyn was frowning, 'I didn't think you were coming to the park with us. I thought you were staying home to have a talk with my dad.'

'We'll see about that when we get there,' Hadyn told her ominously.

Sharon didn't answer. She couldn't help wondering about what it was that her dad wanted to discuss with Hadyn because she knew how touchy Hadyn was about accepting any form of help from him.

She enjoyed her outing with her mother. They talked mostly about old times and about Parry and Gwen and their two children. Elaine was very anxious to know more about Martyn and where they were living.

'I really must come and see you,' she insisted. 'I can't believe that you are living in Tiger Bay; it's always had such a terrible reputation. What sort of place have you got? I still don't know the exact address, only that it's in Clwyd Court and that it is somewhere quite near to Bute Street.'

'I'm sure Dad also told you that we've only got two rooms and that the landlady is a big black woman called Karmu,' Sharon said quickly.

'Only two rooms for all three of you? You do have a kitchen and a bathroom as well?'

'No, we have only the two rooms. A living room where I do the cooking, washing and everything else and a bedroom where the three of us sleep.'

'Good heavens, Sharon, however do you manage? What about all the washing you must have to do for little Martyn? Not so much now, I suppose,' she went on quickly, 'but what about when he was a small baby and you had a pile of nappies to wash every day? Where on earth did you dry them? I don't suppose for one minute that there's a garden there.'

'No, there isn't a garden, and our room is on the second floor anyway,' Sharon explained. 'No, I have to dry all my washing by spreading it around the room and then airing things off in front of the fire.'

'You poor child, it must be appalling for you to have to manage like that when you always had every comfort while you were growing up. Why ever haven't you come home?'

'I longed to do so but I was afraid you might turn me away. When I left, remember, Dad told me never to come back,' she said with a shrug of her shoulders.

'Yes, I know, and we've both regretted those words from that day until now. It's strange the way fate deals with things. If it hadn't been for Hadyn's bravery when that robbery happened, then we might still be poles apart,' she said with a lop-sided smile. That's all in the past, remember,' she added, squeezing Sharon's arm. 'Come on; let's go back home. I've got a special tea all ready and waiting and there're lots of things that this little boy will love,' she added as she smiled down at Martyn.

As they walked the short distance back to Pen-y-lan Road from the park Sharon wondered what sort of mood she was going to find Hadyn in.

As Elaine opened the front door with her key

she could hear both Hadyn and her father laughing about something and her heart lightened.

Her feeling of optimism increased when Hadyn greeted her with a beaming smile and announced, 'Your father has offered me a job and he says I can start straight away even though I might not be of very much use for a couple more weeks.'

'You mean serving in the shop? Oh, that's wonderful,' Sharon enthused.

'There's a bit more to it than that.' Her father frowned. 'Hadyn will certainly be spending some time in the shop but he will also have the use of a car and he'll be going out and about a great deal of the time. The idea is that he will be our travelling representative.'

'What does that mean?' Sharon frowned.

'Hadyn will call on builders and decorators with samples of carpets and paints to save them having to come into the shop to make a selection when they are very busy. He will even take pattern books direct to where they are working, if necessary, so that their customers can have a better idea of what the results are going to look like in their own homes.'

'Something similar to when I used to do paintings of what the rooms would look like after they were decorated,' Sharon said thoughtfully.

'Exactly!'

'This idea sounds even better,' Sharon said, beaming.

'I hope so, but we'll have to wait and see,' her father said cautiously. 'As far as I know there is no one else offering a service like this and we are often asked for colour impressions like you used to paint.' He paused and then went on quickly. 'We could still make use of your talents in that direction, Sharon, if you think you have the time to do them.'

'That sounds wonderful, Dad. I'd love to start painting again,' Sharon told him with a beaming smile.

'Do you really think you will have the time to do that?' Elaine questioned.

'Oh yes. I'll have plenty of spare time after Martyn starts school,' Sharon assured her.

Elaine shook her head doubtfully. 'There will be a lot more for you to do when you move home. I don't know if your dad has told Hadyn yet that there will be a house going with the job. Isn't that right, Elwyn?' she stated in a no-nonsense voice as she looked across at her husband.

'Oh dear, I think I may have forgotten to mention that, Hadyn,' Elwyn Pritchard murmured.

Although she could see that her father was taken by surprise by her mother's statement, Sharon smiled to herself as she saw how quickly he understood what her mother was trying to do and nodded in agreement.

A new job for Hadyn and a new home for the three of us, what more could I ask for? Sharon thought happily. She'd miss Karmu but she couldn't wait to get as far away as possible from Clwyd Court and the Tiger Bay area.

'This is a dream come true,' Hadyn said grinning.

'Well, it is for me, but what about you? I thought your dream was to have your own club...'

'That really was just a dream,' Hadyn said

quickly. 'I knew I had no more chance of that happening than flying to the moon. Anyway, that's all in the past. This is a great chance to prove myself in a job I know something about and always enjoyed doing.'

'And we'll have a proper home to go with it,' Sharon added with a smile.

There was only one thing that worried her and that was the fact that she and Hadyn were not officially married.

It was only a scrap of paper, she told herself, so did it really matter? Not to them, perhaps, but she knew it would distress her parents if they ever found out.

To her surprise, when they went home that night, after Martyn was tucked up in bed and sound asleep, Hadyn himself broached the subject.

'I think we ought to make living together legal, don't you?' he asked as they sat drinking a cup of cocoa before going to bed. 'Do you want to do it quietly, simply, the two of us at a register office, or do you want to invite your parents and arrange something a bit grander? I'll go along with whatever you decide.'

Sharon thought about it for some time, staring down into her cup as if expecting to see the answer there.

'I think we should do it very quietly and not say anything at all to anybody else about it,' she said at last.

'I agree with that,' Hadyn confirmed, 'the only thing is we will have to have witnesses. Who do you suggest we should ask to be there with us?'

'Does it have to be anyone we know?' Sharon frowned. 'I'm sure Karmu would be willing to be a witness, but she's bound to talk about it to people she knows.'

'We will need two witnesses, so what about asking Caitlin and Alwyn?'

'No!' Sharon shook her head firmly. 'If we even mention it to them they're bound to talk about it and everyone will know. Before we know what is happening some newspaper reporter will find out and there will be all sorts of publicity. I don't want it to be reported in the newspaper and I don't think my mam and dad would be very pleased about that either.'

'No, you're probably right. In that case, then, it might be better to tell your parents that we aren't married. At least we would never be afraid of them finding out in the future.'

'I suppose you're right; it's just that I don't want to upset them now that we are reunited and they are doing so much for us.' Sharon sighed. 'Perhaps we'd better sleep on it; that's how we usually solve our problems.'

The next morning they both agreed that since they were going to start a fresh life and move into a new home, it was best to tell Sharon's parents the truth.

The meeting with Sharon's parents was much easier than they had anticipated. They didn't even look surprised when Hadyn admitted that he and Sharon were not married. They listened in silence as he confessed about the number of times he had been in prison.

Hadyn left it to Sharon to explain how she had

lost her second baby when she'd been working in Curran's factory and also to tell them the truth about Martyn.

Both Elaine and Elwyn Pritchard agreed with them that the wedding should be a very simple, quiet affair. They were also emphatic that as far as anyone else was concerned, they should say nothing about Martyn's parentage, not even to the rest of their family.

'It will be far the best thing, especially for Martyn as he grows older, that people assume that he is your child. You've accepted him as your own, Sharon, and if you can do that then that is all that matters, my dear,' her mother told her with tears in her eyes. 'He's such a lovely little boyo and he looks so much like Hadyn with his shock of auburn hair that no one is ever going to question it.'

'Will you both come to the register office and stand as our witnesses?' Hadyn asked.

'Most certainly,' Elwyn declared. 'That's right, isn't it, my dear?' he asked, looking across at his wife.

'It will make us both very happy to do so,' Elaine agreed.

'We'd like Karmu, our landlady at Clwyd Court, to be there as well. She's given us so much help all the time we've been there, and perhaps Parry and Gwen. You have told them that Hadyn is coming to work for Dad?'

'Of course I have,' Elaine told her, 'and they're looking forward to seeing you again and having Martyn as a playmate for their two little ones.'

'I was keeping this to celebrate the day you

moved into your new home,' Elwyn said as he brought out a bottle of champagne and Elaine fetched four glasses, 'but this is an equally momentous occasion.'

'Come on, we'll drink a toast to the future and to drawing a line under the past,' he said as they raised their glasses.

'I want a drink as well,' a little voice piped up.

They all turned to smile at Martyn as he came towards them holding out the mug that, earlier, he'd been given a drink of milk in.

Until then he'd been playing happily in a corner of the room with some wooden bricks which had once belonged to Parry and which Elaine had found for him.

'So you shall,' Elwyn told him as he picked him up in his arms. 'Come on, then, a toast to your mummy and daddy and to your granddad and grandma. Mind you, take only a very tiny sip,' he cautioned as he held his glass of champagne to the little boy's lips.

Martyn took the glass in both his hands and took a little drink. Then he shuddered and pulled a face as he pushed the glass back towards Elwyn. 'It's too prickly, Granddad, it's all going up my nose,' he giggled. 'I'd sooner have a piece of toast.'

The publishers hope that this book has given you enjoyable reading. Large Print Books are especially designed to be as easy to see and hold as possible. If you wish a complete list of our books please ask at your local library or write directly to:

Magna Large Print Books
Magna House, Long Preston,
Skipton, North Yorkshire.
BD23 4ND

This Large Print Book for the partially sighted, who cannot read normal print, is published under the auspices of

THE ULVERSCROFT FOUNDATION

THE ULVERSCROFT FOUNDATION

... we hope that you have enjoyed this Large Print Book. Please think for a moment about those people who have worse eyesight problems than you ... and are unable to even read or enjoy Large Print, without great difficulty.

You can help them by sending a donation, large or small to:

**The Ulverscroft Foundation,
1, The Green, Bradgate Road,
Anstey, Leicestershire, LE7 7FU,
England.**
or request a copy of our brochure for more details.

The Foundation will use all your help to assist those people who are handicapped by various sight problems and need special attention.

Thank you very much for your help.